I STAND ALONE

OTHER BOOKS by Jason Medina

NO HOPE FOR THE HOPELESS AT KINGS PARK

THE DIARY OF AUDREY MALONE FRAYER

A GHOST IN NEW ORLEANS

GHOSTS AND LEGENDS OF YONKERS

KINGS PARK PSYCHIATRIC CENTER:
A JOURNEY THROUGH HISTORY,
VOL. I-III

A NIGHT AT THE SHANLEY HOTEL

MEG

THE UNDEAD NOVELS
by Jason Medina

THE MANHATTANVILLE INCIDENT:
AN UNDEAD NOVEL
(BOOK 1)

AFTERMATH OF THE MANHATTANVILLE INCIDENT:
AN UNDEAD NOVEL
(BOOK 2)

NO MAN'S LAND:
AN UNDEAD NOVEL
(BOOK 3)

I
STAND
ALONE

Jason Medina

Copyright © 2024 by Jason Medina.

Library of Congress Control Number:		2024908064
ISBN:	Hardcover	979-8-3694-2083-6
	Softcover	979-8-3694-2082-9
	eBook	979-8-3694-2081-2

All rights reserved. No part of this book may be reproduced or transmitted in any form or by any means, electronic or mechanical, including photocopying, recording, or by any information storage and retrieval system, without permission in writing from the copyright owner.

This is a work of fiction. Names, characters, places and incidents either are the product of the author's imagination or are used fictitiously, and any resemblance to any actual persons, living or dead, events, or locales is entirely coincidental.

Any people depicted in stock imagery provided by Getty Images are models, and such images are being used for illustrative purposes only.
Certain stock imagery © Getty Images.

Cover photography by Jason Medina.

Print information available on the last page.

Rev. date: 04/25/2024

To order additional copies of this book, contact:
Xlibris
844-714-8691
www.Xlibris.com
Orders@Xlibris.com
860029

TRIBE.

CONTENTS

Chapter 1: Mother 1
Chapter 2: Father 14
Chapter 3: Death 27
Chapter 4: Rooftops 39
Chapter 5: Hopeless 49
Chapter 6: Ready 59
Chapter 7: Alone 69
Chapter 8: Ruins 79
Chapter 9: Sasquatch 90
Chapter 10: Mongrels 102
Chapter 11: Stranded 112
Chapter 12: Night 124
Chapter 13: Lost 134
Chapter 14: Savages 143
Chapter 15: Survival 153
Chapter 16: UFO 162
Chapter 17: Revelations 172
Chapter 18: Gods 183
Chapter 19: Another 194
Chapter 20: Paradise 206

TALES FROM THE RUINS

A World Gone Mad 219
Tomorrow Never Knows 234
The Hunting Party 247
The Meek Shall Inherit The World 261

About The Author 277

CHAPTER 1: MOTHER

Today, I want to tell you about the end of the world. For as long as I can remember, there have been prophecies predicting the end of the world. There are books, where you can read about them. Well, there used to be. Maybe we still have some in our feeble little library. Honestly, I stopped reading about such things long ago. After living through it there didn't seem to be a point anymore. Basically, each so-called prophet had his or her own vision of doom. Each prediction was never the same, but they all had the same end result. Our kind would become extinct for whatever reason.

One person saw visions of fire engulfing the planet and destroying everything. Another said we'd blow ourselves into extinction due to the war to end all wars. One might even argue those two visions are related. People were always afraid of nuclear war because of the destructive power involved, but it turns out that was not to be our fate.

Some said the world would end when the millennium arrived. They believed all of the world's technical systems would somehow crash and cause total chaos and financial ruin for all. Of course, it didn't happen. They were just being paranoid. It's a common human trait. Paranoia. Instead, life went along like it always did. For a few decades anyway.

Years later, there was another would-be prophet, who caused a big stir. Some old guy swore the world would come to an end later that year. He actually built up quite a following. More like a cult. Many foolish people believed him. It's crazy how some people need something to believe in, no matter how terrible it might be. There is something to be said for the power of belief. Some of this man's followers quit their jobs to live out their final days on their own terms. I heard how one guy abandoned his family and drove as far north as he could. As if the end of the world wouldn't reach him there.

Moron.

I bet he had a lot of explaining and apologizing to do when the world continued to go on into the next year. I often wonder if any of those followers were somehow disappointed. I know afterwards that idiotic prophet had the audacity to say he was off by a year, and that the end would come during the next year, instead. This time, no one paid him any mind. He became the butt of many jokes. Soon, he was forgotten and the world went on.

And then came the end of the ancient calendar. No one knew why this calendar only lasted for two thousand plus years. Why was it coming to an end? Why didn't the creators plan for a longer period of time? No one knew the answers. Some believed the end of the calendar meant the end of the world as we knew it, as if time would somehow stop. Conspiracy theorists and myth chasers posed their theories in books and documentaries. There were even spectacular films depicting the end of times. That's what I was told anyway. It was so built up, people actually expected there would be a great disaster when the calendar came to an end. You can probably imagine the terror that might have instilled.

When the time drew near, and eventually arrived, there were numerous mass suicides. These people didn't want to know what horrible fate was in store for the world, but they believed it would consist of great destructive disasters unlike the world has ever witnessed.

Well, guess what happened?

Nothing.

The new year came and went, as it normally did. There was no epic disaster. Aside from a few terrible storms and quakes that year, the planet survived. Business as usual. Humanity continued to survive and thrive, so they could remain the only true danger to the planet for many years to follow. Meanwhile, the powers that be decided to simply continue the calendar from where it left off, so the world could go on. And it did. Genius. Big surprise.

Eventually, pollution, carelessness, and reckless behavior ultimately caused the planet's ozone layer to decline. This led to global warming, which some believed to be a myth. Yet, they couldn't explain how the polar icecaps were melting away more rapidly with each passing year, or how it caused the water levels to rise, forever stealing away beaches little by little. In addition, the constant expanse of civilization destroyed many of the world's natural resources, forests, and jungles, taking away the habitats needed by thousands of species. Once the resources were used up in one region, humans generally moved on to a new location leaving behind deserts and wastelands in their wake. Also, the seas of the world became dumping grounds for waste and garbage, leading to the deaths of so much wildlife. Each year different species would become extinct with barely a notice. Well, there were people who cared and tried to help, but it just wasn't enough. The world was too far gone. The future was beginning to look hopeless.

Of course, the steady attitude was as long as life was okay now, who cares about the future? The people preferred to live in the here and now. They didn't want to waste time worrying about a future that didn't involve them, even if it meant their descendants would have a bigger problem to deal with when the time came. That would be their problem to worry about.

Fast-forward a couple more decades to when I was a little girl. That's when fate finally caught up with us. It wasn't any of the things they expected. Instead, this event took us completely by surprise. Funny how that happens. You hear about how the end is near for so long and when it comes, you're surprised. It seemed the end of the world had finally arrived.

I suppose it wasn't actually the end of the world, but it was pretty damn close. It was the scariest time of my life. That's for sure. I had nightmares about it for years.

It still boggles my mind. Considering all our great technology, how could they not have known about it? They should have seen it coming. I guess they were too distracted by the latest political nonsense going on. There was a lot of that going on back then when politics mattered.

They learned about the asteroid only a month before it was said to strike. It was about three miles in diameter. Many people prayed it would just pass close by and barely miss us. However, scientists were certain it would hit us directly. Apparently, the government wanted to shut them up to avoid worldwide panic, so the scientists gradually stopped talking about it publicly.

In a way, the government was right to worry. As those weeks passed, that huge rock in the sky could be seen moving dangerously closer. At first, it looked like a comet, but within the first two weeks, it began to look like a small moon. Religious fanatics led people into suicide pacts, while looters rioted and took what they wanted, no longer caring about the laws. They knew time was limited and wanted to enjoy their last moments. It was the same as always, but this time, the end was more real and inevitable. There were frenzied orgies of madness all over the world. It was the most chaotic time humanity had ever seen. I've only heard stories, but it was enough to terrify me. I won't dare write about the things I heard.

Luckily, some people were prepared and did their best to survive. That's how we made it through that time. Someone thought up a foolproof plan to stop it, or so they thought. Unfortunately, the plan didn't quite work out like they wanted it to go. A special nuclear packed missile was launched. It was a direct hit.

The end result was still disastrous. The asteroid was blown into three large pieces. The largest piece struck our moon, which caused it to shift its orbit. This led to several disasters caused by tidal shifts. The smallest piece mostly burned up in the atmosphere splitting into hundreds of smaller pieces that rained down over the eastern continents of the world creating massive fires like in that early prophecy. Each of those pieces were about the size of a car and weighed tons. The third final piece landed in our largest body of water causing vast tidal waves, tsunamis, and shaking up the tectonic plates, until great quakes were unleashed upon our coastal region. The sea level at the coastlines increased exponentially and has never truly receded. Well, to the best of my knowledge anyway. Entire cities were wiped out killing billions of people. Maybe trillions! It was an epic tragedy beyond belief, which lasted weeks, before dying down.

And that wasn't all. Several volcanic eruptions were instigated by the quakes. Clouds of black dust had risen to the skies, spreading across the land, and darkening everything for nearly two decades. Those of us, who were smart enough, managed to find lasting shelters underground. All communications satellites were down, supposedly after having been destroyed when the asteroid arrived breaking through our atmosphere. In essence, we were on our own.

It was essentially the end of civilization. The end of humankind, as we knew it. They called it the *"Big Apocalyptic Event,"* which seems fitting. To think, as bad as it was, it could have been much worse. The entire world could have been completely destroyed. We wouldn't be here now. In a way, I suppose we were pretty lucky. I'm trying to think positive. After all, I have a daughter to consider.

I still can't believe that was close to twenty-five years ago. Time flies, as they say. Well, maybe no one really says that anymore. It's something I remember from my youth. I need to hold on to those old memories for my daughter's sake, if not for my own. When she's older, I hope I'll be able to tell her about how the world used to be. That's why I'm writing this. It's for her.

To my daughter, I've been thinking about our situation. We really are lucky. Not only did we manage to survive a disaster of epic proportions, but somehow we were able to form some type of lasting civilization in the aftermath. My dad used to tell me the first few years were the hardest. So many people died. I'm starting to think maybe they were the lucky ones. For many years, it was a living hell for us survivors. We were forced to make a lot of adjustments because the world would never be the same.

It was different everywhere. There were no more communication networks, so we would learn how the world was affected through traveling messengers. The first one came from the nearest city to the south about a month later. He spoke of how the taller buildings collapsed onto the smaller ones. Coastal cities had it worse with flooding and mudslides. We only learned about that a year later when another traveler found his way here. There were pockets of survivors scattered everywhere. Food supplies were running low at a fast rate. Medical supplies were scarce. There was no more government. No one to help us. We were on our own, so we tried to stick together whenever possible. There was safety in numbers.

In the city where we lived the situation was similar to most other cities, but we managed to make it to this underground shelter. In the beginning, we thought our time here would only be temporary. As it turned out, we're still here almost three decades later. This became our home and we quickly learned we needed to keep it secret in order to keep it safe. There was no doubt being in here was certainly safer than being on the outside.

Some groups that tried to survive on the outside became aggressive and protective of their small encampments and shelters. Each group became known as clans. The existence of each clan depended on their location and how desperate their fight to survive had become over time. Some clans joined with one another forming larger clans, but that made their resources run out faster making them more desperate. In some cases, the stronger clans wiped out the weaker ones to steal their resources, their shelters, and sometimes their women and children. Many lived in fear, which is no way to live.

Not that it made a difference. There just wasn't enough food for everyone. While people could have resorted to farming, it took time and required fertile land. Not to mention crops, seeds, and strong hands to work the fields, while also dealing with the dangers of the outside. In the meantime, people were starving. Dying. Even in here. We had to learn how to hunt and fish. It was the only way to survive.

Fortunately, we had some who were experienced in those skills. They had to teach the rest of us. I learned how to fish when I was twelve. Your father learned when he was eleven. He was tall for his age, so it was believed he could handle himself out there with the other fishermen. He learned how to hunt when he was thirteen. Hunting took more strength, since carrying the food back was no easy task. Not to mention, there are many dangers to face out there. Sometimes, the food gatherers need to fight.

There are people out there who choose not to be part of any clan. They are selfish, greedy, and anti-social people. The degenerates, the criminals, the vagabonds, and the insane. They mostly travel on their own, or in very small groups. We call them nomads. Most of them are extremely dangerous. From what we learned, they began hunting the last of the old clans and either wiping them out or chasing them away. We had to limit our hunting and fishing to the daytime hours and are always alert.

One thing that helps is that nomads are usually noisy brutes. This often makes them easier to avoid with the proper strategy. Another advantage we have is most of them lack intelligence, and therefore have not learned to work together like a clan would. They are too uncivilized, which makes them disorganized. Still, don't underestimate them. They will take everything you have to ensure their own survival, including your life. They know no bounds and follow no laws. They are ruthless savages.

We believe the remaining clans have all learned to stay hidden away in their shelters. We no longer communicate with each other, so we can only guess. It's safer this way.

That being said, there is more to fear out there than nomads and potential rival clans. Encountering people is mainly a daytime problem, although that's still the safest time to venture outside. At night, there's something far worse. It began about a year after the *Big Apocalyptic Event*. That's when the first of the sky ships made their presence known. They arrived armed with their powerful bright beams of light. These sky ships hunt down anyone they can find and somehow suck them up into the sky using these beams. Anyone who is abducted has never been seen, again. It took a year before we realized how much more dangerous it was to go out at night. By then, we lost a third of our group.

Before my dad died, he told me the sky ships actually came from space, possibly from another world. I think he called them *yoo-effoes*, or something like that. I really don't recall why. He said sightings of the sky ships dated back to our earliest times. When I asked why he never taught me about them before, he said because he never believed they existed. Therefore, talking about them seemed pointless. Many of the other adults thought the same. Perhaps, if they had believed, they would've been more prepared.

For some reason, in the past, the sky ships tried to remain unseen. Supposedly, there were random sightings of sky ships all over the world throughout the ages. In many cases, they were even documented in books or on film. Despite the evidence, it was always the same. People were skeptical and didn't believe the sky ships came from space. Maybe they were too afraid to admit there was intelligent life beyond our world. Maybe denying it made them feel superior. I really can't say. It was before my time.

What matters now is that we know better. These sky ships no longer hide. Instead, they daringly fly over the ruins searching for survivors. Sometimes, they come in low for a closer look. Other times, they stay high above for a better vantage point. One thing is certain. They are definitely real and they are the most dangerous threat out there. Never forget that.

On a positive note, the sky ships only seem to appear at night. Maybe it's the only time they can use their beams of light. No one really knows the true reason why, but at least, it gives us some kind of advantage. We learned how to avoid them, just as we learned to avoid the nomads. Hopefully, when the time comes for you to venture out, you won't have to worry about either threat.

I'm not sure how it will be for you growing up in the shelter, but for me it was miserable. Well, at first. I was so sad because I was forced to say goodbye to the life I knew. I had to face the fact that I would never return to my real home. My toys were lost forever. We would never see the rest of our family ever again. There was nothing we could do about it. It wasn't easy for any of us.

The only thing that helped was that I was still very young, so in time I'd forget about the things I missed. I'd learn to adjust to my new environment. I'd get used to not having my toys. That's what my parents kept telling me anyway. It actually took a very long time for me to adjust.

I Stand Alone

Having other children here made it a little easier. We all spent a lot of time together. The children were always kept in the same area as a group, since the parents had to work to make this shelter into our new home. It didn't take long before us kids got restless. We were so bored. The adults eventually had to find a way to keep us occupied, so we wouldn't get in the way, or cause trouble for them. School was out of the question, since there were no school teachers. Besides, there was never time for us to have a real school. Still, we had plenty of other teachers, who would take the time to teach us things. They couldn't let us grow up without teaching us how to survive. We began learning our skills at early ages.

It kept us occupied, which satisfied us for a while.

By then, we had all become friends. In a way, us kids felt like we were our very own community among the adults. It wasn't until some of us got old enough to go out hunting or fishing that we began to feel like part of the adult community. It was silly. We were all one community. One clan. There were no separate groups within our shelter. Only separate sleeping areas. We had become a surrogate family for each other. Our real families were lost out there forever, but we still had each other. That had to count for something and it did.

It made our bonds strong. We stuck together and helped each other whenever possible. We were there for each other. We were there with each other through the good and the bad, for better or worse. We were all we had.

When I was a teenager, I essentially forgot about the things I would never have in my life. Instead, I was focused on the things I could have. I knew I could become a productive member of the clan, since I was good at reading, writing, sewing, fishing, and cooking. I helped out as best I could. I also knew that someday I might become a mother, so adding a new person to the clan was another way I could contribute to our survival because let's face it, without children there's no future.

I can't really say what life will be like for you when you get older. I can only do my best to make it comfortable for you now, while I'm around. You're still so young. I sometimes find myself imagining you as a young woman. I can almost picture how you'll look in my mind. Maybe a little how I look and a little like your dad, too. I think it's a nice combination.

What truly worries me most is will there still be an adequate amount of food for you to consume by the time you're my age. Hunting in the same area for decades is bound to have a profound effect on the environment. In time, the animals will be harder to find. Hunters will need to go further away, which puts them in greater danger. I don't even want to think about you being one of those hunters someday, but I know I have to because it's always better to be prepared.

I hope you'll be just fine. I'm probably overreacting, since I'm always expecting the worst. I need to be more positive. I try. It's so hard in this mad world we live in.

I think I'll continue to write in this journal more for you, than for myself. I want you to use it as a way to learn from me. I might not remember all the things I write down. At least, if it's already written, all you'll need to do is read it. I'll do my best to mention any important details that you need to know. I'll also tell you about myself and your father, so you know who you came from. That's important. I also want you to have this journal to read for those trying times whenever you feel alone in the world. Trust me. I know that feeling well. Let these words remind you that you're never truly alone. You have us. Always.

Okay, I've probably written too much for today. I don't want to overload you with depression. Think happy thoughts when you read this. Think of me and of how much I love you. I'll write more for you soon. I promise.

As you should have realized by now, I met your father here in the shelter when I was just a child. We quickly became close friends. We always spent time together. Naturally, as we grew older, we fell in love. It wasn't planned. It just happened. After we had you, things changed for us. We were adults, and as parents we had a greater responsibility than just caring for each other. We had to take care

I Stand Alone

of you, our baby girl. It was a challenge. By then, our clan had been reduced to only about twenty people.

Sadly, my parents were already gone by the time you were born. So were Christian's. That's your father's name. I suppose you probably already know that. Well, if by chance you didn't and only refer to us as mommy and daddy, now you know. My name is Mazzy. I guess you knew that already, too.

Anyway, as I was saying, many of the older people don't last very long these days. They usually get sick and require medications that we simply no longer have. A simple infection could mean a death sentence to a sick person. Some sicknesses are so deadly they have claimed many from our clan, as if we didn't already have enough to worry about. I can only hope you'll never fall ill to any of these sicknesses. I couldn't bear losing you, my dear sweet girl. I love you more than life itself.

I wonder how old you'll be when you finally develop the curiosity to read your mother's old journal. I hope that I'm still around to see it. If you have any questions for me, I'd love to be there to answer them for you. I'll have to make sure you learn how to read as soon as possible. Of course, you're still too young. As I write this, you are only three years old. I was six when I came to this shelter. That's three years older than you. You need to learn math. Ask your father to teach you. He's very good at it. I have always been better at writing. My parents taught me well. Reading books helped a lot. You'll also read the same books I read, which are in our library. It's not much, but it's better than nothing.

I also plan to tell you all the same stories my parents used to tell me. There are some really great adventures I want to tell you about. Mind you, none of them are real, but they are fantastic stories that will make your imagination go wild. I want you to have a better childhood than I had. I'm sorry it'll be spent in this shelter, but we need to keep you safe. Besides, it's always been home to you.

Who knows? Maybe there will come a day when you can safely leave the shelter and see what it's like on the outside. I hope you never have to encounter any nomads or sky ships. I hope you live as good a life as you can in here. There are currently four other children close to your age. Two are boys. Maybe one will become your life partner like your father has become for me. That would be nice.

I'm sorry. I know I shouldn't plan too far ahead. Anything can happen. Life in the shelter cannot be predicted. I sometimes let my imagination get the better of me. Blame my parents. They made sure I had a good one. Just like I plan to do for you. I want you to believe in everything. Don't be close-minded. Be ready for anything. Expect that anything could happen, even seeing the spirits of the dead. If your father and I die, it will be the only way we can ever see each other, again, so it helps if you believe in spirits. We'll always try to guide you and watch over you, even after we die. I promise.

Just in case I'm taken from you at an early age, I want you to know me, to remember me. I have brown eyes and fair skin. My hair is long and brown. It's very curly and often gets in my way when I'm writing in my journal. I'm shorter than your father, but smarter! I read more books. Honestly, he's highly intelligent, as well. He knows math and science far better than I could ever understand it. He's also an excellent hunter. He'll teach you. You need to learn, so don't give him a hard time. Listen to him. He'll keep you safe. He keeps us both safe. He's a good man. Very handy, too. We're all lucky to have him. Someday, he'll be one of the clan's elders. Maybe me, too.

There's something else you need to learn about. Your body will change when you get older. You may experience weird things that scare you. Your chest will grow. Those are your breasts. Use them to feed your baby when you have one. You'll understand when you're older. Read that pregnancy book in the library. It'll help teach you and guide you, if you become a mother. In fact, read all of the books in the library! *Please*. Do it for me. Learn everything that you can from everyone here. Never stop learning.

My greatest fear is that you'll someday be alone. If that happens, remember what I said. We'll always watch over you and guide you, even when we're long gone. Just believe in spirits, and our spirits might even appear to you. I'm only telling you this because I saw my father, after he died. He came to me in a dream and told me he was at peace. I know it was really him. I felt it. It wasn't like a regular dream. It was so vivid. I believe he came to comfort me because I was so distraught. It helped.

There I go, again. I'm so sorry if I'm scaring you. I keep planning too far ahead. I only want you to always be prepared for anything, so you're never caught by surprise. Learn to expect the unexpected. I can't emphasize that enough. Always be ready.

I'm sure I'll be reading this to you someday when you're at the age when you can understand the words and their meanings. Maybe we can have a good laugh about it. That would be nice. I'll explain everything when the time comes. I'll also be sure to have many years of memories written down for you to read about, although I should warn you... my memories aren't too exciting. I've lived a relatively boring life in here. However, I still plan to write everything that I can remember for your sake. Maybe it will comfort you when you need it, in the same way my father's spirit comforted me when I needed it.

Remember, I love you, Evangelina. Always. Forever.

CHAPTER 2: FATHER

"Evangelina? What are you doing?" Her father asked, as he approached. Christian barely entered his daughter's room, lingering at the doorway. It was a fairly big room for one person. She once shared it with another teenage girl, until that girl was killed by nomads during a fishing expedition a year earlier. Christian sighed, as he watched his sixteen-year-old daughter. He hoped she'd live a long life.

She glanced back at him and replied somberly, "Reading," before she turned back to the tattered old journal in her hands. It once belonged to her mother. Evangelina often enjoyed reading it, while lying on her bed alone in her room. This was around the hundredth time, so she skipped through the pages to some of her favorite entries. She had most of it memorized by now. It didn't matter. She enjoyed focusing on what she considered her early beginnings, which basically consisted of the entries regarding the *Big Apocalyptic Event*, the time when her mother and father met, and when they had her. The rest was not as significant. Of course, she read them, too, when it suited her. Not today.

Christian stared sadly at his daughter when he noticed the old journal. It disappointed him how she never really got to know her mother. Mazzy had been taken from them when Evangelina was only a child. Like so many others, she became ill, caught an infection, and they lacked the medicine she needed to get better. His eyes became watery just thinking about the loss of his beloved Mazzy. The pain of her loss still cut deeply. She meant the world to him. He missed her terribly.

He recalled the day they first met. Both were mere children when they were forced to take shelter in this underground bunker with their parents and dozens of strangers. They had no idea it would become their home for the next few decades. At the time, none of them truly comprehended how different their lives would be. It was both an ending and a new beginning for everyone.

Christian was forced to grow up sooner and missed out on having a normal childhood. He learned to fish, hunt, and eventually how to kill another person by the time he was thirteen. It was all part of his survival training. However, he needed other skills to survive, as well.

He eventually became a builder, which meant he was one of the ones responsible for building the various rooms within the shelter, which at first only consisted of a kitchen, storage closet, and one large living area with three subdivisions, and the restrooms. He learned carpentry skills from a man named Gilbert, who was one of the elders. Christian was a fast learner, so he helped to make the shelter into a home for the others. They added several smaller rooms, one for each family. Christian also learned how to build furniture, which would later come in handy when Mazzy became pregnant.

Of course, being a hunter and a fisherman also meant he had to take turns leaving the shelter in search of food. Conveniently, his carpentry skills even came in handy during those food runs. He built a variety of weapons for the people who had to guard the hunters and fishermen. In time, he was such a skilled crafter that the elders preferred keeping him in the shelter, where his artisan skills would not be wasted or lost. That suited him and Mazzy just fine.

By the time he reached eighteen years of age, he and Mazzy had officially become life partners. Two years later, when she became pregnant, his focus changed and he dedicated himself to his family. He built everything they would require for their home, including toys for his daughter. That was important.

Together, he and Mazzy tried to raise their daughter as best they could. They taught her everything she was willing to learn. They also made sure she had some kind of childhood. She was told the stories her parents learned from their parents. They read books to her, until she was old enough to read them herself, and they played games with her. Their hard work paid off because their daughter was a happy little girl. She had no idea what she was missing out there, since she never experienced any of it.

Once Mazzy became sick, everything changed. Christian tried to take care of her, but without the medicine she needed, there was no hope of keeping her healthy for long. She only lasted a few weeks.

After she was gone, he was devastated. He had already lost his parents, by this time, so Mazzy and Evangelina were the only real family he had left. Of course, being in the shelter with the others for so long made them all feel like family, too, but it wasn't the same. Mazzy was different. Losing her was like losing a part of himself. He never fully recovered from that loss.

Fortunately, he still had his precious daughter. She had become his world. He raised her the way he thought Mazzy would have wanted. He taught her everything he could. He tried to get her to read all of the books from the library because it was Mazzy's wish. He tried his best to be a good father like his father was for him. Luckily, he had help from the other adults in the shelter. They all helped each other. It was just the way of their clan.

At the age of thirty-five, he became one of the clan's elders. He was the youngest elder. A couple of years later, he found himself wondering where the time went. Soon, he'd be forty. It was not so long ago when he was playing with his little girl. She was growing up so fast. Too fast.

He watched her silently, still deep in thought. Finally, she realized he was still standing at her doorway. She put the journal down and turned to face him. He looked depressed and distant.

"What's wrong, Dad?"

He snapped back to reality. "Huh? Oh, sorry. I was thinking about you and your mother. I wish she could see you now." There was a twinkle in his eye, which made her smile.

"Me, too," she responded. She sat up and looked down at the journal in her hands. She knew he probably missed her more than she did. She barely remembered her, aside from what she could read in the journal. The memories she had were very hazy. On the other hand, her father had grown up with her mom. They had known each other almost their entire lives. Her death surely must have left a huge hole in his life, in his heart. His daughter wanted to cheer him up, but wasn't sure she could. "I'm sorry you're sad, but at least you got the chance to know her. You got to spend so much time with her. Years. I wish I had more time. I have to read her journal just to remember her." She faked a smile. Now, she was sad.

Her father entered the room and sat on the bed beside her. He put his arm around her and said in a comforting way, "She was like you. Same big brown eyes, same long curly hair, only yours is darker like mine. And she had the same love for reading." He smiled and stared at the journal on her lap.

She leaned her head on his shoulder and asked wistfully, "What's your favorite memory of her?"

He sighed. "Wow. There are so many. The first time we met comes to mind, even though we were both terrified that day. We got to be scared together, which somehow made it easier for us to cope with what was going on. Becoming friends with her made being here easier. And the day we first kissed. That was a great memory. I wish I could relive that moment every day for the rest of my life. It was magical." His mind almost drifted off into daydreaming, but he kept himself in the moment. "The best was when she told me she was pregnant. We were both extremely happy. Scared, but extremely happy."

They both laughed a little.

He added, "Actually, the day you were born is probably the greatest memory that we shared. We were blessed with a beautiful, healthy, baby girl in a world that our parents thought was over. Your birth was proof that life can go on, even when things looked like they were at their darkest. You gave us hope for a future we didn't think would ever come." He smiled proudly at her, while gazing into her brown eyes, which matched his own.

"Aw, Dad." She blushed and looked away bashfully.

His smile faded, as his tone changed. "Long after I'm gone, you'll likely still be here. You're one of the last young people of our clan, aside from Seth and Abby. After we lost Darrick, and then Jana, you became the youngest. The rest of us… we're getting old." He stared down at the floor.

"You're not that old, yet, Dad," she replied. "And don't talk about when you're gone. I don't want to think about it." She began to pull away, but he held her close.

"I'm sorry, but you need to be ready." He looked her in the eyes. "Someday, it will be true. I can't live forever. Who knows how much longer I'll be around? The same goes for the others. You *need* to be ready. Your mother was very determined about that."

"I know, Dad. I will be. I promise. I don't expect you to live forever." She looked at him with pleading eyes. "Just don't leave me so soon like she did." She couldn't fight back the tears anymore.

He kissed her forehead and assured her, "I'll try my best to stick around for a long, long time."

"You better," she stated, and then they hugged.

The winter season was drawing near. Christian stood at the bunker's doorway, as the hunting party went out to gather food. He watched them leave the shelter and bolted the metal door behind them. He was grateful his daughter was not going with them. She began going out on food runs when she turned thirteen. It was unavoidable. Every able body had to help out. Still, he would rather go out than to see her go out. That's why he usually went out with her whenever it was her turn to go on a hunt. The other elders frowned upon his insistency, but they understood. She was the last of the teenagers. Not to mention she was his daughter. Of course, he'd want to watch over her personally.

As of recently, the hunting parties had to venture further out to find any worthy game. The animals in the area learned to stay away from the vicinity of their underground shelter long ago. They were trying to survive, too.

It had been a while since anyone encountered a nomad. Hopefully, there were none in the region. It was hard to be sure when it came to them. All it took was for one to wander into their region and cause trouble. If he were to escape, he'd only be back after learning there were people in the area. People meant food and supplies. The nomads were not too bright, but they knew that much.

Christian tried not to dwell on it. He had work to do. The shelves in the library needed to be either braced or replaced. They were old and falling apart. He couldn't have that. The library was his daughter's favorite place to visit. After all, there were not many places to visit within the shelter.

Every time a family died their former rooms would be converted into public living areas to be shared. Over the past few years, several new rooms had been added. There was a meeting room, which doubled as a dining area. They had a lounge, where people could gather and talk or just relax together. One room became a workshop, where Christian built new furniture, weapons, and tools. Another room near the original storage closet was used for additional storage. Another as a hospital. While another set of rooms had been converted into a guest area, on the unlikely chance someone new would arrive and join their clan.

Christian usually repurposed the resources from old unused furniture to make new pieces. He had a large supply of wood and metal, which he kept in the workshop. He was the only carpenter left in the clan. He wanted to teach his daughter his skills, but she showed little interest in making furniture, although she did enjoy making tools and weapons. It was better than nothing. She even made her own throwing knives, which she could throw with uncanny precision from her belt.

She was not without other skills. She became very good at fishing and hunting, especially when using her knives. She knew how to clean her kills and how to prepare them to be cooked. While her cooking was not great, it was not terrible. She knew enough to get by. She was also a fast runner, which would definitely keep her alive longer on the outside. Her favorite skill was probably her excellent ability to read and write. She had been elected to help keep inventory records of their supplies. Not everyone in the shelter could read or write, as well. There was no school. They all learned from their parents or from each other, as with everything else.

It was difficult to believe out of all the people that once resided in the shelter, they were down to a mere seven. Three of whom were now out there hunting for food. Of the seven, three were elders. One was out leading the hunt. That was Abram. He was the best hunter in the clan, so he often led the hunts. The other elder, Troya, was probably in the kitchen thinking of what to make for dinner. She was the oldest person in the clan and no longer went out at all. And of course, Christian was the third of the elders. Normally, no two elders were allowed to go out at once, just in case something were to go wrong.

Luckily, they had a doctor of sorts in their clan. Avery learned a lot from his parents, who were both in the medical field prior to the *Big Apocalyptic Event*. There were only two medical books in the library that Avery could use as reference guides. Sadly, it wasn't enough to make him a good doctor. Just a competent one. Incidentally, he was not allowed to go on hunts either. He was too valuable.

Christian had become good friends with Avery over the years. He held no resentment over the fact that Avery could not save Mazzy. It was not his fault they lacked the proper medicine to keep her alive. He tried his best, despite a bad situation. It was something Christian appreciated.

When Christian finished working on the shelves in the library, he proceeded to replace the books on the new, improved, sturdier shelves. He looked at the covers of each book, as he placed them back. It occurred to him that it had been too long since he read one. He never seemed to have the time anymore. He was always busy making something, teaching his daughter skills, or out there hunting.

After he finished, he grabbed one of the books and sat down. He skimmed through it briefly and wondered if he should even bother. Why not? He turned to the first page and began reading.

The next day was quiet and peaceful. Christian did his work for the day, before taking the time to return to the library. He continued reading the same book. Across from him sat his daughter. She was also reading a book. They glanced over their books at one another and smiled. It was a pleasant moment.

However, it did not take long for Troya to enter the library and ruin the mood.

"Christian?" She began. "When is the hunting party due back?" Her shrill shaky voice somehow matched her aged appearance. She was very concerned, and had every reason to be.

Still, Christian tried not to worry too much, yet. He knew very well how sometimes it could take a whole day to find any game. Let alone to track and kill it. Bringing it all the way back to the shelter was another story entirely. If it got dark, they'd have to seek shelter for the night and continue during daylight to avoid the sky ships. Keeping that in mind, he replied calmly, "They should be back sometime today."

"Are you sure?" She asked, not convinced. Her silvery hair was unkempt and hung down the side of her wrinkled face like vines from a withered tree. Apparently, she was so worried, she had not bothered to tie her hair back before leaving her room, which she normally did each morning.

"Yes," he replied in a reassuring voice. "You know hunting is not as cut and dry as it used to be. There are barely any animals foolish enough to come near the shelter." He spoke from experience. He knew she was simply being motherly. It was her way. She always tended to worry. To appease her, he added, "If they're not back by dinnertime, I'll head out myself to check on them."

His daughter suddenly glanced over her book at him and responded, "If you go out there, I'm going with you."

He shot her a sharp look, "That won't be necessary. I won't be out there long."

"Doesn't matter. I don't want you going out alone," his daughter insisted.

Troya agreed, "She's right. No one should go out alone."

Christian sighed and gave in. "Fine, but we probably won't need to go out. I'm sure Abram and the others will be back before dinnertime." He hoped.

He tried to sound convincing, but he was starting to have doubts. Their combined concern was becoming contagious. He tried to get back to reading, but noticed Troya was still lingering in front of him. She was involuntarily tapping her foot with impatience. Christian looked up at her. She was staring at him with a raised eyebrow. He waited. She gradually turned to leave. He knew she was not going to let this go. She'd most certainly be back before dinnertime. In fact, there would be no dinnertime, until he went out and returned with the hunting party. He knew he was not going to be able to read the book. Not with his mind on the guys, who were out there. What if something did go wrong?

He got up and placed the book on the shelf. He exhaled in frustration.

"What's wrong, Dad?"

"What do you think? Now, she's got me worried," he admitted. He walked off leaving the library to wait by the door of the shelter. So much for his peace and quiet.

As he walked, a million scenarios began to play out in his mind. What if Abram and the others were abducted by a sky ship last night? Perhaps, they ran into an especially volatile nomad, who was able to catch them by surprise. Not likely, but what if? Could they have gotten injured? *All three of them?* It could happen. Maybe they fell into a pit and are trapped. Maybe one of the ruins collapsed and fell on top of them crushing them, or pinning them to the ground and leaving them vulnerable.

Before he realized it, he was gearing up, grabbing his weapons, and heading toward the door. What he did not realize is he was not alone. His daughter was right behind him.

She complained, "I *knew* you were going to try leaving me behind. I told you I'm going *with* you. I won't take no for an answer." She practically stomped her foot.

He turned to face her, but knew this was an argument he would not win, especially not with Troya watching them both from the hallway looking like a worried mother. Still, tapping her foot.

"I wasn't planning to leave without you," he lied. "I was only getting ready."

"Fine. We're ready. Let's go," his daughter demanded. In that moment, she reminded him so much of her mother. He had to laugh. She asked, "What's so funny?"

"You. You're just like your mother. Stubborn and adorable." She was not amused. He looked over to Troya. "Lock the door. We won't be gone long." He unbolted the door and stepped outside. His daughter was right behind him. They moved the camouflage shrubbery aside and headed out into the ruins of the city above their shelter.

Christian walked slowly and guardedly with his daughter trailing in his shadow. "Stay close," he warned, although he did not have to issue the instructions. He knew she would.

"I always do," she replied curtly.

Both remained alert, as they walked through the ruins of the old city along the hunting trail, which had once been a paved road long ago. It was now scarred by hundreds of cracks and overgrown with weeds and tall grass. The old twenty-foot streetlamps that were spread evenly along the sides resembled trees with years of vines wrapped tightly around them from their rusted bases up to their broken lamps. The nearby building ruins lurked in the background like straight-edged concrete hills that were off limits, although tempting with their open doorways that were more like darkened caves, and their many broken windows that watched them like eyes. Some ruins were so tall they blocked out the warmth of the sun, while casting a cool shade over the trail. Distant ruins were mere faded gray shapes protruding into the sky.

It was still daylight, although the sun was already on its way down to the western horizon's edge, partially hidden by the ruins. It was late in the afternoon, but not yet dinnertime.

Christian fought the urge to call out to Abram. He did not want to attract the wrong kind of attention. Who knew if there might be nomads in the area? For all he knew, some could be watching from the windows of the towering ruins. It was not a chance he wanted to take, so he walked at a fast pace. He made sure his daughter could keep up. She already knew to walk through this area quickly.

They relaxed their pace once they reached the open hunting grounds. There were more trees in that area, so less places where someone could be hiding in the darkness of an old decayed structure. Christian examined the woods. He kept checking the ground for signs of the hunting party. He thought maybe there was a clue as to which direction they may have gone. Hopefully, they stuck to protocol and followed the trail as far as they could. It would make finding them easier.

He had a feeling they'd run into each other sooner or later. Abram would probably ask why he and his daughter were outside, but then would quickly realize Troya sent them out. At first, he'd be annoyed, but then they would laugh it off.

It would be great if they found a nice big deer. Maybe two. Christian suspected this long walk was going to build up his appetite. A nice hot meal would make a fine reward for this unnecessary trip into the wild.

He had to remind himself to remain alert regardless of what he thought about their reason for being outside. It was still dangerous to be out there. He remained extra alert for his daughter's sake. He looked over his shoulder at her. Her eyes were scanning beyond the tall grass on both sides. She was more alert than him. Good girl, he thought.

"Are you watching my back?" He whispered back to her, as he faced forward, again.

"And your sides," was her casual response.

"That's my girl."

He wondered how far Abram traveled. Considering the hunting party had been gone since the previous afternoon, there was a good chance this was going to be a very long walk. It was getting cooler out, too. He had not taken that into account before. The last thing he wanted was to be caught outside on a cold dark night with his daughter.

"We're not staying out here for too long," he said. "We'll go until we reach the water road, then we're heading back. We're not equipped to be out here overnight."

She asked, sounding more curious than concerned, "Okay, but what if we don't find them?"

"Doesn't matter. We won't do anyone any good if we get sick or abducted." He looked up through the trees at the sky instinctively. The clouds were puffier than he remembered, which worried him. He wondered where the sky ships hid during the daylight. What if they hid in the clouds? Watching. Waiting.

His daughter saw him looking up, so she began doing the same, although she watched the clouds with fascination. She wondered how they felt. She imagined they felt a lot like a soft pillow, only smokier. She thought about the smoke created when someone is cooking food. It was something she could not feel with her hands. Was it the same with the clouds?

The temporary silence was shattered by the screech of a low flying bird. The sound acted as a warning causing a nearby flock of birds to launch from the branches of the tree where they sat. They knew a threat when they saw one.

Evangelina was ready, though. She was always ready. It's how she was taught. She threw the knife that was tucked between her fingers and one of the birds went down. Her father was impressed.

"Nice shot!"

"It looks like we won't go back empty-handed," she said with a sly grin, as she warily retrieved her knife and the dead bird. It was not too far from the trail. Her father watched and waited for her. Within seconds she was behind him, once again. "Okay, let's go."

He continued to lead the way, until they reached what they knew as the water road. It was a lengthy river that traveled several miles flowing from north to south. It took them nearly an hour to reach it, but it was someplace they'd been to many times in the past. It's where they usually went fishing. The river was about half a mile wide.

The two stood at the shoreline looking up and down the river, and then across to the other side. There were more trees and ruins stretched along the opposite bank as far as the eye could see. There was no sign of the hunting party. It was more than likely they went either north or south along the river. They had no means of crossing it safely. The current was mild, but most of them were non-swimmers. Christian searched the ground for footprints. He was grateful when he saw some heading southbound.

"They went this way," he pointed. He paused to look up at the setting sun. Time was running out. Soon, it would be dark. The dense trees in the area would surely block out the sun sooner, although they would provide cover from the sky ships. As far as he could recall, there was no shelter close enough on their side of the water road short of another mile to the south. If Abram led the others in that direction, he might have sought shelter when it got dark. Perhaps, they were on their way back.

Christian gazed down the length of the trail heading south, as he pondered their next move.

His daughter stood close to him. She looked up at him and asked, "What do we do now? Do we go that way, too, or do we go back?"

It was a good question, he thought. Was it worth the risk? By the sound of her voice, he could tell she was getting worried. She had never been out at night before. He always made sure of that. This was no time to change his ways, or was it?

CHAPTER 3: DEATH

"We can't take the chance," Christian finally replied to his daughter's inquiry with regret. "We'll have to go back. If the hunting party doesn't return by morning, we'll head out after breakfast. In any case, we can be better prepared, in case we need to stay out overnight. We're not ready for it. Come on. Let's go." He turned to go back to the shelter and urged her along. This time, they walked side by side.

Troya was not pleased when they returned without the hunting party. Christian was hoping they would have already been back by the time he got home. That was not the case. That night, they did not sleep easy.

The next morning, they set out, again, just the two of them. This time, they were dressed warmer and carrying backpacks full of overnight gear, which basically consisted of a bedroll, extra food, water, and what passed for a first aid kit. The kit was basically something that could be used to wrap a wound and a needle with threading for emergency stitches. Their drinking water was also part of the first aid kit.

The father and daughter quickly walked through the city ruins heading straight for the river. They then made their way south and tried to follow the footprints, but they weren't easy to make out on the cold unyielding ground. It had not rained in days, so the ground was dry. The temperature was dropping, which hardened the dirt, leaving little chance for foot impressions. They would have to pay close attention to their surroundings not only to avoid danger, but to find clues that could lead them to the others.

Christian was able to lead them south for several minutes before he began to hesitate. He wished he was better at tracking, like Abram. As far as he could tell, they might have wandered off the trail and he was going in the wrong direction. He kept pausing to look around for signs to guide him.

Finally, Evangelina moved ahead of him and took the lead. "Come on, Dad. It's too soon for you to be tired."

"I'm not tired," he explained, as he adjusted the long bow hanging over his shoulder. "I'm just not sure if we're still going the right way. I'm having trouble tracking them."

She looked down at the ground and replied, "I can still see their footprints and the bent blades of grass." She pointed downward. "They went this way." She continued along the trail.

So, apparently his daughter was a better tracker than him. He shook his head in disbelief and followed her. Meanwhile, he kept an eye on their surroundings, so she could focus on tracking the others.

The trail gradually veered away from the river. That meant they were getting closer to the southern ruins. After several more minutes of walking, the trees began to part ways to a wider trail. The ruins ahead were currently visible like the broken fingers of a hand pointed upward, while the tracks on the ground were getting harder to notice. His daughter took more time to examine the ground before continuing forward, stopping every once in a while to bend down and check the area more closely.

At last, there was a clue that even he could not possibly miss, although it did not reassure them. They found a broken spear. The tip was covered with dry blood. The etched markings on the spear's staff indicated it belonged to Seth, one of the hunting party. He was only a few years older than Evangelina.

"That's a bad sign," Christian stated grimly.

His daughter stood over the spear and scanned the surrounding ruins. A throwing knife was tucked between her slender fingers. Christian readied his bow and stepped ahead of her. He also turned toward the ruins. The others could be inside any one of those vacant structures, or behind them. It was possible they might have moved on to a different location. If so, they might have been running blind. Christian knew whatever, or whoever, Seth stabbed did not die at this location. There wasn't enough blood on the ground.

They stood silent momentarily and listened to their surroundings, but heard nothing aside from the birds chirping from their out of reach perches. The stoic watchers from high above. They probably knew exactly what happened to the hunting party. Too bad they weren't going to tell.

The father and daughter stepped forward moving vigilantly down the cracked old street. They watched everywhere and listened to every sound. The ruins almost seemed to close in on them, as they continued deeper into the uninviting abandoned city. There were so many destroyed structures in the area. So many hiding places. They felt too vulnerable being out in the open.

Soon, they noticed a foul smell coming from nearby. The odor was not too familiar to Evangelina, but her father recognized it. It was the smell of death.

He held out his hand in front of her. "Wait. Do you smell that?"

She nodded, "Yes, what is it? It smells really bad, like food when it's gone rotten." She was partially covering her nose with the back of her wrist. It was the same hand holding the small knife.

"Exactly. It's death we're smelling. Something dead nearby."

She immediately understood. It was probably one or more of their clan they were smelling. The reason they hadn't returned was because they were likely dead. She wondered if it was really necessary to confirm it visually. She wasn't sure she wanted to do so. She'd seen recent death before in the shelter, but never old death that smelled like that. It was like rotten meat.

"Gotta find it," her father said. He simply followed the flies.

His daughter swallowed and forced a lump down her throat. She thought he'd want to do that. It didn't take long for them to locate the nearby pile of corpses on the side of a decayed two-story building. Surprisingly, there were more than three bodies on the ground and plenty of dried blood. The hunting party was definitely among the bodies. So were five other unknown strangers. They weren't dressed like nomads. They looked like they might've been civilized. It was odd how someone piled them all together. Abram was at the top of the pile right next to poor Abby. She looked like her chest had been ripped open. It was too hard to look at. Evangelina turned away from the ghastly scene, as tears filled her eyes.

She was filled with sorrow, anger, and curiosity. Who could have done such a horrible thing? And why was the hunting party placed with the corpses of these five strangers? Were they from another clan? Did they fight each other or fight together against a common threat?

Christian examined the corpses and noticed large bite marks on some. It looked like an animal attack. One corpse was missing a few fingers on his left hand. Another looked like his face had been clawed to the bone. There were five distinctive claw marks. Abram had the same marks across his chest. One person had a missing arm, and then there was Abby's chest. It looked so unreal.

Christian knew right away. They certainly didn't fight each other. Something killed them all. Something big and vicious. He immediately checked the area, fearing for their safety.

"It's not safe to be here. We should go," he warned. "There's nothing more we can do for them." He would've liked to bury the bodies, but it was too risky. He grabbed his daughter by her arm, and led her back the way they came. He was walking fast. "Hurry, before whatever killed them comes back for us."

She didn't complain. His fear made her afraid. She had never seen her father afraid before. It terrified her. She kept expecting something deadly to leap out from the windows at them.

It was a long walk back to the shelter, but they made it back in record time. Fortunately, they did not encounter anything along the way.

They were both relieved once they were safely within the shelter and the door was bolted shut. Evangelina was distraught, but she did her best to keep it together. The thought of seeing her friends' bodies was disturbing. It was going to take an extremely long time before she got that image out of her head. She was glad to be back home. At last, she felt safe enough that she could look to her father for answers to some of the questions racing through her haunted mind.

"Dad? What do you think could've done that to them?"

"I don't know." He shook his head. "A bear? Mountain lion?" He was just as confused as her. "Whatever it was, it's nothing we want to face out there. If it took out eight people and still got away, I'd rather not see it in person. Not to mention, we have no idea who piled the bodies there."

"How can we be sure *it* got away?" She asked. "Maybe whoever piled the dead together killed whatever it was. There may have been a bunch of others, if there was another clan," she supposed. "Do you think there was another clan?" She almost sounded hopeful at the prospect of more civilized people.

"Maybe. I suppose it's possible," he agreed. "They could've been traveling as a group, and then ran into trouble. Maybe our people showed up just in time to help the other group by fighting whatever large beast attacked. It killed those we found. The others probably chased it off. I doubt they'll return, after finding danger there."

"How do you know?"

"I don't. I'm just speculating. We do know they had time to pile the bodies before leaving."

"Oh, yeah. You're right," she nodded, as she realized he was correct about that.

"We'd better break the bad news to Troya and Avery," her father said. The thought of their clan being suddenly reduced to four left him feeling uneasy. Hunting and fishing would ultimately fall to him and his daughter alone. They were in for a rough winter. They lacked a sufficient amount of food, since the hunting party failed, which meant he and his daughter would have to go back out very soon. The thought was troubling. He did not wish to run into whatever beast killed the others. Nor did he want to put his daughter at risk, while something so dangerous was on the loose.

Of course, Troya and Avery did not take the news well. Life had been hard enough when there were seven of them. It wasn't going to be any easier with only the four of them remaining. The rest of the day was spent in mourning for their losses and worrying about their future. It was also unfortunate they could not bury their dead, which was their normal custom. Christian hated leaving the bodies out there to rot, but it did not seem reasonable to try burying them with the threat of danger being so immediate.

That night Evangelina stared at her ceiling, while lying on her bed in the darkness of her room. She thought about the sad fact that she was the last young person left in the shelter. She also thought about what her mother wrote in her journal when she stated her concern that someday Evangelina might end up alone. That possibility was starting to feel a little too inevitable. Troya was old. She wouldn't last much longer. Once she was gone, it would only be a clan of three. A trio was hardly a clan.

She shut her eyes and tried not to think about it. Instead, she tried to think about the wonderful things she read recently in the books from the library. She thought about castles made of glass, beautiful gardens full of colorful flowers, large puffy white clouds close enough to touch, fishing at the water road, and ruined cities covered in dense foliage.

Just great. Ruined cities were in her head. So was the smell of death. And the sight of those dead bodies piled together like logs waiting for the fire.

Her friends. Her clan. Her family.

Abram, Seth, and Abby were gone. Dead and gone. Forever. And they were rotten. Tears filled her brown eyes, especially for Abby. It was time to stop holding back. Abby had always been like a big sister to her. She and Seth had just become life partners only weeks earlier. They were so happy together. It was hard to believe they were gone. And Abram! He was the toughest, strongest person in the clan. What could possibly have killed him? Was it really a bear or mountain lion, or was it something far worse? Perhaps, it was a sasquatch, if they even existed. Surely, they are much bigger than bears. She had never seen one in real life, only in books, and the images weren't very clear. Her father didn't believe they were real. Many felt the same. However, she had found them fascinating since she was a little girl.

Then again, maybe the sky ships did it. They are supposed to be the biggest threat out there. Do they only abduct people or have they resorted to killing, too? There was no way to know the truth. It was a mystery that would probably never be solved.

Another question came to mind. How much longer would the clan be safe within their shelter? What if there might come a day when they must leave to survive? Anything was possible. Even that.

She didn't know what was scarier. The memory of seeing her dead friends, the thought of murderous sky ships, a wild beast on the loose, having to leave the shelter someday, or being completely and utterly alone. One thing was certain. Once again, she wasn't going to sleep well.

Over the next few weeks, the clan had to adapt to becoming a clan of four. Each person had to shoulder new responsibilities to make up for those, who had passed on. The need to learn from one another was more urgent than before. Troya made sure they all knew how to cook, so they could survive on their own, while Avery taught them all some first aid skills. Christian showed Avery and Troya how to build useful tools and weapons. His daughter already knew that. There was really nothing she could teach to her elders. They knew most of what she knew. She was the youngest and least experienced in the clan.

The warmer days were spent with her father hunting, fishing, and foraging. They managed to gather plenty of food to sustain them through the colder winter months. Troya made sure to ration the food for each meal she prepared to make it last longer. Fortunately, she was not a big eater. Neither was Evangelina. Avery was also quite lean and liked being that way. It was Christian who ate the most. He was the largest and strongest of them, considering Abram was gone. He had a healthy appetite, although he tried not to eat more than he should.

The shelter was much quieter than it used to be. Everyone kept busy during the daytime hours. Most of them kept to themselves at night. Only Christian and his daughter spent time together at night, since they resided in the same living quarters. Each still had their own privacy with separate bedrooms.

Some nights when Evangelina was alone in her room and her father was asleep next door in his room, she would try what her mother suggested in her journal. She'd try to communicate with the spirits of the dead. She had been trying to reach her mother for years with no luck. Recently, she tried speaking to Abby to see if she'd appear to her. It wasn't working, which was frustrating. She tried hard to believe in the spirits like her mother said, but it made no difference. They wouldn't appear for her. Not even in her dreams.

Well, she did dream about Abby, Seth, and Abram, but it was more like memories of times they shared. She missed them dearly. So many people had died since she was a little girl. She remembered most of them. However, she only missed some of them. The rest just sort of faded into the past.

Winter went by without incident. The weather was warming up. Soon, it would be time to go out and hunt, again. While Evangelina was dreading going back out there, her father was actually looking forward to it. He needed a change of pace. He spent much of the winter reading books, much to his delight. Still, he was bored being in the shelter and wanted to venture outdoors, so he could work on building up their food supply. He was tired of rationing. He longed for a decent meal.

He and his daughter went out on their first spring hunt of the new year and managed to find a large deer within minutes. It was surprising to find one so close to the shelter. It had been a long time since that occurred. They ate well that week.

As more weeks went by, winter was rapidly becoming a distant memory. Evangelina was getting used to going hunting with her father. They had been fairly lucky the past few times finding food within a short distance of the shelter. Of course, they both knew that would not last. Soon, they'd have to go further away either to the north or south. Going east across the river, or water road, wasn't an option. There was nothing to the west, aside from more city ruins, which they preferred to avoid.

Avery wanted to join them on a hunt, but Troya forbade it. If anything were to happen to him, they would be in trouble. His skills were far too important. It left him feeling depressed. If Christian was bored from being cooped up all winter, imagine how Avery felt. He had not left the shelter in over two years. The last time was to help bury someone who died. He was going out of his mind being stuck in the shelter all the time. He had no idea how Troya could manage to stay content, considering she had not left the shelter since she was a young woman.

Troya was not fond of being on the outside. She was never a strong fighter or a good hunter. Being outside actually terrified her. There was a chance of danger at every turn. She preferred being within the safety of the shelter, where the biggest risk to her health was an accident in the kitchen or a bad fall. Those were risks she could accept. She even kept away from the workshop to avoid any accidents from happening to her in there. She knew her way around the kitchen well, so that's what she stuck to each day. Cooking breakfast, lunch, and dinner.

The rest of her time was typically spent reading books. She had already read every single book in the library more than once. Whenever she felt the urge to read a book, she'd choose one of her favorites. She liked to read in her room, where it was quiet. She never had a life partner, nor did she want one. She was happy being alone in her room, and content with sharing the company of the others at the dining table.

Avery, on the other hand, was lonely in that regard. He knew there was no chance of ever having a life partner, unless it was with Christian's teenage daughter, which didn't seem appropriate. She was far too young for him. He was close to her father's age, so that was unlikely. He had to settle for the lonely boring life he had with the knowledge that nothing would ever improve.

Needless to say, he was not a happy man. No one ever noticed his depression, since he typically spent most of his time alone. Not even Troya, who was usually so observant, noticed his sorrow. He hid it well. The only motivation Avery had to go on was the fact that the clan relied so heavily on his medical knowledge and first aid skills. He was grateful when the others finally showed an interest in learning from him. Teaching them first aid gave him something to look forward to, for the most part. It also made him feel like they might not always need him so desperately, which brought him some comfort.

At last, summer had arrived. It was time for another hunt. Christian and Evangelina had to travel a little to the north along the water road. The trail in that direction was thicker with trees. That path had never actually been a road, so it was heavily overgrown compared to the south trail. It was more of a game trail than a foot path, meaning it was mainly used by animals. It was also muddy due to a recent heavy rainfall.

There had actually been a severe thunderstorm that passed through the area the night before. From within the shelter they could not hear it, so they were not always aware of whenever it rained. Not until they went outside and saw the ground was wet with puddles of water, or covered with mud, instead of the usual dry dirt.

Another way they could tell if it rained was if they heard the pipes drain into the cistern, which was connected to the shelter. Whenever it rained, it would catch water that would feed down a filtered pipe into the shelter's water storage tank. Pipes would then feed water to the kitchen and community bathroom. It was a plumbing system that already existed from when the shelter was first built, and it worked well.

The rain made everything smell different, as well. Christian enjoyed the smell of the grass, after a rainy day. It was different in a nice way. His daughter wasn't very fond of walking over mud, but he didn't mind so much. It gave him a reason to clean his boots.

His daughter's mind was on other things besides rain and mud. She was still worried about that unknown large beast that was on the loose, even though months had gone by since it killed the others. She kept knives in both hands, just to be safe. She wasn't as good with a bow like her father, so she didn't bother to carry one. She did carry a big hunting knife on her belt and kept more small knives all along the sides of her belt in small holders. The belt was custom made by her father, who learned a few tailoring skills from her mother. Evangelina also had a spear strapped to her back. She hoped it would be enough.

After a few minutes of walking behind him in silence along the trail, she asked, "Dad?"

"What is it?" He did not turn around when he answered, nor did he stop walking.

"What if we run into that beast?"

Confused, he stopped and turned to ask, "What beast?" He had not thought about it in a long time, unlike her, who could not get it out of her mind. Therefore, he forgot about it.

"The one that killed Abram, Seth, and Abby!" She rolled her eyes unable to believe he had forgotten.

"Sweetie, that beast is probably long gone. It's been months. Besides, it was to the south. We should be okay up here." He stepped over a large puddle with his long legs. "Okay. Let's not talk too much, otherwise we'll scare away the game."

"Right. Sorry, Dad." She hopped over the puddle behind him. A few moments later, she added, "It's just that I can't stop thinking about it."

He sighed. "Try. If you let your fears overwhelm you, life is going to be extremely daunting for you," he said.

She knew he was right. She decided then and there never to mention it again. She tried to push it out of her mind to no avail.

They soon emerged from the trees and came upon a small grassy clearing, where they saw a plump brown rabbit. Her father held his hand up to stop her from going further. He readied his bow and took aim. He shot an arrow, which swiftly struck its target on the first try. It wasn't too bad for the first catch of the day.

A moment later, his daughter scored a squirrel with one of her knives in the very same clearing. It wasn't much, but combined with the rabbit it was adequate for dinner.

They tried to find more game as the day went on, but were not successful. They did manage to gather a few berries on the way back to the shelter. All in all, it was not too bad of a hunt. Tomorrow was another day. They could try to find something more. The recent rainfall would have brought out the worms, so fishing might be a better idea, since there would be plenty of bait.

As they went through the ruins on their way back to the hidden stairway leading down to the shelter's entrance, they walked along a path they had always taken without a second thought. So, when a piece of debris fell from the top of one of the abandoned four-story buildings, it caught them completely by surprise. It seemed the lightning from the previous night's thunderstorm had struck the roof's ledge of that particular structure, which loosened some of the wall. It just happened to fall when they passed beneath it.

As the large pieces of debris crumbled and fell, Christian heard it. He looked up in time to see it. He only had seconds to react. He immediately pushed his daughter back and fell to the ground in front of her. Just then, the rubble crashed down on top of him.

His daughter could only look on in horror.

CHAPTER 4: ROOFTOPS

From within a cloud of dust Christian cried out in pain. It was a pain like he'd never felt before. When the dust cleared, it became obvious the debris had fallen onto his right leg crushing it. He couldn't move.

Evangelina picked herself up and hurried over to her father. She looked confused, but soon realized what happened. It occurred so quickly, she barely had time to register it until it was too late. She stared in disbelief at the pile of debris. It could have just as easily fallen onto her head and crushed her skull, instead. She was lucky her father pushed her back, but now it was him lying on the ground. He needed her help. There was no time to think about it. She needed to act fast.

She tried with all her might to move the debris off of his leg. It was so heavy. She tried, again. This time, she was able to get it off of his leg. He cried out, again.

"Sorry!"

He struggled to speak through clenched teeth. The pain was intense. "It's... fine. You did... good." He tried to breathe. He glanced over at his leg. It looked like it was in pretty bad shape. "You'll need to help... help me back to the shelter."

Her eyes gaped with fear. She was afraid if he tried to stand, he'd only make it worse. She didn't want to contribute to it. She hesitated. They weren't far from the shelter, so she decided to get Avery. He'd know what to do.

"Dad, please, hang on. I'll get Avery to help me bring you inside. I don't think I can do it alone without hurting you worse. Your leg... it's..." She couldn't even say it. She didn't want to think it, but it was obvious. His leg was broken beyond repair. She didn't need to be a doctor to know he was never going to walk, again. She raced to the shelter before he could protest.

Christian closed his eyes tight, trying to block out the pain. It was no use. He wanted to cry. The pain was unlike anything he'd ever felt before. He came close to fainting.

Seconds later, his daughter returned with Avery.

Avery quickly went to work applying a splint to the injured leg. "Hang on, buddy. I know it hurts. We'll get you inside, as soon as possible. Be strong."

Evangelina found herself looking back up at the rooftop. She wondered if the debris fell on its own or if it was pushed. She stepped back to give herself a better view. She saw no one up there. Still, she felt like someone or something was out there with them. She turned her attention back to Avery and her father. "Hurry," she urged. "It's not safe out here." She stated the obvious.

"Almost done," Avery replied. "Chris, we're going to get you up on your feet. Be sure not to put any pressure on that leg. Use our shoulders to brace yourself. Evie, I need your help." She moved closer. He issued instructions to her. "Stand on the other side of him and help me lift him, so we can get him inside." He turned back to her father. "Okay. Are you ready?"

He nodded weakly.

Together, they were able to gently help Christian back toward the shelter. The two had a hard time getting him down the stairs. They moved down slowly. Somehow, they managed and brought him back into the safety of the shelter. Troya closed and bolted the door, once they were inside. Christian was led to their hospital room and placed on a bed.

It was a long while later when Avery briefly realized he finally got to see the outside. It was a shame he never got the chance to enjoy it. Considering what happened to Christian, he began to think he was better off staying in the shelter, where he was less likely to get injured or killed. The rest of the day went by with him tending to Christian's leg. He wrapped it and tried to give him something to ease the pain. Evangelina helped in any way that she could.

Many thoughts began to go through her mind. She hoped she was wrong and that her father would eventually walk, again. In the meantime, hunting and fishing would now be her responsibility alone. Avery could go with her, but would that be wise? What if something happened to him? Without a doctor around, her father may suffer. And there was no way Troya was going out on a hunt. Evangelina knew her father wasn't going to like her going out alone, but what choice would she have? They needed food to survive and supplies were still low. Even if they rationed what they had, someone would have to go hunting or fishing by the end of the week.

She frowned. Life was about to get a lot harder for her. She was ready. She had to be. She always had to be ready for anything. It was how she was taught.

Her mind drifted back to that rooftop. Could it have been an accident? It was possible, but she really wanted to know for sure. How could she know without going into that building and investigating the roof? It would have to wait until tomorrow. She could use the excuse of going fishing to go out.

The next day, she went out alone. She told the others she was going to the water road to catch fish. Her father had even told her it was a good time to fish, so who was going to argue with that logic? They needed food. She left at dawn. It was the best time for fishing. As soon as she found a good spot, she gathered worms from the dirt to use as bait. Once she had enough, she returned to the building near the trail.

The dark open doorway stared back at her. It almost dared her to enter. Did she dare? She looked up at the rooftop and down at the scattered debris that crippled her father a day earlier. It was sufficient to motivate her. She entered the building. It was the first time she'd ever done such a thing.

Her small knives were clenched firmly between the fingers of both hands, as she stepped into the abandoned building. Right away, she noticed the unfamiliar smells of mildew and mold. Ages of junk and broken furniture littered the lobby. There was an open doorway on either side of the staircase on the ground floor. She had no interest in investigating those apartments. Instead, she climbed the stairs with caution.

The were two more open doors on the second floor. There were also two broken windows in the hallway facing the front of the building. She peered through and looked down at the trail. For the first time, she realized it was actually wider than how it looked from the ground. She could see it far more clearly from above. It was easily noticeable that it was once a road. Years of vegetation covered the sides closer to the structures, giving it the appearance of a small trail. She wondered if vehicles once rode over it.

When she was ready, she continued up to the third floor hallway and looked out the windows from there, once more ignoring the open doorways to the vacant apartments. She listened thoroughly for any sound, but there was only the crunching of the debris on the floor beneath her hand-me-down boots.

Every time a person from the clan died, their personal belongings and clothing were shared with the other members of the clan. That was the custom, since the beginning. Every article of clothing she owned used to belong to someone else. Most of it belonged to her mother. Her clothing fit her well.

Soon, she reached the top floor. She noticed one apartment still had its door barely hanging from the hinges. The other apartment door was missing. The one with the broken door caught her attention, for some reason. She found herself drawn to it.

She peeked inside. The smell was horrendous. She immediately noticed a huge hole in the ceiling, where daylight was shining through. A puddle of stagnant water was directly under it. Water dripped down from the hole. Waterlogged items littered the floor of that room, which was a complete mess. There was so much junk on the floor. The actual floor was barely visible, except near the door. She put one foot inside. The floor felt soft and weak when she stepped inside. It made her hesitate.

Just then, a bird flew through the apartment and up through the hole in the ceiling. The sound of its flapping wings startled her causing her to almost stumble. She shifted her feet to steady herself.

One foot began sinking through the old wooden floor, so she quickly stepped back out to the hallway.

Her eyes turned to the two windows in the hallway. She moved closer and gazed down to the street level. Each floor she climbed made her feel queasier from the height. Still, she found herself fascinated with the expanded view from each height. Her vantage point kept improving. She could see more and further than she ever imagined. It was exhilarating.

She turned and looked up at the last flight of stairs. It led to an open door. The roof. She walked up the stairs cautiously and slowly stepped out onto the roof. The floor was covered with a black material she'd never seen before. It felt like walking on rubber. It was spongy and soft. She stepped carefully. She could see the gaping hole that led down to the apartment below. She tried not to get too close.

The roof seemed empty for the most part. There were some strange structures and items spread out randomly across the surface. One was metallic and shaped like a large stove pipe. There were some odd metallic branches sticking out from the ground connected to wires. That's what the antennas looked like to her. Branches. She had no idea what they were. She also saw some type of dish-shaped item lying on the ground. It too was made of metal with wires connected to it. It was heavy when she tried to move it.

At last, she noticed the broken wall at the edge that faced front. The rest of the wall looked weak, as if it would probably fall eventually. She kicked it and saw bricks fly off the roof falling to the ground below. She stepped closer to the edge and peered over the side. It was the highest she'd ever been in her life. She began to feel dizzy, so she stepped back.

She closed her eyes momentarily and regained her senses. When she opened her eyes, she stared across at the opposite rooftops to the south of her. They were similar looking and mostly level with each other. Some of the same items were on those rooftops, as well. She counted the roofs. There were five. She walked to the sides of the roof, where she stood. She noticed two rooftops to the west, and another two to the east of her. Five on each side of the trail.

Her eyes searched the distance beyond that block. She had no idea there were so many ruins. There were buildings and rooftops as far as her eyes could see going to the south and west. They came in all shapes and sizes. Some looked extremely tall, but those were far away. There were mostly trees to the east. The north was a mixture of both with the structures being further apart from one another.

A new fascination came over her. She wondered what the view would be like from some of the other rooftops. She could see everything for miles in each direction. The city must've been huge. Of course, there was a grave risk that came with entering the abandoned structures. She got lucky this time. She might not be so lucky the next time. Would there even be a next time? She kind of wanted there to be one. She loved the view from high up. It was spectacular. Something she would never forget.

She tried to imagine how the view would look at night. Night was something she'd only ever seen in books. She imagined it was so pretty in real life. Of course, her father made sure she was never outside at night. It was too dangerous. Nobody from the clan ever went out at night. It was one of their rules.

Only sky ships were out at night. She wondered, where were they at this very moment? Where did they hide during the day? Did they return to space? To their world? She gazed upward, but couldn't see beyond the blue sky. As much as sky ships scared her, she was curious to see how they looked, even if seeing one could mean the end for her. If they caught her in their beam of light, she'd be gone forever.

What did they do with the people they abducted? Did they eat them? She felt disgusted.

Her attention turned back to the view below. There was so much green! She enjoyed how she could see over the trees just like the birds. There had to be thousands of trees everywhere, even on the buildings. It was more than she ever imagined. They seemed to go on forever in every direction.

She let her eyes follow the line of the trail toward the water road. She could even see the water road and how far it stretched in both directions. It seemed to have no end. It just kept going on and on. It suddenly seemed more like a barrier that she could never cross.

It occurred to her that if she didn't get to the water road soon, there'd be no fish for her to catch. She sighed and took one last look around her. She was in awe. The beauty was truly breathtaking. She found it funny how the clouds still looked too far away to touch, even from all the way up on the roof. It made her smile.

She noticed something else she never knew about. Just beyond the distant faded ruins in the north, there were real mountains. If it had been a cloudy day like yesterday, she probably might not have noticed. As it happened, it was a bright and sunny morning. It saddened her how the mountains seemed so very far away. She figured it would take a year to reach them on foot. Too bad.

Finally, she turned to leave. There were fish waiting to be caught. She didn't want to be outside too long. She hoped to be back in the shelter by mid-afternoon.

Later that night, she lay on her bed still thinking about being up on that rooftop. She wished it were safer outside, so she could explore more rooftops. She would love to check every rooftop view in the ruins. She wanted to see the view from every angle. She also wanted to see what it looked like beyond the ruins in the south, and where the water road ended. Did it open up into a large sea?

Her mother wrote about large seas that covered large portions of the world. There were a few photos in the library books that showed vast blue seas. Some of the images had giant fish called whales leaping out from the surface. What a magnificent thing to witness. If only they weren't extinct. So many of the sea creatures were extinct long before the *Big Apocalyptic Event*.

Her mother said it was due to various reasons, such as global warming and pollution. Plus, humans hunted a lot of the sea creatures for their resources, until there were no more. Humans were also the cause of global warming and pollution. Her mother speculated that humans were always the biggest threat to the planet. She blamed humans for most of the things that went wrong in the past.

Could it really have been that bad?

Evangelina wondered what the world must have been like before the cities became ruins. Based on photos she'd seen in the books, there were so many people. Hundreds of people lived in those abandoned structures she saw from the rooftop. Probably a lot more than that. It must've been so crowded.

She closed her eyes and tried to sleep, but she couldn't. As usual, her mind was racing. Suddenly, she had the urge to go to the library and look through the books, which had photos. She wanted to see what life looked like before, now that she had a new perspective on things. She fought the urge to leave her bed, although it wasn't easy.

Her curiosity was eating away at her. She had gotten a glimpse of how people used to live when she stepped into that wet messy apartment. Apparently, they had so many possessions that everything was scattered across the floor. They likely had more things than they needed, as opposed to her clan who only had what they really needed. She thought about when her mother wrote how she had to leave her old toys behind when she entered the shelter. It made her wonder, exactly how many toys did she have? It must have been a lot. No wonder she was miserable. It had to be difficult adjusting to having so much less than what she was used to.

Evangelina had a feeling people took many things for granted in the past. They probably never learned to appreciate what they had because there was so much to have, unlike now.

And what about the hunting trail? How did it look before it became overgrown with so much greenery? Was it similar to that cracked black road down in the southern ruins? How did it change so drastically? She always thought it was some old dirt trail. Not a paved road. However, from high up, it looked like it might have been a real road. A street. That was a word she recalled from the books.

It was amazing how the world looked so different from high above the ground. It was so much bigger than she imagined. Everything was much more fascinating. It all had so much depth to it. From the ground the ruins seem so intimidating, but from the rooftop they actually look more like a city. A city with its maze of buildings just waiting to be explored. Sometimes, it's so easy to forget that the ruins were once cities. She never really thought of them that way, until standing on that rooftop.

She wondered what else she could see from different rooftops. Maybe there were better hunting grounds where the animals were plentiful. Perhaps, she could see herds of deer from certain rooftops. She might be able to know which direction she should go to hunt, rather than guessing every time. It would certainly save her a lot of time. It would be a great advantage for a lone hunter.

Naturally, it would mean going into more abandoned structures, which was the tricky part. Not to mention climbing a lot of stairs, while going past numerous apartments. Was that something she really wanted to do, especially while alone? What if she ran into trouble? What if she ran into a nomad, or a group of them? Worse! What if she encountered that beast that killed Abram, Seth, and Abby? Did she really want to take that chance?

Probably not.

Maybe she was better off staying away from the ruins, considering she'd have to go out on her own. There would be no one to watch her back or her sides. That building had a lot of windows, so there was plenty of light on the upper floors. However, the ground floor had been darker and kind of spooky. Many of the other ruins are also dark. Much darker and spookier.

"There could always be danger hiding in the shadows." It's something her father used to tell her when she was younger. He emphasized it often, until she was old enough to remember it. She knew he wasn't merely trying to scare her. It was true. It was something she had to consider, before she dared risk her life just to find deer easier or to get a better glimpse of the world from a higher vantage point.

There was another problem she had to consider. How was she supposed to bring a full-sized deer back to the shelter by herself, if she killed one too far from the shelter? She wasn't strong enough to carry one alone, so was it really worth the risk?

She became frustrated and was finally able to fall asleep. That night she dreamed about flying over the ruins like a bird without a care in the world. It was a wonderful experience. It seemed her initial fear of heights was fading and had been replaced by awe and wonder.

CHAPTER 5: HOPELESS

A week had passed since Christian's injury. Almost every bone in his right leg had been crushed. The pain he felt was still intense, although he was able to bear it enough to not cry. He was crippled. That fact had plenty of time to sink in for him and for his daughter. The dynamic of the clan had shifted for the worse, once again.

He was still lying in the hospital, where Avery could watch over him more closely. There was no telling how long it would be before he could sleep in his own bed. It was torture.

So was the thought of his daughter having to go hunting and fishing on her own with no one to watch her back, or her sides, as they always joked with each other. While she was technically old enough to handle herself on the outside, she was still his daughter. He was never going to stop worrying about her. He had plenty of faith in her skills to know she would be careful. Not that it made a difference to him. There were simply too many dangers out there.

Avery came in to check on him. He used a stethoscope to check his heart. Next, he checked his blood pressure. It was high. A thermometer was placed into his mouth. Avery raised an eyebrow.

"You still have a fever. I believe it was brought on by some kind of bacterial infection," he said.

"Great," Christian frowned. His situation just kept getting worse. There wasn't much he could do about it. He'd been lying in the bed like he was supposed to be doing.

"I can give you something for the fever, but we're running low on antibiotics," Avery added. "Hopefully, your temperature will go down by tomorrow. I'll keep a close eye on the infection."

"Okay. Hopefully the bones in my leg will grow back by the end of the week, so I can leave. Right?" Christian smirked, and then winced from the pain in his leg.

Avery pouted. "I'm so sorry this happened to you, my friend. I wish I could say your leg will get better soon, but the cold reality is you'll probably never walk again. We don't have one of those old chairs with the wheels on the sides, so you'll probably remain bedridden."

"Your bedside manner is fantastic. I think I'm feeling better already."

Avery managed a slight chuckle. There really was nothing he could do for Christian's leg. All he could do was try and keep the fever down, while trying to make his patient as comfortable as possible. Ultimately, Christian would have to be moved to his own bed, where his daughter would have to help take care of him. He was going to need help getting cleaned up and using the bathroom. His meals would have to be brought to him. Avery did not envy the responsibilities his daughter was going to be stuck with for the rest of her father's life. She was most likely not going to be ready for it. She lacked the experience.

Meanwhile, Christian had gone back to staring into the distance and feeling sorry for himself. There wasn't anything else for him to do.

Over the last few days, his daughter would visit him during the morning, afternoon, and night. She had even sat beside him and read to him. She read him the book he had started, which pleased him. He enjoyed her company, while he had it.

Other times, he was left wondering where she had gone. She had begun going on hunts every other day. She claimed she couldn't find sufficient food to last longer than that, so she needed to keep going out. He hated the fact that she was constantly going out alone. He wanted to be there with her.

Instead, he was stuck in the hospital bed unable to go anywhere. Unable to do anything about his predicament. Was this going to be his life from now on? He felt absolutely miserable. This was no way to live. Life was hard enough. He had to remind himself it had only been a week. How was he going to deal with being bedridden after a month, or a year? And then there was the infection. It worried him.

Sometimes, he felt like death would be a better alternative. The easy release from his burden, and from becoming a burden. He didn't want his daughter to get stuck with taking care of him for the rest of her life. That was no way to live either.

He tried to think of something else to occupy his mind. Mazzy. She died from an infection. He missed her so much. Thinking about her always made him sad, but considering his current situation, it actually made him happy to think about her. Remembering all the good times they shared helped cheer him up slightly. At least, it got his mind off of his injury and infection. The fever didn't bother him as much.

When Mazzy was still alive, life was so much easier. For one thing, there were more people in the clan! It was still hard to believe there were only the four of them left. Times were getting desperate. Would he be the next to go? It was a terrible way to think, but he could not help himself. He felt so useless. Maybe the others would be better off if he were gone.

No. He couldn't think that way.

He closed his eyes and tried to think back to when he was a child. His parents took care of him back then. They always made everything better. Well, they tried. He missed them, too. He wished they had not died so long ago. They never got the chance to know their granddaughter. They would have loved her so much, and she would have loved them.

Tears formed in his eyes. He wanted so badly to give up, but he could not break his promise to his daughter. She didn't want him to die. She already lost her mother. She wasn't ready to lose her father.

The only time he seemed to not think about his injury was when his daughter was sitting in the room reading to him. Those small moments brought him peace of mind. The subtle sound of her voice reading to him made him forget his problems. Instead, he would focus on the story she told him.

He tried to focus on that, as he attempted to fall asleep. Eventually, he was out cold.

Early the next morning, he found himself being woken up by Avery. "Chris, wake up. I have bad news."

Instantly, his mind went to his daughter. Did something happen to her, while she was out there hunting? He became agitated and tried to sit up. "Where's my daughter?" He demanded.

"Easy," Avery gently pushed him back down on the bed. "She's asleep in her room. She's fine. It's not her. It's Troya. She's gone."

"Gone?" Christian was confused. "Where would she go in the middle of the night? That woman hates going outside." He wondered if it had been the sky ships. Did they somehow manage to take her away, while she was in her bed?

Avery replied, "She's dead."

The death of Troya was inevitable due to her old age, but that fact did not make her passing any easier to accept. The other three members of the clan still mourned her loss. They would miss her, and her cooking. They would miss the way she mothered them all, and how she gave good advice. She was the last person of the clan, who actually remembered how the world used to be. She would often tell them stories about her life before the *Big Apocalyptic Event*. They were always so fascinating to hear.

It had only been days since her passing. In her absence, Avery and Evangelina were forced to share the responsibilities of preparing meals for the three remaining members of the clan. If one could even consider three people a clan. The clan was practically extinct.

Evangelina tried to get her mind off of Troya's death. It was too depressing. The woman had been like a grandmother to her. Now she was gone. Another family member lost forever.

As a distraction, she had been exploring the rooftops of the same block over the past week. On the opposite side of the trail from that first building she could easily walk from one rooftop to the other, so she did. She stood on the roof closest to the west. They rarely went west since there was nothing to hunt in that direction. She wondered if there were nomads hiding out in the many buildings on that side of the ruins. She had no intention of finding out. There was nothing for her in that direction, but danger.

She walked across the rooftops as far east as she could go, and then gazed over the woods that stretched out toward the water road. She dared not lean on the waist high ledges, for fear that the short walls might crumble apart and collapse to the ground below like the one that crushed her father's leg. She still had no idea lightning had been the cause of the accident.

As usual the clouds drew her attention to the sky. She noticed a lone bird flying high overhead. It soared over her and continued south. Her eyes followed it. At that moment, she wondered what it would be like to fly. To be able to see the world from high above. The view had to be so much greater than what she could see from the top of four-story tall structures. Looking down from high places no longer made her feel dizzy. Height had become too much of a fascination to her. She knew there was nothing to fear from being on the rooftops, as long as she didn't fall off the side, or fall through into one of the apartments below. She stepped delicately wherever she went, always expecting to find a weak point. So far, she hadn't.

While exploring the rooftops, she also had plenty of opportunities to explore some of the vacant apartments of the buildings on that block. She found many items that were foreign to her. She wished her father was exploring with her, so he could explain what the items were. She collected quite a few souvenirs. Mostly small useless trinkets. One was an old rusty keychain. She had no idea what it was, but liked the metal ring at the end. She picked up an old coin that no longer had any value. She also found a screwdriver, which she knew was a tool. It could also be used as a weapon. Another thing she found was a small, colorful, cube-shaped puzzle toy. She'd never seen anything like it before.

Exploring the ruins had become sort of a side hobby for her whenever she went out hunting or fishing. First, she'd explore some nearby ruins, and then she'd follow the trail to her destination. She never spent too much time in the ruins. Finding food was always her main priority.

When she was ready, she headed back to the shelter carrying two rabbits she bagged earlier. As she entered through the metallic door, she noticed Avery pacing back and forth. Curious, she bolted the door behind her and turned to face him. When he saw her, he approached with desperation in his eyes.

He asked frantically, "What took you so long? I've been waiting for you. It's your father. His fever has gotten worse. I can't seem to do anything about that damned infection."

She allowed the words to sink in, before reacting. Her mother died from an infection when she was sick. She became worried and was already expecting the worst. She tried to remain calm, as she inquired, "What does that mean exactly?" She knew what it meant, but she asked anyway.

"It means he could die." Right away, he could see the pain in her eyes. It was not what she wanted to hear. The thought of losing her father was more than she could bear. "I'm sorry," he added.

"Why aren't you in the hospital by his side?"

"There's really nothing I can do. We don't have the medicine I need to help him. I've been giving him everything I have just to keep the fever in check. It's no use." He felt defeated.

He might have said more, but by this point she stopped listening. She handed him the rabbits and walked toward the hospital. Her father seemed to be asleep. She could tell he was still breathing, although his breaths were shallow. She moved closer to his side and stared down at him. The tears fought their way down her face. She wasn't ready to lose him, especially not right after losing Troya.

Evangelina spent nearly every waking moment by her father's bedside. There may not have been anything Avery could do for him, but there was something she could do. She could make him feel loved during his last moments. She could let him know how much he means to her. And she did. She told him how much she loves him over and over. She talked to him about everything she had been doing outside. She made sure to finish reading that book to him. She held his hand and kissed his cheek.

The only problem was he was barely awake for any of it. For all she knew, he heard nothing she'd said to him. Maybe she was only talking to herself. Maybe not. Either way, she was going to do it anyway. Just in case he could hear her.

"Dad. I don't want you to worry about me. I'll be fine. You just focus on yourself. Get better, so we can spend more time together. I know I'm being selfish, but I don't wanna let you go. I love you so much. Please, be strong, Dad. Please..." Her voice broke off, and she cried.

She continued to speak to him softly in a soothing voice. He could hear her. He listened to every word she said. He heard her talking about exploring the buildings of the ruins. How she stood on the rooftops and looked out across the ruins at the abandoned world. She told him about the items she found. Her souvenirs. She described each item, since he could not see them.

He wanted to tell her she was crazy for exploring the ruins. He couldn't believe she would be that careless to risk her safety like that. After a while, he could hear the fascination in her voice. He could tell how much it meant to her. She had not shown such excitement, since the first time she killed an animal on a hunt. How could he think to take that joy away from her, knowing he was about to leave her? Realizing he was going to abandon her, the way her mother did so long ago, made him feel terrible.

Gradually, the pain in his leg was fading, until he barely noticed it anymore. Was it getting better? Was he going to make a full recovery? Maybe he wasn't going to die, yet. Maybe by shutting down, it was his body's way of healing. A glimmer of hope gave him the strength to gently squeeze her hand. She stopped talking once he did.

"Dad? You can hear me?" He squeezed, once more. Her heart skipped a beat. She pulled his hand closer and kissed it tenderly. "I love you, Dad."

In his mind, he responded. I love you, too. He tried to say the words out loud, but could not. He wanted to get up from that wretched bed already. He was so tired of lying there. It was more than he could take. In the past, he had always been so strong. Why couldn't he be strong now? Why couldn't he just stand up, or maybe open his eyes? He tried with all his might to lift himself up.

At last, he felt himself moving. He felt himself rising from the bed. He sat up and pushed himself further. He forced himself to stand. The pain was gone. It was all mind over matter and the pain no longer mattered. He was stronger than it. He could beat this. He would. Nothing was going to stop him. He turned to face his daughter. She was still sitting beside the bed next to his body.

It was then that he realized he was dead.

His daughter was now crying over his body. Her head was on his chest, which no longer moved up and down from his breathing. His body was completely still. And so was his spirit momentarily.

Finally, he said, "I'm so sorry, Evie," except she couldn't hear him.

"Don't blame yourself," a familiar voice said from behind him. When he turned he was almost blinded by the light. A figure stood there across from him. It was a woman. She moved closer and her features became clear to him.

"Mazzy?"

"It's time to go, Christian," she said to him. She reached out her hand and he took it. "We can still watch over her. This is her time, now. Our time is over."

He nodded and stepped into the light with her. He took one last look at his daughter and his body. Now it was Mazzy, who squeezed his hand. He faced her and said, "I'm ready."

Avery walked into the room and saw that Evangelina was crying over her father's sleeping form. He had a feeling he knew what it meant. His friend was gone. Her father was dead. He bowed his head and stepped closer, placing a hand on her shoulder.

"I'm so sorry, kiddo."

And then there were two.

Early the next day, Avery was outside digging yet another grave. This time, he was doing it alone. He couldn't bring himself to ask Evangelina to help him dig her own father's grave. This was something he needed to do for her. He dug close to where they interred Troya. He had to keep stopping to rest. He hated how he had to dig another grave so soon after the previous one. It was way too soon.

He jammed the shovel into the dirt and leaned on the staff. He took a moment to cry for his dead friend. "Damn it, Chris. Why couldn't you just get better?" He wiped the tears away angrily, smearing dirt on his face, and then continued to dig the grave.

Once it was ready, he went into the shelter. The body was already wrapped. There was no way he'd be able to carry it out on his own. He was going to need her help.

Evangelina was crying on her bed face down when he knocked on her front door. She ignored the knocking, at first, but then realized he was the only other person left in the shelter with her. She didn't want to be rude or cruel. He was mourning, too. She forced herself up and out of her room. She walked over to the door, but first she wiped her tears away. She could hide the tears, but not the redness of her puffy eyes. When she opened the door, she saw Avery standing there looking pitiful. In that moment, she realized he always seemed to look that way to her. She waited for him to speak. There was nothing she wanted to say. She wasn't in the mood to speak. Not yet.

In a weak voice, he informed her, "The grave is ready. I'll need your help."

She said nothing. She only nodded.

They went into the hospital to retrieve the body. Right away, the tears poured down her face, again. Seeing her father wrapped up in a dark shroud struck her hard. Avery waited until she composed herself. He understood her pain. He had to bury both his parents long ago.

When she was ready, they grabbed the body. He took the head and shoulders, while she grabbed the legs. Christian was heavy. It took a lot of effort for them to carry him out of the shelter, up the stairs, and over to the grave. They needed to take a few breaks, which only prolonged their misery.

At last, the body was placed into the grave. Once they both caught their breath, it was time to cover the body. Avery decided he could do that part alone. There was no reason to make this poor young girl bury her own father.

"I can do this part," he said softly. She looked up at him. He was already holding the shovel. "You shouldn't have to do this." He shook his head.

She sighed sadly and nodded, before turning away. She didn't leave, though. Instead, she cried some more. She made no effort to hide it, this time. What was the point?

Avery began placing dirt over the body at a steady pace. He worked as fast as he could, but he was so tired from carrying the body. It left him drained. Regardless, he pushed himself to get the job done. He figured if the body was completely covered, perhaps it would somehow make it easier for her to look at the grave. He knew he had to do this for her. He felt like he owed her. It was his fault both her parents were dead. He was the doctor, but he failed to heal them both. Each pile of dirt he tossed in was another futile attempt to make amends for his failure.

Finally, it was done. Avery was out of breath. He thought he was going to have a heart attack, considering how hard he pushed himself. Even if he wanted to say something, he lacked the strength. That suited Evangelina just fine. She didn't want to hear anything from anyone, at the moment. For a long time, they both stood over the grave in silence.

Eventually, it began to rain on them. Still, they remained in place.

This was the third time Avery found himself outside of the shelter in the past month, yet he could not relish in the moment. As badly as he had wanted to leave the shelter, now all he wanted to do was run back inside. He felt so vulnerable standing out there for so long, but he dared not leave Evangelina alone. Not in the condition she was in. He tried to ignore the rain like her, but it was such an uncomfortable feeling to be drenched. He was not used to it. All the same, he would stand by her, until she was ready to go back inside no matter how long it took.

The dynamic of their group had changed, once more. While none of them would ever say it aloud, they both knew it. They were no longer a clan.

CHAPTER 6: READY

It's been a month since my father died. I still can't believe he's gone. And Troya, too. It's crazy. Almost everyone I've ever known is gone, except for Avery. I hate to think it, but sometimes I wish he was gone, instead. Things have been kind of weird with him lately. I no longer feel comfortable being around him. I don't want to be alone with him for too long.

It began about two weeks ago. I had just woken up in the morning. He knocked on my door to tell me breakfast was ready. I know he lingered by the door longer than necessary. I think he was listening to me get dressed. That was when I began sleeping with my knives under my pillow. Just in case.

Whenever we eat our meals together, I notice him looking at me too much. I don't like it. He never did that before. I don't know why he had to start doing it, at all. Sometimes, I'm tempted to take my food to my room, so I can eat in private. I just don't want to be rude. We're the last two left. We should spend time being social like we always did in the past. It was better when there was more of us eating together.

The other day, when I got back from fishing he was waiting for me at the door. He surprised me. I wasn't expecting to see him as soon as I came into the shelter. Shame on me. I should've known better. I need to expect the unexpected. I'm still learning to do that. It takes so much focus to always be alert. The shelter was the one place I thought I could let my guard down. Not anymore.

Avery has become the unexpected.

He keeps finding excuses for us to talk. We never really spoke before, so we don't have a lot to talk about. The only time we really spoke was when he was teaching me first aid skills. Maybe we'd share a word or two during a meal, but it was always while talking with everyone else. Never just me and him alone. Now, whenever he approaches me and wants to talk, I get a bad feeling. I don't want to talk to him because I don't feel like he really has anything he needs to say to me. He just wants an excuse to stare at me. That's what it seems like. I don't like it. It makes me cringe. I could be wrong, but I don't think so.

To avoid the awkwardness, I spend more time outside than before. I take longer when I explore the ruins near our shelter. I enjoy it anyway. It's fun looking for rare artifacts. There are so many hidden mysteries beneath the piles of junk.

I wonder why there are so many piles of junk everywhere. Did people just throw things into large heaps for no reason? Maybe it was the nomads. I heard they like to destroy things. They supposedly do things that make no sense, since they aren't intelligent.

It's odd how I haven't seen any nomads, considering how often I go outside. Come to think of it, I've never seen a nomad in my entire life. I wonder if they still exist. Maybe they were all taken by the sky ships. I think so. How else is it that I've never seen one? It makes no sense. There are definitely no signs of them in the ruins near the shelter. Everything always looks the same way I left it. Nothing is ever out of place. I keep track, so I'd know. No one moves a thing. I'm the only one out here.

The bad thing about that is I tend to feel safe when I explore these nearby ruins because I've come to expect them to be unoccupied. I've got to keep reminding myself to be ready for anything. I could easily run into someone, while exploring them. As long as I'm always ready, I know they won't catch me by surprise. If I do run into a nomad, I need to be ready to kill. I won't be able to reason with them. They'll try to take what's mine, including my life, and I can't let that happen.

The question is will I be able to do what needs to be done? Can I kill another person? Am I really ready to take a human life? I've never had to do it before. There probably won't be time to hesitate. I'll have to do it fast, before they kill me. I hope I'll be ready. I need to be.

Now that I'm thinking about it, I keep expecting to see one in these ruins. I should focus on what I'm doing and stop distracting myself with other thoughts. I always need to be ready. It's still early in the day, so there's plenty of daylight coming in through the windows. Of course, each one is broken.

There used to be glass on the windows, but not anymore. My dad said the nomads broke them all long ago to stop clans from making their shelters inside. Without the glass to block the wind, it gets very cold during the winter months. The cold air can make the ruins feel just as cold as being outside with all the windows broken. I learned that from my dad, too. He taught me so much. I'm lucky he did.

I'll return to the shelter soon. I'd rather stay out here exploring, but it's getting late. That means it'll be dark. I've never been outside at night. It's against the rules. I've got no idea how it'll look, but I do know it gets darker. My dad said at night the day sun goes away and is replaced by the night sun, which is also called the moon. I don't know why. There are also millions of tiny lights that appear in the sky. Those are the stars. It's where the other planets are, far up near the stars. That's where the sky ships are from.

To be honest, I'd love to be able to see the stars. It's too bad I can't. It's way too dangerous to be out at night because of the sky ships. It's not worth the risk. Maybe someday, I'll feel brave enough to take a chance, even if it's against the rules. Stupid enough is more like it. Then again, if Avery keeps driving me crazy, I might feel safer being outside at night, than I do being in the shelter.

I've noticed going down the stairs from the rooftop level is always easier than walking up. The climb takes a lot of energy and leaves me feeling tired. Still, I do enjoy the view and the air smells much better from high up, than while on the ground. The ruins smell damp and dirty on the inside. However, there are all kinds of smells on the ground level outside of the ruins. Some aren't so bad. I like how the grass smells, but only when away from the ruins.

Okay, it's time to leave these ruins and head back to the shelter. I'm not looking forward to it, although I'm getting hungry. It would be nice to eat something. I sure miss Troya's cooking. She made everything we brought back taste delicious. Avery doesn't always do that. Neither do I.

When she opened the door and entered the shelter, Avery approached her practically running. "Where have you been?" He demanded. "I was worried about you!" He noticed she wasn't carrying any dead animals. "So, you weren't even hunting?" He almost looked upset.

She rolled her eyes and lied, "I *was* hunting. I just didn't find anything. That's why it took so long. I was looking. There wasn't anything out there. I didn't want to go too far. Besides, we should have plenty of food for a few days. Didn't you make anything for dinner?"

"Yes, I did, but I was waiting for you before I ate." He seemed to calm down. "I didn't want to eat without you, or for you to have to eat alone."

"Well, I'm here, so let's eat. I'm hungry." She walked past him toward the kitchen.

"Me, too," he managed an unseen grin. He followed her to the kitchen.

Moments later, they were seated at the table eating the meal he prepared. It was another roasted bird with some vegetables on the side. The same thing they ate the night before. It was the only meal he could make that tasted fairly good.

For a while, they dined in silence. It suited her just fine.

He thought differently. He broke the silence. "I'm sorry about before. I guess I should be more understanding. You're the only one who goes out there to hunt, while I've basically taken on all of the interior domestic responsibilities. Mind you, I'm not complaining. It just bothers me that I've never really felt as comfortable being outside like you. You shouldn't have to do all the hunting and fishing."

"Don't worry about it," she responded. "Going out there doesn't bother me." She wanted to tell him she enjoys it, but decided it was best to keep that information to herself. Otherwise, he'd never believe her when she spent too much time outside. He would assume she was taking her time out there. Of course, he'd be correct in that assumption.

The conversation ended there.

I Stand Alone

Sometime later, while she was sitting in her room reading, there was a knock at the door. She rolled her eyes and asked, "What is it?"

"I was hoping we could talk," he answered from the other side of the door.

"About what?" She responded, while still sitting on her bed with her door closed.

He sighed exaggeratingly. "Can you please open the door? Talking like this is ridiculous."

"Fine." She put the book down, grabbed one of her knives, and walked toward the door. She opened it halfway and stood blocking the way into her living area. "What's on your mind that can't wait, until tomorrow? I have a headache, so I was trying to read peacefully hoping it would help."

"Oh, I'm sorry to bother you." He looked guilty.

No, you're not, she thought.

"I was thinking," he began. "Maybe we should come up with some new rules of how to do things, since it's just the two of us now."

"Yeah, sure," she nodded in agreement. She actually liked the idea. "Not now, though. I really don't want to think about it. I just want to read for a while, before I go to bed. It relaxes me."

"Okay. No problem. I'll leave you alone then." He backed away slightly. He began to turn to leave, but then said, "I just thought you might want to talk, rather than being locked away alone all the time, since before you used to have your father around."

"That was different. I'd rather be alone now. You're not my father, so you don't need to try and take his place."

"Oh, I would never try to take his place. Far from it. In fact, I was thinking that maybe we could spend more time getting to know each other."

That wasn't going to happen. "Goodnight, Avery," she said, as she began to close the door.

"Uh, okay. Goodnight."

She closed the door in his face and locked it. She let out a long sigh of irritation and returned to her bed. It took a while before she could focus on the book, again. He ruined her mood.

Avery skulked off slowly to his room. He was extremely disappointed their conversation didn't go as he planned. He even practiced it in his head several times, before knocking on her door. Somehow, it all went wrong. Instead of taking a step forward, their relationship took three steps back.

He sat alone in the darkness of his room. It was not what he wanted to be doing. Not at all. He began thinking of her, as he had been doing the past few weeks. It was never something he thought about before they were alone, but now he couldn't help himself. She was the only person left to think about. She was the only person left for him to talk to, even if she wasn't much of a conversationalist.

By now, he hoped they'd be much closer. Friendlier, at least. If that didn't happen soon, it was going to be very lonely living in the shelter apart. It was such a shame. He wanted so desperately to gain her trust, but had no idea how to go about it. He wanted them to be able to sit together and have a pleasant conversation. He wanted them to be more like partners in everything they did. Maybe something more.

Why was she making it so difficult? Surely she was just as lonely as him. She was young and still had so much to learn. So many experiences that lie ahead of her, and if she just gave him the chance, he would be able to help her through those experiences. It could be fun for both of them. Perhaps, magical. Even if he was twice her age.

Besides, why would that matter anymore? Times were different. The old rules no longer applied. Those rules belonged to a society that was practically extinct. It was time for them to make new rules. She agreed to that much.

For now, he resorted to touching himself. He promised himself that someday it would be her turn to do it for him. He longed to touch her body. To feel her warmth against his skin. He craved the taste of her lips. He knew once she had a taste of romance, she would never get enough.

In the meantime, he had to be patient.

A week later, he approached her before she decided to leave on a hunt. He realized it was the only way he'd get a chance to talk to her. Their small dinner talks were not going well. She was always tired and eager to hurry off to her room. It didn't help how she seemed to go out more often and stayed out far too long leaving them little time for conversation.

"Hey," he knocked on her door causing it to open wider. "We should talk." He poked his head into her room, but did not step inside. He took in the scenery, since he rarely got a glimpse of her living area. He noticed there were a lot of books on the neatly organized shelves. She had her own library. It was no wonder she could stay locked up for hours. What he didn't know is that some of those books had been recovered from the ruins only recently. She had built up quite a collection.

She cursed herself for leaving the door ajar, while putting on her boots. She should have closed it. She wasn't planning to be in her room for long. She was almost ready to go. Her intention was to go out to the southern ruins, since it was early in the day. She wanted to explore someplace new. She was eager to find new souvenirs to add to her collection. Not to mention, she also wanted to see the view from those rooftops.

"I've been thinking," he said, not waiting for her to respond. "Now, hear me out. This is extremely important. It's bigger than you and I." She glanced up at him with curiosity. Satisfied, he continued, "You and I might be the last hope of the human race." He paused and allowed his statement to sink in.

She quickly responded, "No. There are others out there." She finished putting on her boots and stood up from the chair. She was ready to go.

"We don't know that for sure," Avery said.

"Yes. We do," she nodded. "My dad and I saw proof of it."

"That was months ago. For all we know, those people could be dead. Probably killed by whatever deadly beast killed Abram, Seth, and Abby."

The beast. She had almost forgotten about it. Perhaps, a trip to the southern ruins might not be so wise, after all. She began to reconsider her plans for the day. As usual, he managed to ruin her mood. Avery saw her moment of hesitation and seized the opportunity.

"Hey. I know it may seem awkward, but we should really think about the future of our clan," he stated. "I believe we can make this work."

The beast was forgotten, once more. She scowled at him and asked, "What clan?"

"Exactly! There are only two of us now, but we have the power to change that, Evie. We can make a family. A new clan! If you and I…"

"Ew!" She put up her hand to stop him from speaking. She didn't give him a chance to finish his sentence. The mere thought disgusted her. "Forget about it! No way! You're old enough to be my father!" She pushed past him and pulled her door closed behind her. She began walking toward the exit of the shelter with him hot on her heels.

He tried to plead his case using reason, "I also happen to be the only man left, in case you haven't noticed."

"Or so you assume." She unbolted the door.

Before she could open it to leave, he grabbed her by the arm and turned her to face him. "Look around you! I don't see anyone else here! Do you? Face it, missy! It's just you and me! The sooner you get used to that idea, the sooner we can turn this into a real clan, again."

She shook her head. "It doesn't matter, Avery. That's not something I want."

"Evie, please." He eased up on his grip. "Think about what I'm saying. Please. Try to imagine this shelter in about ten years. What do you see? I see emptiness."

She stopped to think about what he said. It did seem kind of profound. She wondered what if he were right? What would become of them in another decade? She sighed and realized what he said made sense, from a certain point of view. She just wasn't ready for what he wanted.

"Maybe in a few years, I'll change my mind," she finally replied, somewhat calmer. "I just can't get used to the idea. Not now." She shook her head. It still didn't seem right to her, even if it did make some sense. Still, she hoped it would be sufficient to get him off her back for a while.

He stared her in the eyes and declared, "If we wait too long, we could be dead. Maybe in a few years. Maybe less!"

"Then why even bother? Do you want to leave a baby to fend for itself?"

He hated that she threw his own words back at him leaving him speechless. It made him angry and frustrated. He was tired of her being so stubborn all the time. Why couldn't she just listen to him? Why did she always have to make everything seem so much harder than it had to be? He was done with it. Done with her nonsense. He was the older and wiser of the two. It was time she start listening to him. He was the elder now. She needed to learn how to fall in line. She needed to follow the rules. It was time for a hard lesson. His mind was made up.

He grabbed her with both hands and pushed her against the door. His strength even surprised him, considering he was so lean.

"Damn it, girl! You're going to do as I say from now on! I'm the elder! What I say is law! And I'm tired of your anti-social crap!"

"No!" She immediately went on the defensive. Her right knee shot up and smashed into his groin hard. Rather than keel over like she expected him to do, his hands wrapped around her long hair. He yanked downward and let out a scream of frustration in her face. She was forced to bow her head forward causing her to face the floor. His legs instinctively squeezed together making another strike to the groin unlikely.

He continued to pull her hair, while leading her back toward her room. It made it hard for her to resist. He then slammed her back against her door. In that moment, he let go of her hair and gave her the opening she needed. She could barely see through her hair, which was a tangled mess, but she could see enough to do what she needed to do. Her right hand moved up and across with an almost lightning speed. He barely realized what she had done, until it was too late.

For a split second, he stood there in shock with his gaping eyes staring dumbly at her. His slack jaw was locked open, yet no sound came out of his mouth. She stared back into his eyes and waited almost holding her breath in anticipation. His hands gradually moved up toward his throat. They wrapped tightly against his neck, but it made little difference. It was too late. The blood was gushing out of the gash she made with her knife. There was nothing he could do to stop it. His legs began to feel like jelly. He only managed to stand another few seconds before his legs buckled and he fell backwards to the floor.

At last, she caught her breath, as she stood over him. She watched with indifference, as he bled out. The blood pooled around him soaking into his clothing. Moments later, he was dead. His eyes and mouth were locked in that same gruesome gaped reaction.

She scoffed briefly almost with no emotion. As it turned out, she was ready to kill someone, after all. Now, she was alone.

CHAPTER 7: ALONE

Today I turned eighteen years old, not that it really matters anymore. In a way, it's kind of funny. Why am I still keeping track of my birthday or any other dates? It seems kind of pointless. There's no one here to celebrate it with me. I guess in a way, I do it because of my mom. Specifically, because of her journal. She kept track of dates. It's what I learned to do from reading it. Therefore, it seems normal.

I suppose something has to be normal around here.

I made myself breakfast, before I sat in my room to read. A few hours later, I ate dinner. Now, I'm back in my room. I wanted to go outside this morning, but I noticed it was raining. Normally, we never went out when it rained. I'm not really sure why. It's only water. I've been wet before. It doesn't bother me. Maybe it's time to change that rule.

Oh, wait. Now, I remember. Avery said we could get sick.

Wow. Avery. I haven't thought about him in a while. It's for the best. I'd rather forget him all together. He turned out to be a huge disappointment. My dad would've killed him, had he still been alive. I still can't believe that lunatic attacked me.

Speaking of my dad, I miss him. I think about him from time to time. I'm used to being alone, but I do miss him a lot. I miss his voice. His smile. That twinkle he'd get in his eye. I loved whenever we would sit and talk about Mom. I especially enjoyed hearing him talk about his memories of her. My memories of her are too hazy. I barely remember how she looks. I remember Dad's face, though.

No more of that. It's too depressing.

I really hoped to return to the southern ruins today. The last time I was there, a few weeks back, I found some great books. It was an effort to carry them back. I stuffed them into my backpack, which made it very heavy. Luckily, I brought my backpack with me. I always do. It's best to be prepared. Sometimes, whenever I go out, it's just to explore the ruins. Not to gather food. Exploring the ruins has become a hobby of mine. I'm always careful when I enter any of the abandoned structures.

Who am I kidding? They're *all* abandoned! The whole world seems abandoned.

One book that I found was a very thick fantasy adventure novel. Amazingly, it was in pretty decent shape. It still had the cover and none of the pages were missing or damaged. The book was buried under several boxes, so it was protected and preserved. It took me about two weeks to read it, which is longer than usual. Like I said, it was thick. There were so many pages! It was such a great story, though. It was a tale about a journey across another world sometime in the distant past. There were fantastic creatures and beings called elves, dwarves, orcs, dragons, and even powerful wizards. I might read it again, someday. While reading it, my mind was transported to that world. I felt like I was there with them every step of the way. That's the best thing about a good book. It was great.

I've felt lost in stories before, but never like that. This story has become my favorite. Ever since reading it, I find myself fantasizing about going on my own grand adventure beyond the ruins. That would mean leaving the shelter for days. Maybe even weeks. Unfortunately, I can't really do that.

I've started writing in my own journal. I can only wonder if anyone will ever read it. I'm mainly doing it for myself. I want to be able to look back and read what I was doing in the past during my younger days, assuming I can last that long on my own to become old enough to give a damn.

I think so. I do pretty good on my own. I only have to hunt and fish for one person, so food lasts longer. Sometimes, I'm not even hungry, like when I was reading that thick book. I was so preoccupied with it that I would forget to eat. Yes, it was that good!

I do get lonely sometimes. It's difficult to be completely alone. Not only am I the only one here, but I'm the only one in this entire region. I haven't seen anyone else out there since the bodies my dad and I found. I've never seen a nomad. I never ran into that beast either. It's probably long gone. The world is just a big empty place

I Stand Alone

to me. As it is, this shelter seems so much bigger now that it's just me in here. There are too many rooms for one person. I still haven't done anything with Avery's old living area. I took what I needed from inside and closed the door long ago. I haven't gone back inside. I don't have any use for his rooms. I have more than I need already. I rarely go into my dad's old workshop, too. It's depressing. Only once in a while, when I need to fix something. The tools are kept in there.

I spend most of my time in my room. It's the only place that really feels like home to me. Being in here reminds me of my parents. It's where I go when I want to feel close to them. It's where I sleep. It's the only room that matters to me, and it's where I am now. I keep my journal on the desk Dad made for me. It's right next to mom's journal. They belong together.

In a way, I continued her story with my own. I began by telling all the old memories I could recall from my childhood beginning with the earliest. It was mostly memories of me playing and learning, or describing the people who've died. There have been so many. That stuff took up close to a third of the notebook I'm using. It was nice thinking about those days. Remembering all those people was sad, but now they won't be forgotten. Even Avery.

I don't write in my journal every day. If I did, it would be very boring to read. I only write when there's something significant to tell like when I explore somewhere new. I decided to write today because it's my birthday. It seemed like an important date to document.

My dad told me people used to celebrate their birthdays in the old days at large gatherings. There would be fancy desserts to eat called cakes, and people would give gifts to the birthday recipient. He only experienced something close to that as a child. The tradition died out a few years after being in the shelter. There were no more cakes. It's too bad. I've never eaten one.

This is actually my first birthday since my dad's death. I used to enjoy spending my birthday with him. He always made it feel like a special day. He would usually make something new for me. A gift. Now, it just seems like any other day without him here. Another lonely day.

Tomorrow should be better. I'll go to the water road to catch a few fish. It'll be a good day for fishing. Thanks to the rain, the worms will be easy to find, so I should have plenty of bait. If I catch a good amount of fish, I won't have to do anymore hunting this week. It'll give me time to do some exploring.

If all goes well, I'll go back out on the following day to explore the southern ruins. I love the view from the rooftops down there. It's magnificent. The ruins seem to go on for miles, although the forest has swallowed up most of the shorter structures. In the distance, there are taller gray spires that go straight up into the sky almost touching the clouds. They're much further away, so I haven't been able to explore them. I wish. I wonder how long it would take to climb to the roof of some of those towers. Probably hours. It would be dark before I got halfway up, even if I set out at dawn. I'd love to try someday.

I find myself thinking more and more about staying out until dark, and then sleeping out in the ruins. I've noticed a few that could be barricaded to make a safe place for myself, at least for one night. The only thing, which leaves me feeling vulnerable are the broken windows. The sky ships would still be able to get to me with their beams of light. That's unacceptable.

I wonder. Am I really the last person left on this world? I find it hard to believe, but then why haven't I ever seen anyone else out there? Where is everybody? Did the sky ships take them all away, even the nomads? It's a scary thought. I hope it's not what happened. I don't want to be the last person on this empty world. There has to be someone else out there.

Do I really want to find anyone else, though? It's something for me to consider.

Well, I think it's time to get some sleep. I have to be up early tomorrow, if I expect to find some worms.

The next day was a beautiful day to be outside. The temperature was warm and comfortable. It was a nice spring day. The grass gave off a pleasing aroma due to the recent rainfall. It was definitely a great day for fishing, and that's exactly what she was planning to do. She'd

I Stand Alone

already gathered the worms she needed, and was now heading east along the trail toward the water road. Of course, the trail was muddy also due to the rain. She always hated walking through mud because her boots got so filthy. Regardless, she learned to deal with it. It just meant having to clean them before returning to the shelter.

As she walked, the birds above watched her from the trees like they always did. She was tempted to take one down with a knife, but she already had an ample supply of poultry. What she needed was fish.

"You're lucky today, little birds," she said. In a way, she thought of them as her guardians. She knew if danger came near, they'd warn her by flying away all at once. "As a hunter, one needs to pay close attention to their surroundings." That's what both her father and Abram taught her.

She learned to pay close attention to everything. That's what her mother taught her.

At last, she arrived at the water road. She went straight to her favorite rock. It was actually a large boulder that extended out into the water. She always preferred fishing while sitting there because it easily placed her at an elevated position overlooking a deeper part of the river. Plus, there were no trees in the way, so she usually stood there to cast her line as far out as she could. She knew she'd have a better chance of catching fish that way. While there were plenty of fish in the shallow area near the shore, her line would be more likely to get snagged on the plant life growing there. She learned that the hard way when she was younger. It was a lesson she never forgot.

Once her line was in the water, she sat down on the rock to play the waiting game. In addition to skill, fishing typically required a great deal of patience and time. She was fully aware the waiting could sometimes take longer than she preferred. She didn't mind today. She dedicated the day to catching fish. Well, until it got closer to the evening. Other than that, she had no intention of going back to the shelter without any fish. She already had her dinner planned for the evening and it included fish. She wasn't about to disappoint her stomach.

It only took fifteen minutes before she made her first catch of the day. She tossed it into a wicker basket she carried with her whenever she went fishing. She caught another fish a few minutes later. Within the first hour, she managed to catch seven fish. It was more than adequate to last her into the next week. This way she could alternate between fish and poultry for the next few meals.

She gathered up her equipment and prepared to return to the shelter.

Suddenly, she caught a glimpse of movement on the other side of the river. She had to do a double take. She couldn't believe her eyes. There was something moving on the opposite shore. It looked like a furry animal down on all fours. However, when she looked closer, she realized it was a person. It was hard to tell whether it was a male or female from her distance. Plus, the person had shaggy, long, dark hair covering their face. It still hadn't noticed her staring across the river.

Evangelina wasn't sure if she should hide or try to get their attention. She wondered if it were someone from a clan or was it a nomad? She had to resist the temptation to call out. Instead, she kept watching with curiosity from her seated position on the rock. The person appeared to be alone.

They were crawling around as if searching for something on the ground. Perhaps, foraging for food. She noticed the person stopped and placed something into their mouth. They gradually moved closer toward the water's edge. That's when the person looked up and froze. They'd seen her. Now, they were making eye contact from across the span of the river.

She considered turning to leave, but she was too interested to just turn away. This was the first living person she'd ever seen out in the wild. She wasn't sure what to do, so she waited to react. What would the other person do? They seemed to be looking back at her with the same curiosity.

Unfortunately, the moment didn't last very long.

The person stood up straight and howled like a wild animal leaning their head back to shout up into the sky. They became excited. Agitated. They howled, again, more desperately. Soon, another figure appeared from the ruins behind them, followed by another emerging through some nearby bushes.

At this point, Evangelina knew this wasn't a good sign. Whatever they were doing, it didn't look friendly. She knew they had to be nomads based on their primitive behavior. Still, she studied them. She found it odd how they were acting as a group. It went against everything she heard about nomads. They weren't known for acting together, unless this was some kind of clan. Either way, she knew it was time to go. These people weren't friendly. That much was obvious based on their hooting and howling.

She turned to go, but looked back once more. The first one near the shore ran toward her into the water splashing up a storm. The others soon followed. At this point, she became nervous. Would they be able to reach her? She put down her fishing rod and basket of fish. Both items were replaced by knives. She was ready to fight, if necessary. She dared not risk running away and leading them back to her shelter. It's location needed to remain hidden. She only hoped she could handle all three at the same time.

However, the further they ventured out into the water, the more they splashed. They were no longer approaching. It seemed they were moving away toward the south. She watched in confusion, as the water road seemed to take them away. They looked just as confused. The current carried them south, until they were no longer within view. One disappeared beneath the surface and wasn't seen, again.

She waited a few moments, but there was no sign of them anymore. The previous serenity had returned. All she heard was the sound of the birds, which was a welcome relief.

In time, she gathered her things and turned to leave. She looked back a couple of times before she decided it was safe to go back to the shelter. As she reached the ruins near the shelter, she wiped the mud off her boots using grass. The rest of the trail from there going toward the shelter wasn't too muddy.

I saw other people today. Finally! There were three of them, although I only saw one, at first. I think he was foraging for food.

Was it a he? I don't know. It was hard to tell. The voice sounded male. When he saw me, he howled like a savage. After he did, two more people appeared. They looked just like him. Savage. I know they must've been nomads. The whole experience was kind of creepy. They looked like they wanted to kill me. Luckily, they were on the other side of the water road.

It's no wonder I haven't seen anyone else. Maybe that's where everyone else is hiding. On the other side of the water road. I wonder how they got there. It doesn't seem possible to cross the water road on foot. They tried. It proved to be a fatal mistake. The water swallowed them up and washed them away to the south. They obviously didn't know how to swim. It was foolish of them to try crossing the water road. I doubt I'll ever see them again. I doubt they even survived the ordeal. It looked scary, being dragged away by the water like that. They sure seemed frightened. I don't blame them. I think I would've been terrified, if I were in their position. It was kind of scary watching it happen. I've never seen someone killed by nature. I almost feel sorry for them.

At the same time, I felt relieved because I knew I wouldn't have to fight them. I was safe. Still, I hate that the only people I've seen out there had to die. It's a shame, but I know it was for the best. It's such a huge disappointment.

They were far too aggressive, though. They're definitely not the kind of people I'd want to run into. I know they would've attacked me. They probably wanted my fish and my supplies. I don't know if I could've taken them on all at once. The only other time I had to fight someone else to the death was with Avery. I had an advantage over him. He was unarmed and he lacked experience.

I didn't have a choice when it came to the nomads. I knew I couldn't run back to the shelter. They might've followed me back here, and then I'd never be rid of them. They would've had the advantage over me. They could've set up an ambush for the next time I had to go out for food. Standing my ground and fighting them was my best option. I'm just glad it didn't come down to that, considering it most likely wouldn't have turned out well for either of us.

Without a doctor to help me, I can't afford to get injured. I only know a little bit of first aid. I really need to read both of those medical books in the library. I've tried. They're just so very boring.

Getting back to those nomads... they were too far away for me to get a good look at them. It would've been nice if I could see what they looked like. I haven't seen anyone else in a while. I did notice they were wearing animal furs, which means there are animals to hunt on the other side. It also means those people knew how to hunt and how to make clothing, which means they did have some intelligence. No boots from what I could tell. They each had long hair like me, only theirs was wild and messy. I didn't notice any tools or weapons in their hands. In fact, it didn't look like they were carrying any supplies at all. For the most part, they appeared to be primitive with limited intellect.

It was interesting how they had an animalistic way of calling each other. It meant they could communicate, as well. At least, to a certain extent. I'm making a note of that for future reference.

I wonder if there were more of them out there. I thought they were nomads, but I might be wrong. What if they belonged to a clan? It could've been a clan that was forced to survive out in the wild for many years. Maybe they've got enough sense to avoid the sky ships at night. That would be interesting. I wish I knew for sure.

Whatever the case, I'll have to be more careful in the future whenever I go to the water road. I don't want to run into any more of them. Maybe I'll need to find a new spot to fish. It's too bad. I really like that spot. I've been using it for years. It's usually very productive. It used to be peaceful, too. Maybe not so much anymore.

Wait a minute. I wonder why I've never seen anyone there in the past. I've been fishing from that spot since I first went out at the age of thirteen. We all have. That's where my dad and Abram taught me how to fish. We never saw anyone on the other side of the water road before. Why now?

It makes no sense.

I think those people were just passing through. Maybe they were nomads. One thing's for sure, this experience has left me with a lot to consider. A lot of questions, too. I was planning to go exploring tomorrow, but I think it would be wise if I waited another day. Just to be on the safe side. In case there are more and they come looking for their friends.

So much for being alone in the world.

CHAPTER 8: RUINS

I waited two days, before venturing out to the south. As I walked through the mangled ruins of what was once civilization, I found myself distracted by the events of the other day. I hoped I wouldn't be interrupted by another group of nomads, if that's what they were. This time, I was ready. Ironically, I just wanted to be left alone, so I could explore the myriad of ruins in peace.

I looked up and around me, as I pushed forward. The jagged shards of forgotten edifices had become shells of their former existence. Scattered piles of bricks, stone, wood, broken glass, and sharp rusted metal had become the new foundation of the abandoned wasteland that went on for miles and miles. I wondered how long ago it had been when some of the taller towers collapsed onto the smaller structures. I could see there was evidence of it along the roads between the decayed buildings, which had become no more than overgrown trails for lone wanderers like me.

Unless I'm the only one left to walk these desolate pathways and explore the surrounding ruins. Was I somehow becoming a nomad? It's an amusing thought.

When I look around at these fragile old constructions I can't help wondering what they must've looked like before they deteriorated. Before they began collapsing and crumbling into piles of rubble and dust. According to mom's journal, it's been about three decades, since these mountains of debris resembled an actual city. That's more time than I've been alive.

How majestic it must've been to walk along the paved roads in between. Riding vehicles from one place to another. I bet it was a lot faster than walking. I could only imagine how it felt to gaze up and see the shining glass of hundreds of windows reflecting the sunlight of a beautiful summer day. And all the busy people that must've been walking around going from one place to another. I always imagined the old cities being overcrowded like in the picture books of the library.

I can't even begin to understand how difficult it had to be building the taller structures. How did they get the building supplies to the upper floors? It was probably a nightmare carrying everything to the top. Who has that kind of energy? I get tired after walking up to the fifth floor. I bet they had the younger people working on it day and night, taking lots of breaks. Those are the things that aren't shown in my books, so I can only speculate. I never thought to ask anyone. Now, there's no one to ask.

While walking through the ruins, I found myself searching for things. Nothing specific. Mainly small things. Just more artifacts to add to my collection. I'm always eager to see what lost treasures I can find hidden beneath the rubble. I've already found quite a few items over the last year. Some things are kind of hard for me to identify. They aren't in any of the library books. Other items are things I can recognize. I usually find a lot of metallic objects, mainly old tools and pieces of broken machinery. If there's anything I want to keep, I place it into my backpack. Sometimes, the items are so small they fit in my pocket. I like small things like that.

Now that I mention it, I found a small, round, silver object today that kind of looks like a ball. It's made of metal and is fairly lightweight. It's about the size of my thumbnail. I'm not sure what it's for, but I like it. I wish I knew what it was supposed to be.

If only my dad were still around. It would've been nice exploring the ruins with him, although he probably wouldn't have let me. Sometimes, I wonder if he was afraid of entering the ruins. I used to be, but not anymore. I'm used to it now. I enjoy it.

I once read in a book that these cities had names. Sadly, I don't know the name of the one near the shelter. Nor do I know the name of this one. Not that it would make a difference. Most of these cities are the same these days. Broken statues of rock and durasteel surrounded by trees and greenery for as far as the eye can see over carpets of broken glass, rock, metal, and bones of the dead. Ruins. There are clingy green vines creeping up the sides of everything giving the structures an almost organic appearance, as if they were alive.

On the inside they all smell the same. Moldy. Outside there are different odors, depending on where I go. Some areas are covered in dust. Other areas stink of chemicals, while others are just plain rotten. I'm not sure if it's death I smell. It could be old food. When I smell that odor, I leave. I don't want to find out where it's coming from. Some mysteries are best left unsolved.

I learned a long time ago the ruins aren't the place to go for foraging. That's done in the forests and along the water road. Any food that was worth eating in the ruins was scavenged long before I was born. I know the early hunters of my shelter used to scavenge food from the ruins. Mostly processed canned food or old candy. I never got to see any of that stuff, but I heard about it often.

Troya used to like telling me about the things she used to eat as a young girl. I'm not sure why. It seemed like she was teasing me by telling me about things I'd never be able to eat. I never complained to her, though. Talking about such things seemed to make her happy. She was rarely happy, so I let her have those small moments.

I miss her. She never liked leaving the shelter, but she sure loved talking about the days before she was forced to live there. I wrote about her memories in my journal. She told me how she used to travel to different places. She told me about all the pretty colorful clothes she owned. I also heard about how she went to a school to learn things from teachers, who only taught her about academic things. Not about how to survive in the world. Some of it sounded like useless knowledge, if you ask me.

My dad taught me about science and math, but I don't see that as useless knowledge. It comes in handy to know how things work or knowing how much food you have. Without science and math, there would be no buildings. No ruins. No shelter. No me. My mom taught me how to read and write. It isn't very useful knowledge for survival in this dead world, but it sure helps to pass the time when you're completely alone like me. I'd go insane, if not for my books and my journal.

I wonder if there's at least one city on this planet that doesn't look like an utter wasteland. That would be awesome. I guess I'll never know.

I hated thinking I was the last person in the world. Now, I know I'm not. It doesn't really matter. It's possible I may never see another living person, again. I need to get used to that idea. I'm better off being alone anyway. It's much safer that way.

She filled the afternoon by exploring the southern ruins and began to lose track of time when she came upon a small collection of hardcover books. They were situated on the shelves of an old wooden bookcase in an isolated back room of an apartment that didn't have any water damage. Therefore, there was very little mildew and mold. Aside from the broken door, shattered windows, and ransacked kitchen, the rest of the apartment was in decent shape. Everything else was covered with a thick layer of dust, but mostly untouched.

There were about two dozen books on the shelves of the back room, which had no windows, and therefore very little light. Fortunately, there were a bunch of old candles throughout the apartment, and she always carried a book of matches in her bag. They had so many at the shelter that had been saved by smokers, until there was nothing left to smoke. She collected the candles and lit one to allow her to see.

She was in all her glory. She gently cleaned off each book and looked through them one at a time, while creating a pile on a nearby table of the ones she wanted to take back with her. She actually wanted to take the entire stack, but there was no way she could fit them all into her backpack. Plus, their combined weight was too much for her to carry across the distance to the shelter. In addition, some books were a lot heavier than others. This would have to take several trips. Maybe three or four.

One of the heavier books was a reference encyclopedia. While there was already an encyclopedia in the library at the shelter, this one had more photos. She definitely wanted to spend time examining this book in the comfort of her room. It would be taken in the first batch, along with a few other interesting looking novels and textbooks.

She glanced out of a window in the next room and realized it was becoming late in the day. It looked a lot darker than she thought it would be. Dark rain clouds had moved in from the west blocking out the sun. There was also a breeze in the air. Then she heard rumbling thunder in the distance.

"Oh no. That's not good. I need to get back to the shelter," she said to no one in particular. She quickly closed her backpack and flung it over her shoulder. She blew out the candle, and then hurried down the stairs to the lobby. She came to a sudden stop at the exit of the building. Something in her gut told her it wasn't a good idea to try making the long trek back to the shelter.

She looked up at the sky and saw how dark it had become. It didn't seem that cloudy earlier when she left the shelter. She wasn't sure what to do. It looked like it was about to rain at any minute. There was no way she'd make it back to the shelter in time. While she really didn't mind getting wet, she didn't want the books in her backpack to get damaged. Nor did she want to risk being out when it got too dark, which looked like it would be a lot sooner than expected. She cursed herself for not paying closer attention to the sky for its warning. She had been stuck in that back room with no windows for too long.

Then it occurred to her. Perhaps, she could return to the apartment and hide in that very room. The sky ships shouldn't be able to reach her with their beams of light, if she remained hidden in there with the door closed. It seemed like the best idea based on the circumstances.

She went back up to the third floor apartment. Since she couldn't properly secure the damaged front door, she placed the dusty sofa in front of the doorway to hold the broken door closed. She then went into the back room and shut that door. There was a lock on the door, so she locked it. The room was pitch black. She relit the candle and sat down on the chair that she cleaned off earlier.

"Well, it looks like this is home for tonight," she grumbled in a worried voice. Resigned to stay in that room for the night, there was nothing she could do about her situation. She decided not to waste the time she'd be spending there, so she sorted the books into two more piles. That way she'd know which ones to bring back to the shelter on her next two trips.

Afterwards, she pulled the encyclopedia out of her backpack and began looking it over. She'd start at the beginning. She knew it would keep her occupied, until she was ready to get some sleep.

Would she even be able to sleep? This would be her first night sleeping outside away from the shelter. Her father and her had always been ready to do so, in case of an emergency. However, that never happened. He always made sure to get them back to the safety of the shelter before nightfall, or before the rains got heavy. Being so far from home made her feel nervous. She tried not to think about it and focused on her book.

Suddenly, the booming sound of thunder shattered the silence and caused her to jump nearly two feet from her seat. The heavy book flew from her lap to the floor. She found herself on the floor beside it covering her head with her arms. It was the first time she'd ever heard thunder this close. It was so loud. The rain began falling immediately afterward, making a pitter patter sound on a piece of metal outside of the apartment's living room window. The rain came down hard and fast. She read about thunder and lightning, but had never seen the flashes of electricity brighten the sky. She noticed the flash under the crack of the door. She began to relax a little after hearing the steady sound of the rain. She realized there was nothing to fear. Regardless, it scared the hell out of her.

Falling asleep was going to be a problem, if the storm continued on like that. She was on high alert, especially when she heard the thunder crackling a second time. It sounded way too close for comfort.

She must've eventually fallen asleep because she had the strangest dream. The room was filled with a bright light so white that it felt warm. Was it due to lightning? The whole room had warmed up. Her body became as light as a feather, causing her to float off the chair. The sensation didn't scare her because it felt so relaxing. There was a gentle pull at her stomach, and then she noticed she was floating face up moving out of the room toward the light. She never noticed if the door had opened or if it was already open.

Her body moved slowly through the air out of the nearest window. She tried to turn her head, so she could look down, but trying to move took so much effort. It left her feeling drained. She managed to get a glimpse below her. She couldn't see the ground that should've been three stories down. There was only the warm bright light wrapped around her like a blanket. That's all she could see, as she floated higher and higher into the sky. It was hard to tell if it was still night or daytime.

Her body felt so light. It was easier to just float and not worry about a thing in the world.

She wanted to close her eyes and turn away from the blinding light, but couldn't bring herself to do so. Her eyes were fixed on what was ahead. There was something dark beyond the light. A shape. The higher she went, the more she could see it. It was huge. This thing was so big, it literally blocked out the sky. She noticed there was no more rain or thunder. Only the light and the enormous dark object beyond it. She felt herself gradually being pulled closer to the object.

A moment of panic came over her. Was it a sky ship? Was she being pulled up by its beam of light? She didn't want to be taken away. She tried to resist with all her might, but found that she couldn't move at all. Her entire body was paralyzed. It was terrifying, yet relaxing.

She soon floated into what looked like an open doorway at the bottom of the… sky ship?

Her body came to rest on a cold flat surface in a completely white room, which almost glowed. She was shocked when she noticed her clothing was gone. How did her clothes disappear? She didn't remember them coming off. She still couldn't move a muscle. The surface beneath her felt so cold against her bare backside. Her heart was pounding in her chest. She wanted to escape so desperately.

The room became brighter, as if it weren't already bright enough. It occurred to her she wasn't alone. Someone was there standing over her. The light made the person difficult to see. There were only indistinct shapes moving like a blur. Dark eyes leaned close looking down at her. She became even more frightened. Something metallic poked her belly. It didn't hurt, though. Something else was probing her ears. It felt wet and cold. There was a warm tickle at her feet. What was happening to her?

She was freaking out, until she heard a gentle voice in her head. It was neither male, nor female, as far as she could tell. It was a very soothing voice. It wasn't very loud. Just loud enough for her to hear it.

"Relax," it said. "This will not take long."

"What are you doing to me?" She wanted to say the words, but instead could only think them. Her mouth wouldn't move. Somehow, her lips were frozen shut.

"You're being examined," the voice replied.

The calm response surprised her. She immediately thought, "How can I hear it in my mind?" Rather than waiting for a response, she pleaded mentally, "Please, let me go. I want to go home." A tear emerged from the corner of her dry eyes. She tried to blink, but it felt like something metallic was holding them open. The paralytic feeling was driving her mad. She wanted to leap off the cold table, but even if she could move, where would she go? How far up was she?

Finally, she had control over her eyes. She shut them tight instinctively. They felt extremely dry and irritated. She blinked away the tears and tried to look around her. Her vision was slightly blurred. She could only see the brightness of the light. A numbing sensation moved through her body. It made her feel weak. Tired. She tried so hard to fight it, but her eyes closed.

Everything turned dark. She still heard the voice in her head. Maybe there were two voices. It was difficult to know for certain. She no longer understood what was being said. The voices sounded like they were moving further and further away, and then everything became quiet. She still couldn't move, but felt like she was floating through the air like before. That was the last thing she remembered.

A loud noise woke her from her sleep. It sounded like something crashing. The racket came from outside down in the street. At first, it didn't fully register with her. She tried to open her eyes, but she felt utterly exhausted. She stretched out her arms and legs, rubbed her eyes, and sat up. Her whole body ached. There was a powerful hunger stirring in her stomach. She felt like she hadn't eaten in days.

She pulled out a few berries from her backpack and devoured them.

When she was ready she gathered herself together with no memory of her apparent dream of abduction. It sounded like the rain had stopped. It was quiet outside, aside from the noise she suddenly remembered woke her moments ago. She wondered what could've made the noise. She pulled her backpack on and stood from the chair. Her legs felt weak. She had to steady herself.

Cautiously, she unlocked the door to the room. She peeked through and saw that the living room was just as she left it. The sofa was still against the front door. She stepped out of the back room and attentively peeked out of the living room window to see the street below.

It appeared to be empty. She stared down for nearly a minute. She guessed some bricks might've come loose from somewhere and fallen off one of the buildings like what happened when her father's leg was crushed. That had to be it. She knew she was alone out here.

As soon as she turned away from the window, she could've sworn she heard another sound coming from the street. She turned back and looked out of the window, a second time. This time, poking her head fully out. She wanted to see down to the building entrance. She watched for a long time, but still saw nothing out of the ordinary. She waited and listened. There was only silence.

Somehow, that didn't ease her mind one bit. She remained in place, leaning out of the window. There was a strong temptation to throw something down to see what would happen, but if she did that, she'd be giving away her position. Instead, she just waited.

Minutes dragged by. There was nothing.

She wanted to return to the shelter. It felt like a reasonable amount of time had gone by. If she didn't see or hear anything by now, there was likely no one down there. It was probably like she thought.

Something had fallen from a building. Considering how the thunder was crashing the night before, it was highly possible something was damaged by it.

Satisfied by her reasoning, she pulled the sofa away from the door and peeked out to the hallway. It was empty. Exactly how she thought it would be. Regardless, there was a knife between the fingers of each hand when she left the apartment.

The walk downstairs was almost ninja-like, as she tip-toed quietly down each step not making a sound. She was careful not to step on anything that would make a crunching noise, which wasn't easy in an abandoned building. Her eyes watched vigilantly staring at each open apartment door she passed on the way down. Descending the three flights of stairs so carefully took a lot longer than she would've liked. She couldn't wait to be back on the trail heading north along the water road.

At the moment, it seemed so far away.

At last, she reached the ground floor. Now, came the tricky part. Going outside and hoping nothing was out there waiting for her. Either way, she was ready for a fight. It didn't make her any less nervous. As she approached the doorway leading out, she heard a soft growl coming from outside, which made her freeze in place. She immediately tensed up.

It had to be some kind of animal. She hoped it didn't pick up her scent. Just then, she noticed its foul odor and wondered how she didn't smell it before. It was horrendous and unlike any animal she'd ever smelled before. She had to hold her breath, in order to stop it from infesting her nostrils.

She considered turning around very slowly and going back toward one of the open apartment doors. She figured she could hide inside and wait, until whatever it was left the area. She didn't want to take a chance with an encounter, in case the animal wasn't alone.

Abram used to tell tales about packs of mongrels roaming the ruins in search of food. They were relentless hunters, who worked together to take down their prey. They tended to follow one alpha male, who was usually the strongest of the pack. If it were a pack of mongrels out there, she wouldn't be able to fight them off. Nor would she be able to outrun them. They'd catch her and kill her.

She forced the fear out of her system and tried to remain calm. Abram used to say some animals could smell fear. She turned slowly and tiptoed back toward the nearest apartment door. She hoped it would be able to lock. Of course, the open windows weren't going to keep her safe for long. They'd smell her eventually. Then the hunt would begin. It wouldn't be hard for them to jump into the open windows of a ground floor apartment.

New plan.

She began up the staircase with every intention of hiding in one of the second floor apartments, instead. That way she could look down and see when they went away. It might've been a good plan had she made it up the stairs, or had it been a pack of mongrels.

It wasn't.

She heard the sound of heavy footsteps crunching on the ground behind her. She turned her head and saw an enormous apelike bipedal beast covered with hair. It stood about nine feet tall. After reading about it so many times, she knew what it was instantly. The large creature hunched over slightly and had to duck in order to enter through the doorway of the building. With it came the overpowering stench. It saw her immediately and let out a loud thunderous roar that shook her to her core.

Her blood went cold, as she froze in place. Only two words slipped through her shuddering lips. "Oh shit."

CHAPTER 9: SASQUATCH

The tall monstrous sasquatch stood in the open doorway, salivating as it leered at her. The beast was covered with long, unkempt, dark, brown hair everywhere except on its face, hands, and feet. Its hands and feet were three times the size of hers. If it were to grab her, it would likely crush her bones to dust. The apelike face scowled at her small frame, as it balled up its rocklike fists. There were extended sharp fangs in its open mouth gaping hungrily at her making her feel like a snack waiting to be devoured.

For a few short seconds, they stood there and sized each other up.

It didn't take long for Evangelina to realize she was no match for it. She turned quickly and raced up the stairs to the nearest second floor apartment. She ran inside and slammed the door shut behind her. The lock was broken! She had to think fast. She grabbed the nearest chair and jammed its backing against the doorknob. There was no way that was going to keep that thing out for long. She needed a plan.

Rapidly, she searched the room for weapons and a place to hide. All she had was her knives, which seemed way too puny to make a difference against that massive beast. It would be like poking him with thorns. As for the apartment, there was nowhere she could hide, where it wouldn't find her. There was one other option. Going out one of the windows. She hurried to the nearest one and looked down. It was a longer drop than she would've dared to jump on any other day, but she didn't really have a choice at the moment. It was either jump out of the window, or stay and fight that thing. Easy decision.

She began to climb onto the windowsill, but then stopped to think. What if she jumped down and injured her ankle or her leg? What then? She'd never be able to get away in time. It would easily be able to get her. There was no doubt she'd be thrashed to a pulp in seconds. That certainly wouldn't be good.

No. There was no escaping from it.

She had to be brave. There was another possibility, but it would take precise timing, skill, and a lot of luck. It would also take a lunatic to even consider it. She supposed that meant her.

"Think crazy," she told herself in a whisper. "Be crazy."

Within seconds, the door burst open sending the broken chair flying across the room. Splintered pieces of wood flew in every direction as the door fell apart. The brief explosion caused her to flinch. She almost changed her mind about jumping out of the window. It began to seem like a better idea.

No! Be crazy!

The creature scanned the apartment and locked eyes with her. It was looking directly at her, but surprisingly she didn't back down. She held up her measly three inch knives and prepared for the fight of her life. She then forced a lump down her throat and stood ready by the window. She could barely keep her knees from wobbling. Beads of sweat slid down her face. She gripped her knives firmly and focused her mind. *Crazy!*

The creature snarled at her. It almost seemed like it was smiling at her, or was it her imagination? Did it find her amusing? Maybe it admired her bravery, or stupidity. Then again, it was likely just showing off its fangs. Whatever the case, it actually hesitated, before attacking. It was studying her. Watching her intently. She stood her ground and waited for it to make its move.

It growled and so did she. BE CRAZY!

As a show of strength, it tossed a table to the other side of the room, before letting out a roar. It watched her still, but she didn't move away from the window. It heaved its bulky chest and clenched its fists. Within seconds, it was charging at her like a bull in an arena. She waited for the absolute last second, before dodging it, and jumping onto its back. She stabbed both knives into its eyes from behind, while it blindly crashed through the open window. She held on tight, as she rode the beast's back down to the street.

It slammed down hard face first, just as she pulled her knives out and rolled away landing nearby flat on her back. Both of them lay on the ground not moving for several seconds. She stared up at the sky and tried to catch her breath. As far as she could tell, nothing was broken. The fall only knocked the wind out of her. When she was able, she looked over at her hairy opponent, who was now blind.

As it pushed itself up, blood was dripping from its damaged eyes. It shook its head and got onto one knee. It was definitely hurting. There was no doubt about that. The fall only dazed it. Otherwise, it was able to stand. Once it did, it tried to look around. No, it was sniffing for her scent. It was now facing her with bloody eye sockets, while breathing heavily. It didn't look too pleased.

She propped herself up on her elbows. Damn. This wasn't over. Not yet. She forced herself onto her knees. Both knives were still in her hands covered in the creature's blood. She took a deep breath and got to her feet. It was still facing her.

"I'm sorry about your eyes, but you attacked me. I didn't want to fight you," she found herself saying instinctively. It's what she had been thinking. The last thing she wanted to do was fight a beast like that. Even blinded, it would likely pummel her once it got a hold of her. She no longer had the luxury of a doctor, so not being injured was a high priority for her.

At the sound of her sincere voice, it seemed to react. Its facial expression changed. No longer angry, but pensive. It relaxed its posture, before standing straight and proud. For a second, she could've sworn it bowed its head at her, before turning away to leave. Perhaps, it was bowing its head in defeat. It slowly began to walk toward the trees south of their location, where it disappeared from view. It didn't look back at her.

She sighed with relief, as she watched it leave. It occurred to her this was more than some simple beast. It gave her the impression it understood her. If so, it had advanced intelligence. This realization made her feel guilty for blinding it.

She wondered, was this the same beast that attacked and killed her friends more than a year ago? It was possible, considering how it attacked her. Was it merely protecting its territory?

What if it wasn't the one who killed them? What if something else was responsible, and this creature somehow chased it away, then piled the bodies neatly, so they could be found? That was also a possibility, although a bit of a stretch.

The more she considered it, the more she was tempted to follow it. She thought maybe she could at least try to wrap its wounds. Would it even let her, or would it take the opportunity to strike back? It was a risk she dared not take. She couldn't afford to make a mistake like that, now that she was alone.

She was curious. Why did she even care about this creature that tried to devour her only moments earlier?

No. It was too dangerous. Let it go. It's time to stop being crazy.

In any case, she knew it wasn't going to attack her, again, in its current condition. Maybe not ever. One less threat to worry about on the outside, unless there were more of them. She had never seen one in person. It was something she only read about in one or two books. Some believed them to be extinct creatures from a forgotten age. There were rumors of sightings. Blurry indistinct images always taken from a distance. Nothing in the old encyclopedia from the library.

Why was that? Surely, they exist. She just saw undeniable proof.

It was a good thing her mother taught her to believe in everything. To keep an open mind. Expect the unexpected. That's how she lived her life. Everything was possible. Everything. She found herself gazing up at the sky and had a vague recollection of a strange dream from the night before. The memory came to her in a few broken images. Nothing that she wanted to remember.

She gathered her belongings. It was time to return to the shelter.

Over the next couple of days, her mind remained fixated on her recent encounter with what she firmly believed to be a sasquatch. She looked through the books in the library, until she located the few vague references. The descriptions matched what she had seen. She then recalled the new encyclopedia and looked through it. She quickly turned the pages toward the letter S, until she found an entry on sasquatches. It was listed as a large mythical apelike beast covered with hair, which was believed by some people to exist in desolate woodland areas or mountainous regions. There was a lot more, but she focused on the image. It was the same blurry indistinct photo she'd seen before. No wonder no one believed in them.

The word "mythical" stood out and distracted her. It wasn't mythical. It was real. She had just seen one. What else could it have been? As far as she knew, there was no other creature in the world like it.

She documented every detail into her journal.

Why had she never seen one before? Her father never spoke of them. Neither had Abram or any of the other people who went on hunts, although Abram did often mention how there were some dangers out in the world that she could never imagine. Was this what he meant? Were there other extraordinary dangers like it out there? Did she really want to know?

Of course, there was also the sky ships. They still remained a mystery to her, but the thought of seeing one terrified her. She preferred to keep them a mystery. A distant one. The last thing she wanted was to be taken by them, never to return.

At that moment, a brief memory flashed through her mind. Was it even a memory? She imagined herself lying on a table and being held down, unable to move. Just as quickly as the image appeared, it was gone. Was it from a dream? She couldn't recall. Why had the image come into her mind?

The thought seemed too disturbing to dwell on. She instantly changed her line of thinking. It was something she preferred to forget. Instead, her mind fell back on that poor blinded creature. How would it be able to survive now? Would it still be able to hunt, or would it starve to death? She felt responsible for its suffering. Why? It attacked her!

For the time being, she dared not venture back to the southern ruins. She remained close to the shelter for the next couple of weeks, only venturing out when she needed to hunt.

Someday, when she was ready, she would have to return to that area. She wanted the rest of those books she found in that apartment. She hoped they were still undisturbed. It wasn't as if she saw many other beings out there, who would take them or damage them. Therefore, she had a feeling they would be waiting in that back room, right where she left them. She only hoped that she wouldn't encounter anyone, or anything, when the time came for her to retrieve them.

Soon, she thought.

In the meantime, she made room for the new and future books she would acquire by reorganizing the library shelves. She also went through the books she managed to bring home. They were more than adequate to keep her occupied, until she was ready to get the rest. It was a good haul. She spent most of her days and nights reading the new books and perusing any photos they contained.

Photos fascinated her to no end. Her father once explained as best he could how the photos had been captured back in the days before the *Big Apocalyptic Event*. The process fascinated her. She wished she had the capability to capture photos, as well. Alas, it was a lost artform.

Eventually, she got that itch to go exploring. She longed to explore new rooftops. She also wanted those books desperately. She wondered what hidden photos they might contain that could reveal more parts of the lost past to her. It had already been three weeks, so she felt more than ready. It was time to go back to those ruins. Naturally, she would be swift and careful. This time, she wouldn't be taken by surprise, if there was anything else out there. She would be ready for it.

It was decided. She'd leave the next morning.

That night she lay in bed thinking about the potential dangers she might face during her morning expedition. Her mind was also on the sasquatch. Would she ever see it, again? Did she want to? She tossed and turned half the night, barely getting any sleep. Her mind kept racing from one thought to another. Eventually, she decided to get out of bed and make herself breakfast. Simply lying in bed was beginning to feel like a waste of time.

She had a hearty meal, since she didn't know how long she'd be out. She made sure to pack plenty of rations for her trip, in case she got stuck overnight a second time. She hoped not. She didn't find the last overnight experience to be enjoyable.

When she was ready, she left the shelter.

She reached the ruins without incident. Before entering the building, she stared at the wooden debris from the broken window on the ground. She couldn't see any blood stains. Perhaps, it was washed away by rain. She couldn't recall if there was a lot of blood on the ground the last time she was there.

Carefully, she entered the main doorway and paused to listen. She waited for nearly an entire minute before proceeding toward the staircase. Once she was satisfied with the silence, she began up the stairs to the apartment, where the cache of books was located. She hesitated for a moment, when she passed the second floor and noticed the open doorway to the apartment where she hid from the sasquatch. It had destroyed the door when it entered after her. There was splintered wood on the floor.

She promptly resumed her climb to the third floor, and went straight to the back room, where she began stuffing her backpack with books. The urge to take them all at once was overpowering, but it simply wouldn't be possible. The bag was already gaining too much weight and was stretched to its limit. It was going to take no less than two trips. There was no way around it.

Tomorrow was another day.

She made her way back to the shelter as quickly as possible. Normally, the new books would've been sufficient to keep her busy for another week or so. However, she didn't want to wait any longer than necessary to get the rest of those books. She went back out the next day to retrieve them.

Just as on the previous day, she used extreme caution when entering the building. She then hurried up to the apartment and stuffed the rest of the books into her backpack. It was going to be another heavy load, but she could handle it. She slipped the overloaded backpack on with a grunt and quietly descended the staircase to the ground floor. She didn't want any surprises.

After a quick peek to make sure the coast was clear, she left the building, and followed the path leading back toward the shelter. On this day, it seemed longer than usual.

Somewhere in the distance, she heard a shrill shriek that echoed throughout the ruins behind her. It stopped her in her tracks and sent a chill down her spine. It was a scream unlike anything she'd ever heard before. Her body was frozen in place, as she listened for any other sounds. There were none.

She faced forward and quickened her pace, as she followed the trail going north, along the water road. Her eyes kept glancing across the water to the other side. She wasn't sure where the eerie noise had come from, but she hoped it was on that side of the water. Whatever it was, she wanted it to be as far from her as possible. If it was across the water, it wouldn't be able to reach her easily. She hoped.

The truth was she had no idea which direction the sound came from. It could've been behind her on her side of the water in the very ruins she had been exploring. That seemed more likely. In any case, she didn't want to think about it. Her steps hastened with knives at the ready. Her mind remained alert for the entire trek. Despite her fatigue, she was practically jogging when she reached the ruins near the shelter.

Almost there, she told herself. This trip was going to mean another journal entry for certain. She had to document that creepy scream. The more she thought about it, whatever it was that made the sound must have been in torment with how it sounded. It was almost like a wailing sound. Maybe it wasn't a sound to fear, but to pity, she thought.

As soon as she was back in the shelter, she bolted the door shut and removed the heavy backpack allowing it to drop to the floor. It felt great to be rid of that weight. She panted from her exhaustion and slid down to the floor, where she sat for several minutes. Her back was aching.

There was one thing she hated about leaving the shelter. She was unable to bolt the door from the outside. It always made her worry about what she might find upon her return. True, there was a simple combination device that locked the door from the outside, but what would happen if she ever forgot to set the locking mechanism? Someone could get inside, even if the door was hidden by brush and branches. What if someone was watching when she left? They'd know where the entrance was located. These are thoughts that went through her mind, as she sat on the floor with barely enough strength to stand.

She realized she was being silly and childish. Paranoia was not one of her typical traits. However, that creepy shriek she heard left her feeling rattled. Fortunately, she did set the lock, so there was nothing to worry about, this time.

Now that she had the rest of the books, she figured perhaps it would be best to remain indoors for the remainder of the week. She had plenty of food, so there was no need to go back out anytime soon.

The new books were thoroughly entertaining and intriguing. They did indeed keep her quite occupied for several days. She had already read halfway through one book. A novel. She might have finished it had she not kept stopping to examine the other books more thoroughly. She was hoping to learn new things that would help her gain more insight into the past she would never truly know. It was always a goal when it came to reading a new book. After all, these books were the only teachers she had left.

One book described space travel in great detail with an array of color photos. That immediately became a new favorite. She found it odd how it made no mention of sky ships. It did mention rockets and space shuttles, which were equally fascinating. Seeing her world from the point of view of space was an added bonus. It was far more beautiful than she could ever imagine. So radiant and full of color. Yet, surrounded by such infinite darkness with only the tiny scattered lights of the stars to light the background. While this pleased her, it also made her sad because she knew she'd never be able to see this point of view through her own eyes. Space was something more of fantasy to her, than reality.

Another book that piqued her interest was a culinary book. In it were numerous recipes for tasty looking meals she'd never be able to sample. The glossy color photos that accompanied each recipe were to die for. Each and every meal pictured in the book was a tease, which looked extremely delectable. Many of the listed ingredients were foods and spices she'd never even heard of before. It frustrated her. She hated how so many things of the past were lost forever.

She focused a lot of her free time on the new encyclopedia, as well. She found herself going back to the entry on the sasquatch. Sometimes, she'd stare at the blurry image and wonder why it was the only one ever taken. How could a creature that large and frightening be so elusive to avoid photographers for so long? It was hard to believe. There was a very lengthy description, which was amazing, considering it wasn't even supposed to be real. She read it repeatedly. It mentioned how they are known to let out strange howls or screams. Could that mean wailing sounds, as well?

Her mind drifted to the one she encountered. Did it have anything to do with that loud scream she heard? It didn't scream like that when it was about to attack her, although it did roar like a bear. Maybe they only screamed like that during certain instances. It didn't scream when she stabbed its eyes, nor did it scream when it crashed out of the window and fell to the ground. Therefore, it didn't feel the need to scream when it felt pain or anger. Perhaps, it screamed when it felt sorrow. Surely, it had reason to feel sorrow, if it was hungry and unable to hunt due to being blinded.

The thought distressed her. She didn't want it to suffer. It boggled her mind how she felt more compassion for that creature than she did for Avery when she killed him. Both had attacked her. Yet here she was feeling sorry for this creature, which she didn't even know. For all she knew, it could've killed her friends. Would it have been any different had it been a lion or a bear? Another man?

She had to get this beast out of her mind. There was no use obsessing over it. It was long gone, by now.

She turned the page and continued looking through the encyclopedia. There were plenty of other fascinating creatures pictured in the thick volume. There were large underwater creatures that she'd most likely never see. Many were already extinct.

Even humans were nearly extinct.

It was a scary thought. If only there was a way for her to know exactly how many humans were still living on the planet. Whatever the number, it had to be significantly lower than thirty years earlier. She had to be one of the last humans left. Maybe she was the last one. It was a profound thing to consider, but was it really unlikely? She barely saw any others out there in all the years she'd been going on hunts. Most of the ones she'd seen were dead. She was pretty much alone in this world.

How much longer would she last on her own? Another year, if she was lucky. Maybe more, if she were very lucky and extremely careful.

The world would likely go on without her species. How would everything look a hundred years from now? Would the ruins completely decay and collapse, by then? Would all signs of humanity be erased by the erosion of time? The world would belong to nature, once more. Come to think of it, the world already belongs to nature.

She was only a visitor taking what she could, whenever possible. A thief.

She once read how there were billions of people on the planet. Billions! There was no doubt the past three decades have had an astronomical impact on her species and their ability to survive and thrive. It was crazy.

It occurred to her these dark depressing thoughts weren't going to make falling asleep easy, so she closed the book and set it down on her desk. Besides, there was no point in dwelling on what she couldn't change.

She washed up and retired to the cozy welcoming comfort of her bed for the rest of the evening. She'd read her novel, instead, until she felt sleepy. Hopefully, it would fill her mind with happier thoughts. It was a fictional story about a young princess who was able to travel through time. How remarkable would that be? She pondered to herself. To travel to when the planet was still in its prime. Being able to see the world how it used to be before it became a vast wasteland of lush ruins. Experiencing the things even her parents never got a chance to experience. If only that were possible. That would be a true adventure. She smiled to herself.

If only she knew this was the last time she'd ever sleep in that bed, she might enjoy the moment for all it's worth. She might take time to realize and appreciate how lucky she is to have such a safe shelter. A place to call home. Maybe she'd think twice before leaving it, again. If only.

When she finally fell asleep, she had a wonderful dream about traveling into the past to when the world was still vibrant and full of life. She experienced many magnificent new things and saw all the things she'd never be able to see in real life. She was also able to eat every one of the meals shown in that cook book. It was amazing, even if she had no idea how they actually tasted. In her mind, they were all delicious. That was all that mattered.

Sadly, it was the last peaceful sleep she'd ever experience at the shelter. Her life was about to change.

CHAPTER 10: MONGRELS

After eating breakfast the next morning, she decided it might be a good idea to go on a hunt. Food supplies were starting to run low. She managed to remain indoors for a week. During that time she went through a good deal of her food stores. It was time to stock up. This time, she'd go up north into the forest, where she could hunt for meat. If she couldn't find anything reasonably sizable, she'd settle for a few birds or rodents. They would be easier to carry back anyway.

Besides, she could use a break from exploring the ruins in the south. It was a long walk, which always made it a time consuming journey. She told herself it had nothing to do with the scream she heard, even though it was a deciding factor.

As soon as she stepped outside, she looked up at the sky. It was bright and blue with puffy white clouds scattered across the vast expanse. Just the way she liked it. The sun was still low in the east, so it was fairly early. She locked the shelter door and covered it with its camouflage coverings.

She began the usual trek through the local ruins on her way to the eastern trail near the water road. That trail was the best one to take when heading north, or south, for that matter. The grass along the trail was worn down from years of trampling footsteps belonging to the hunters of her clan. Abran called it a game trail because the animals also used it to travel along the water. Back when she was younger, they used to still find evidence of animal droppings along the trail.

Not anymore. The animals learned to keep away from the region to avoid being hunted. As far as she could tell, they rarely used the trail these days. It probably stunk of humans to them. She knew animals were more sensitive to smells than humans. She learned that much from reading her books.

Her eyes checked the buildings on either side of her from time to time. The ruins near the shelter have always been abandoned and unoccupied during her lifetime. After exploring them, she knew each one rather well. She knew which would make the best hiding places for an ambush. She was ready. There was a knife in each one of her hands.

Always be ready. Her mother's lesson had become like a mantra.

As she walked, she couldn't help wondering if the sasquatch was still out there in the southern ruins, or if it had moved on to a different region. She refused to accept that it might've starved to death. It could still hunt by smell. Probably. Well, she thought so anyway. It smelled her without any difficulty.

A few minutes later, she reached the water road. She paused momentarily to look across to the other side. There was no one out there, as far as she could see. Good.

Ever since being alone, the places she grew up believing were safe, seem to feel more dangerous to her. She felt like nowhere was truly safe anymore. Again, she remembered her mother's teachings. Always be ready.

She turned north and continued walking. While following the trail, she glanced up at the trees that lined the path. The birds were looking down at her, as usual. They were always watching. She grinned briefly. They might've been watching, but they certainly weren't ready to avoid her knife, which she threw with lightning speed and precision. An unlucky bird fell from a nearby tree onto the grass. She casually walked over to retrieve it, as the other birds fluttered away in retreat.

That's the first kill of the day, she thought to herself. Too easy. One or two more should be plenty for today, unless she spotted something larger. Unlikely, but one could hope. After seeing the water road, it got her thinking. Maybe tomorrow she could catch some fish. She still had a few worms leftover in her tackle kit back at the shelter.

As the day went on, the trail took her further north than usual. An hour had gone by, since starting north. After the first bird, she hadn't seen any other easy ones to target. The rest remained too high and far out of reach. They were avoiding her. It's as if they knew she was hunting them. Smart little critters, she thought.

It was slim pickings in the forest today. Even the squirrels and rabbits were keeping out of sight. At this point, she'd settle for finding a mouse. Where were all the rodents she normally saw when hunting in this direction? Did they know something she didn't know?

As if in answer to her question she heard a howling sound coming from further north. It sounded far enough away that she wasn't too worried about it. All the same, there was no point heading any further in that direction. She didn't want to run into anything she couldn't handle.

Disappointed, she made an about face and began heading back south. She looked up at the sky. The sun was approaching noontime. There was still time to catch fish, instead.

Before she got too far, there was another howling sound. It came from the south, probably in response to the previous howl. She immediately stopped walking. The last thing she wanted to do was walk right into a pack of mongrels. Even if it were only one, it could still do some serious damage before she killed it. It wasn't so bad during the winter when she was dressed with thicker clothing to protect her skin from bites. However, it wasn't winter. She was only wearing a thin black jacket, which was hardly adequate to protect her arms if she was bitten.

She considered her options. There weren't many that seemed good. She could head west into the forest, but that was largely unfamiliar territory to her. Getting lost would be very bad, especially now. She typically stayed near the trail when going north and wasn't really in the mood to explore the denser forest. Not today, and not with wild mongrels on the loose. On the other hand, if she went too far east, she'd be blocked by the water road. She could still hear it rushing by from where she stood, even if she couldn't see it through the trees anymore. It wasn't too far from the trail. She examined the trees nearby to see if maybe she could climb one and stay out of sight for a while. None looked worth the effort. There was nowhere to hide.

If she waited too long to decide, they could potentially surround her. There was no telling how many were out there. Soon, there would be no escape. Time was running out. Whatever she was going to do, she needed to decide and do it. Thinking about it was only wasting precious time.

"Think faster," she ordered herself.

She hurried into the forest west of the trail. Maybe she could get lucky and find some kind of structure, where she could hide and wait, until they went by. Of course, what if they picked up her scent and decided to follow her? That was another problem she had to consider. They had an excellent sense of smell. She hated dealing with mongrels.

She picked up the pace and pushed through the branches that kept blocking the way. Each one slapped and scraped her as she went by. The woods were becoming denser with each moment. Everything had become so wildly overgrown over the years. It was almost impossible to keep going forward, which was frustrating her.

Ultimately, she had to stop. Going any further west seemed utterly pointless. She could barely walk between the trees. The trees and bushes were so thick, there were practically no spaces between them. At this rate, the mongrels would catch her for sure.

She tried going south, instead. Perhaps, if she continued far enough in that direction, she'd emerge somewhere behind the ruins near the shelter. At the moment, it seemed like her only best option. Of course, going south through the forest didn't seem much easier, but she was able to push her way through. The rough branches kept brushing against her body and breaking. Had she been wearing short sleeves, there would've been cuts and scrapes up and down her arms.

To top it off, there was still a chance she could get lost in the woods. That's all she needed. It was taking way too long to navigate the dense foliage, which was making her feel anxious. She hadn't heard anymore howls, yet. That was a good sign. Was it possible she managed to elude them?

She wondered how much further she'd have to go through the woods. The effort was draining her energy. She was grateful it was still early in the day. That meant it wouldn't be dark anytime soon. If it got too dark, she wouldn't be able to see where she was going. It was dark enough being beneath the shade of the trees that seemed to block out the sky. She longed for freedom from the labyrinth of trees, which were closing in on her, again.

If only she could find a structure, where she could hide. It would be a great help, right about now. She just needed somewhere to hide for a short time. Someplace where she could barricade herself inside and be a lot safer than she felt, at the moment. She hated being out in the open with nowhere to go, if one could consider where she was as being out in the open. It certainly felt enclosed.

It occurred to her the mongrels could be following the scent of the dead bird she was carrying. The fresh blood was probably attracting them. It's scent would most likely lead them straight to her no matter where she went. On a good day, mongrels could easily smell blood anywhere within ten to fifteen miles around them, if not more.

She did the only safe thing she could think to do. She tossed the dead bird as far to the north as she could. Unfortunately, her meager throw didn't get it very far, considering the thickness of the branches surrounding her. She heard it hitting a branch nearby and falling to the ground.

"Aw, crap. There goes dinner," she thought.

Her eyes moved upward ahead of her. Where's a nice high rooftop when you need it? She kept moving south, until she reached a small clearing. She hesitated to enter it. At the same time, she was tired of being surrounded by trees. The open area looked too inviting to resist. She paused in the clearing to rest and catch her breath. It was exhausting trying to move through the thick forest. What was she thinking by going through it?

From the clearing, there seemed to be a slight path heading southeast. She wondered if it would lead her back to the trail, or even to the ruins. Any one of those would be better than being stuck in the forest. She took the path and was able to move faster. Alas, she couldn't move quieter. The faster she went, the noisier she became. Her feet stomped along the dirt, crunching dead leaves and fallen branches along the way. She had to keep alternating from looking forward and down just to avoid tripping over something. If she fell and hurt herself, she was as good as dead. She had to be careful, while also trying to be fast. Her heart was pounding so hard in her chest. If they wanted to find her, all they had to do was follow its thumping sound.

The path gradually opened up and she saw sunlight ahead. It was the eastern trail! She made it back. Hopefully, the mongrel to the south had already gone north. When she reached the trail, she broke off into a full sprint. She ran south, glad to be back in familiar territory. She knew exactly where she was from this point. It wasn't far from the intersection, where she could head west toward the shelter. Even being near the ruins would be a lot better. She knew them so well that she could hide there with ease and find a safe place to wait it out.

The only problem was the full-sized, dark, gray mongrel standing ahead of her in the middle of the trail. It appeared to be waiting patiently for her. How inconvenient.

She stopped abruptly kicking up a cloud of dust. It glared hungrily in her direction. "Oh, you've got to be kidding me," she uttered.

It let out a low growl, while flashing its sharp fangs at her. She was frozen in place. It arched its head upward and began to howl, calling for the rest of the pack. Within seconds, it was on the move. The hunt was back on.

Evangelina had two choices. Fight or flight. There was no way she'd be able to outrun an adult mongrel. It would likely catch up to her and take her down, giving it the advantage. Surely it would bite her. Maybe in more than one place, before she managed to fight it off. By that time, it would be too late. The other mongrels would soon be on her. Fighting it didn't seem any smarter. She would probably still get bitten, but at least she'd be facing it. That would give her an opportunity to do some harm, in return. If she injured it in a way, where it couldn't follow her, she might have a chance to run to safety. The choice was easy. Lucky for her because her time was up.

The mongrel leapt up onto her chest. It was going for her neck, but she quickly blocked its teeth with her left forearm ready for the pain. It's full weight knocked her back to the ground. She winced when she felt its fangs ripping through her jacket sleeve and sinking into her flesh. There was no time to think about the pain. Instead, she stabbed with the knife in her right hand. She jabbed it into the mongrel's neck repeatedly as many times as she could, until it released its grip on her arm. She took that moment to push it off of her. It whimpered and crawled away with its blood soaking the fur on its neck.

Instantaneously, Evangelina was back on her feet and running south. She heard the howling from behind her, and more off to the side. It was coming from the woods west of her position. Probably back where she tossed the dead bird. She just had to make it back to the ruins. That was her goal. If she could get there, before they caught up to her, she'd be okay. She wouldn't lead them to the shelter.

Within moments, she heard the footsteps rushing through the grass beside her. She didn't look. There was no time. She kicked it into top gear and ran as fast as she could.

They were still faster. They managed to get ahead of her emerging through the woods onto the trail. Without skipping a beat, she veered left going east toward the water road to avoid them, leaping over a fallen tree as if it wasn't even there. The mongrels didn't seem to have a problem following her through her new route. She heard several of them behind her.

It didn't take too long to reach the water road. There was nowhere left to run. It was the end of the line. Swimming wasn't an option. The strong current would most likely drag her to her death. As it turned out, she had one more trick up her sleeve. She jumped up and grabbed onto a thick branch of a large oak tree near the water. She pulled herself up, while pushing herself up with her foot against the tree trunk. She climbed up to the next branch and stopped to look down, just as a mongrel jumped for her leg and missed.

The first of the mongrels had gathered at the foot of the tree jumping up and trying fruitlessly to grab her legs. She was already too high for them to reach. As it turned out, mongrels weren't very good at climbing trees. Lucky for her. The rest of the pack had finally caught up. There were six of them in total, not counting the one she maimed with her knife. That one had given up on the hunt.

For the moment, she was able to catch her breath. She knew the moment of rest wouldn't last. She was trapped in a tree with nowhere else to go. She didn't like the idea of them being directly below her. She searched for a way to possibly climb higher, or to move further away. She saw another branch from a nearby tree extended toward her branch, so she slowly made her way toward it. It didn't seem any safer, but it made her feel better if she was still moving and trying to get away.

Delicately, she crawled along her branch, until she was near the other one. She had to stand up and jump to it, which made her nervous. First, she made sure there was something to grab onto with both hands. Once she saw a few other branches she could use to brace herself, she made the leap of faith. The mongrels watched with anticipation from below, waiting for her to slip and fall, so they could pounce on her.

However, they were robbed of that chance. She made it safely to the other branch and was able to balance herself. Next, she moved along that branch and tried to reach another one that extended out over the water. It seemed more appealing to not have a pack of hungry mongrels directly below her, so that branch became her next goal. She had to shimmy across the current branch, until she could grab onto the other one. It was a bit out of reach. She had to jump, again.

She took a deep breath and made the attempt. Surprisingly, she reached it, but had to pull herself up onto it since it was slightly higher. It wasn't easy because she barely had the strength to do it. If not for the adrenaline rush she felt, she probably would've lost her grip and let herself fall into the water. However, it was her adrenaline that had been driving her through this entire experience from the start. Plus, she wasn't about to give up now.

Once on the other branch, she crawled along its length, until she was over the water. At last, she felt a little safer. It was another opportunity for her to catch her breath. The pain in her arm reminded her of the injury she obtained moments ago. There was no time to check it, yet. It could wait. There was no point in enticing them further by the sight of her blood.

For a brief moment, she simply stared down and watched the water rushing past below. It was moving rapidly. She wondered how deep it was at that point. If she were to fall in, would she drown? Would the mongrels be able to jump in after her? Could they even swim? She hoped not. Then again, swimming wasn't one of her best skills either.

The continuous barking distracted her and brought her attention back to her four-legged pursuers. This time, they kept their distance. It seems they didn't want to get too near the water, or maybe they felt confident enough that they'd catch her eventually. She was literally out on a limb with no other means of escape.

"Go away, you mangy mutts!" She shouted down at them to no avail. Apparently, they were immune to verbal taunts. She remembered how Abram had once told her they were intelligent animals. People actually kept them as pets. It seemed hard to imagine from her point of view.

The mongrels remained in place watching her patiently, and waiting for her to fall within reach of their combined teeth. However, she had no intention of becoming anyone's meal. She'd stay up in that tree all day, if she had to. Just the thought of being torn to shreds was all the inspiration she needed to hold out as long as she could.

As for the night time, she'd worry about it when the time came. It was still early in the day. The sky ships wouldn't become an issue for another few hours. She hoped the mongrels would eventually get bored and grow tired of waiting for her by that time. Maybe one of them would catch the scent of an easier prey to hunt.

She taunted them a second time. "Bark and growl all you want, for all I care. I'm not coming down, until you leave. I have my backpack, so I have something to snack on, while I wait." She was truly amazed how fast she had run, while wearing her backpack. At some point, she forgot it was on her back. Her main focus had been getting away. Hiding in a tree was as good as it was going to get.

That's when she heard a disturbing sound. It ripped right through her thin fabric of safety she thought she had. Her heart instantly leapt to her throat. Hearing the wailing scream from the other day would've been a thousand times better than the sound she was suddenly hearing. It started very subtle, at first. She barely noticed it, until it began to grow louder. The tree branch was beginning to crack under her weight. She felt it tilting downward toward the water. Before she could crawl back to the previous branch, it broke.

"Oh, shhhiiit!!!"

The next thing she knew, there was a huge splash, and then the water current was washing her away.

CHAPTER 11: STRANDED

Life in the shelter never required learning how to swim. Even for those, who went fishing often, it wasn't something they learned. Everyone was taught to stay near the shore. Therefore, swimming became irrelevant. In time, there were fewer and fewer experienced swimmers to teach the following generations. A small number of the older people had a vague idea of how to swim because they mainly learned as children, but that knowledge wasn't generally passed along. The idea of swimming across the river, or water road, was frowned upon for safety reasons. That being said, Evangelina never learned how to swim, and neither did her parents. Otherwise, her father would've surely taught her.

When her body hit the cool water, instinct took over. Her arms began flailing, while her feet kicked out desperately in an attempt to gain a foothold on the ground, which was out of reach. Fortunately, she was able to grab onto the thick branch that had formerly supported her. Like her, it was floating down the river, pushed along by the current.

By this time, she had already swallowed plenty of water and was coughing it up, while holding onto the branch with both arms for dear life. Her legs floated behind her like dead weight. She didn't know to keep kicking. Not that it would've made a difference. The current was taking her where it wanted to take her. She had no say so in the matter. She was simply going along for the ride.

The mongrels were startled by the suddenness of the breaking branch and the loud splash it and its passenger made when hitting the water. A few jumped back. Two of them took it as a sign to take their leave and head back north. It was possible they went to check on their companion, who was probably near the brink of death already. The alpha of the pack stood at the edge of the water watching its former future meal float down river. Another was tempted to jump in after her. It hesitated only because it had enough sense to know the current was too strong for a swim. Then again, maybe its duty was to remain with the alpha. Meanwhile, the last two mongrels decided to run along the trail heading south, so they could follow their prey and keep an eye on her, in hopes that she'd somehow be pushed closer to the shore within reach, at which point they'd howl to let the others know. They were indeed intelligent animals.

Meanwhile, Evangelina noticed she was quickly approaching the southern ruins. She wondered how fast she was moving. More importantly, she wondered how she was ever going to reach the shore. She didn't dare let go of that large branch. Wherever it was going, that would become her destination. She only hoped it would stop soon. As far as she was concerned, she'd already been taken too far south.

She didn't even notice the mongrels trying to keep up with her pace. They were partially hidden from view by trees, bushes, and rocks along the shoreline. She believed the mongrels were way back where she left them, and were no longer a threat to her. It seemed she was wrong. For the moment, she had other problems to worry about like keeping her mouth closed and her eyes open.

The branch briefly got jammed up against a protruding rock near the center of the river. She took the opportunity to see if she could feel the ground with her feet. She couldn't.

Suddenly, she heard that same eerie wailing sound coming from the western shore just south of the ruins. When she glanced over her shoulder, she saw the sasquatch standing near the shore. It was facing her direction. The mystery of where the sound originated was solved. She wondered if it could smell her. If so, did it recognize her scent?

From out of nowhere, she saw a pair of mongrels attack the sasquatch. Even blinded it was a formidable foe. It grabbed one of them by its hind legs, and slammed it hard against the ground like a rag doll. There was a whimpering sound, which died down almost immediately.

Moments later, the branch was pushed free and she was on the move, again. She tried looking back to see how the sasquatch was doing, but lost sight of it. Little by little, she was drifting closer toward the eastern shore. That certainly wasn't her intention. She needed to get back to her side of the water road. The last thing she wanted was to end up on the wrong side. However, her ride was far from over.

In the next few seconds, the current took her further and further away from her shelter to a new unexplored region. She had never come this far south before. Everything was unfamiliar to her. After about another minute, the force of the current was finally subsiding. By this time, the current had dragged her several miles downriver.

Eventually, she was just drifting along with the branch. If she knew how to swim, she probably could've done so, at this time, although the water road had become wider than before. It seemed to open up into a large lake. It continued going south, but apparently this was to be her stop. The branch was gradually being pushed by gentle waves toward a small lagoon, where there was a beach.

It seemed to take forever, but she could finally feel the ground beneath her feet. She began walking toward the shore, while still pushing the branch along with her more out of habit than for safety. The water was becoming shallow. Soon, it was only up to her waist. When she reached the shore, she dropped down onto the beach to rest in a seated position facing the water.

She gazed longingly across to the other side, where she belonged. It looked so far away. How was she ever going to get back to that side? She was at a complete loss. Of course, she could've probably used the very same branch to float over to that side, while kicking, had she known anything about swimming. It was too bad for her that she didn't.

"Just great. I'm stranded on the wrong side of the water road," she protested to herself. "How am I supposed to get back to my shelter?" She looked behind her beyond the trees and saw ruins. There were more along the water road to the south. Hopefully, there was no danger hiding within to worry about. She then looked down at her clothing. She was soaking wet. At the moment, she really didn't care.

It seemed like a good time to check on her wound. She rolled up the sleeve of her left arm and winced from the pain. There were canine marks from where the mongrel bit into her arm. It wasn't as bad as she expected it to be, but it did break skin. She was bleeding and it hurt.

It was an effort to pull off her backpack. She was exhausted, after her misadventure. It took her a couple of minutes, but she managed to wrap the wound. For several minutes she remained seated on the beach, while keeping watch around her. It gave her time to rest.

Once she was ready, she got to her feet. Her backpack was still lying on the sand. She took another good look around continuing to take in her surroundings. The nearby ruins would require exploring. For one thing, she wanted to make sure she was alone. She'd also need to find an adequate shelter before nightfall. She'd begin by searching the few structures situated near the water, although she had no intention of staying in those. They looked too badly damaged and open to the elements.

She heard a continuous splashing sound coming from the water, so she turned back to face it. She couldn't believe her eyes. One of the mongrels was swimming across the water toward her.

"I should've known. So much for expecting the unexpected." She pulled out her knives and waited.

She realized there was still time for her to gain an advantage before the mongrel reached her side of the shore. There was little doubt, it would follow her wherever she went, so she picked up her backpack and ran south along the sand. Fortunately, it was a short beach. She climbed up a waist-high concrete wall at the end to what was once part of a small dock. The wooden pier was long gone, destroyed by years of stormy weather. Only the wooden support pylons remained sticking out from the water like strange chess pieces on a submerged board waiting to be played. They only drew her attention briefly. She had no idea what purpose they served, but figured further investigation could most likely wait until she wasn't preoccupied with her survival.

She warily walked along the concrete surface toward the nearest structure, which was just a few feet away. It was an old one-story concrete pump house. It's door was missing. There were two small open windows, one facing north and the other facing south. A quick peek of the interior revealed it was only one room. It appeared to have been used as an office of some kind. An old metallic desk covered with a multitude of junk and debris from the damaged ceiling stood in the center of the small square room. There was no chair. Ancient waterlogged pages littered the floor like a soggy carpet. She noticed old rusted two-inch wide pipes clinging to one wall. They were connected to larger pipes that ran along the ceiling.

She placed her backpack down and grabbed a pipe from the wall. She yanked it off with ease on the first try. It felt sturdy enough and was about the length of her arm. The rusty edge was jagged and sharp. It would serve nicely as a weapon, she thought.

All that remained was to wait for her hunter. She moved her backpack to the side and leaned back against the desk, which luckily seemed strong enough to support her weight. The pipe was held with the jagged end pointed outward toward the doorway. If she was correct, the mongrel would come in ready to pounce on her. She was ready to welcome it.

Of course, the mongrel was smarter than that. It leapt in through the north window smashing through what little window panes remained. The shattering noise of broken glass and wood startled her. When she turned to face it, the mongrel was already leaping up onto the desk ready to bite into her right shoulder. She quickly pivoted her body to avoid it, while swinging the pipe as hard as she could. It struck the mongrel on its right side knocking it sideways behind the desk.

It yelped in pain.

Evangelina stepped away from the desk and waited for it to emerge for its second attack. It slowly stepped around the south side of the desk snarling its teeth at her. Its dark piercing eyes, lit by the daylight coming through the windows, stared directly into hers. It was breathing heavily. So was she. It growled angrily at her, watching her every move. She braced herself and waited for it to attack, but it remained in place, waiting for her to make a move. When she took a step back toward the doorway, it took a step forward toward her.

"Okay, so that's how you want to play it, huh?"

It let out a low growl in response, wrinkling its snout at her and brandishing its fangs.

She stepped back through the doorway, until she was outside exposed by the sunlight. The hungry mongrel moved closer, but remained inside the dimly lit structure. It was standing in the shadows between the doorway and the windows, but it wasn't hidden. She could see its black and gray fur just fine. She only wished there was a door, so she could slam it shut.

"Fine. Let's play it your way," she said.

She turned and immediately ducked around the south corner of the building. The mongrel emerged from the structure's doorway at a trot. She then charged at it stabbing the pipe forward like a spear into the mongrel's left side. As she did, it tried to bite her hand, forcing her to let go of the pipe and back away.

It stood there defiantly with the pipe sticking out from its side. She pulled out her knives and waited for what was coming next. She knew. When it leapt toward her, she held out her hands firmly in front of her with both knives waiting for their target. It dived right onto them, knocking her back to the ground onto her behind. The mongrel still actually tried to bite her, even in its weakened state. She easily pushed it off and crawled back away from it.

"You lose," she said triumphantly, while sitting on the ground. She watched patiently as its eyes rolled upward with its tongue dangling from its open mouth, dripping with saliva. Blood poured from its belly and side. It died quickly. The pipe stood erect like a flagpole planted into the ground, marking her kill.

She lifted herself to her feet and dusted off her pants. After retrieving her backpack and pulling it over her shoulders, she stared down at the mongrel. One thought came to mind. Lunch.

She had never eaten mongrel meat before. It wasn't too bad. Normally, she had a light lunch, but after the morning she had, she was able to build up quite the appetite. There was no way she'd be able to eat it all, nor would she be able to store any of the meat in her wet backpack, or take any of it back to her shelter. It bothered her to waste food. She removed its pelt and washed it. It would serve her as a decent blanket, since she'd be camping tonight. The fur should keep her warm. She collected some of the stronger bones to utilize as tools. The rest of the carcass was left to be absorbed by nature.

After eating, she put out the small fire from the firepit she constructed at the beach. Next, she gathered her things, which were still wet. It was time to explore the ruins beyond the trees. Hopefully, she could find a secure place to sleep for the night.

First, she took a moment to examine the pylons of the old pier, but couldn't make heads or tails of them. Had there been any remnants of an old boat, she might've figured it out, but there was none. The only other structures near the dock was a ransacked garage and a small rundown shed. There were stacks of tires in the garage, but not much else. She found an old screwdriver, which she took. The rest of the stuff was garbage. The shed was empty and stunk of old urine.

The walk through the trees didn't take long. She soon emerged at the ruins of what had once been a small fishing village. No structure was taller than two stories. There was a wide dirt trail that stretched between the ruins, which she guessed served as a main street. A rusty old vehicle had been abandoned in the middle of it. All four wheels were missing. There weren't many structures still standing. There was an old fueling station, a burnt out store, a dining establishment with no roof, a few unmarked buildings, and some houses hidden away by the trees off to the side. She hadn't seen any homes like those before, except in her books. The city ruins she was used to mainly consisted of brownstones and tall buildings.

Her curiosity drew her closer. She had to fight her way through the tall weeds surrounding the nearest home. It was a one-story white house. When she reached the entrance, she pushed open the fragile old door, which was barely hanging by a hinge. She stepped inside and marveled at the design. It was quite different from any building she'd ever seen. It seemed so much cozier. Brighter. The many windows made it easy to see, where she was going. It was a nice change from the darkness she often encountered.

She checked each room. The décor wasn't too different from what she'd seen in the apartments of the abandoned buildings and brownstones. There was unmolested clothing in the drawers of an old dresser in the bedroom. She was amazed at the design, colors, and fabric of the clothing she found. She was even able to find warm dry clothing that fit her. She changed her outfit, but kept her wet clothing with her. After all, it was hers. There was no way she'd leave it behind. It had been handed down to her from her mother. For now, she carried her wet clothing draped over her wounded arm.

While the small house was fascinating to her, it couldn't keep her safe. She continued exploring the village, until she found a strong brick building with a door that she could close and barricade. She blocked the windows with furniture and locked herself in a windowless back room, after lighting one of the candles from her backpack. By this time, her matches were fairly dry, even if they were a little flimsy.

It was late in the afternoon, but she knew it was pointless to explore any further. There wasn't a lot to see at the small village. That much was clear. The building where she hid appeared to be the best place to camp for the night. She was pretty tired and wanted to rest her aching body. It had been a rough day. The following day would also be challenging. She'd wake up early and begin searching for a way back across the water road.

She wished she had a book with her. If only she packed her novel, so she could read it. Of course, if she had brought a book, it would've been damaged by the water. It was just as well. She pulled out the mongrel bones she collected and began scraping them with one of her knives. She'd create a simple set of tools. It would give her something to do. She also had the screwdriver, which could be helpful. Her wet clothing was laid out to dry.

Once she began to feel tired, she pulled the mongrel pelt over her and closed her eyes. It took a while before she could fall asleep. Her mind began to drift. She found herself dwelling on her predicament. How was she ever going to find a way to cross the water road? It apparently went on for miles in both directions. Were there no bridges anywhere? She'd seen huge elaborate bridges in her books. She'd also seen small simple ones. Why wasn't there any kind of bridge crossing this water road? A bridge could've made things so much easier.

She then remembered that time she saw those nomads trying to cross the water road. It took them away, just like it did her. At the time, she believed they perished. Yet here she was safe and sound. What if they also survived their ordeal? What if they were washed up onto the same beach as her? What if they had come through the same ruins? Maybe it was one of them, who left the stink of urine in that old shed. Would she encounter them, again? If so, would she have to fight them?

No. That was so long ago. Even if any of them survived the water road, they had to be very far away, by now. Nomads were always on the move. Besides, they were from this side of the water, so they probably just returned to the north, where they came from. North. The same direction, where she needed to go, so she could get back to the shelter.

Home.

It was funny. She never liked to think of the shelter as home. It was always "the shelter" to her. Home was only her room. It was the only place that ever felt like home to her. That was her happy place. She wanted so desperately to be there now.

She blew out the candle and allowed the darkness to envelop her.

I need to get back to the shelter. I don't know how much longer I can last out here. For the second time, I had to sleep away from my home. This is all so new to me. Being stuck in the ruins overnight. I used to think it'd be fun and adventurous, but it's not what I expected. It's a wonder I was able to sleep at all last night. I guess I was too tired to care.

I suppose yesterday was an adventure. Now, comes the challenge. Getting back home.

When I woke up this morning, I had to hunt for my breakfast. I thought it'd be simple. It wasn't. I ended up skipping breakfast and having lunch, instead. Not by choice. I tried hunting for birds all morning, but couldn't catch any. I even lost a knife, after throwing it into the trees and missing my target. Next, I tried catching fish, which is no easy task without a fishing pole. I was forced to build a temporary fishing pole using that pipe I found and some wiring from one of the ruins. It took a while to find decent bait, as well. The beach was too shallow, so I climbed back onto that elevated concrete area where I killed the mongrel. The carcass was starting to smell, so I walked to the far end before casting my line. Eventually, I was able to catch a fish sometime during the afternoon. One fish.

By that time, my wet clothes were completely dried, so I collected them from the place where I slept. While the clothing didn't smell very good, I wasn't going to leave them behind. I folded them and shoved them into my backpack.

It was time to move on. I intended to leave the ruins much earlier in the day. I knew I had a long way to travel. Despite that, I took a little extra time to make sure there were no useful supplies in the other structures I skipped past yesterday. I'm glad I did because I found better footwear. A practically new pair of black boots, which were still in their original box. They were hidden in an old closet. They're way more comfortable than mine. My old ones were falling apart. My ride through the water road combined with all the running I did yesterday had taken its toll on them. The rubber bottoms were starting to come off. It was time to discard them. They served their purpose for many years, but they're no good to me anymore. I'm sure mom would understand. They were hers. Hopefully, these new ones should last a very long time. I've already had plenty of time to break them in.

When I left the ruins, my goal was to travel south, first. Since I had never come down this far, I wanted to see if maybe I'd get lucky and find a bridge beyond the wide body of water that the water road had become. While it did eventually narrow out further south, the separation of both sides seemed to go on forever. I've only succeeded in putting myself further away from the shelter, while losing precious hours of daylight.

So, now I'm heading north, which is what I should've done in the first place, rather than wasting valuable time. I've already gone past the ruins from earlier. Maybe staying there another night would've been smarter. Too late. There was a trail leading north from there, although it veered away from the water road going slightly eastbound. I took it regardless. I didn't think I'd have to walk so far for so long. The trail took me in a northeasterly direction. A little too far east.

Fortunately, not long ago, I came upon another trail that crossed the one I was on. This one appears to be taking me northwest, which is more promising. I can see ruins in the distance whenever I reach a hillcrest. That's a good sign, since I know there are ruins across from my old fishing rock. Maybe the very same ruins. I hope.

I find it curious how some of these trails are numbered. There are metal signs with numbers, which appear every once in a while. I've noticed each trail seems to have its own number, if any at all. Some don't have signs with numbers. Instead, there are destinations listed that no longer exist. Names that mean nothing to anyone any more.

As of yet, I haven't seen any nomads. Thankfully. In fact, I haven't seen much of anything. No animals either. I hope that changes soon. I'll need to eat dinner at some point. I'm getting hungry. I have rations in my backpack. Berries and meat jerky. I'd prefer to go further before I resort to eating them. I don't like being out here on an unfamiliar trail in the middle of nowhere, far from any structures. If the darkness comes before I reach the ruins, I'll be at risk. I need to keep moving. Eating can wait. What bothers me is I probably would've been there had I not gone south earlier.

Of course, had I found a bridge, I would've been back at the shelter by now. No. I can't waste time thinking about what could've been. I need to focus on the here and now. I need to stay alert.

I don't like how this trail is surrounded by so many tall trees. The forest around me is too thick to enter. I might get lost in there. It looks dark, too. I can't tell if anything might be in there watching me. It's best to stick to the trail, until I reach the ruins. Not to mention, following this trail makes it easier to know which way is north. These trees are too tall for me to see the sun. I can't tell how close it is to dusk. I don't know how much time I've got left, before it gets dark.

I'm getting hungrier. My stomach is complaining. If I need to, I'll eat my emergency rations from my backpack. Not yet. Just a little further. I should save them as a last resort. Besides, I can't afford to stop, yet. I'm still too far from the ruins. If only I could find something to kill. I'd eat it raw just to save time.

Not a bird in sight.

It's getting darker. Much darker. The moonlight is helping. I can see where I'm going. Need to walk faster. So hungry.

Wait. Why is it getting windy all of a sudden? What's that low humming sound? I think I see a light up ahead. Oh, no. No!

It's a sky ship!

CHAPTER 12: NIGHT

The sky ship was flying fairly low in the darkened sky. It moved slowly directly over the trail, following it southbound. It's bright beam of light shined down illuminating the trail, and turning darkness into light, as it went. As the sky ship grew near it also kicked up loose leaves from the ground. The deep hum of its engines grew louder with each passing second.

The powerful ray of light seemed to emerge from an even brighter light source. It was impossible to see the sky ship beyond the brightness of its lights. It didn't matter because Evangelina had no intention of stopping to look up.

She didn't have a lot of time. She hurried into the nearby woods on the left, moving deep enough to stay out of sight, but not so deep that she might get lost. The light from the sky ship made it easy to see the trail from where she hid in the woods. However, she knew once it flew past, everything would return to near total darkness. Therefore, she had to keep an eye on which direction the road stretched from south to north. She couldn't allow herself to become distracted and lose sight of it. Staring at the bright light would mean taking time to adjust to the darkness, once more. A problem to worry about later. Staying hidden was paramount, for the moment. She dared not get caught by the sky ship. She needed to put plenty of distance between her and it.

It seemingly hovered along without taking any notice of her. Good. She waited until it was completely out of sight before she moved an inch. Once it was gone and she couldn't hear it any longer, she knew it would be time to move.

That only took a few seconds. As she suspected, it took more time for her eyes to readjust to the darkness, so she waited. When her night vision was restored, she gradually began making her way back toward the trail. She tried to move quietly, as if the sky ship would somehow hear her footsteps and return for another pass. She wasn't taking any chances.

When she reached the trail she picked up her pace and continued north. She moved at a slow jog for several minutes, but then there was a familiar hum sneaking up behind her. Instantly, she turned back to look and saw that it was practically upon her. The bright beam was zooming fast up the trail.

Without a second thought, she raced into the woods for a second time automatically running for the east side of the trail. She dodged through the trees and didn't stop, until she ran straight into one. It was so dark she hadn't even seen it. The sudden impact knocked her to the ground temporarily dazing her.

She silently cursed herself for not paying attention to where she was going, and then checked to see if she felt any blood on her face. Luckily, there was no wetness, but she'd probably have a bump on her forehead, if not a bruise.

For a short time, she remained on the ground, recovering, and waiting for the sound of silence to return to the darkened woods. While she rested, she wondered why it had come back. Did they detect her presence somehow? The thought was terrifying, although she realized that couldn't be the case, or they would've found her now. She hated being out in the open with that thing flying around hunting her like she was prey. It definitely knew she was out there, hiding.

For nearly an hour, she sat in the forest. Hiding seemed like a good idea. Being in the darkened woods, unable to see anything around her felt a lot safer than walking along that road with the sky ship making passes with its dreadful beam of light. She closed her eyes and waited even longer. The temptation to sleep was strong. It had been a long walk. A good night's rest would've felt great. However, sleep wasn't something she felt comfortable doing in the middle of the woods. Hunger was another thing on her mind. She wanted to eat something so badly, but it was too dark to remove her backpack. Something might fall out and get lost. It was too risky. She'd have to wait a little longer.

The longer she waited, the less she felt alone. She could hear birds up in the trees. There were insects all around her. Small critters crawling around the ground through the fallen leaves and twigs made only the slightest sounds. Every tiny movement was amplified by the near silence. It never occurred to her how noisy it could be at night when one just sat and listened to the darkness.

She opened her eyes and could actually see a little. Her eyes had adjusted, once more. The idea of sitting there all night didn't seem too bad to her. It was probably safer, until she felt something creeping onto her hand. She shook it off. Another thought occurred to her. How many things were crawling over her body that she couldn't feel? She began feeling disgusted. Almost immediately, she stood up and brushed her hands along her body hoping to knock off any bugs that might be crawling over her clothing. She even shook her hair wildly and pushed her hands through the dark strands. Everything itched.

"Gross," she whispered to herself.

In her opinion, an adequate amount of time had gone by. No more waiting. Not in the darkness, where she couldn't see everything that wanted to crawl over her. The sky ship must've moved on. It had been a while since she heard it. She turned back the way she had come and began walking slowly toward the trail. Her hands had to guide her for part of the way whenever it got too dark to see the trees in front of her. Running smack into another tree wasn't on her agenda.

After several minutes of wandering through the woods, she made it back to the trail. It still didn't feel quite safe. She hesitated before stepping out from the cover of trees and onto the trail. For a moment, she considered walking through the woods, while keeping close to the trail. It didn't seem like a bad idea, so she tried it for a short time, but kept tripping over branches, the roots of the trees, fallen signs, tires, and rocks. There was a lot of debris along the sides of the trail. It just wasn't worth the effort.

She gradually moved back onto the trail, remaining alert. The difference was noticeable beneath her feet. The trail felt hard, as if it were paved under the dirt and weeds. It probably was, she figured. It must've been a road that was driven on by vehicles long ago.

She scoffed at the notion. A vehicle would've certainly made her experience so much easier. Simpler times. Not that she would ever know.

Thinking about the sky ship made her feel paranoid. It couldn't be helped. She kept looking back frequently to make sure it didn't sneak up on her a second time. The problem was she wasn't sure if it was behind her, or somewhere up north. It could come from any direction.

"This sucks," she mumbled. She hated not knowing where it went last. She hated being hungry. She also hated walking through the woods at night. Most of all, she hated being so far from her shelter.

She reached up and felt her forehead. It felt sore to the touch. She could feel a bump where she hit her head against the tree. She checked her fingers. No blood. One small reason to be thankful.

At long last, she could see the ruins getting nearer. Reaching them tonight became the new goal for her. Once she found someplace fairly safe where she could hide for the night, she'd eat some of her rations. It was something to look forward to, although finding shelter had to be her main priority. She didn't want the sky ship to return and find her. She got lucky earlier. Hopefully, she'd seen the last of it.

Eventually, the trail curved slightly, as it entered the outer limits of the city ruins. The first of the abandoned structures had been reached. It was a burnt down fueling station. There was no shelter or supplies to be found there, so she continued on her trek. The next structure she came across was a large storefront. There were too many large broken windows, so she didn't even stop.

Moments later, she reached a series of small homes, much like the ones she saw back at the small fishing village. Surely, one of them could serve well as a temporary shelter. It would be great to finally eat something. She was starving.

Just then, the sky ship emerged from behind the homes and raced toward her location with its bright light scanning the ground. She took off running toward the ruins of the city.

She had to run partially uphill, as she went, which only made it more difficult to escape from the fast approaching light. All the same, she was determined to get away. She hurried past the inviting houses, which could've made such a nice place to hide, and finally eat, and maybe even sleep. Who knows what supplies might've been hidden in their closets? If only she'd been faster.

Instead, she was running away from the homes and toward the first intersection of the city's ruins. Taller buildings began to surround her like another forest. This time, made of brick, concrete, and durasteel. Perhaps, it could work in her favor, she hoped. The sky ship would have to fly higher to avoid crashing. There were also more places available for her to hide. She wasn't planning to waste the opportunity.

She ran blindly into one of the nearest buildings. Stupidly, she thought just because she was indoors, she could stop running. There was only a brief respite, barely long enough for her to catch her breath, before the sky ship shined its light at the doorway where she entered. No good. She couldn't let it find her.

While it was focused on the front entrance, she began moving through the darkened lobby toward the light at the end of the hallway. There was an open back door that led to an alley. She took it and ran through the alley toward the next building. She climbed into an open ground floor window and rushed through the apartment carelessly without taking any time to look around her. She didn't care. Within seconds, she was out the door and moving up the stairs to a second floor apartment. She stopped when she entered an apartment facing the side of the building and ducked down behind a sofa. She only needed to hide long enough for the sky ship to move on to a different location. Hopefully, she managed to lose it.

Only then did she consider the possibility that someone else could've been in the building. Right now, all that mattered was avoiding the sky ship. She cursed to herself when she spotted the bright light just outside of the windows. How did they find her, again?

She got to her feet and raced back down the stairs. She went through a first floor apartment and climbed out of a rear window. She hurried down the next street, which she noticed was paved. Her boots made a louder reverberating sound against it, as she ran. This time, she cursed her new boots for making too much noise, but didn't stop running. She turned the corner and hurried through some kind of shop exiting through its rear door into yet another alleyway. This one stunk of old garbage.

The alley led her to another street near some park or wooded area. She wasn't sure. She could see ruins on the other side, so she ran through the trees hoping the canopies would hide her better. The sky ship could be heard humming closer. It's light was searching for her, but in the wrong direction. It lost sight of her.

At last, she began to feel safer.

She emerged on the other side of the park and entered another building. She noticed a staircase that went down into a darkened basement. Carefully, she descended the steps into the waiting darkness. She had to hold her breath because the stench coming from the basement was so foul. For a second, she almost turned back. However, either she learn to deal with the odor or risk being caught by the sky ship. Not really a choice. She continued down the steps, stopping when she reached the bottom.

It seemed like a good place, where she could stop to rest. There was no way the sky ship would find her down there. For the moment, she was safe, even if she couldn't see a thing. It gave her time to catch her breath, which helped. This was way too much running for one week. She leaned against the wall, not wanting to go too deep into the basement. Lighting a candle wouldn't be necessary. She didn't plan on staying down there for too much longer. Just long enough for the sky ship to finally move on.

It was a total mystery to her how it somehow kept tracking her every movement. It always seemed to know exactly where to find her. She wondered if maybe it had a way of detecting humans. How else could it keep showing up everywhere she went? It was too much of a coincidence. Unless she just had extremely bad luck. Probably.

In the meantime, she'd have to wait it out. There wasn't much of a choice. She was too tired of running. The basement appeared to be safe, despite the odor emanating from within. She found herself trying to guess how much longer she'd have to wait until daylight.

Would the sky ship simply leave once the sun came up? It seemed silly to think so, but it's what she was hoping. She figured it would have to land, and its occupants would have to exit the safety of their ship to follow her down to the basement, which was highly unlikely.

What did they look like anyway, she wondered? No one really knew for sure. There was a lot of speculation over the years, but no hard proof. Very few people ever returned, after an encounter with a sky ship. The few who had seen them managed to run and hide, like she did. Nobody knew how the occupants looked. They probably liked it that way. She was fairly confident they wouldn't come for her on foot.

She would've remained in the basement until dawn, except for the fact that it wasn't empty. It didn't take long to realize she wasn't alone. There was a noise in the darkness. Breathing. She swallowed nervously when she heard the sound. The urge to run back up the stairs overpowered her. What was down there with her? Was it an animal? A nomad? Something worse?

Apparently, she was about to find out.

From within the darkness there was a sudden movement. She backed up the stairs watchfully, not taking her eyes off of the basement. A large dark shape became visible, as it slowly rose to its full height and approached. It was taller than her. The foul smell was coming from whatever was in there. She panicked. Was it another sasquatch? A bear? She really didn't have the strength to fight something that deadly, after all the running she'd done. She was tired and hungry.

When she reached the top of the stairs, she was holding her knives. Whatever was down there hiding in the dark, if it chose to follow her up, she was ready to fight it. She couldn't run anymore. It was time to make a stand, and she had the higher ground. That gave her an advantage. Didn't it?

A smirk appeared on her face when she noticed it was only a man. A nomad. He was hairy and unkempt. His clothing were mere filthy rags hanging from his pale blotchy skin. The teeth he had left were stained yellow. A salt and pepper, shaggy, full beard hid the rest of his face. He was older than her by a couple of decades. His wild, bright, blue eyes looked like sapphires staring up at her with lust.

"If you come any closer, I'll hurt you," she warned. Her voice was young, but it was also firm and unshaken.

He hesitated at the sound of it. It had been so many years since he heard anyone's voice. The feminine sound threw him off his game. Her confidence was intimidating. It took him a moment before he decided whether or not it was worth the risk to come after her. While he waited, her confidence grew. She brandished the knives to let him know she meant business. At that point, he must've decided she was worth the risk because he accepted her challenge and began climbing the steps with a wicked grin on his face. It turned out, he was armed, as well, with a long hunting knife held in his rugged left hand. His large fingers wrapped around the handle like sausage links. He grinned, as he made sure she saw his knife.

She gaped at the large blade and knew all it would take was one wrong move on her part and she'd be severely injured or maimed. He could do an intense amount of damage with that weapon, especially if he knew how to wield it. On the other hand, if she somehow managed to defeat him, she could claim the knife and keep it for herself. It was an inspiring thought, if she could only pull it off without bleeding to death. That was the real trick.

The nomad paused before getting too close to her. Was he hesitating, again, or was this part of his strategy? She had been hoping to kick him back down the stairs. However, charging recklessly toward her wasn't something he was willing to do, which implied he did have some intelligence.

Somewhat disappointed, she opted to try reasoning with the brute. "We don't have to fight," she said, shaking her head and hoping to appeal to his apparent intellect. She slowly put her arms down to show she was no longer a threat. She also tried another word, unsure if he'd even understand. "Friend?" She even smiled at him to seal the deal.

He eyed her curiously, squinting and tilting his head. He was confused by her strange combat strategy. She backed away from the top of the stairs slowly, hoping he'd return to his hole in the ground. She'd be okay with that idea. Getting his knife wasn't that important to her. He stood his ground, so she slowly turned away, and then hurried toward the doorway of the building. Before exiting, she peeked outside. There was no sign of the sky ship, which was a relief.

The rapid sound of steady footsteps informed her that her new friend wasn't quite ready to let her leave the premises. At least, not without a fight. She quickly turned and threw her knives in succession directly into his chest, which made him ease off from his charge, giving her plenty of time to pull out two more of her much smaller knives. He gazed down curiously at the tiny blades protruding from his chest, perhaps wondering how she managed to toss them so fast with such precision. Practice, of course. The distraction was just the time she needed to slap him across the face with a two-by-four piece of wood she found on the floor, likely part of the broken front door. The big knife fell from his hand with a loud clank, as it hit the dirty tiled floor.

Like a savage, she seized the opportunity and tackled him to the ground by throwing all her body weight against his upper torso. He wasn't expecting the attack. When they hit the floor, she stabbed him repeatedly with her other two knives in the chest, stomach, and neck alternating between each targeted location, so he wouldn't know where to expect her next strike making it nearly impossible to block. She continued the brutal onslaught at an unbelievably fast pace driven by adrenaline, until he stopped grunting and moaning, or rather until she was completely drained and out of breath.

When it was over, she stared down at his lifeless body taking in what she had done, while again, using the time to catch her breath. This was her second human kill. As with Avery, she was left with little choice. There was no point in dwelling on it any longer. She refused to become anyone's victim in this post-apocalyptic nightmare of a world. Her conscience was clear, as far as she was concerned.

She retrieved her other knives from his chest and wiped off the blood on his rags. She then reached over to pick up his huge knife from the floor, before standing up. Tenderly, she placed it into her right boot. It would serve her well, if she was forced to fight another nomad. Unfortunately, she had a feeling that would be the case. Until she could reach the shelter, she'd be in danger every step of the way.

Considering it was still dark out, it wasn't safe for her to leave the building, yet. She decided she could return to the basement stairs and wait it out there. Going down into the darkened room didn't appeal to her. For all she knew, the nomad hadn't been alone down there. It was even possible he was protecting his family from what he might've believed to be an intruder. Her.

She hoped not.

When she reached the top of the stairs, she called down into the darkness. "Hello? Is there anyone down there?" She waited, but there was no reply. Only silence. That suited her fine. She sat down at the top of the steps and waited.

And she waited.

An hour went by. Still nothing. No sky ship. No noise coming from below. Only then did she feel safe enough to remove her backpack and eat some of her rations. It took everything she had to resist from eating it all. She knew she'd need the rest later. It was still a long way back home. For now, she'd sit and wait some more. Soon, the daylight would come.

CHAPTER 13: LOST

After the night she had, she was more than ready to get back to her shelter. The only problem was she had no idea if that were even possible. At the moment, she had no idea where she was or which way to go. She was lost and tired. She hadn't slept all night. How could she when she was so busy running and hiding? Not to mention there was her little encounter with the big, hairy, smelly nomad.

At least, she gained a new weapon from that experience. It was a small reward for the hardships of the night.

The miniscule number of rations she permitted herself to eat was barely going to sustain her. She needed to find food. She'd have to hunt, before she could even think about going home. The sun had just unveiled its morning light onto the day. The birds would be up in their trees singing happily, as usual. She'd get one with one of her small knives. There were a lot of trees in that park she ran through earlier in the night. That's where she'd hunt for her breakfast. She might even kill two birds, so she could eat lunch, too, while she was at it. She felt that hungry.

Leaving the temporary shelter of the building's basement steps did give her a brief moment of hesitation. What if the sky ship was still out there waiting for her to emerge from her hiding spot? At this point, she wouldn't put it past them to be waiting for her during the daylight. Of course, their beams of light would be rendered useless during the daytime. Well, she hoped so. They were certainly bright enough to be seen during the daylight.

No. That would be stupid. No one had ever seen one of them during the daytime. She was only being paranoid. It should be safe to go out.

When she exited the building, she couldn't help but glance upward at the sky. Seeing the lovely dark blue sky with a blast of orange and yellow from the dawn was a welcome sight. It brought a smile to her face. She loved the mornings. It was so rare that she glimpsed a sunrise, even if she couldn't actually see the sun, at the moment. There were too many buildings in the way.

In the last couple of days, she'd not only experienced sunrises, but sunsets. While both were breathtaking to observe, she decided she could do without the latter. She wasn't too fond of the night. The night sun, or the moon, as it was called, didn't bring the safety of the daylight that came with the morning sun. Morning was also a good time for fishing, if only she knew which way to go for the water road. She looked up, again, and tried to see where the sun was hiding.

Frustrated, she turned around to go back into the building, and took the staircase up to the roof. The building had four floors, so walking up wasn't too bad. It was a necessary climb, as well as a good way to get her bearings. Once on the rooftop, she could finally see which way to go.

East became easily apparent. She stared at the glow over the eastern horizon. It was amazing. The mixture of dawn colors made it look like the sky was on fire, but only in the east. She had a hard time turning away from its beauty. When she looked west, it was a darker shade of blue than the usual daytime sky. That told her how early it was in the day. Too early! It was good, though, because she'd have a good many hours of daylight to accomplish her next goal. Going home.

First things first. A quick look down at the street level told her where that park was located. It was time to go hunting.

While going downstairs, she allowed herself time to explore the apartments she went past. If the door was closed, she skipped it. However, those that were wide open were fair game. During her search for supplies, she found two books that she barely shoved into her backpack. Her spare clothing made it difficult to fit anything. She also didn't want to add too much weight. However, she had a feeling she could deal with having two books to choose from the next time there was a chance to stop and read. Not today.

She also found more matches, another candle, a fork, and a small metal cup she could use for drinking, if she ever found clean water. Her water bottle was nearly empty.

When she finally left the building, she headed straight to the park. From the rooftop, she noticed it was a rectangular park covering about four square blocks. It was a sufficiently large hunting ground to find a bird. Maybe even a rodent of some kind. She'd take anything, but bugs. That was where she drew the line. No eating bugs. Ever. She didn't care if she starved to death.

It didn't take long to reach the park, since it was only a block away. The park didn't have a surrounding wall or fence, so she simply entered. Her small knives were out, as she stalked through the trees searching for prey. Her steps were steady and quiet. Slowly, she searched the trees, until she heard them singing. She followed the sound and saw a flock spread out along the branches.

She aimed and tossed one knife with the same accuracy as always, hitting her target in its chest. A large bird fell from the tree onto the grass. Perfect. Before going to retrieve it, she took a chance and threw the other knife. She hit another bird, also knocking it from the tree. Grateful, she walked over to retrieve both kills and her knives.

That's when she noticed a small pond beyond the grassy clearing. Her smile broadened. She'd be able to refill her water bottle, as well. The day was starting out pretty good.

Minutes later, she lit a small fire by the pond, where she opted to cook her breakfast. It would be necessary to boil her water, before it was safe to drink. She had a metal container for just such purpose in her backpack. Abram called it a canteen. She preferred to think of it as her water can.

She cooked both birds and devoured them with no remorse. The second one was rather small, so it wouldn't have filled her empty stomach. Removing the feathers was tedious, but it gave her time to boil her water. She kept a tailfeather from each bird. The longest she could pluck. They would someday remind her of the time she spent in the ruins across the water road. She smiled. Soon, she'd be home.

After breakfast, she packed up her gear and headed west through the ruins. The sky over the west was a pleasant light blue, by then. The usual puffy white clouds were stretched out thin. As they slowly dragged across the sky they didn't appear to reveal any sky ships, for the moment.

 Little by little, she trudged through the ruins of the city on her way westward. She figured, as long as she kept going in that direction, she'd reach the water road eventually. It was such a long road, there was no way of avoiding it. The walk wasn't as simple as she hoped it would be. There were many obstacles and roadblocks that caused her to make detours, so she could circumvent them. It was an annoying waste of time, which she didn't appreciate. Over the years, some of the taller buildings had crumbled down creating enormous walls and mounds, which she didn't want to risk climbing. The jagged rubble and sharp objects sticking out through the ruins made climbing over the rubble a terrible idea. It was best to go around.

 As she went, she came across a large grid of blocks that had been completely leveled. Every structure had been brought down to the ground, leaving behind a huge flat field of ruins and rubble. Going around it would've most likely taken twice as long as simply going directly through it. She gazed up at the sun and sighed. There would be no shade.

 She imagined herself as a tiny insect crawling through those forever fields with the heat of the sun beating down on it. It could possibly take eons to cross. Well, not for her.

 Her first steps through the open space were rather casual. However, the further she walked through the flattened ruins, the more she began to feel far too vulnerable. Being there left her out in the open. There was absolutely nowhere to hide. Her steps hastened, as she decided she wanted to cross that section of ruins as fast as possible. It was as if she couldn't reach the other side fast enough. Maybe she was like an insect, after all. Panic set in, and she came close to a slow run, but moving too fast could lead to tripping and falling. An injury would be ill advised, so she had to tread carefully.

 Her eyes kept moving from looking down to looking ahead, and also to looking around her in every direction. While she didn't see anyone, it felt to her like someone was watching her. Maybe from the taller buildings in the distance. She probably stood out like a fly on a white platter. A lone figure moving across an open field of rubble and dust. If it had been nighttime, there's no way she would've dared to attempt crossing the field. The sky ships would be on her in seconds. Lucky for her it was still morning. She could see the sun hadn't yet reached its noon position.

It bothered her how her mind kept racing. She tried to keep her focus on where she was going. Hurry and cross this field, she told herself in her mind. Stay alert.

She couldn't help herself. As a way of keeping herself distracted, she tried figuring out what could've happened to cause so many structures to be razed so low in such a concentrated location. Did something fall on them? Maybe something really big. Perhaps it was an explosion, she thought. Whatever it was had apparently been so powerful it took out about a square mile of buildings. There were several scattered weeds trying their best to grow through between the shattered pieces of concrete and metal. No trees, though. It was unlike anything she'd ever seen. She estimated it must've occurred years ago.

It made her realize there might be a whole lot in this strange world to experience. Chances were she wouldn't understand half of it, and there was no one left to explain the mysteries. She once yearned to explore the world beyond her ruins. Now, she wasn't so sure anymore. Being too far from the shelter wasn't the magnificent adventure she imagined, after reading her fantasy books. The eerie urban decay and vast barren wasteland in front of her was far from magnificent. It wasn't even remotely interesting.

Right now, the only thing she wanted to do was get back to the shelter. She longed for the safety she enjoyed when closed up in her room. Her home. She missed her home desperately. Her cozy soft bed. She missed her fascinating books. She missed the clean bathroom and the comfortable kitchen. She missed her father, and her clan. Her family. She missed not having to worry about hiding from sky ships. Most of all, she missed the mother, whom she barely knew.

I Stand Alone

She looked up at the blue sky and felt a moment of defiance when the brightness of the sun forced her gaze away. No doubt, the heat of the sun was getting to her. It was a very warm day. She paused from her walk and felt a strong urge to shout up at the sky, but realized it would accomplish nothing. Her sudden anger was overwhelming, but misplaced. She was really angry at the sky ships. Angry at space for sending the stray asteroid that left her world in utter ruins, but then her anger gradually turned to confusion.

Space was so black just like the nighttime sky, so how was it possible for the sky to look so blue during the daytime? Where did the stars go during the day? Did the sky ships have anything to do with their disappearance each morning? They were also only visible at night. Maybe they were invisible during the day, but were still up there… watching and waiting for night to come.

Just maybe they couldn't touch her now.

At that moment, she noticed a single star in the sky. Was it a star? She noticed it was moving across the daytime sky. It moved slowly, but at a steady speed. What was it? A second later, it zipped out of view and was gone, leaving her more confused than before. Had it been a sky ship, or maybe it was something else?

The great wide open around her suddenly didn't feel as large. The end was in sight. With her eyes facing forward, once more, she focused on her goal. No longer did she worry about anyone watching her. Her mind was only on one thing, getting back home.

When she finally reached the end of the leveled field, she looked back the way she had come. The mystery of what caused the catastrophic mess no longer mattered to her. It was irrelevant. A feeling of satisfaction came over her knowing it was behind her now. It was time to resume her trek west. She needed to reach the water road. Once she did, she'd find a way to cross it. She no longer thought it was impossible. After all, she already crossed it one time, even if it was beyond her control when it happened. Regardless, she got to the other side of the water road. Therefore, she could find a way to do it, again. She had to.

First, she'd have to get through the ruins. Hundreds of abandoned buildings still surrounded her path to the west. She looked back up at the sun. It was noon. She hoped she wouldn't lose track of which way was west. Going straight through the ruins wasn't always possible, but she'd surely try her best.

At the same time, she couldn't forget the many potential dangers around her that could be hidden throughout the ruins. There could be more nomads, another angry sasquatch, a pack of hungry mongrels, a bear, lions, and even traps that could be set waiting to catch a lone unsuspecting traveler. She'd be ready. She had to remain alert. Always. It was her mantra. Be ready for anything.

She watched the darkened empty windows of the decayed buildings she passed. She glanced up at the looming rooftops, as well. She always slowed down when reaching the end of a block, using extreme caution before crossing any intersection. The open spaces were the worst places to be complacent. There was no cover. No place to hide. Crossing those areas had to be done rapidly and with extreme caution. She tried to avoid places that looked ripe for an ambush. It meant taking a few unwanted detours.

After a while, she began to think she might've made one too many detours. How long could it possibly take to reach the water road? She hadn't gone that far east that it would take this long to get back to the west. Perhaps, she'd gotten turned around somehow.

She looked up for the sun and realized she wasn't going true west anymore, but at more of an angle. She needed a better confirmation. It was time for a visit to a rooftop, so she could get her bearings. There was a six-story building at the end of the block. That would make a good place to take a look around. The idea of climbing six floors didn't appeal to her, but there was no other way to reach the top. If she had known anything about elevators, she never would've gone to a rooftop without complaining, but elevators remained an unknown invention to her. Oddly, she'd never even read about one.

Entering the building was a little harder than expected. There was a crashed vehicle that knocked down a utility pole, which was blocking the door from opening. It was meant to open outward. She had to stack up piles of rubble, until she could reach the ladder of the fire escape. In the past, she tried to avoid using fire escapes, after stepping onto one that immediately began to come loose from the sudden weight of her foot. She planned to climb into the first window she reached.

Both second floor windows were boarded up with wood, but the glass had been shattered. She easily kicked the wood free from one knocking it inward. Much to her surprise, the apartment was actually in pretty decent shape. It hadn't been ransacked and scavenged like all the rest. In fact, the front door was locked from the inside and barricaded with heavy furniture. Everything was covered in layers of dust. She wondered when the last time was that anyone had been in there. She imagined it might've been from before everything went to shit.

It looked like there were some potential supplies for her to snatch up. She wasn't about to pass up the chance. She checked the kitchen, first. As expected, the cupboards were bare. There was no food at all. She searched each room of the apartment, until she came across two skeletons in the bedroom. They were wearing fancy clothing. One wore a dark suit, while the other had on a long white gown with laces. There was a thin veil covering her face.

All of a sudden, she felt like she was intruding on their privacy. This was their tomb.

"Oh. Sorry." She felt bad. The couple likely managed to hold out as long as they could, before giving up. They probably died before there were any clans, but maybe not before there were nomads, since they felt the need to barricade their door. Too bad. Somehow, it didn't feel right going through their things. Not with them still there. Unburied.

She left the bedroom and quietly shut the door behind her. She tiptoed across the living room and proceeded to remove the barricade from in front of the door. She then unlocked it and peeked out at the hallway. It was quiet out there. She left the apartment and located the door that led to the staircase. She climbed the other five floors to the roof landing. Once at the top, she pushed open the door leading out to the roof and stepped out.

Normally, she admired the view from high up, but when she found herself looking back down at the barren field she crossed moments ago, it left a bad feeling in her stomach. The area looked somewhat smaller from high up, although it was a fairly large region. Whatever caused that area to flatten must've been something great. Not good, but great.

She turned her attention toward the other ledge facing west. That's where she needed to focus her attention. There were more buildings and tall trees stretched out across that direction. Actually, more trees than buildings. It was as if the trees had grown large enough to swallow up the smaller buildings on that side of the city. It was hard to tell if the water road was beyond the trees because they were so tall.

There were grayed out faded ruins far beyond the trees and more to the southwest of her location. She recognized some of the shapes. The familiar towers and spires. She was almost home. Those were her ruins and the ruins to the south that she explored so often. She knew them well by their distinctive shapes. The broken fingers of a hand. A smile flashed across her face, as relief washed over her.

It wasn't that far. She could make it to the water road before it got dark. After that, she'd have to figure it out.

She hurried back down the stairs and remembered how the front door was blocked, so she went through the same apartment that allowed her entry into the building. Once inside, she locked the door, again, and then ritualistically replaced the barricade of furniture. She would preserve the tomb of the married couple.

When she was done, she climbed through the open window and down the ladder of the fire escape. She allowed herself to drop down to the sidewalk. Her direction was clear from there. She hurried down the street heading west.

As soon as she reached the next corner, she came face to face with a handsome man.

CHAPTER 14: SAVAGES

Had she been moving any faster, she would've bumped right into the unsuspecting man. She found him to be very attractive, which made her feel awkward. Going into fight mode didn't seem like the appropriate response, especially since he was simply standing there. He appeared to be a few years older than her, but not too much older. Maybe in his late twenties. From his cleanshaven appearance, he didn't look like what she believed to be a typical nomad. He wore clothing much like hers. The clothes were dirty, but in decent condition. He even had on shoes.

Who was this guy?

She froze in place. He stared back locking eyes with her. She didn't want to look away. His eyes were a mesmerizing hazel color. Her first instinct was to suspect he was part of a clan, which meant there might be others nearby. She snapped out of her stupor, and then her eyes quickly scanned her surroundings. He noticed her hesitation and studied her suspicious movements, but still made no move against her. She wondered if there were others with him, would they be friendly? Was *he* friendly? She wasn't quite sure, yet. He hadn't attacked her, so that was a good sign.

"Um, hello?" She opted for the friendly approach. She followed up her greeting with an awkward smile.

He grinned happily and took a step closer.

Instinctively, she took a step back. She wasn't used to meeting anyone at all outside of her clan. Her apprehensive actions seemed to offend him because his expression changed to one of anger. He then reached out to grab her, but she pulled away angrily.

"Hey! No grabbing!"

He shouted over his shoulder without taking his eyes off of her, "Girl!"

A man appeared at the doorway of a nearby building. Another peered out from a second floor window of a neighboring building.

There was another three she didn't even notice. One on a rooftop and the others were behind her. So, he definitely wasn't alone. This time, he moved toward her menacingly.

She wasn't having it, although she knew there'd be too many for her to fight. This was a fight she'd lose. That was obvious, so she dodged his advance and ran past him. He immediately gave chase. The others soon joined in the pursuit.

Running from a group of dangerous men was much scarier to her than running from the pack of mongrels from the other day. The mongrels were merely hungry animals. It was normal. This was different. These men wanted to hurt her. She knew if they caught her, they'd want to do terrible unthinkable things to her. They might not have been nomads, but they were just as bad. Maybe worse. They were desperate savages.

Her heart pounded in her chest, as she struggled to keep her distance from them. She was already tired from staying up all night, walking half the morning, and climbing stairs to the roofs of two buildings. She wasn't sure how much further she could run. She knew she couldn't run toward the water road, since there would be no where left to go. Instead, she headed in a northbound direction, while trying to remain parallel to the west, so she wouldn't get lost, again.

She had to leap over a crevice in the ground, which she nearly missed. She was truly beginning to hate being out in the ruins. Everywhere she turned, there was another threat waiting to get her. She was tired of running from things. It was extremely frustrating. It didn't help how the terrain was so unfamiliar to her. For all she knew, they could be leading her into a trap and she was heading straight into it.

The thought made her turn the next corner. She ran west for a block, before turning back toward the north. She was closer to the tall trees. Going into the trees was tempting, but the buildings offered more places for her to hide, if she managed to lose them. Therefore, she remained close to the buildings, hoping to find an opening, where she could duck into and keep out of sight. It would have to be someplace that wasn't too obvious, or they'd guess where she went.

She turned another corner heading east, but ran into the first doorway she came across. She hurried up the stairs to the second floor and into the nearest apartment, where she closed the door and hoped they wouldn't find her. Just in case, she hid behind the large sofa near the window.

The handsome man and two of his friends stopped when they reached the corner where she disappeared. They took a moment to catch their breaths. The handsome man called out to the other two, "Find girl!" He pointed at the buildings on that block. She couldn't see them from where she hid, but she heard them. They'd find her sooner or later. She couldn't just sit still and wait to be caught.

She quietly exited the apartment and proceeded up the staircase, as silently as could be. She was already so tired. All she wanted to do was rest. When she reached the fourth floor, she heard someone enter the building. One of them was down in the lobby. It was only a matter of time before he found her.

At least, he'd be alone.

She kept climbing the stairs to the last floor careful not to make a sound. If she could only reach the roof without him hearing her, it would give her time to set up an ambush. She'd have to take him out fast. There was no way she could let the others hear, or they'd come for her, too. Being thrown from the roof would probably be the nicest thing they could do to her. It wasn't likely. Maybe after they were done with her ragged body.

It was best not to think about it.

Once she reached the rooftop, she closed the door and quickly took a breath, and then she searched for anything that could be used as a back-up weapon. There wasn't much up there. Just some buckets filled with stagnant water. It was odd. There were weeds growing on the roof. There was even a small skinny tree at the far end.

While looking at the buckets, again, an idea came to mind. It wouldn't really stop her pursuer, but it would distract him long enough for her to strike at him. She picked up the smallest bucket and had to empty some of the water because it was too heavy for what she had in mind. She hurried toward the door to set up her plan.

Waiting for the man to finally come up to the roof took close to an hour, but she waited patiently. He searched every single apartment of the building before finally reaching the rooftop. When he opened the door and stepped onto the roof, the bucket of water fell onto his head. The old-fashioned prank startled him. The last thing he expected was to be doused with warm water, which had been heating up for hours under the warmth of the sun.

Evangelina followed that up by stepping around the roof shed from where she had been hiding, and jamming the large knife from her boot into the quickest spot where she knew would both silence him and kill him. His throat. However, she didn't stop there. She pulled him through the doorway letting it close behind him, while tripping him with her foot. When he fell face first the knife was pushed deeper into his throat, until it was sticking out the back of his neck. He was dead within seconds.

She rolled him over and removed the knife, which took some effort because it was lodged in pretty good. Once she got it out, she wiped it clean on his shirt. She noticed he wasn't the handsome one. It was the one standing in the doorway of the building behind him. He was ugly. Not that it mattered.

She checked his pockets. He didn't have anything useful on him, other than a sharpened stone. She tossed it aside and stood over his body. At last, she had time to catch her breath, even if for a few seconds. It was a small win for her.

It was too bad the moment couldn't last too long. The others would eventually come looking for him. Maybe they'd come together, or maybe one at a time. Still, it gave her time to plan her next move. She figured she could try resetting the bucket over the door. Of course, she'd have to refill it with water from one of the other larger buckets. It was possible the trick could work a second time, but if there were more than one person coming through, she wasn't going to be able to strike at them in the same way. She might get the first one, but the second one would certainly be a fight. She hoped to avoid fighting them on the roof. Then again, she was probably going to have to fight one of them, no matter what. Maybe even all of them at once. It was a scary thought.

Then again, fighting them was the only way she was truly going to get away from them. She couldn't have them hunting her the rest of the day. Waiting for each one to come, one at a time, would certainly take a good part of the day, as well. She really didn't want to be on the roof longer than she needed to be. The afternoon sun was bearing down on her. She needed a good plan.

Moments later, she was looking down over the edge of the roof. The handsome man met up with four other men in front of the building where she hid. Five guys?! Great. That was going to be a heck of a fight. She studied them. One looked much taller than the others. Another had a beard. The men all wore clothing like her, although she doubted they belonged to a clan. Maybe once, long ago.

They appeared to be talking, although she couldn't hear them clearly. It sounded more like grunts than actual words. The handsome man appeared to be the leader based on his gestures, and the fact that he did most of the grunting. She guessed they were waiting on their friend to exit the building. It was going to be a long wait. Sooner or later, they'd come looking for him.

She was counting on it.

She waited for the right moment to implement her plan. It had to be timed perfectly. It was only a matter of time before they approached the building. It might only be one of them. It didn't matter, as long as she did what needed to be done at exactly the right moment. Timing was everything. If her plan worked out, it would show them she meant business, while also eliminating at least one of them. Of course, it would also get their attention. She only hoped she was ready for what would follow. The fight of her life.

At last, the group began walking toward the entrance of the building. This was it, she told herself. There'd be no turning back.

Apparently, the group of men had grown tired of waiting for their friend. They agreed to conduct a search. His disappearance could only mean he found the girl, or she found him. They walked toward the entrance when suddenly something large fell from the sky and landed on top of one man crushing him. It was their friend.

Evangelina wasn't even sure if she hit her target. She didn't stick around to find out. She aimed the body at the group hoping to hit one or two of them with it, and then pushed it off. As she turned and ran for the access door to leave the roof, that's when she heard the splat coming from the street. It definitely got their attention based on the startled screams she heard. If she managed to hit one, great. If not, maybe she scared them a bit. Unless she only pissed them off. That was inevitable.

She hurried down to the floor below the roof landing, trying to be as quiet as possible. They were already making a ruckus as they rushed into the building. She closed the doors to five out of six apartments on that floor, leaving only one ajar near the staircase. She hid within another that faced front. The door was closed to that apartment. Next, she waited for them to come. She figured most of them would hurry to the rooftop. Maybe one might be smart or alert enough to investigate the apartments. It was even possible one might go for the open door, first. She was counting on that, too. She needed them to spread out. It would be easier than facing them together.

It was time to wait, again. The waiting was torture. At last, she heard the hurried footsteps coming up the stairs. The commotion in the hallway made her tense. They were just outside. They weren't hurrying up to the roof. The closed doors caught their attention. Moments later, the door to her apartment crept open. Someone stepped inside. It only sounded like one man.

The bearded man cautiously examined the apartment, while remaining at the doorway, before entering any further. When he was satisfied the first room was empty, which was a dining room and kitchen combination, he moved deeper into the apartment. He checked on the first closed door. It led to a darkened bedroom. The room appeared to be empty. He entered to make sure. He threw open the closet door, ready to defend himself. There wasn't anyone inside. He walked past the bed and bent over suddenly. While on his knees, he could see there was no one under the bed. Satisfied, he left the room and moved on to the next door, which led into the bathroom. He immediately yanked the shower curtain away, once again, ready to fight. Again, there was no one there.

He decided to head back out to the hallway to rejoin his friends, but as he walked toward the door, he failed to notice someone sneaking up behind him and pulling a large knife across his throat. She had exited the bathroom just in time to move behind the kitchen counter, where she waited for him.

She let his body fall gently to the floor and snuck out of the apartment. She moved quickly to avoid being seen. She went for the staircase and hurried down to the next level, where she entered another apartment, except it turned out this one wasn't empty.

A very large hand grabbed her from behind and everything went black.

She came to when the water was splashed over her head. There was a brief flashback of being dragged away by the water road, which made her panic. She tried to move her arms and kick out with her feet to reach the ground, but felt restricted. When she opened her eyes, everything looked blurry. She shook off the water droplets from her long eyelashes. The pain in her head was maddening. Apparently someone must've hit her. There was someone laughing nearby. A tall rugged looking man with large hands. He was the only one with her. She wondered where the others were lurking.

It took a moment before she realized her hands were tied behind her back and she was lying on the ground. Her feet were also tied together. She wasn't wearing her backpack. It was nowhere in sight. It was probably with the others. A quick look at her surroundings told her she was back on the roof. It was hard to tell how much time had gone by. It was still daytime, but she couldn't see the sun, which meant it was down by the western horizon behind the trees. Soon it would be dark.

After she became a teenager, her father used to tell her to stay far away from the nomads, in the likely event that she ever encountered them. He said they were extremely dangerous savages, who'd try to enslave her, beat her down, use her for their sexual pleasure, and then probably eat her. Part of her thought he was merely exaggerating to frighten her, but she played along. She would respond by telling him she certainly didn't want to be enslaved, beaten, and most definitely not eaten.

She enjoyed what little freedom she had, and was never fond of pain. The thought of being eaten both terrified and disgusted her.

However, she was confused about how sexual "pleasure" could be something bad, since it was something of an oxymoron with how he put it. He had to explain what he meant. How they wouldn't care about her needs. It would be forced upon her and it would hurt. The pleasure would only be one-sided. He explained nomads were filthy animals with no compassion or remorse. They were incapable of feeling love or hate. There was only the need to cater to their natural instincts. In that regard, they were more like animals than humans. That's how he described them. Animals.

She thought it was such a shame because the world was already so lonely without having to avoid what few other people remained outside of their clan. Little did she know, the world is filled with all kinds of stupid. Her ignorance included. At least, she was smarter than her captors. She could feel the large knife still hidden in her boot. They never bothered to check her for weapons. It was something she would've done. It showed their ignorance, which was an advantage for her.

The way she saw it, if she were going to attempt an escape, now was the time. It would be a lot harder once the other men joined this fool who was left to watch over her. The wheels in her mind began turning, as she thought of a way to cut her ropes and get to her knife. She instinctively checked her belt for her small knives. She usually had about a dozen shoved into small holders along the sides and rear. They were there, too. She scoffed at their stupidity.

It was fairly simple to slide one knife from its holder behind her and begin cutting the ropes that bound her hands together. She just had to move slowly, so it wasn't obvious. It would also help to keep her guard preoccupied.

"Hey!" She called out to him.

He stepped closer toward her, but said nothing. He loomed over her blocking out the daylight with his massive frame. He was extremely tall. She figured he was about six and a half feet. Almost like a mini sasquatch. The thought would've made her laugh had she not been in her current predicament.

She looked up at the sky overhead and asked, "Aren't you guys worried about the sky ships? It'll be dark soon." Her gaze turned back to him. He stared dumbly at her, but didn't respond. She raised her voice, "Sky ships!" She then looked up, again, pointing with her face.

"Yoofohs," he responded in a deep voice. He glanced up at the empty sky and shook his head. "No," he said, while still looking up. He turned back toward her and added, "No yoofohs." He then gave her a big grin. Some of his teeth were missing, just like the hairy nomad she killed the night before.

"Yes," she nodded vehemently. "Not yet, but soon. Only at night." She felt silly when she realized she was dumbing down her conversation for his sake. "There's still some daylight left, but once it's dark, they'll come. They've been following me," she warned. It wasn't a lie. "We're both in danger. *Danger?*"

"Day-jur?"

"DAN-GER!" She emphasized, again, feeling frustrated. She looked past him at the access door leading back into the building and asked, "Where are your friends?"

He turned to see what she was looking at. She cut faster when he turned away. He walked toward the door and opened it. It seemed he was curious, as well. He looked down the stairs, but couldn't hear the others. She figured there had to be around two or three, depending on whether or not she got someone with the dead body she pushed from the roof. Her current companion knew they were in one of the apartments below, where they found their other friend's body. It's where her backpack was, too, but she didn't know that. He guessed they weren't ready to join him, yet. He turned back toward his captive and his eyes gaped wide when he realized she was gone.

"Huh?" He grunted in confusion.

Before he could turn back to call the others, she appeared beside him. She was so much smaller than him. Faster, too. She had already considered which would be the fastest way to take him down without a fight. She instantly plunged the large knife up into his chin, pushing it deep into his brain with all her might. They locked eyes for that final moment of his life. She tried to gently guide his large body to the ground, but he was far too heavy for her. Plus, she was so tired. His body slipped from her hands and fell hard, hitting the ground with a thud.

"Oh, no. That's not good." She yanked the knife free, knowing the sound of him falling would likely attract the others.

She was correct. It was only a matter of time before they'd come for her.

CHAPTER 15: SURVIVAL

The handsome man and his shaggy redheaded companion were rummaging through her backpack in the apartment below, tossing her belongings out onto the kitchen counter. The redheaded man reached for the two books and examined them curiously. Finding them to be uninteresting, he threw them to the floor and kicked them aside. The handsome man pocketed her matches and the screwdriver. The mongrel bones were pushed from the counter to the floor. The rations and full bottle of water were a nice surprise. They wasted no time and began devouring them without thinking to share with their taller friend, who was still on the roof with the girl. They took turns washing down the scraps with the water.

Afterwards, the handsome man thought about the girl and grinned with lust. She was very young and pretty. She appeared to be unmolested. He felt himself becoming hard. He was going to enjoy breaking her in. He'd have her, first, of course. Maybe even several times before he allowed the other two to get their chance. After all, he was the leader. The smartest of the group. It was his right as the alpha male. She seemed like a fighter, which meant she might even last longer than expected, especially since they no longer had to share her with the other three, who that small seemingly harmless girl managed to kill on her own. The handsome man was quite impressed by her prowess. He hoped she'd put up a fight when he mounted her. That was how he liked it best… with some resistance. He was really looking forward to the experience.

Suddenly, a loud thump was heard on the ceiling shaking him from his perverted fantasy. The two men eyed each other and instantly knew what it meant. It came from the roof. They hurried out of the apartment leaving the empty backpack behind, and raced toward the staircase.

The redheaded man stepped onto the roof, first, merely by chance. As soon as he came through the doorway, two small knives were thrust at him with precision. One struck him dead center in the chest, while the other hit him in his face on his right cheek, getting stuck in his bone. He shrieked from the pain, doubling over angrily, while the handsome man shoved him aside without a care, and charged forward at the teenage girl, holding her screwdriver. He glanced only briefly at the tall dead body lying on the floor in a pool of blood. How she managed to break free and beat him was a complete mystery, but he didn't care to find out. All he cared about was not letting her go. Not until he had his way with her. He was determined.

The redheaded man tugged at the small knife in his face, yanking it free. His face had grown red with blood and fury. He screamed from the pain, but then allowed it to fuel his rage, as he rose to his feet holding the small knife in a threatening manner. He screamed his war cry defiantly, ready to kill the girl, no longer caring if he got his chance to ride her. He wanted her dead for everything that she'd done.

She stood across from both men poised to fight, holding the large knife in her right hand. Both men hesitated at the sight of the large blade. They wondered where such a huge weapon came from. How could they have missed it? It was enormous! The handsome man glared back at the tall dead body on the ground. It was his fault. He captured her. He should've confiscated her weapons, but he failed.

He leered at the girl and spoke, changing his tone, "Friends." The word sounded foreign coming from him. He then smiled and relaxed his posture. The redheaded man was confused by his actions and didn't know what to do, but he dared not go against the alpha male of their pack.

She locked eyes with the handsome man and responded coldly, "I don't think so, pretty man. You had your chance. Now, we're enemies. Where's my backpack?"

Whether or not he even understood what she was saying, he didn't show it. Instead, he stared at her without saying another word. His smile faded and was replaced by a sinister grimace. He scowled. If she wanted to fight, so be it. The redheaded man moved to his side, no longer confused, but also ready to pummel this girl, once and for all. He paid no mind to the blood pouring down his ruddy face. He was brandishing the small knife that caused his wound, while the other small knife was still stuck in his chest.

At this point, Evangelina knew she'd have to go through both of them, if she wanted to leave the roof, unless she planned on jumping. That certainly wasn't going to happen, not from five stories up. She wasn't sure if she was going to survive this fight, but she planned on taking at least one of them with her. They stared each other down for what seemed like an eternity. She hated having a standoff with the two men, but the longer they waited to fight, the longer she got to live. It also gave her time to think.

Meanwhile, it was getting darker by the minute. The sun was setting, casting a beautiful orange glow on the western horizon behind the men. The clouds had turned a darker color silhouetted by the setting sun. For the first time, she got to appreciate the beauty of a sunset. Quite possibly for the last time, as well. She thought she may as well enjoy the view before fighting to the death.

For the briefest of seconds, she imagined being alone on a rooftop, but back in her familiar ruins. If only that's where she was, instead. If only she had never ended up on the other side of the water road. She might've been in her shelter right now, reading a good book.

Instead, she was far from home, across the water road with no way of getting back, facing off against two savage nomads on a rooftop at the brink of nightfall. It was just like a scene from one of her fantasy adventure novels. The hero of the story was either about to die, or do something great. Was that her? Was she the hero? The heroine? Was she about to die, or was she going to do something great?

At that moment, she smiled, which impressed the hell out of the handsome man, but then her expression changed to one of fear. Her eyes opened wide. She cowered and took a step back. It looked like she was about to scream. Unexpectedly, she pointed up at the sky behind them, but said nothing. It was as if fear had robbed her of the ability to speak.

The men became confused by her actions. What was she looking at that caused her to become so fearful? Whatever it was had to be somewhere behind them based on where she was pointing. They both looked at each other, and then nervously turned around simultaneously to see what she was looking at. However, there was nothing there.

At first, the handsome man wondered if she could be seeing something they could not. His redheaded companion became paranoid when he realized it was night. His gaze turned up toward the darkened sky. He no longer wanted to be on the roof, where the sky ships could get to him. The same look of fear was now on his face.

When the handsome man realized what was going on, he became furious. He gave the redheaded man a backhanded slap, shocking him into a state of calm. He pointed angrily to where the girl had been standing. She was gone.

He shouted, "LIES! GET GIRL!"

After almost breaking her neck skipping steps as she ran down to the lobby, she burst from the building's exit and raced out into the night. She hated leaving her backpack behind, but there was no time to stop and search for it. She'd have to come back for it later, if she somehow survived the night.

The two men exited the building less than a minute after her. They spotted her nearing the end of the block and gave chase. They followed her relentlessly through the maze of runs and into the darkness of the western tree line, where she hoped to lose them.

The lush greenery surrounding the abandoned buildings there was completely overgrown, more so than any other place she had seen. Thick vines had completely covered the surfaces of many structures, crawling from the ground and spreading to the rooftops. Trees were growing through the buildings and emerging from the windows. The night sky was hidden by the canopies of the large trees. Running through the street was like going through a tunnel, Bats flocked around excitedly overhead when their solitude was disturbed by the sound of heavy footsteps echoing into the distance.

She had unknowingly left the ruins and entered the forest. It wasn't long before she realized she could no longer keep running. She lacked the strength to go any further. If she continued, she wouldn't have the strength to fight, and she knew this was going to end in a fight. There was no avoiding it.

Resigned to face her fate, she slowed down and came to a halt. She promptly turned to face them, still holding the large knife in her hand.

The redheaded man wasn't in the mood for another standoff. He continued running toward her and recklessly rushed into her, tackling her smaller body to the ground. They both cried out in pain when they hit the hard dirt, and slid slightly across the ground.

The handsome man followed closely, but strategically remained behind his companion, planning to use him as a shield from her deadly blade. He didn't intend on getting stabbed or sliced.

Upon impact, Evangelina had plunged the knife deep into the redheaded man's abdomen, using his own momentum against him. He remained lying motionless on top of her, moaning from the pain. The handsome man haphazardly pushed him aside, so he could get to her. She used the opportunity to quickly roll out of the way.

Before she could get to her feet, he grabbed her from behind and snatched her away, so she couldn't retrieve the knife from the redheaded man's stomach. The handsome man gripped her tightly, as she frantically struggled to break free. Despite feeling completely drained of energy mere moments ago, her adrenaline had kicked in and pushed her to fight for her life. She kicked out wildly and managed to catch the redheaded man in the chin with the heel of her boot, just as he was struggling to stand up.

He fell over, once again, holding his chin with one hand, while gripping the knife in his gut with the other. It just wasn't his day.

The handsome man tried desperately to get the firecracker of a girl under control, but she wasn't making it easy. She was flailing too wildly with her arms, legs, and even her head. Her long dark hair kept getting in his face, making it difficult to see anything. Eventually, she managed to slam the back of her head hard into his face, breaking his nose in the process.

He cried out in pain and tossed her to the ground in annoyance. Before she could crawl away, he kicked her once in her side. She rolled away in pain, but was still able to toss a small knife from her belt in his direction. Due to her condition, her aim was off, and he was able to avoid it.

He rushed toward her, wanting to hurt her very badly. Earlier he had been hoping for her to put up a fight, but he didn't expect to be bleeding when she did. It was more of a challenge than he expected. He wasn't too pleased. He was going to make her pay dearly.

When he got near her, she tossed dirt up into his face, blinding him momentarily. She crawled hurriedly over toward the redheaded man and yanked the knife from his body. She then turned and threw it at the handsome man, just as he sprinted toward her. She was aiming for his neck, but her aim was off, once again, because it hit him in the mouth, instead. It's always harder to hit a moving target. Well, except in this case.

He stood there staggering over her for a moment, completely in shock, until he dropped to the ground. He no longer moved.

At last, she could breathe. By this time, she was completely exhausted.

Just then, from behind her, the redheaded man reached out and grabbed her hard by the hair. She screamed because it hurt. He began pulling her closer to him. She managed to pull out another one of her small knives. She let him pull her closer, and then turned around abruptly. She stabbed him in the eye with the small blade, at which point he let go of her hair and now it was him who screamed. She then shoved a handful of dirt from the ground into his mouth. She quickly covered his mouth with both hands putting all her weight on him. He tried to cough it up, but he was also weakened and tired. He began choking on the dirt, but she refused to ease up, until he stopped moving.

Finally, both men were dead.

For several minutes, she remained lying on the ground, barely able to move a muscle. The urge to sleep and slip into oblivion was so very strong, but she did her best to resist it. Now wasn't the time to sleep. All she needed was to rest her body for a short time. That's all.

As she lay on the ground, she stared up at the darkness above her. It was almost like looking at the nighttime sky, but without the stars or the moon. After a while, she finally began to make out the shapes of the vast trees above her. Her eyes were adjusting to the darkness. She could see the thick heavy branches stretching out and spreading, crossing into each other. It reminded her of arms reaching out with many hands holding one another, and their thin bony fingers intertwined.

She heard flapping wings above. Perhaps, more bats, she thought. In the past, she'd only come across them in darkened basements. Never at night, until today.

When she was ready, she forced herself up, so she could stand. It was an effort just to do that simple task. She had no idea how she was going to do anything else. The first thing she wanted to do was retrieve her backpack from the building, except as she looked around her, it occurred to her she might be lost. She had absolutely no idea how to get back to the building where she left it. At least, she hoped it was still there. For all she knew, those savages threw it from the roof and it could be lying somewhere in an alley with its contents sprawled across the ground.

She wasn't too far off. She got it half right.

The more she thought about it, it was also too dark to see which way to go. Every direction pretty much looked the same to her. Dark and wooded. She was extremely tempted to lay back on the ground, but she really didn't like the idea of sleeping near two dead men. As it was, she could barely see their bodies on the ground. They looked more like mounds of dirt. It was that dark. She hoped to gather up her weapons, before she went anywhere. Leaving them behind would be unwise.

She began to think maybe waiting there until daylight was probably the best thing she could do, under the circumstances. Despite being out in the open, her covered isolated location might prove to be safe from being detected by any passing sky ships. That was also something to consider. She didn't have the energy to run from a sky ship. Not at the moment.

She dropped down to the ground, where she stood, so she could consider her options. While seated on the ground, she collected her knives. She felt around the ground and felt the knife sticking out of the formerly handsome man's mouth. She pulled it out and made an attempt to wipe it clean on his dirty clothing.

It wasn't long before she heard the creeping sound of small critters scurrying in the darkness around her. The second she felt something with several legs crawling over her hand, she was back on her feet in an instant. She shook her hand wildly to be rid of whatever had violated her person. Her abrupt movements caused more scurrying nearby.

"Damn bugs," she uttered.

She decided to keep the large hunting knife handy, as she began walking forward in the direction she hoped would ultimately lead her back to visible ruins. It would be better than the creepy pitch black forest that surrounded her.

She kept bumping into trees, while stumbling along in the dark. This was harder than she thought. At this rate, she could be walking through the woods all night and barely move a block's distance. Still, she pressed on for lack of a better idea.

After several minutes of moving blindingly forward at a slow pace, she heard a wonderfully familiar sound. To her, anything familiar was extremely welcome. It caused her to stop in her tracks. She had to be sure. Yes! It sounded exactly like the water road. She was filled with excitement. Even though she knew she couldn't cross it, just seeing it would make her feel so much closer to home. How could she resist?

She clumsily hurried through the trees, following the sound. Eventually, she exited the forest at the edge of the river bank. It was still hard to see, but she could see a lot better than when she was in the thick of the woods. Everything wasn't covered in darkness. She could see the moonlight reflecting on the rushing water, which looked black as tar. It was a beautiful sight. Her eyes turned upward and she could see dozens of stars, as well. Much to her surprise, she could even make out the other side, although it mostly looked like shapes and shadows.

Right away, she recognized it. It was the same place where she climbed the tree to get away from the mongrels. That tree was unmistakable.

An intense feeling of happiness came over her from being able to see someplace recognizable, after days of being stranded in unfamiliar territory. She felt relieved, as if her journey were nearly at its end. In a way, maybe it was.

However, she soon became frustrated because she still couldn't cross the water road. She sat down on a rock and gazed longingly across the black water. She tried skipping a stone across the surface and watched how easily it crossed to the other side, before disappearing into the rushing water. Tears filled her eyes. It hurt to be so close to home, but to have it so far out of reach. She wondered if this nightmare would ever end.

At that moment, a bright light appeared directly overhead, accompanied by a low humming sound. It shined down upon her, surrounding her in an intense beam of white light. Damn it. They found her. She didn't even try to run, not that she could.

CHAPTER 16: UFO

The bright light held her firmly in its gaze like an invisible vice. She found that she couldn't move, while under its spell. Nor did she really want to. She just didn't care anymore. After everything she'd been through recently, there was no fight left in her. Her life was beginning to seem hopeless.

Her father's injury was the beginning of the end for her. It was all downhill from there. The deaths of Troya and her father, followed by the incident with Avery, only added to the gradual disintegration of the small world she knew. Things continued to decline, afterwards, mainly starting from the day she was chased by mongrels, even if her small world did grow, as a result.

She didn't mind the sasquatch encounter as much because it proved to her they existed.

However, the day she fell into the water road and was washed ashore on the wrong side was the day everything changed completely. Her life hadn't been the same since. It had become a nightmare. There was one hazard after another. The danger never seemed to end.

Now, she lost her backpack and all the very necessary supplies within. Without that stuff, she had nothing left. Nothing but the clothes on her back. It wasn't enough.

She longed for her shelter. Her home. The many books from her library collection waiting to be read and examined over and over. Lying in her cozy bed, instead of somewhere dirty. Things she took for granted, such as taking a shower and using a toilet. She needed to be embraced by the creature comforts and familiarity that came with being at the shelter.

Without those things she didn't care to go on. She was ready to give up. Let them take me, she thought. What did it matter anymore? Let them do their worst.

She felt herself slowly being lifted from the ground. Her view had tilted, so she could see the sky above her, but all she saw was a white light. It engulfed everything around her. She saw nothing, but the light and its whiteness. Her body floated gently upward away from the forest and away from the water road. She moved through the sky like a feather in the wind, up toward the source of the powerful light beam.

She closed her eyes, since it was the only movement she was allowed. She wanted to avoid looking directly into the blinding light. Once her eyes were closed, it almost felt like being in a dream.

In that instant, she felt a familiar sensation. It was as if she'd experienced this before. Maybe it was in a forgotten dream. She wasn't sure, but she remembered feeling this way. She remembered being taken by a light and floating up toward the sky, toward a sky ship. How could she remember that, if it never happened before?

What did they want with her anyway? As far as she was concerned, she had nothing to offer. She was just a girl. What was the reason they were abducting people for so many years? She longed to know the answer to that question. Perhaps, this was her chance to find out. She wondered why they hadn't come for her when she was on the roof with those men. She remembered thinking about it then, which was why she pretended to see a sky ship, Aside from it being a great distraction.

It was strange because she felt a feeling of intense calmness. There was no fear. No stress. Only wonder and curiosity. She couldn't even feel any pain from her injuries, not that they were serious, but they did hurt earlier. The bump on her forehead, the headache from when they knocked her out, the kick she received from the formerly handsome man, and when she was knocked to the ground by that redheaded buffoon. All of those things had caused her pain, even if she hadn't been focusing on them before. How was it possible that she no longer felt any pain?

Was it because of the light? Did it somehow heal her? It felt warm and tingly.

The thought only made her more curious than before. She wanted to see where this unexpected new journey was taking her. What would happen to her once she was aboard? How would it look from the inside? Would she be their prisoner? And who were they? What did they look like? Would they hurt her? Kill her? Eat her? Why did they choose her, instead of the men? Was it because she was far more intelligent? More civilized? Or did they simply require a female specimen?

So many questions went through her mind. Would she even get the opportunity to find answers?

She opened her eyes, but still couldn't see anything but the whiteness around her. She wished she could look down and see how high she had come. It was a shame she couldn't move. Then again, it was too dark to see anything anyway. Maybe it was just as well that she couldn't look down. Seeing nothing but darkness below probably would've been too disturbing. It was a shame she couldn't even see the stars. The light was so bright, she barely made out the shape of the sky ship. It was rather large. Maybe circular?

The angle of her body changed slightly, as she was brought aboard the sky ship.

This was it, she thought to herself. She'd either get some answers, or be overwhelmed with more questions. She hoped she'd be able to move soon. The stiffness and helplessness she felt was beginning to scare her. What if she'd never be able to move freely, again? That would be a bigger nightmare than what she was going through back on the ground.

Fear. She could feel fear, again. The door closed behind her, as the brightness of the light faded. The room was white. She was placed on a flat surface, lying down, and facing up. There was a flash of air, which passed over her. It felt cool and wet. Her clothes were gone. They had been replaced by a soft white layer of living fabric that wrapped itself around her body, covering her from neck to toe.

The ceiling seemed to glow with brightness, as if it were one huge light. She realized she was able to move her head. She looked from side to side. The walls were white. The floor was white. She didn't notice any doors. She was alone.

Her hunger was gone. She had been hungry, but not anymore. She no longer felt tired either. How was that possible?

As if in answer to her question, she noticed she wasn't alone anymore. Someone had entered the room. It wasn't human, but it looked humanoid. It had two arms, two legs, and a head with a mouth and two eyes. There was no nose and no ears, but there were two holes for nostrils. The eyes were large and black. They were shiny and reflective like small, oval, black mirrors. The mouth was small, and there were no lips. No hair either. The creature standing over her was tall, thin, pale, and bald. In a way, it looked sickly. It moved as if it were extremely fragile.

She tried to speak, but still couldn't move her lips or her mouth. It was locked shut. She wanted to ask what it wanted with her. Why had it taken her?

It stepped toward her and studied her a moment. The large eyes blinked kindly at her. It then reached out a long thin arm, extending its hand and forefinger. There were only four fingers. It aimed the probing finger at her forehead and moved closer. She flinched and closed her eyes tight. It gently touched her forehead. The touch was cold. She immediately felt a tingling sensation surge throughout her mind. It felt electrifying, as if her senses were reawakening for the very first time.

Her eyes shot open and she demanded, "What did you do to me?" At first, she hadn't realized it, but she thought the words. Her mouth still hadn't moved. In that moment, she heard a soothing voice in her head that sounded neither male nor female.

"We have been watching you for a very long time."

The soft voice in her mind continued, "Please, communicate with your mind. We find your voice to be excruciatingly loud for our sensitive hearing. It often disrupts our concentration. We shall be able to hear your thoughts now because your dormant mental communicative abilities have been unlocked."

"*My what???*" She asked feeling confused. Again, she had only thought the words. They wouldn't come out of her mouth. She wondered how the strange being was mind-speaking to her. She thought, "What have they done to me?"

"I have allowed you to utilize an ability that has always been within you. It is called telepathy. It is a form of communication using only our minds," it responded in the same asexual soft voice in her mind.

"If I always had this ability, then why couldn't I use it until this moment? None of my clan ever did this, as far as I know," she thought, not really sure if it would hear her thoughts. It did.

"Most humans only possess the limited capacity to utilize a small percentage of the abilities locked within your minds. We have the key to unlock the rest, as needed. A certain percentage of neural *dark matter* is only for our use. It is useless to your kind."

"So, are you implying that you, and your kind, can somehow control us?"

"In a word, yes. It has always been so. I shall explain further. Soon."

"Always?" The thought was disturbing. She would wait until later for the explanation. In the meantime, she wondered, "Is that why I can't move or use my mouth, at the moment?"

"Indeed. You will be permitted bodily movement shortly. However, I have temporarily blocked your vocal ability, until you learn to control it around us. Your kind tend to speak with excitement. As I have explained, the sound of your voice has a tendency to become far too loud for our sensitive hearing receptors." It pointed to a small cavity on the side of its head. She assumed there was probably another on the opposite side.

She thought, "How can you know if my voice is too loud, if you won't let me say anything?"

"You are not our first human visitor. We have been studying your kind over many millennia," it answered with a slight knowing smile. "We learned long ago to be vigilant."

"Is that how you know my language?"

"On the contrary. We do not know your language. Therefore, we cannot speak it. However, through telepathy we can understand one another's thoughts and meanings."

"You said I'm not the first human to be here, so what does that mean? Why are you studying humanity? Why am I here?"

"We have studied humanity since its earliest inception. I will explain more to you in time. Let us first prepare you for what is to come. You have already been cleansed and reclothed. Your injuries have also been repaired. The next step is to prepare you for the journey."

"Journey? What journey?"

"In time." It blinked at her. "Please, be patient. Allow me to complete my tests, and then all will be revealed to you."

"What tests?"

"The ones I have been conducting since your arrival."

She felt even more confused. After a quick visual inspection of her body, she didn't notice anything attached to her. What tests did it mean? Just then, the bright ceiling lights seemed to gradually dim. The room began to appear less white and more of a metallic silver.

"There. The tests are complete," the being informed her telepathically. "You are now ready. You may rise to your feet, if you wish to do so."

Her ability to move had returned. She sat up attentively, while taking in the full scenery of the rounded room. It looked quite plain. The table where she lay was the only piece of furniture and the only thing with edges. Everything else was curved.

She looked at the being. It wore a similar white outfit to what had been placed on her. The strange clothing felt comfortable. Not too tight and not loose, as if it were made for her.

She hopped off the table. It surprised her when her nearly bare feet didn't feel cold against the hard floor. It was actually warm to the touch and felt rather nice. There was a tingling sensation that seemed to be massaging her feet, right where she stood. She couldn't help but look down in surprise.

The being spoke in her head, again, "The sensation you feel on your feet is to prevent them from growing weary. It also cleanses them, while curing them of all maladies. The organic clothing you are wearing will keep you warm or cool, depending on your environment, but it is only temporary."

She nodded, and asked in her mind, "I was tired and hungry before, but I don't feel that way anymore. How is that possible?"

"The initial cleanser has temporarily removed those inconveniences. If you are prepared, please accompany me to the next area. I will take you somewhere you will find quite interesting."

"If you say so. Hey, what do I call you? Do you have a name?"

"My designation is Azculepus."

"Um, okay. It's nice to meet you, *Azculepus*. My name is Evangelina."

It nodded. "Please, follow me, Evangelina." It began walking toward the wall, and then a doorway suddenly appeared before it.

"Wait! What about my things? I left them back down on the surface."

Azculepus replied without facing her, "You will no longer require those possessions."

The tall slender alien led her through a corridor, which looked as plain as the room they had just left. Somehow, she expected to see more technology on a sky ship. It was nothing like what she thought it to be. The walls were smooth and silver. She felt them. They were metallic and hard.

Azculepus allowed her to satisfy her curiosity, as they walked through the curved corridor. She was taken to another room. Once more, a doorway opened out of nothing. She never noticed the door, until it opened.

They entered a room with a window. It was some type of observation deck. Outside, the clouds were visible and within reach. Without thinking, she rushed over to take in the view. Azculepus did not stop her. The clouds were right outside the window. They moved by so fast. The sky ship seemed to be moving through the upper atmosphere just above the top of the clouds. Millions of stars could be seen above, spread out like a background mural that looked alive. Stars seemed to twinkle and blink at her. It was astonishing.

Azculepus spoke to her mind, "I had a feeling you might enjoy the view."

"Oh, yes! It's wonderful!" Had she not been thinking the words, she might've shouted them a bit too excitedly. As soon as she realized it, she finally understood why she wasn't allowed to speak using her mouth.

"Yes," Azculepus confirmed her thoughts. "At least, you understand why we must keep your mouth closed for you. In your excitement, you can inadvertently injure us. In time, you can learn to control your emotions and excitement with proper training. However, we still would not understand your speech."

"I understand," she nodded. "It's okay. I get it. You're right. I'm sorry. I promise I'll try to control my excitement in the future. It's not easy." She stared out of the window. "This view is incredible! I've always wanted to see a view like this."

Azculepus smiled, "I ascertained that much from your mind earlier. Therefore, I wanted you to experience it, before we leave."

"Leave?" She turned to face Azculepus. "What do you mean leave? Where are we going?"

"You will see. In time. All shall be explained to you when you meet with the historian," Azculepus informed her calmly.

"The historian? How many more are there up here with us?"

"Not many. You will miss the view." Azculepus pointed toward the window.

Evangelina turned back to look outside. The sky ship flew through the clouds and entered the atmosphere, once more. The dawn was breaking through the darkness, as the sun was rising in the distance on the eastern horizon. The sky ship dropped down low over the ocean, practically skimming the surface. She could see miles and miles of water stretching to the north. It was magnificent. A broad smile extended across her face. Her eyes lit up with joy, as the sun reflected in them. This was something she'd only seen in her books. She couldn't believe her eyes.

"It's so blue!" Once more, her thoughts were filled with excitement.

"Actually, it does not have a color," Azculepus corrected her. "It is clear. What you see as blue is the sky reflecting on the surface. That is why it appears blackened at night."

"Oh. Well, it's still beautiful." She then asked, "How is it that we are able to fly around during the daylight? I thought your sky ships were... nocturnal."

"That is a silly notion. We are fully capable of flying day and night. During the daytime, we tend to cloak ourselves from view, while the darkness of the night already hides us well."

"Cloak?"

"It is a way of making our vessel disappear. Our vessel essentially becomes invisible, while cloaked. It was a necessary deception, mainly during the prime of your species."

"Wow!"

Amazed, she turned her attention back toward the window. The sky ship began flying over land. The beach passed by like a blur, followed by lush green grass. Below them were now thousands of trees moving by at top speed. Soon, they were replaced with the ruins of a great city. It was one she couldn't recognize, although she imagined they probably looked a lot different from so high up in the sky. The architecture looked different from what she was used to, though. Some were almost castle-like. They flew over towering spires, as if they were mere spikes sticking up from the ground.

"Where are we?" She asked her guide without turning away from the view.

"We have crossed the ocean to another one of your continents. This land is likely foreign to you. I do not know the designation, as you might call it. This is not my world. It is yours."

"This world is as strange and unknown to me as it is to you. I've only ever known my shelter and the ruins near it. I read things in books, but there's so much I don't understand. So many things I've never seen. If this is another continent, I have no idea what it's called. I didn't even know the name of the one where I lived." Her eyes never left the window, as she thought the words. She remained glued to the glass, afraid she'd miss something fantastic, if she looked away for a second. Everything was moving by so quickly. It was hard enough to see. They flew over another stretch of water followed by mountains.

After a while, Azculepus asked, "Are you ready?"

"Huh?" She was still distracted by the view. "Ready for what?"

"Ready to say goodbye."

She turned to face Azculepus. "Goodbye? Where are you taking me?"

Azculepus' head tilted to the side, studying the young human for a moment. "You are quite the inquisitive one. I admire that about you. We will take you someplace new. It will be a fresh start. A chance to do things differently. You are perfect for this opportunity. That is why you were chosen."

"Oh." She never thought of herself as perfect. What seemed even stranger was the fact that she had been chosen specifically. "I don't understand. Why was I chosen?" While she thought the question, she didn't notice the scenery changing drastically behind her. Outside the window the blue sky slipped away and was replaced by blackness. They left her world and had ventured into space.

"Yes," Azculepus confirmed with a thought. "Congratulations, Evangelina. You have been selected as a new prime. This is a great honor. It is why we had to test you so thoroughly, and you passed each exam. You are the perfect human female specimen. It was absolutely necessary that you were young, healthy, strong, intelligent, and capable of bearing children."

Evangelina stared blankly at Azculepus, not knowing what to say, or what to think. She turned back toward the window and saw millions of distant stars gazing back at her. Had her mouth not been locked shut, it would've been gaping open like her eyes.

CHAPTER 17: REVELATIONS

Before she could recover from the shock of what she'd been told, she was taken to another section of the sky ship, which was located on an upper level. There were no stairs leading to it, but there was a strange type of teleportation device. It would be her first time riding anything even remotely close to an elevator. The new experience was somewhat unsettling for her, while also being extremely fascinating. It began when they stepped onto a square pad that was glowing lightly. An instant later, they automatically ended up on the next level above them. The destination had been chosen by Azculepus' mind. She heard the thoughts as the location was selected, and therefore knew they were no longer on the same level. She also felt the movement in her stomach, but never noticed any change with her eyes since the upper level corridor was identical to the one they were on before.

"Whoa! What just happened?" Her startled reaction was once again a confirmation as to why she wasn't permitted to voice her words aloud.

Azculepus explained with a slight smile, "We have been transported to the next level above us, as you surely must have heard me thinking when we stepped onto the telepad."

"But how is that possible? There were no stairs! We just ended up here somehow," she thought, feeling confused. She held her stomach from the queasy sensation of being abruptly lifted and coming to a sudden stop. The speed of the movement felt like an extremely short rollercoaster ride.

"My apologies for not warning you," she heard Azculepus think. "I expect you will likely become acclimated with using telepads, while you are with us. Most things work significantly different here than what you are accustomed to back on your world, as you are quickly learning. Come. I shall take you to meet with the historian, who will explain everything to you."

She followed her guide through another doorway that seemingly opened out of the smooth wall like magic. She wasn't sure if she'd ever get used to that, or the telepad, let alone traveling through space. It was all so crazy to her.

For a brief moment, she wondered what her parents would've thought of everything she was experiencing. How would they have reacted to it all? She found herself smiling, but then felt sad because she knew she'd never see them, again. She had a feeling their spirits had been left behind on her world, even if she never got the chance to see them that way.

In the room was another gray alien being, who was slightly shorter than Azculepus. She figured it had to be the historian. Aside from the height, he or she looked almost exactly like her guide. It was still difficult to ascertain if either of them were male or female. She began to think these alien beings had no sexual differences whatsoever.

The only other noticeable difference between the two, as far as she could tell, were their mannerisms. The historian carried itself in such a way that made it seem older and wiser. It moved much slower than her apparently middle-aged guide, who seemed a bit livelier. Right away, she wondered if there were any younger aliens aboard the sky ship that might be closer to her age.

"Not as young as you," the historian replied in her mind. This new voice sounded much older. The historian watched her closely, as she entered. She kept forgetting they could hear her thoughts. "I am called Atrus," the historian thought with a slight nod of the head. "I understand you have many questions. That is to be expected, considering your current situation. You may now set your mind at ease. I shall answer them all."

"Thank you, Atrus. My name is Evangelina." He nodded at her. "Can you please start by telling me where you're taking me?" She noticed there were no windows in this room either. Half the room was dark, making it hard to see what else was in there with them. She could only make out a large shape.

"To another planet," was Atrus' response, drawing her attention, while ignoring her suspicions. The reply was simple and to the point, although not as specific as she would've liked. Of course, it really didn't matter. It wasn't as if she knew the names of any planets, including her own. Hearing the name of her future home world wouldn't have made much of a difference to her, so she let it go.

She immediately thought of her next question. "Why have your kind been abducting my kind for so many years?"

"We have mainly been monitoring the progress of humanity, as we have always done in the past. However, in recent times, we have also been searching for the right kind of individuals, such as yourself. It has become harshly apparent that much of your kind has regressed into a rather simplistic state of mind. It is quite unfortunate. Until we found you, we have not had much luck in securing a female prime."

She raised an eyebrow. Again, they called her a prime. "Why me?"

"As I have explained, you are an ideal candidate to serve as a female prime. You shall be placed on a new world quite similar to the one you left behind."

She stared at the historian with so many more questions flooding her mind. It felt as if her mind might explode from the pressure. Her eyes lingered away toward the dark side of the room.

Atrus thought, "Perhaps, if I showed you the early history of your world, you would comprehend more clearly. We have a simulation available at the viewing table, which you can observe. Visualizing everything, as I explain it to you will be far easier."

"Yeah. Okay," she thought. She liked that idea. She wondered if it would be anything like the movies her mom wrote about in her journal. That was a concept she never truly understood. Movies. She smiled, "That sounds good. Thank you."

"You are most welcome," Atrus responded, while moving slowly across the dimly lit room toward a large rectangular table that had been in a corner of the darker part of the room. She followed. The ceiling light over the table lit up when they moved toward it, while the lights in the other half of the room dimmed to darkness. The table hummed to life emitting a realistic holographic projected image of the universe that covered the full surface of the table. The table itself was no longer visible.

I Stand Alone

She was amazed by what she was seeing. Her eyes lit up with the same excitement she felt at looking out the window earlier. The image appeared to be so real. It kept her completely enthralled. She barely heard Atrus' thoughts explain, "It might be best if we start at the earliest possible moment."

She heard Atrus' voice in her head, "In the beginning, there was darkness."

Every light in the room turned off, including the table. The room was engulfed in darkness, but only for the briefest of moments. On the viewing table the most spectacular visual effects scene began to play out. From that darkness came a magnificent blinding explosion, which launched billions of would be stars far across the universe, gradually shaping the earliest cosmos.

"And then the galaxies were born."

It was the scene sometimes referred to as "The Big Bang," except that phrase was unknown to the captivated girl watching it. She knew absolutely nothing of how the universe came to be. The books she read only posed theories, at best. She watched in awe, as Atrus explained what she was seeing.

"We learned how the atomolecula, the dark matter you observed at the start, consisted of a high concentration of a flammable gas called hydrogen. When the nuclei within that dark matter collided, they created a cosmic explosion, which essentially began the formation of the universe."

As the scene rotated on the table, tiny planets were gradually formed from the remaining debris surrounding the newly created stars. More debris formed asteroid belts that orbited these stars, along with the planets.

"From virtually nothing, everything gradually came into being, beginning with the stars, which came together to form galaxies, followed by the planets, which gravitated toward the stars that would ultimately serve as their suns. Finally, the planets themselves came to life."

She watched the scene focus on one particular planet, which was a reddish brown color. As the viewing table zoomed into the planet's erratic atmosphere, she could see the planet was covered in volcanic explosions that oozed rivers of molten lava. Meteorites struck the planet, creating additional mayhem and leaving behind craters. Over time, the lava seemed to seep away into the planet, hardening and breaking into rocks. Powerful quakes shifted the land, reshaping the landscape into mountains and canyons.

"On the surface of each planet a beautiful chaos ensued, as they continued through their creation process over a long period of time, which you are watching at a faster speed. The raining down from the heavens also continued. It is something that would never end, but it would lessen… eventually."

She watched as more meteorites smashed onto the surface, leaving their marks. The view switched to space. Not all planets had formed, yet. Stray asteroids were crashing into one another in the solar system, causing some to be pushed and drawn in by the atmosphere of closer planets. Many of the larger asteroids were frozen and covered with ice.

The ice brought the first moisture onto the world. As it evaporated into the upper atmosphere, clouds began forming and taking shape. Soon, the first rain began to fall. The first of the rains came down heavy. Rainwater gradually filled the craters, canyons, and valleys becoming ponds and lakes. The flooding waters created streams and rivers, which led to the formation of waterfalls that settled into other bodies of water. Some of these waterways connected to one another becoming seas, and in time, oceans.

Evangelina was completely mesmerized by the scene and looked on silently. Nature had always fascinated her. She was startled, when she heard Atrus' next thoughts in her mind.

"With water always comes life. Some worlds developed faster than others."

The first sky ship appeared in space. It approached the planet, followed by another, and another. They entered the atmosphere and did a flyby. As they flew over the planet, they began dropping hundreds of thousands of seedlings.

These seedlings became single blades of grass, which quickly spread across the land with the help of rain and wind. New plants were born, growing into trees, which eventually became forests and jungles. The new world had become ripe with greenery and covered with numerous bodies of water.

It was ready for the next stage of life.

The sky ships had returned, but this time they dropped tiny particles into the waters. From the deepest depths came the first signs of animate life. It first learned to swim through the waters, before evolving. From the waters, it emerged, crawling onto the shore and taking its first steps on land. New creatures were formed and evolved from those earliest lifeforms.

Time shifted on the table. The world became something more familiar to her. All manner of creatures were roaming the world undisturbed, but there was still something missing.

The sky ships returned, only this time, they planted the seeds of humanity, which would also evolve over the centuries from primates into a more familiar intelligent species that could ultimately change the world to suit its own needs. She watched humanity as it went through many historic eras, advancing when new technologies were developed or learned. There was so much to take in. She wished the scenes would move slower, so she could examine every little detail.

It became apparent the sky ships continued to return, influencing humanity's advancement.

"Throughout the progress of your world, one of our vessels arrived each year primarily to observe each species' evolution. Our interactions were always minimal, so as to not inspire too much advancement too soon. Humanity became the favorite subject, although the point of the experiment was to allow humans to thrive on their own. That was essentially what happened. It was all part of the larger experiment."

Evangelina repeated the word in her mind, "Experiment?"

"All life on your world had been part of the larger experiment. As time went on, my forebearers and their descendants would continue to check on the experiment for many generations. The constant observations were necessary to see how things had progressed. However, each new visit would often lead to more advancements in technology, as the humans became wiser, more observant, and adaptable."

Atrus went on, "At last, humanity had reached a new height of civilization." The first skyscrapers came into view on the table and were surrounded by dozens more. "With their great constructs they began to reach for the stars, until they finally ventured forth into space." A rocket launched from the planet and went into space. "It was only a matter of time before they would extend their reach to beyond their solar system, as we had done so long ago." Satellites were now orbiting the vibrant planet at a regular basis.

"Unfortunately, due to an unforeseen cataclysmic event, your world was doomed to suffer greatly over the next decades. You may already be aware of this part."

She saw the enormous asteroid that caused the *Big Apocalyptic Event* as it approached, was broken into three pieces, and struck her planet and its small moon. For the first time, she witnessed the massive destruction it caused with her own eyes, something she had only read about, or heard about in stories passed down by her clan. Watching it play out like a movie made it seem a lot scarier than she ever conceived. It literally left her speechless, and in tears, when she thought about all the death and destruction.

"Your kind are dying out," Atrus told her. "Soon, humanity will be extinct, despite its great potential. In an effort to salvage your kind, we have been searching for pristine specimens to mark for relocation. We can no longer conduct our research here, so we wish to restart the experiment on a more suitable planet. That is why you were chosen. You will be the prime female on this new world."

She forced down the lump in her throat.

"Do you understand now?"

"Yes," she nodded reluctantly, but Atrus already knew the answer.

The lights from the table shut down, as the rest of the room lit up, once more. The show was over. Atrus studied his guest for her reaction to everything she had just witnessed. She was deep in thought, but hadn't directed any questions toward him, yet. He waited for the questions he knew would come when she was ready to ask them. There was a lot for her to absorb, so he allowed her the time she needed.

When she was ready, she looked to him and wondered, "Now that you have me, does that mean the experiments on my world will come to an end?"

"Only partially. We will continue to monitor things, even long after humanity is no more. Keep in mind, your kind was but one part of the experiment."

"Were there any other experiments that you haven't told me about?"

"Yes. There were many. On a few occasions, we have taken entire communities and relocated them to other worlds, leaving villages abandoned. Those situations were limited to the earlier eras in humanity's developmental stage, and only done as additional experiments. It was not something done regularly. In some cases, those civilizations thrived on their new worlds, while others failed miserably."

Atrus turned away from her and added, "One other particular experiment consisted of creating hybrids with our kind. The earliest of these experiments occurred more than a century ago with failed results." Atrus seemed ashamed of these experiments. "The children were born with obvious mutations and considered outcasts." Atrus turned back to face her. "Fortunately, as time went on, these hybrid breeding experiments were improved. The differences were less noticeable, although they sometimes resulted in pale humans known as albinos."

She cringed at the word. It was a word she once read in her encyclopedia. For some reason, she thought negatively of it. The only albino she'd ever seen was in the same book.

Atrus continued, "These advanced hybrid experiments also had other unexpected results. Some of the humans involved and many of their descendants that followed were able to access that portion of the mind set aside solely for our use. A small percentage developed psychic abilities, which came directly from my kind."

She became intrigued.

"We hoped to find one of those humans, but ironically there does not seem to be any left," Atrus seemed disappointed, but then a grin formed. "However, we were fortunate enough to locate two surviving descendants from such individuals." She was interested to know more and was very surprised at the next revelation. "You are one of those humans."

"Me?"

"Yes. One of your ancestors possessed such rare abilities of which I have informed you. Your lineage was revealed in the tests performed on you by Azculepus. It is primarily why you are here, along with the other qualifications you meet."

"Does that mean at least one of my ancestors was… an albino?"

"That is precisely what it means," Atrus answered. "It makes you uncomfortable to know this information."

"No. I mean. I don't know. I guess. Maybe." She shrugged. "I'm not sure why. When I read about albinos in one of my books, I got the impression it wasn't something normal. Does this mean you're my… family?"

Atrus smiled warmly. "No, young one. Those experiments were done many years ago, long before my time. In each case, cloned DNA had been implanted into a female human carrier, who would eventually give birth to the child. In your situation, that mother was several generations ago, as part of your mother's family line. Sadly, you also lack any psychic abilities."

"Wow. That's okay. I guess. Hey, I have another question. What about sasquatches? The larger humanoid species covered in hair?"

"I am aware of that species. As with every other species on your world, they were initially placed there by us. They were a significant part of the experiment, although their kind was forced into hiding to avoid the apex predator of your world. Humans. We believe when the last of the humans are finally gone, that world will likely belong to them."

"So, there are still many of them?"

"Sadly, not as many as there used to be," Atrus frowned upon thinking the words.

"Oh." She also seemed saddened.

She thought of another question, unrelated to what they had been discussing. Still, she hoped Atrus would know the answer.

"Recently, I came across a portion of a ruined city that was completely flattened. It was a very large area, so it stood out to me. I couldn't figure out what could've happened to leave that area looking that way. Would you happen to know why? I was just curious."

Atrus replied, "As I have not seen this location, I can only speculate. What you are describing could have been caused by any number of reasons. It could have occurred before the asteroid struck."

"No, I don't believe so," she replied. "If that were the case, it would've been a forest by now. It looked like everything was destroyed on purpose." She remembered how it looked.

"I see. The mental image you are showing me could very well be the result of a powerful energy weapon," Atrus suggested. "I should inform you this vessel is not the only vessel observing your world. Nor are we the only alien species to visit it, especially in recent times. There are others, who are curious to witness the downfall of humanity. I venture to guess at least one species might be aggressive toward your kind, possibly due to past transgressions. Perhaps, they might even fire a weapon upon sight, hoping to finish off your species that much sooner."

A look of worry came over her at the thought of other aggressive aliens out there, who might want to destroy humanity. Atrus noticed her fear and tried to ease it. "Of course, I could be wrong. I am merely speculating."

Somehow, the last thought wasn't very convincing. Suddenly, she wanted to ask about these other aliens. She felt she needed to know more about them, but was almost afraid to ask. Maybe it didn't really matter anymore, considering she was no longer on that world. Perhaps, she'd never have reason to worry about these other alien species. At least, she hoped that was the case.

"I assure you, there is nothing to fear, as long as you are aboard this vessel," Atrus told her. "My kind has no quarrel with any other species."

"That's good. I suppose," she responded, but her curiosity got the better of her. She needed to know more. "Can you tell me about these other aliens?"

Atrus smiled.

CHAPTER 18: GODS

"The universe is a big place," Atrus began. "There are a great many galaxies and each possesses its own intelligent forms of life. During our explorations, we have encountered a few different species that are also capable of long distance space travel."

Evangelina listened intently to his thoughts. She was finally getting used to telepathy. It was starting to feel like normal speech to her, perhaps even better. There was no misunderstanding. Each thought was clear and concise. Some even appeared with images, which was extremely helpful.

Atrus described the first of several alien species to her, which she could imagine clearly.

"The *Plei* are quite different from us in appearance, aside from having the same grayish skin tone. They are taller beings with the ability to grow hair, much like humans, except their hair is only a silvery color. There are no blacks, browns, reds, or yellows. All hair is silver and usually grown very long. Their eyes are bright colors, unlike our darker eyes. The colors can vary between different shades of blue, green, yellow, red, or gray. We know they have visited your world in the past. We found evidence of their own experiments, as well."

"Didn't that bother you?"

"Not so long as they did not disrupt our experiments."

"Oh."

Atrus continued, "The *Arcturians* hail from the Arcturus star system. They are possibly the most advanced beings we have encountered. They have managed to shed their corporal forms and as a result have evolved into other dimensional star beings. They are a peaceful species, who only wish to achieve a higher consciousness."

She tried to imagine what a star being might look like, but her idea seemed silly. It was too unrealistic. Atrus showed her their true form with his mind's eye.

"The next species were the *Anunnaki*. They are magnificent brightly glowing winged beings that are capable of flight. When their distant world became too small for them, they created space vessels and ventured forth into space."

When she initially tried imagining how they looked, she thought of the many birds she killed with her knives and felt guilty. Thinking of her world reminded her of the alien species with the alleged grudge against humanity. She asked, "What about the ones you mentioned earlier? You hinted at transgressions that were made against them. What did you mean?"

"I was referring to the *Reptillans*, an aggressive warrior-like species with reptilian features covered by green scaley skin. Long ago, one of their vessels was fired upon by flying vessels from your world's military forces. Not surprisingly, this happened to my kind, as well. Humanity cannot be blamed for their fear. I imagine we must have appeared as invaders from space. That is typically why we kept ourselves hidden, to prevent negative interactions.

The Reptillans are not as forgiving as my kind. They were greatly offended by the unprovoked attack. Fortunately for your world, they lacked the resources to retaliate, let alone to begin a global invasion. Their world is much too distant for that. It was not worth the effort. Instead, they simply made their visits less frequent.

I should inform you one of their leaders, a being by the name of Orion, has been suspected of making certain that large asteroid struck your world all those years ago, leaving it in its current state. My kind believe he somehow managed to manipulate its trajectory. It is only a theory, which has yet to be proven by facts. Again, this is merely based on speculation."

She knew he was being truthful. Regardless, she found the thought to be distressing. If her world's near destruction had been caused purposely, it meant her entire civilization was essentially slaughtered. Annihilated. The world she could've known was taken away. It bothered her, but what could she do about it? Nothing really, although she wondered if it were true. It pained her to think about it. So many lives lost. So much destruction.

Of course, the only reason she was born was because her parents met in that shelter in the first place. Otherwise, she wouldn't even exist. Perhaps, it was meant to be.

She figured maybe those Reptillans had also been the cause of so many abductions over the years. If so, she suspected their guests were not treated as well as she was being treated by her hosts. It made her upset, so she changed the subject.

"Why were so many alien species visiting my world?" She practically demanded.

Atrus replied, "Curiosity. They wanted to observe the experiment. Over the eons, our various experiments had become widely known across the galaxy."

Somehow, that bothered her, too.

"Mind you, it was no secret, except to your world," Atrus explained guiltily, while frowning.

"Fine. Whatever." She became upset, so she tried to change the subject. "What about your people? Tell me about them." She wasn't sure if he or she would. If there was a need to keep the experiment secret from humanity, then perhaps there was more that needed to be kept secret, even from her. The alleged chosen prime female. She huffed to herself.

Atrus sensed her growing animosity and informed her, "The need for secrecy has come to an end, young one. I shall tell you whatever you wish to know, if the answers are within my ability to do so. I am not your enemy, nor are my kind. We are commonly referred to as 'the Greys' because of our color. However, we are *Ebens*. We originate from the Recticula galaxy. My kind are longtime explorers, scientists, and historians of the universe. We are a nonviolent species."

She seemed to calm down a bit. "Why did you begin this *great experiment*?"

"For the same reasons why anyone does anything they don't understand. Curiosity. Knowledge. The need to learn more is strong. We all seek knowledge, even you." He smiled at her.

She sighed. There was no arguing with that. It didn't stop her from feeling like someone's toy. She hated being part of some cosmic experiment that she didn't even know about, until today. Just thinking how her people had been manipulated since the very beginning of their existence made her angry. She didn't blame Atrus or Azculepus. It had been going on long before they were born, or hatched, or created. She wasn't quite sure how they came to be. This was just their way. It's what they knew.

She tried to think about every book she'd ever read. It was difficult to believe there wasn't any information about these Greys, let alone any of the other species that were mentioned to her. She knew sky ships were mentioned, but that was it. Some people didn't even believe they were real. Just like with the sasquatches. It amazed her. How could humanity have existed for so long in ignorance, while being observed every year? There were no writings of it in any of the books. It made no sense.

"Think," she told herself. Both Atrus and Azculepus watched her with intrigue, and perhaps some amusement. It bothered her.

Then she remembered something from a distant memory. When she was a child, there were a few people from her clan, who used to do strange things she didn't quite understand. It was something she could barely recall. What was it? Praying! They prayed to gods. Or was it one god? It was difficult to remember the exact details. Once those people died, their customs died with them. It wasn't something the rest of the clan continued, for whatever reason. She never thought to ask about it. Instead, she simply forgot about it, until now.

Who were these gods?

Atrus answered simply, "It was us."

"Over the centuries we learned that humans have a need to believe in something, most notably a higher power. It gives them hope, which is one of humanity's greatest strengths. Like most beings, they require a logical way to explain everything they cannot comprehend. One flaw is when they cannot find a reasonable explanation, they tend to create one. If the idea becomes strong enough, others will follow. That is another flaw in your species. The need to be led by someone. It is not a trait you all possess, but far too many did. The individual mind is a rarity amongst your kind. You are one of those few, who do not require someone to follow. It is simply another reason why you have been chosen."

She nodded in agreement. It was true. She preferred being on her own and doing whatever she wanted to do. For the moment, she listened to Atrus tell the tale. She glimpsed at the viewing table wishing there was another show to watch.

Atrus told her, "Not all conversations are shows to be seen. I shall tell you how we came to be known as gods by your kind. During the earliest visits from my kind, there was little justification, or so my kind thought, to remain hidden. They openly visited humankind, once it had found a way to formulate the first languages. There was finally an intelligent way to communicate, even if the various human languages were quite primitive, at the time.

I always found it fascinating how humanity had created separate languages and separate cultures, based on their location on the planet. You are all from the same world. It would make far more sense to speak one basic language, as it is with my kind."

She agreed. It didn't make much sense to her either.

"While humanity had advanced enough to communicate in those earlier times, they had not yet comprehended the concept of space travel. At the time, they had not even mastered the ability to create ground vehicles, let alone anything that could fly. Space was still something far from their reach, although they did take notice of the stars. Therefore, you can imagine their wonder at seeing our brightly lit vessels descend from the heavens. To them, my kind were gods, seemingly omnipotent beings to be worshipped. In time, that is what they did. They worshipped us, and my kind enjoyed it for a while. Each culture on your world had different names for my kind, but in essence it was always some form of deity.

It was not only my kind, but other visitors to your world. The Plei, Arcturians, Anunnaki, and the Reptillans all became known as gods. The Anunnaki were also called angels because of their wings and bright ethereal appearances. For a long time, each species paid many visits to the early humans. However, in doing so, the experiment had been compromised.

Once we realized, there were various religions based on our existence, it became apparent we had intervened far too much. We had inadvertently affected the development of our experiment. The damage was done. It was a grave mistake, but we learned from the error of our ways. Afterwards, my kind took a more distant approach. The new directive was to observe without being observed. We also discouraged any further interactions from the other alien species. Unfortunately, we could not control their actions. We could only hope they heeded our request. For the most part, they respected our wishes.

In time, we were virtually forgotten by humanity. We became the stuff of myths and legends. Humanity had learned to move on without the direct guidance of their so-called deities."

She suddenly recalled reading about gods from the heavens in one of her fantasy novels. It never occurred to her that it could be something based on fact. She wondered how many other references she may have missed in the books she read. It was something she never thought to look for, but now she wished she had her library in front of her, so she could rummage through each book for clues.

It was embarrassing. How could her people have been so gullible?

"You should not blame them for their beliefs," Atrus admonished her. "It is normal for your kind to believe."

She thought of what her mom wrote in her journal. Always believe in everything. And so, she did. However, she always thought of it as a safety mechanism. If you believed in everything, then you can't be surprised. Always expect that anything can happen. Always be prepared. It had been her way of thinking since she was a child.

There was something she wanted to know. "Do you ever think of yourself as a god?" Of course, she knew the answer, as soon as she thought of the question.

"No, not at all," Atrus replied immediately. "We are the architects of the great life experiment. As such, we monitor and make observations, which we record for historical reference. We are far from being gods. We are just beings like yourself."

For a split second, she was about to shout, but then she remembered her mouth was still locked shut. It only made her angrier. She shot back, "Except no one is taking you from your world! Nobody watches or controls what you do! You don't have to worry about being abducted! You're not a prisoner on some sky ship with your mouth locked shut!"

Atrus frowned and admitted, "Yes. You are correct, young one. However, keep in mind, you are not our prisoner. You have been selected for something far greater than the existence you would have lived back on your world. While we may have temporarily blocked your ability to speak, it was only for our safety. With your uncontrolled outbursts, we surely would have been severely injured, by now."

She became less angry and felt a little sorry. He was right. She had to control her anger.

Atrus added, "Perhaps, we are not the same, although we are not very different. We are both living beings driven by our curiosity for knowledge. Now then, is there anything else you would like to know?"

"At the moment, I think I need a break," she replied. "Time to think things over."

"Very well. Azculepus will take you to a room, where you can rest. You have been through a long ordeal. The knowledge you have been given will no doubt take time to settle into your mind. I am confident we shall communicate, again, when you are ready. After all, it is a long journey to our destination."

She nodded, and then followed Azculepus through a doorway, which led out of the room.

They walked in silence toward the room, where she would be allowed to rest. She hoped there would be a window. The idea of seeing space with her own eyes still excited her.

"Yes," Azculepus confirmed. "There is a window for your entertainment. You shall also be fed. Your body requires sustenance."

Her temporary room was located on the same level, so there was no need to step onto a telepad. She was grateful. The doorway opened onto the smooth wall and revealed a similar room to the one she used when looking down at her planet. The only difference was this room had a bed.

"Will I be confined to this room?"

"You are not our prisoner. I understand you have a need to explore your surroundings. It is also part of your entertainment. That is acceptable, although I doubt you will find anything of interest."

"How do I open the door?"

"That is simple. You walk toward the wall and think of a door. It will open, if there is one there to be opened. Try not to get lost. I shall return shortly with food from your world."

That sounded pretty good to her. All of a sudden, she felt incredibly hungry. She hadn't eaten since the day before. She figured it had to be the next day, at this point. It was going to be very hard to tell when it was day or night, if all she saw outside was the darkness of space. She moved toward the window and watched the stars. There was so many. It would be impossible to count them all. She noticed they barely seemed to be moving, so she wasn't sure if they were flying or if they had stopped. It was tricky to detect any movement on the sky ship. It felt as steady as being in a building on the ground. Then again, she wasn't exactly an expert on riding moving vehicles.

This entire experience had been like a bizarre adventure to her. It was still hard to believe she was on a sky ship flying through space. How far had they traveled? Where were they going? Atrus said it was going to be a long journey to this other planet, but how long? Days? Weeks?? Months??? YEARS???!!! Maybe she should've at least asked how far they were going.

She tried to open her mouth, but still couldn't. She frowned and plopped down on the bed. It was fairly comfortable. It wasn't as soft as hers, but it wasn't too bad. The blanket felt strange. It was unlike any material she ever felt. It felt smooth and thin. Maybe a little too thin. She hoped it would keep her warm. Not that she was cold, or tired. Sleep could wait. Currently, she wanted to eat.

Azculepus mentioned food from her world. That would be great. What would it be? Meat? Fruit? Vegetables? She was so hungry that she could eat it all.

The doorway opened and Azculepus appeared holding a tiny silver packet, which was handed to her. She looked at it with intense curiosity and disappointment. Before she could ask what it was, she was told, "It is a packet containing a small pill, which is packed with the nutrients and proteins your body requires. The taste will be exactly similar to your most favored meal. It will also fill your stomach in the same way."

She eyed it suspiciously and glared at Azculepus. "You'll have to excuse me, if I find that hard to believe."

"Try it. You will not be disappointed."

"How am I supposed to eat when my mouth is locked shut?"

"I have unblocked your mouth, for the moment. Please, refrain from speaking aloud. Keep in mind, I do not know your language."

She opened her mouth and felt completely elated. She grinned happily from ear to ear. "Thanks," she whispered softly with a nod of appreciation. She also thought the word when she remembered her language was foreign to her host. Azculepus nodded, as Evangelina popped the small brown pill into her mouth and began chewing it. Her eyes gaped wide. It was absolutely delicious! It tasted exactly like pancakes, which was her favorite meal. It was also something she hadn't eaten for a long, long time. She made sure to chew every last bit, and swallowed it all. Once she was done, she felt fully satisfied, as if she had eaten an actual meal. It was unbelievable.

"Okay, I'll admit that was perfect," she thought the words.

Azculepus smiled and informed her that her mouth had been closed, once more. "I apologize, but it is necessary. We would not want you to snore when you sleep. Some of your kind have been known to do so. I shall return to see you in approximately six hours of your time."

"My time?" Confused, she asked, "Isn't time the same for you?"

"Your measured units of time are based solely on the rotation of your world and its orbit around its sun. It is the same for me, even while we are here deep in space. We continue to measure time based on our world's rotation around our sun. I assure you the difference is significant. Time moves much slower for us."

"Oh." It was all so strange. She didn't question it. What was the point?

"Precisely," Azculepus agreed. "You may choose to rest, or you may explore, as you wish. You may also explore, and then rest. I strongly advise you to make time to rest your body and mind. If you require any assistance, think my name and I will hear you. We can communicate throughout the vessel. It is not necessary for us to be in the same area. The same applies in regard to the historian, if you think of any other questions you might have."

"Thank you. You're very kind. I'm sorry, but I can't remember how to say your name."

"Az-cul-e-pus."

"Okay, I got it. I think," she smiled.

The door closed and she was alone, at last. She laid back on the bed to consider her predicament. Six hours was plenty of time for her to explore, and then take a long nap. Then again, maybe she could take a nap, first, and then explore. A dreadful thought occurred to her. What if she had to use the bathroom? Where was it? She got up from the bed and decided exploring was the top priority.

She stepped toward the wall and thought the word, "door." Like magic, it opened. She got a cheap thrill from it. She went through and looked down the corridor in both directions. Everything was identical. How was she supposed to remember which was her room? There were no doors to mark the location. She could be walking through the corridor for hours thinking "door," but if she were in the wrong spot, nothing would happen. Either that or she'd be opening several wrong doors before she ever guessed the right one. The whole thing was giving her a headache.

Suddenly, going for a little walk didn't seem like the best idea. She went back into her room and the door closed when she wanted it to do so. She sat on the bed and pouted. If only she had her books with her.

I Stand Alone

Since there was nothing else to do, she laid down on the bed. She wanted the lights to turn off, but wasn't sure how to do it. As soon as she thought about it, the lights went off. Her eyes turned toward the window, which only let in the tiniest amount of light. Space was exceptionally dark. There was no light from the moon. Not anymore. There was no moon.

As she lay there thinking, she thought about something else that had been bothering her earlier. There was so much going on that she kept forgetting to ask about it.

"Hello? Can you hear me, Atrus?" She called out in the darkness.

"Yes, I can. What is wrong, young one?" The voice sounded as though they were in the same room.

She couldn't stop the smile from appearing on her face. It amazed her how they were able to communicate, while in different areas of the sky ship.

"I have another question, if that's all right with you?"

"It is," was the response. "You may proceed with your query."

She posed her question. "I've been thinking. You've told me I'm supposed to be this chosen prime female for some new world, which I must admit sounds totally crazy to me, but whatever. I know it means I'm supposed to somehow help populate the world with humans. Right?"

"That is correct."

She cringed at the thought, but then continued. "Well, you do realize it takes more than one human female to make a baby, right?"

Atrus was amused. "That depends on how we proceed. However, we were hoping to do things the traditional way. By doing so, we are fully aware we shall also require a human male. As I mentioned to you earlier, we were able to locate two descendants of those hybrid experiments. You and a male. You are not the only human aboard this vessel. Nor were you our first."

She instantly sat up in her bed and thought, "Door!"

CHAPTER 19: ANOTHER

She moved through the corridor quickly, not sure where she was going. Her memory from earlier had been fuzzy. There was so much on her mind. She was too distracted. Now wasn't any different. When she reached someplace she believed to be familiar, she thought the words, "Door!" A door opened.

Atrus was there waiting for her. It was the right room. Atrus was impressed by her ability to locate the history room on her own, considering how she thought everything in the corridor looked alike.

"We could have communicated just as easily, if you remained in your room."

"I like talking to people face to face," she replied. "With my mouth, but this will have to do."

"You have my apologies, but I cannot take that chance with your state of mind. Humans are too predictably unpredictable. There is also the fact that I do not understand your language."

"Right. So, why didn't you tell me there was another human here with us?"

"You did not ask. I was only answering your questions and telling you what you wanted to hear. His presence is no secret."

She rolled her eyes. He was probably right to keep her mouth closed. She wasn't too pleased. "You should've told me. Of course, I would've wanted to know. Considering you can hear my thoughts and see into my mind, then you should've known I was lonely for my kind. I thought I was the last normal person left." Then it occurred to her. What made her think it was a normal person? She hadn't seen a normal person, since her father died. What if it was a nomad? It had to be! She felt disgusted at the idea of mating with an apelike nomad.

"He is not what you might call a *nomad*," Atrus assured her. "We found him quite far from your previous location, several of your days before we located you. He is indeed capable of communicating intelligently with us, as you have been doing. He is near your age, only slightly older. He is also taller than you. Like you, he is a fighter, a thinker, and a seeker of knowledge. However, he is less volatile. He is definitely not filled with as much anger as you." Atrus frowned.

She sensed the disappointment, and it made her feel ashamed. She realized she did have anger issues, although she couldn't help how she felt. Why should she have to pretend not to be angry when she felt furious?

"You should not pretend to do anything," Atrus' voice answered in her head. "Always be true to yourself, young one. At the same time, learn to control your feelings. Do not allow them to control you. You are a very intelligent person. You are capable of so much more than you exhibit." She listened. "If you do not learn to control your anger, it will get the better of you. Heed my warning for humanity's sake."

She nodded shamefully. "I'm sorry, but I wish you told me about him. It's something that's important to me, especially if he's normal, and not a nomad."

"Understandable. If that is how you feel, I apologize to you for not informing you of his presence in a timely manner."

"Can I please meet him?" She was eager, but also nervous.

"I must apologize, once more. He is already in his extended sleep cycle."

"Huh? What's that supposed to mean?" She became worried.

"We must travel to another galaxy in order to reach the world where we are taking the both of you. It shall take far longer than you could possibly imagine. Once you had an opportunity to rest, my intention was to inform you there would be only one more of your days to be awake, so you could eat another three meals, before we must place *you* into your extended sleep cycle. If you were to remain awake for the entire trip, you would not survive the experience. You will age and you will likely die, long before we arrive at our destination."

The words sent a chill down her spine. "Why do we have to travel so far away?"

"That is where the world we have chosen for you is located. It is almost an exact match. We have cultivated it for quite some time in preparation. It is nearly ready for humanity except this time we shall skip the evolutionary process. By the time we arrive, it will be ready. However, rather than begin a new experiment as we did on your world, we have opted to simply place two fully grown humans, instead."

"That's incredibly risky. What if we don't get along? What if he turns out to be a jerk, and then I need to kill him? Or worse, what if *he* tries to kill *me*?"

"You really do have a violent mind. Please, try to change your way of thinking for the sake of humanity or this entire process will have been a waste of time. We have chosen a perfectly civilized match for you with similar interests. There should be no reason for any of you to kill each other."

"Good. I hope not." She really didn't want to make this whole thing a waste of time. They were giving her a second chance to survive on a world without nomads. A world where she wouldn't have to worry about being abducted anymore. She could finally enjoy the sunrises *and* the sunsets. Nighttime would no longer be forbidden. It would simply be another time of the day, where she could venture out and explore, if she wished.

"Will that world have the same time measurements as my world?"

"The days and nights are slightly longer and vary with the seasonal changes, but it will be as you thought. You will be free to enjoy both times equally without fear. I can promise you that much."

"What else can you tell me about this man? What does he look like?"

"His hair is dark like yours, only shorter. He does have some facial hair. He is in perfect health. Like you, he is a prime male. Therefore, he has few noticeable flaws, if any. He also lacks any psychic abilities, and no, he is not an albino. His skin tone is like yours."

She felt relieved. "Does he speak my language?"

"I do not know the answer to that question, since I am unfamiliar with his or your language." She was shocked. It was the first time

Atrus couldn't answer one of her questions. "We communicated through telepathy, so I never heard his voice. Nor have I heard yours."

"But you're hearing my thoughts now. That's my voice. Isn't it? I hear your voice in my head. It sounds different from Azculepus' voice. Doesn't my voice sound different to you?"

"You are correct. I suppose his vocal voice would sound identical. It has never occurred to me. You have given me much to think about since your arrival, young one. I would like more time to commune with you, but that would be unwise. You do need to rest."

"Okay, I'll go back to my room," she gave in reluctantly.

It amazed her how she was able to find her way back to her room with little difficulty. She only missed the door twice. Now, she was back on her bed. This time beneath the blanket. It was much warmer than it looked, although the room wasn't really too cold. She had forgotten how the special clothing was intended to keep her warm, as well. Plus, the floor was also warm to the touch on her nearly bare feet. Her outfit came complete with partial socks that wrapped around the bottom of her feet, but left her heels and toes exposed.

As she lay on the bed, sleep was the farthest thing from her mind. There were so many thoughts going through her head. She wasn't sure if she'd get any sleep at all. Her mind was on this unknown human male. She still found it hard to believe there was another human on the sky ship, which was actually funny considering she was normally one to believe in anything.

The typical questions raced through her brain. How did he look? Would he be handsome? Would they get along? Would he treat her nicely? If he had similar interests, exactly which ones did they share? Was he a lover of books like her? Could he even read or write? Was he any good at throwing knives? Did he crave adventure, or was he a homebody like her dad? Was he a skilled hunter or fisherman? He had to be, if he was still alive. Could he cook? Did he have any medical skills?

And then there was that other question. Would they fall in love?

She had never known that kind of love, except in her books, or from how her dad spoke about her mom. She read about romance in many of her novels over the years. It was always described as being magical in some strange way. That seemed a bit absurd. She didn't doubt it would be special, but magical? How could that be? It seemed silly to think so.

Her parents came to mind, again. Her dad used to tell her so many wonderfully romantic stories about him and her mom. It always pleased her to hear these stories, mainly because she wanted to hear about her mom. If only she had more memories of her.

She wanted to experience something like what they had, but without the fear of losing him too soon. Her heart couldn't take it. It was a relief to know he was in perfect health. That bit of information was very important to her. She didn't want to experience the same kind of loss that her dad experienced. It was too heartbreaking. She already had enough sadness in her life. She was ready for something different. Something good.

She rolled over and faced the window, pulling the blanket closer to her neck. It felt cozy, but it wasn't home. She was tempted to sit up and stare outside for a while, but there really wasn't much to see. It all looked the same as before. Billions of stars blinking at her. Still, it was a beautiful sight. One she was never able to enjoy back on her world. One she would never forget.

What the heck. She sat up and pressed her face against the window, trying to see more than the window would allow. Maybe there was something else to see out there, if she looked hard enough. She watched for several minutes, imagining tiny planets around each little star. She wondered how many of those unseen worlds also had life. She came to the conclusion that space was fascinating.

Eventually, she dropped back down on the bed. She dug her head into the pillow and turned sideways. She always slept better on her side. Her mind drifted back to her world. She thought about her shelter, which she'd never see again. She missed it. She longed for her books. There would be no books on the new world, unless she wrote them herself. Where would she find paper? And a pen?

She closed her eyes and tried to clear her mind.

It was not long before she was dreaming. She was more tired than she thought. In her dream, she was already on this new world. She found herself in a beautiful magnificent city, except it wasn't in ruins. It was all like new. The streets were nicely paved. There were trees, but not in excess like on her world. She could actually see the full surface of each building, as they were meant to be seen. Unbroken windows with shining glass that reflected the beauty of the sky. She looked up to see the sun. It was early in the day. She had time to explore, so she did.

The buildings were clean. Not filled with litter and debris. There was no rubble in the streets. It was perfect, and this was her new home. Her city. Well, it was hers and his. Whoever he was. He wasn't in her dream. Not even there would she be allowed a glimpse at him. She'd have to wait for reality.

A short while later, she was seated in a room. The room was brightly lit with large bay windows overlooking the city. She was high up. She enjoyed the view, but she wasn't there to look out of the windows. She held a book in her hands, so she read. It was a good book, too. Someone was there with her, but he was behind her. It was him. He was cooking food for them. He was making pancakes because it was her favorite. She smelled it and cherished the aroma. It made her close her eyes, even in her dream.

She slept well.

When she awoke, Azculepus had returned, as promised. He brought her another pill for breakfast. She devoured the tiny morsel. This time, she tasted eggs with toast. She even thought of a fruit juice drink and tasted that, as well.

"Today, you will require three meals to prepare your body for the extended sleep cycle. Your next meal will be sometime later to allow this one sufficient time to digest."

"I understand," she nodded. "When will I have to sleep?"

"Not until after you have digested your third meal." She thought about what she'd like to taste for dinnertime. "Yes, upon completion of your *dinnertime*, as you call it," Azculepus told her.

"Okay. Good. I suppose that gives me a few hours to enjoy my last day of being awake. What do you guys do around here for fun?" She was half joking when she asked the question. At the same time, she was curious if there was something she could do to entertain herself, aside from star gazing and wondering about her future mate.

"You will have an opportunity to view him before you enter your sleep cycle. I will be placing you beside him. All sleep chambers are situated in the same area of the vessel."

"Really?" She was quite pleased with that idea. An optimistic smile appeared on her face. "It will be really nice to see what he looks like. I wasn't sure it was possible."

"It is. As for your entertainment, I am sorry to inform you there are few options. There is the observation deck, as you are aware. You may explore, since you enjoy doing so. Another activity for you was suggested to me by Atrus. You are permitted to utilize the viewing table. Atrus will show you how."

"Yes! That sounds awesome! Thank you!"

"I see you still have not learned to control your excitement level."

She sighed heavily through her nose, while rolling her eyes. "I know. Sorry. I don't think I can." She shook her head. "I guess I'll just have to remain mouth-locked for the rest of the ride." She smirked.

"At least, your temper has subsided."

"Yeah, sorry about that, too. I was pretty upset yesterday. Um, it was yesterday, right?"

"If you feel like it was, you may describe it as such to allow yourself an impression of normalcy. For the rest of us, it is still early on the same day we acquired you."

"Wow. That's strange. How long did I sleep?"

"Approximately five to six hours. If you recall, you were given six hours of rest time. I returned exactly six hours later, as I said I would."

"You guys are pretty precise with everything, huh? Or girls? I'm sorry. I don't mean to offend you, but I'm not really sure how to think of you."

"I am not offended by your comment. It is typical for you to be curious. We are asexual beings. There is no male or female amongst our kind. Each of us is perfectly capable of reproducing new life, but not in the same manner as your kind. There is no need for sexual intercourse. We reproduce by..."

"Okay, okay," she interrupted. "I'm sorry, but that's way too much information for me." She definitely didn't want to think about sex, especially since her mind was an open book. Some things needed to remain private. "Let's think about something else, such as that viewing table. I'm ready to give that a try. Can I?"

"Very well," Azculepus was slightly amused at her embarrassment, revealing only the tiniest smile. She was led back to the history room, although she already knew the way. It was the only place she knew how to find, besides her room.

Atrus was there to greet her. "Welcome back, young one. I trust you have rested well and are ready to engage the viewing table for entertainment purposes?"

"You trust correctly. I'm really sorry that I was angry earlier. I wasn't angry with you. I was angry at this situation I'm stuck in. My life has been a bit chaotic the past few days." She recalled being chased by mongrels, dragged away by the water road, hiding from sky ships, and her ordeal with the nomads. She hoped Atrus would be able to see the memories.

"That does seem somewhat chaotic for such a short time period. Thank you for sharing your experiences." There was a brief pause. "I am aware you are upset about your situation. It is understandable, considering you have been forced to give up so much of what made your life comfortable, especially your books and your home. I noticed they are on your mind quite often. In the end, you will realize you are better off. You will be safer on this new world." It almost sounded like a promise.

"I sure hope so," she thought, still not really convinced. "So, how can I use this table? Can I view my world?" She walked toward it.

"Yes, you may, but I thought you might prefer to view your new world, instead."

"I can do that?" She became excited.

"Yes, indeed," Atrus smiled.

"Then yes, please. And thank you."

The viewing table came to life, as the lights dimmed. She was able to see her future world spread across the surface. It was unexpected to see how similar the landscape was to her former world, except without the ruins or nomads. She didn't see any structures whatsoever, but there were forests, mountains, water roads, lots of animals to hunt, and a beautiful blue sky filled with lovely white puffy clouds. It was beautiful. She liked it already.

Sure, she'd miss exploring the ruins of her old civilization, but the idea of no longer having to worry about nomads was a tremendous relief. The new world was going to be so much better. It would be peaceful. She watched it in real time motion for several minutes, rather than at fast speed. It was important for the experience to feel genuine. Everything looked so serene. She wished she could be there at this very moment. For the first time, she was actually eager to see this place in person.

The thought of sharing that experience with another normal human was exhilarating. It also made her a bit nervous. What if they didn't get along? She wanted to believe everything would be fine, but her suspicious nature wouldn't allow it. She had to be ready for anything, even for him to be a jerk. If she expected the worse, then she wouldn't be disappointed. If he turned out to be a nice person, even better. She'd be ready either way.

Her thoughts were interrupted by Atrus. "I have communicated with your male counterpart at length, prior to your arrival," she was told. "I do not believe you will be disappointed."

She turned toward Atrus. "I hope you're right," she replied.

"Only time will tell. Try to think positive."

She nodded.

Sometime later, she was fed her second meal, which she chose to have at the observation deck. She sat there for a while, staring out of the window and allowing her imagination to take her on a journey across the stars. It amazed her to think how many potential inhabited worlds there were out there among the billions of stars before her. What kind of species resided on each of those worlds? Were they anything like her?

Afterwards, she explored the corridors for a short time, but ended up getting lost. Atrus had to guide her back to her room.

When it was time for her final meal, that was where she had it. In her room. She wanted time to be alone with her thoughts with no distractions. She laid on her bed thinking. There was so much for her to think about. How was she ever going to fall asleep with her mind so awake?

Several hours later, the time had arrived for her to be placed into her extended sleep cycle. She was nervous about that, as well as suspicious. She really wanted to trust Azculepus and Atrus, but it wasn't easy when she thought about being put to sleep for an undetermined amount of time. It made her incredibly uncomfortable.

Azculepus tried to ease her mind, as she was led to the cryogenic sleep chambers, explaining how there was nothing to fear. "The extended sleep cycle is not painful. Try to think of it as normal sleep, except when you awaken a lot more time would have passed."

She nodded solemnly.

When the door opened, she finally got to see him. Her future mate. The chamber was equipped with a frosted glass cover. He was sleeping so peacefully. She stepped closer to get a better look at him. He was a beautiful man, she thought. Maybe even perfect. She smiled. She couldn't wait to meet him. For a split second, she was tempted to ask his name. However, she decided it would be best to hear it from his voice, instead, when they were properly introduced.

There were numerous other sleep chambers in the room, which were empty. She turned toward Azculepus and asked, "Will you also be going to sleep?"

"Yes, but for a shorter time period, since time moves much slower for us. Therefore, we do not require as much sleep as you. We shall take turns."

"How many more of your kind are here with us?"

"There are five others, along with me and the historian. There is the pilot and co-pilot. There is also an engineer, the mechanic, and a researcher. Seven crew members is the typical compliment for an exploratory science vessel, which is our designation."

She suddenly realized they identified one another by using their professions, rather than their names. It amused her.

"That is true," Azculepus agreed with a smile.

"Will I be able to dream, while I am asleep?"

"Perhaps. My kind do not dream, but I am fully aware your kind does, while asleep. It is normal for your kind, so it is highly likely you will dream quite often, considering you will be asleep for a very long time." She wondered how long it would be. "Using your measurement of time, you will be asleep for several decades. The rest of your body will be placed in a form of suspended animation, while your mind will continue to function."

"Several decades??? Wow! That is a long time," she swallowed nervously. She looked up at the tall alien with pleading eyes. "Please, promise me one thing."

"Very well."

"Promise me that I'll wake up from this sleep. I'm not ready to die. I thought I was, but I was wrong. I want to live."

Azculepus nodded with a smile, "Yes. Of course, and you shall. I promise you shall both awaken, once we reach your new world. When you do, you will look no older than you are currently. It will be as if no time passed at all. If all goes well, I expect you should live a good long life together."

She smiled gratefully. She really wanted to believe what she was being told. She had to believe it. She imagined her mom telling her to believe everything. Maybe this moment was the reason why those words had been engrained in her mind so long ago. She needed to have faith.

Azculepus nodded in response, while opening the sleep chamber. It looked like a metallic coffin with a glass cover. She tried not to think about it. When she was ready, she climbed inside. It was a tight fit. There was little room for tossing and turning. She heard Azculepus' voice explain she wouldn't be doing any of that during this sleep. Her body would not be moving at all. Somehow, it wasn't as reassuring as he intended it to be.

She laid back onto the pillow, and gazed up at the alien's large black eyes, which were looking down at her. They blinked at her.

"Are you ready?" She heard the soothing voice in her head.

"I think so," she nodded with reluctance.

"Close your eyes," she was instructed. "It will be fine." The chamber was closed.

She did as she was told and closed her eyes. At this point, what other choice did she have? There was a brief moment of panic when the cryogenic gas entered the chamber. The hissing sound startled her. The gentle voice in her head told her to relax. It was going to be okay. She stared through the glass, back into the large black eyes and nodded, wanting to believe the words. She closed her eyes, once more. Her body began to feel numb. A feeling of calm came over her. Soon, she felt tired. So sleepy. Within seconds, she was asleep.

"Sleep well," Azculepus said, while turning off the lights and leaving the room.

CHAPTER 20: PARADISE

After traveling across the galaxy, the bright oval alien starship had begun its approach toward the previously distant planet. They had just entered the solar system. The starship was coming up on a small lifeless moon. Just beyond the moon would be their destination. The home of their next life experiment. The crew was excited about this vibrant young world. It was another chance to make this experiment work. They anticipated it would work out better than it had on the previous world.

As they navigated around the uninhabited moon, the planet had come into view. It was a beautiful bluish planet rich with life. The pilot and co-pilot sent the image they were seeing from their minds to the rest of the crew.

Atrus began a new holorecording of their approach at the viewing table. Azculepus hurried to the cryogenic chambers to awaken their human passengers. It was time for them to prepare for disembarkation. They would have to be cleaned, acclimated, and fed, after their long slumber.

The room containing the chambers was dimly lit. Their eyes would be sensitive to the light, after being asleep for so long. It was necessary to get the humans accustomed to being awake. Afterwards, Azculepus would monitor their vitals using a small handheld device.

A button was pressed and a new gas was fed into the chambers, gradually clearing away the frost from within. Lights along the side blinked with excitement. There was a blast of air, and then the glass covers became clearer. Both humans had been cleansed. The chambers opened simultaneously.

It was the man, who opened his eyes, first. His hair was damp from the cleansing, while his vision was blurry. For a split second, he thought he was having another dream. There had been so many during his slumber. Dream after dream filled the decades of time. Sadly, most would be forgotten, now that he was awake. He took a deep breath through his nose and tried to move. His entire body felt stiff, although his vision was slowly beginning to clear up.

Azculepus sent them both the same mental message, "You will both feel limber once more, in due time. It takes a moment to recover from the effects of the extended sleep cycle, even for my kind. Take your time. When you are ready, you may exit the chamber. We are approaching our destination, but we shall remain in orbit, until you are ready."

The young man looked toward him and instinctively tried to speak using his mouth. He had forgotten that he couldn't. Instead, he responded mentally. "How long have I been asleep?"

"You have been asleep for precisely seventy-seven years of your time," was the message sent to them, since they were both eager to know. Each looked surprised and finally turned to face one another. They stared at each other with wonder and curiosity.

The male tried to speak to his female companion's mind. He asked how she felt, although she didn't respond. He wasn't sure if she couldn't or if she chose not to.

Azculepus answered for her. "She feels much the same way you do, at the moment. I am sorry to inform you she is unable to hear your thoughts. Only my kind can communicate with your kind in that manner. You must both resort to vocalizing your thoughts to each other, if you wish them to be known. Therefore, you shall have to wait until we land. Rest assured, once your voices are no longer a threat to my kind, control over your mouths will be fully restored."

The man looked at Azculepus with disappointment. He turned back toward the girl beside him. She was still looking at him. He didn't mind. She was remarkably beautiful for someone who had been asleep for several decades. It appeared she was just as eager to climb out of the chamber, but neither of them was ready for that kind of physical effort. Their legs still felt stiff and weak. For the moment, they remained seated within their chambers.

Eventually, the man pushed himself to rise. He had to hold onto the edge of the chamber to steady himself. When the teenage girl saw him, she did the same, not to be outdone.

Azculepus watched them with interest and informed them it was not a competition. "There is no hurry, nor is this a race. Please, take your time. Rise when you are ready, not before. I do not wish for either of you to fall and injure yourself."

The man forced a smile, while looking at his lovely female companion. He felt so unbelievably weak. He wondered if she felt the same. Judging by how little she was moving, he believed so. He straightened his back, as he stood up. There was a tingling sensation in his legs, which felt the same as when a limb falls asleep, and then is moved too suddenly. He waited for the tingling to subside before trying to move, again. At least, his vision was almost back to normal.

He wondered how he must've looked to her, after being asleep even longer than her. Probably like some uncivilized nomad. He smirked at the thought. He wondered how long it had been before they found a suitable mate for him. Was it days? Weeks? Months? Plus, was she actually suitable for him? Better yet, was he suitable for her? He would've liked very much to have met her before being put to sleep. At least, that way he might've had a few dreams about her. The thought made him smile, again, and he allowed his eyes to wander in her direction. He needed another look at her.

She noticed him checking her out and furrowed her eyebrows. She frowned. He looked away and felt embarrassed. He didn't want her to think he was some kind of perverted savage. Surely, that wouldn't be a good first impression. If only he could apologize to her, but he dared not look at her now. It would have to wait.

Instead, he tried focusing on himself. At last, the tingling sensation was gone. He felt ready to walk, so he took a step forward. It wasn't too bad. He didn't fall flat on his face and embarrass himself further. That's a good start. He let go of the chamber. He was still standing. Also good.

He took another step forward, and then another. Before going toward the door, he turned and looked at her. Was she ready, as well? He would wait for her, before taking another step. He held out his hand and offered it to her, so she could join him.

She looked down at her feet as if willing them to get strong. She let go of the chamber and took a step. She didn't fall either. While still focusing on her feet, she walked toward him, but didn't take his hand, so he dropped it back to his side. She was determined to do it on her own. He had to admire her strength. It was better than her being a weakling, who he'd have to coddle.

Azculepus gradually led the couple to the observation deck, keeping an eye on them both to make sure they didn't fall.

Once they were in the room, they glanced at each other, still feeling curious. They were soon distracted by the view outside of the large window.

"That is your new world," Azculepus told them with a smile.

Evangelina looked amazed. She couldn't believe how much it resembled her home world. It could easily be mistaken for the same planet.

"I shall allow you time to enjoy the view, while I get something for you to eat." Azculepus left the room, leaving them alone.

Aside from not being able to speak, even if they wanted to, it was an awkward silence. They kept their eyes glued to the window. Both sat next to each other. Neither of them wanted to move apart. It felt nice being next to another human. It was also nice to enjoy the view together. Someday, they might be able to discuss this first moment alone. The man couldn't wait to hear the sound of her voice.

When Azculepus returned, they were each given a pill, which would suppress their hunger for several hours. They were both made fully aware how their next meal would have to come from their own combined effort on the planet.

It was also nearly time for Azculepus to bid them a fond farewell. "This will be the last moment we spend together, while you are aboard our vessel. I am positive I shall see you both sometime in the future, but for now, this is goodbye. I wish you both the best, as you begin anew. Atrus will escort you to the surface, once we locate an appropriate place to land. In the meantime, I shall remain with you."

The couple regarded the kind alien scientist with fondness.

Over the next few minutes, they watched the approach in silence. Within seconds they entered the planet's upper atmosphere. They passed through a thick blanket of white clouds before bursting into the light of day. Seeing how excited Evangelina was by the clouds caused the man to smile. Her eyes twinkled with joy. He admired her childlike enthusiasm. It gave him the impression she had an innocent heart. That made her more attractive to him. There was so much he wanted to know about her, but that would have to wait, until later. In the meantime, he focused his attention on the view outside.

The sun was shining brightly in the eastern sky. It looked to be early in the day. They both looked in its direction together. The slight tint on the thick window made it possible for them to stare at it without harming their vision.

The ground below was lush and green. There were grayish mountains far off in the distance, and clear blue water over to their right. The colorful flowers stood out even from high up. The same familiar animals from their world were looking up at them, but how was that possible? A quick thought from Azculepus confirmed they were indeed the same animals. Each type of animal on this world had also been on their previous world. It was part of the experiment to restart humanity by utilizing the same set up, while striving for different results. Improved results was more like it.

In more ways than one, this was the start of a new day for the young couple because it was also a new beginning. A rebirth of humanity. A second chance rarely afforded to a species, let alone to an entire world. The young couple had both been thinking the same thing, as they turned to each other and smiled. This time, the experiment would be a success.

After flying over the land for several minutes, a landing site had finally been selected based on the needs of the human passengers. It wasn't far from the nearest fresh water stream that flowed into a large lake surrounded by forests of trees bearing fruit, edible plants, and fertile fields of grass and wheat.

Animals scurried away and fled in every direction to hide from the oval-shaped metallic starship, as it landed in a small field. Its lights weren't as brightly offending during the daytime. The curious animals watched from their hiding places as a door opened near the bottom of the vessel, and then a landing ramp was deployed extending to the ground.

They watched anxiously as the human male was the first to emerge, stepping out through the doorway, and down the ramp. A beautiful female came out after him. They were both still wearing the skintight white outfits given to them when they were brought aboard. None of them wore footwear, although it was requested. They were told this had to be a fresh start without any of their former possessions. Otherwise, the experiment would be off to a bad start.

Atrus followed them closely down the ramp to see them off.

The couple shielded their eyes from the brightness of the sunlight when they stepped out from under the shade of the large starship. Atrus remained in the darkness of the shade, not wanting to be exposed to the direct sunlight. It is one reason why their kind prefer to operate during the night. Their pale skin is far too sensitive and will get sunburned faster than a human's.

Flocks of birds flew overhead spying on the new arrivals.

"The clothing you wear will not last long out in the elements," Atrus said. "You have been wearing them for a very long time. You will need to hunt the animals for pelts to make new suitable clothing, as well as for food to ensure your survival. You may also eat freely from every tree of this bountiful garden. The fruits are ripened and waiting to be picked."

This new world would be their garden to sow. It contained all of the familiar wildlife from their former world, so they'd know which animals they could hunt and which ones to avoid. The world itself was almost an exact duplicate of their home world based on its earliest times prior to the birth of humanity.

"This is so beautiful," Evangelina thought.

Her male companion also enjoyed what he was seeing. He was eager to walk around and explore the area. There was so much they needed to do. They'd have to find or build a shelter, they needed to acquire food and water, and apparently they were also going to need new clothing. However, he was more eager to talk with his female companion. He still didn't even know her name!

Atrus moved closer to both and informed them, "Before you venture forth, come closer under the shade." They did. "Once I touch my finger to your foreheads, you shall no longer hear my thoughts. Control over your mouths will be returned. I ask that you please refrain from speaking too loudly, if you must speak, until I have boarded our vessel. Remember, I will not understand your language."

The couple nodded in agreement.

"Will we see you, again?" Evangelina asked using her mind.

Atrus smiled in response, "Naturally. My kind shall return someday to check on your progress. I shall likely be amongst them to record the interactions. We shall see each other then."

Again, the couple nodded. They both felt the same, even if they didn't make it known. Whenever these aliens returned, they would no longer be considered a threat. There would be no reason to run and hide. They would be welcomed as friends, so long as it was the Ebens, or the Greys, who returned.

As promised with a gentle touch from Atrus' cold slender forefinger, they felt the difference in their minds. Somehow, everything seemed quieter. They had lost a certain amount of awareness that they didn't even realize they gained. Their thoughts were their own, once again. Each was able to open their mouths, which they did as a test. None spoke, yet. Not while Atrus was walking back to the ramp. They waited for the ramp to close. As the starship began to rise slowly over them, it caused a gentle breeze.

And then the man finally spoke, "Who knew?" She looked at him, as he continued through an unexpectedly thick accent, "The road to the stars descends from the sky." He smiled. Despite his accent, she understood his words. His voice was confident and deep. She liked the sound of it. She wondered how she would sound to him, although she didn't make a comment.

I Stand Alone

Instead, she looked up at the rising sky ship, as she still thought of it. She thought about how long she wasted trying to avoid sky ships. Her clan feared them for so many years, and with good reason. What ever happened to those, who were abducted and never returned? Were they taken to other planets, as well? Were they taken by one of the other alien species, such as the Reptillans? Unfortunately, she'd never know the answers to those questions. All she knew was that she was lucky. This world would be a better place to live. And safer.

She only wished she was able to keep her boots and her knives. She looked down at the white outfit and at her feet. While the outfit felt comfortable and was capable of feeling warm, or cool, as needed, it certainly wouldn't last long. It was going to get dirty fast. It was a good thing she had experience with sewing. Too bad she lacked the necessary tools and materials that she had back at her shelter.

It was going to be a rough start. There was no doubt about that.

When the tiny gleaming silver starship finally disappeared into the clouds, they realized they were alone. There was another awkward silence between them, but they both had a good feeling about this new beginning.

"My name is Evangelina," she finally said. It felt so good to use her mouth for talking, after not doing so for years. She wasn't even sure why she hesitated, at first. All of a sudden, she wanted to talk for hours and scream at the top of her lungs, but she refrained. It would be a shame to scare away the only other human being on the planet with a temporary fit of insanity.

Wow, she thought to herself. It was only the two of them against the world. This time, she wasn't speculating, as she had done on their previous world. It was a stone cold fact, and she didn't even mind.

He responded to her announcement by trying to pronounce her name. As it turned out, he did so rather poorly. "Ivin-ja-leera," he struggled to say the long name. His accent was brutalizing it.

It would've been amusing to her, if it didn't bother her so much. They needed to be able to communicate with one another. It was only them, from now until who knew when? It worried her that he couldn't even pronounce her name. She found herself wondering if he heard her voice with an accent. That seemed even more amusing. What if all this time, it was her who had the accent and didn't even know it?

She scoffed slightly at the thought, and then he chuckled believing she was laughing at his mispronunciation. She found him adorable.

Trying to be kind, she repeated her name for him, "*E-van-ge-li-na.*"

Again, he didn't get it quite right. It was becoming a little frustrating. Maybe he wasn't as smart as she hoped. She decided to make it easier on him.

"Okay, this isn't working. Just call me Eve. Okay?" He watched her curiously, as she pointed to herself and repeated, "*Eve.*"

He looked at her apologetically, nodded, and then pointed to himself. "*Adam.*" He smiled at her, feeling silly for not being able to say her name right. His gorgeous smile made her want to melt away. She blushed and smiled back. She also giggled unconsciously. At least, he was exceptionally handsome, she thought. That was going to make being here alone with him a very pleasant experience.

Now that the pleasantries of introductions were behind them, they needed to find shelter for the night. If they didn't find someplace quick, they'd have to begin constructing something temporary, until they had time to make one that was permanent. They were on the same page when it came to that, so getting started was easy.

It didn't take long to set up a makeshift lean-to shelter using wood. It would serve them well for the first night or two. The first few days were spent gathering fruits and vegetables for food. They then began working on their new home. It wasn't easy without any tools. They had to make some, first. It was a good thing Evangelina, or Eve, had experience making tools, thanks to her father. Adam was especially impressed by her skills. Fortunately, he was not without skills of his own. He knew a lot about making temporary shelters. They worked together to knock down some skinny trees they could use. Within a week, they had something they could call home. It was a hut made of wood, stone, and mud with heavy branches and leaves for the roof.

One afternoon, while taking a break from working, they sat down on rocks in front of their new home. It occurred to them they still had no idea what to call their new world. Eve really didn't care what they called it. She had no idea what their previous world was called, so what did it matter what they called this one? It was Adam who insisted on a name. His name for the soil was earth, so he decided it would be a good name for the planet their soil came from. And so, they called their world Earth.

They filled their days with fishing, hunting, and farming their land, while making improvements to their home. Eve had picked up on some of her father's carpentry skills, so she began making small simple pieces of furniture. She had a sharp stone that served as her main cutting tool.

The time the young couple spent together did well to strengthen their bond. They became good friends, before becoming lovers. Neither of them wanted to rush things, since they had their whole lives ahead of them. It was only them, so there was no point in rushing. Taking it slowly worked out better. They gradually fell in love and were happy together.

A year had gone by when Eve realized she was pregnant. It was a happy moment for the couple because it meant humanity had been saved, although Eve was the only one who had any kind of medical training. She had to teach Adam what to do, so he'd be ready when the time came.

During her pregnancy, he took good care of her. He made sure she got plenty of rest, which was no easy task. She always wanted to be on her feet doing things, since there was so much to do. She even built a bassinet for the baby, while she was pregnant.

Months later, when she began to go into labor, Adam did just fine with delivering the baby despite his nervousness. It was a miracle all the creatures living in the forest didn't run for the hills with how Eve was screaming during childbirth. Luckily, it all worked out, and the couple had their first child. It was a boy. They named him Cain, after Adam's father.

Taking care of a baby was a lot of extra work for the young couple, but they were ready. They had it all planned out thanks to the books Eve read back on their old world. At this point, the couple came to a major decision. They wouldn't inform their offspring of their previous world. That detail would forever remain their secret. It was part of their past. This world was meant to be a fresh start for them, and for humanity. They knew any focus wasted on their past might affect their future and possibly hinder the development of this new world. Therefore, they agreed to never speak of their former world ever again, for the sake of all humankind.

In time, their son was followed by a second son, whom they named Abel. Both children would eventually grow into adulthood. During those years, Eve bore Adam many sons and daughters. Of course, it might be best not to get into too much detail on how their descendants procreated throughout those early years of humanity's growth. Therefore, this story will end here.

If any of this story seems somewhat familiar, it's purely coincidental. Then again, history does have a tendency of repeating itself. Let's hope not.

THE BEGINNING

TALES FROM THE RUINS

BONUS STORIES

TALES
FROM THE
RUINS

BONUS STORIES

A WORLD GONE MAD

Jakayla was a pretty average woman with shoulder length wavy brown hair. She had an average body. She wasn't too pretty or too smart. She didn't cook well, but she cooked well enough. Recently, she lost her job due to budget cuts, so she also wasn't too happy. She lived in an okay apartment on the second floor of a decent six-story building in a not so bad neighborhood. In her opinion, the only thing she had going for her was her wonderful husband. He was the best. The light of her life. And so tall and handsome. If not for him, she would've given up a long time ago, but he was her rock. He always got her through the tough times. He was always there for her. She loved him more than anything.

Brendon loved his wife just as much as she loved him. He cherished every moment they spent together, which wasn't a lot now that he was working longer shifts to make up for her unemployment. He didn't blame her. It wasn't her fault. Just a case of bad luck. He often felt like bad luck was all he ever got dealt, with exception to his loving wife. She was the greatest part of his life. His dream was to buy her a beautiful home in the suburbs, and then have a baby. Maybe two. He wanted a boy, first.

Today was like most days. He was at his job, working hard, and thinking about when it was time to head home. He checked the time. That was still a few hours away.

While he was out, his wife had been keeping busy. She started her day by doing the laundry. At the same time, she swept and mopped the apartment. She then placed the clothes into the dryer, before getting started on dinner. She wanted to make sure it would be ready by the time Brendon got home. He was always hungry when he got home from work. He was the only person who ever liked her cooking. She wondered if he was only being nice, not wanting to hurt her feelings. *She* didn't even like her cooking.

Once the clean clothes were folded and put away, and dinner was in the oven, she finally had a break in the day. She decided to stream the local news on her computer, while eating some strawberries. She would've preferred to have them dipped into chocolate sauce, but she was all out. After taking the first bite, she frowned. It just wasn't the same without the chocolate sauce.

Something on the news caught her attention. She thought she heard the word asteroid, but missed the first part of what was said. She listened closely to the rest of what the male reporter was announcing.

"They're saying it's nearly three miles in diameter and it could strike our planet in less than a month. The government will neither confirm nor deny this claim. They've essentially put a stop to any further talk about this probable impending asteroid. In fact, we're…"

The news broadcast was cut off abruptly, and a commercial came on. Oddly, there was several minutes of advertisements, before the news returned. When it finally came back on the air, there was a segment about an upcoming fashion show, and then it went into the weekly movie reviews. The focus had changed to entertainment. There was no other mention of the asteroid, which she found strange.

She switched off the newsfeed and played some music, while she checked on dinner.

Later, when her husband got home from work and the couple sat down at the dining table to eat, she told him about what she heard on the news.

"It was weird. The newsfeed was cut short and they never went back to it. I checked the Internet and couldn't find anything about it there either."

Brendon smirked and replied casually, "It's probably nothing to worry about. Just another near miss, which was why it wasn't too important. We get those all the time. The government has ways of blasting them to bits or pushing them away from our path. I wouldn't waste time worrying about it."

"Then why was it cut short like that?" She asked, not believing his reasoning.

"The network heads probably shut them up to avoid starting a panic over nothing. Apparently, they didn't shut them up soon enough because they got you going." He chuckled.

"Don't tease me. I was really scared," she pouted.

"Well, don't be. I promise everything will be fine." He reached out and held her hand. "By the way, thanks for having dinner ready when I got home. I was starving and this tastes so good. You always know how to make my day." He winked at her.

She smiled at him. He always knew how to make her feel better.

In time, she forgot all about the asteroid. That night, they made love and all her problems seemed to fade away. She felt blissful, as she lay in his arms. It was her favorite way to fall asleep.

A couple of weeks went by and there was no mention of the asteroid. She sat down and listened to the news, while sorting bills. She hardly paid any mind to what was streaming on her computer, until she heard the word asteroid. At once, she stopped what she was doing and focused on the screen.

"Apparently, the government was sorely mistaken. I'm pretty damn sure they regret their decision to silence us," the nerdy looking thirtysomething-year-old male astronomer declared angrily to the middle-aged female newscaster interviewing him. "Well, it won't matter now. It's too late. There's nothing that can be done to stop it. We estimate it should reach us in less than three weeks' time. And I promise, it *will* hit. Don't let the skeptics disillusion you. In fact, it's trajectory takes it right over our continent."

"Are there any tips at all on how we can avoid being in danger?" Asked the naïve and partly skeptical interviewer.

The astronomer scoffed, "Avoid? Yeah, catch the next space shuttle to another planet! This thing can't be avoided! It's three miles wide! It's a freaking planet killer!" He tried to calm himself. "There's a very strong chance none of us will be here in about a month. Even if you somehow managed to survive the impact, the devastation that will follow will leave the world in ruins. Trust me." The camera zoomed in on his face. "It's going to be chaos. You want my advice? Go home to your loved ones. Spend every last minute with them. Stop wasting your time at work or watching these stupid videos. I'll tell you something. I'm done, after today. In fact, this interview is done. Good luck. I mean, goodbye." The astronomer began walking away. "Luck won't save us," he said over his shoulder, leaving his stunned interviewer with a gaping mouth.

Finally, she turned to the camera. "Well, you heard it here."

The camera switched back to the main news anchors, who were speechless. The looks in their eyes were as if they just watched a dead man rise from the grave and began dancing.

"Planet killer?" Those were the only words that slipped from Jakayla's lips. Whether or not there was any truth to this asteroid story, the seeds of fear had been planted firmly in her mind. She was terrified. Her thoughts went to her husband, who was out there at work probably with no idea of what was going on. She hoped he'd find out and rush home to her. If they only had a few more weeks to live, she wanted to spend every second with him, rather than being home alone.

She grabbed her bag and hurried out to the market. She had a feeling it might be wise to stock up on food, just in case. When she got there, she realized others had the same idea. The market was packed with people trying to buy up all the food. It was madness. Two women were even fighting over the last deluxe pack of bacon. Someone else was filling their cart with canned foods. She bought what she could, not wanting to get into any fights with anyone. She couldn't wait to get out of there.

When she got home, she put away the groceries and began cooking dinner. She considered making less food than usual, thinking it might also be a good idea to start rationing their food. If the market was crazy today, it was only going to get worse as the weeks went by. She wasn't looking forward to another trip there.

As the day went on, she looked at the time with concern. It was an hour later than the usual time when her husband typically got home from work. He hadn't contacted her to let her know he might be late, so she immediately began to worry. She hoped he was okay.

Dinner was ready, so she lowered the heat on the stove to keep it warm.

Another hour had gone by. She was starting to panic. What if something went wrong? What if something happened to him? She became almost frantic. She paced back and forth and kept looking out of the window. It took all her strength to remain sane. She wasn't even hungry. Food could wait. Her mind was too preoccupied with his safety.

"Please, be okay," she pled with her eyes shut tight. She was visualizing his handsome face and wondering if she might never see it, again. Tears began streaming down her cheeks, just at the thought. No. She couldn't think that way. It was better to think positive. He probably just got caught up in traffic. Maybe he's having car trouble in an area with a bad signal, so he can't contact her. He might even be stuck at work. He probably forgot to let her know. No way. She knew that wasn't the case. He'd never leave her worrying like that. It wasn't in his nature to be that forgetful. Something definitely happened.

Finally, she heard his key in the door. When it opened, she launched herself at him and wrapped her arms around his neck. She didn't want to let go. He was a bit overwhelmed by the intense greeting.

"Whoa! Hey, what's wrong? Aw, were you worried about me?"

She pulled away and glared at him. "What do you think? I thought something happened to you!"

"Hey! Wait a second!" He became defensive. "Don't go getting mad at me now. It's not my fault I'm late. The roads were a nightmare. I can't believe how packed they were with cars. There was a big accident, too, which didn't help. A fuel truck crashed into a diner. It's crazy out there!"

"I know. It was the same at the market. I'm just glad you're all right. All sorts of things were going through my mind." She touched his smooth face gently. "I thought something happened to you."

"Well, I'm fine, and I'm so very happy to be home with you." He smiled at her and kissed her on the forehead. "I'm sorry I'm late. Did I already miss dinner?"

"Of course not. I waited for you. I've been keeping it warm," she finally let go of him and pointed over to the pots on the stove.

"You're the best wife in the world." He kissed her on the lips and they embraced.

As they sat at the dining table to eat their dinner, she asked, "Did you hear about the asteroid? It was on the news, again."

"Again? Now what?"

She looked disappointed. "So, you haven't heard. It's definitely coming. In a few more weeks, it should reach us. They say it's going to hit us, and that's not all. It's a planet killer." She stopped eating and waited for his reaction.

He chuckled. "You're messing with me, right?" He filled his mouth with a spoonful of rice.

"I'm dead serious, Brendon. I swear on my dead grandparents." Tears filled her eyes and he immediately knew she wasn't joking. "I'm so scared." She broke down and cried.

He stood up and bent down beside her. He put his arms around her and held her, as she cried for several minutes. He didn't know what to say. Telling her everything was going to be fine wasn't going to cut it, this time. He was starting to get worried himself.

After dinner, they checked the computer and listened to the ongoing video reports. The news of the asteroid had been spreading like wildfire all day. People everywhere were in a state of panic. This was serious business.

Brendon stayed home from work the next day. There was no way he was going to leave Jakayla in the state of mind she was in. She was too distraught. She needed him to be at home with her, so he called out sick. His boss didn't believe him, but he really didn't care what his boss believed. His wife came first. Always.

That day, he tried to keep her mind off of the asteroid. They stayed in bed and watched movies, and then took a shower together. When they were done, they made love. Afterwards, the couple did a jigsaw puzzle, which took up a good part of the day. In the evening, they had a nice quiet candlelit dinner, before making love, again.

Later, they reminisced about how they met, and then watched the first movie they ever saw together. It was a perfect romantic day.

Unfortunately, Brendon had to return to work the next day, if he wanted to keep his job. He couldn't afford not to keep it. They needed the money. The roads were hectic, just as he expected them to be. When he got to work, there weren't a lot of other people there. One person quit. Another person hadn't even bothered to show up the last two days. Suddenly, he didn't feel so bad about calling out sick. He had to pick up the slack left by those who didn't come in, so he had a hard day. It was longer than usual, too, but he was able to let his wife know he would be going home late. He even told her to eat dinner without him, this time.

Later, on his way home, the traffic was ten times worse than it had been the other day. It was practically at a standstill. He found himself looking up at the sky frequently. It went from dark to black, and he still wasn't home. The drive was taking so long. He could see the asteroid glowing in the night sky like a giant star. While it was kind of cool, but also terrifying because of the danger it foretold.

Jakayla was so happy to see him when he finally got home close to midnight. She hugged him tight and he hugged her back. At that moment, he knew he would not be going back to work. Instead, he was going to stay home with her. He wasn't even going to bother letting his boss know. Screw it.

The next two weeks weren't easy. At first, there was the thought that if the asteroid did manage to pass them by, Brendon was going to be out of a job. However, if it was going to hit their world, it meant they might all die. Needless to say, it was a depressing predicament either way.

Not to mention, it quickly became evident how the asteroid was coming closer with each passing day. During that first week when it appeared in the sky, it resembled a comet. Everyone outside kept looking up and hoping it might somehow fly past their world, barely missing them. However, by that third week the asteroid began to look more like a small moon. There was no doubt it was aimed right at them. If the government had plans to do something about it, they'd better act fast because time was rapidly running out. According to the news updates, they had less than a week to go.

These updates were becoming more and more alarming. "We repeat, a large asteroid is on a collision course with our planet," said the reporter. "If you haven't seen it, by now, it's unmistakable in the eastern sky. Take a look. It looks like a small moon, but that's no moon. This thing is massive and believe me it will change *everything* on this planet. We only have days before it reaches us. God save us all."

Jakayla was filled with terror, as she listened. She turned to her husband with tears forming in her big brown eyes. "What are we going to do?"

"I… I don't know." He was at a loss. "Maybe we can try to drive far away from here, but the roads will be congested with traffic. It has to be so much worse than before. We'd never get far enough away." He frowned. "I think we should just hunker down and stay here. Ride it out. You know?"

She turned away from him and walked toward the window. She couldn't believe that was the best idea he could come up with, but she couldn't think of anything better herself. Deep down, she knew he was right. The roads would certainly be congested. She looked down at the street. People were running around like maniacs. On the news, there had been reports of looting and rioting. Religious fanatics coerced people into suicide pacts. There were mass suicides across the globe. Some preferred to go out on their own terms. Others were using the mayhem as an excuse to create their own. No one was trying to stop them, so they were out of control. It wasn't safe to be outside. There was no escaping the asteroid. What else could they do, but stay home? She began sobbing like a baby.

Her husband took her in his arms and tried to comfort her, except he was just as scared.

Over the next couple of days, the asteroid had appeared to grow in size. It now looked larger than their moon. Every day, the sounds of violence coming from outside reminded them how it was better to stay home. There were gunshots, screams, crashing sounds, windows being broken, and people shouting at each other.

Jakayla asked Brendon, while lying in his arms in their bed, "Why do times like these always bring out the worst in people?"

"Some people are savages. Don't worry. I won't let anyone hurt you. I'll kill someone, if I have to. I don't care anymore. This is about our survival now." He was dead serious.

The next day, he barricaded their front door with heavy furniture. They had no intention of ever leaving. At the same time, no one was getting inside.

Finally, the government had a plan. They launched a nuclear weapon at the asteroid hoping to split it in half, so both pieces could end up bypassing the planet on either side. It might pass close, but their hope was that it wouldn't strike them.

All the world watched the live footage in anticipation, including Brendon and Jakayla. The flaming tail of the missile could be seen with smoke trailing behind it, as it climbed higher into the sky. And then, came the thunderous impact. It was a direct hit! The asteroid shattered into three large fragments. Unfortunately, now all three were currently heading toward the planet. However, none of them appeared to be coming toward their city anymore. Maybe they might survive this, after all.

Brendon became hopeful. He tried to convince his fearful wife that they might be able to survive. She didn't believe it. As far as she knew, they were living their final moments. She wanted to go out in his arms, so they made love all day for the next two days.

At last, that fateful day had arrived. It sounded like thunder rumbling in the sky, except the sound didn't stop. It kept rumbling causing everything to vibrate. Jakayla tucked her head into Brendon's chest and he held her tight. They hid in the bedroom closet, as if it would make a difference. The rumbling increased. Everything was shaking, until there was a huge explosion in the distance, although it sounded like the world was coming apart. Jakayla screamed into her husband's chest and he closed his eyes waiting for the inevitable to claim them.

The quake that followed lasted for nearly an entire minute, which normally isn't a lot of time, until you find yourself in the middle of one. The building shook violently, but not to the point of collapsing. Most of the buildings were essentially quake proofed long ago. It didn't stop everything from falling off the shelves. Small trinkets and glass picture frames shattered as they smashed to the floor. Outside the ground opened up in random areas, swallowing a few people unlucky enough to be out there.

When the shaking stopped, there was an eerie calmness about the silence. It was over. The world had not exploded. It was still there. The city was still standing, for the most part. As were many others. A few structures collapsed in the aftermath. Electrical towers, streetlamps, and trees fell. The destruction was different everywhere across the world. In some places, it was on a massive scale.

There were countless deaths. Thousands had been killed instantly upon impact of the sizable asteroid fragments. The shockwaves killed millions more in the regions surrounding the impact craters. The quakes and floods that followed killed so many others. The quakes also caused volcanic eruptions that spewed lava, which devastated the country sides. Clouds of black dust filled the sky, spreading darkness over the world, which would last for years. In the wake of the impacts, the human civilization on the planet had been brought to the brink of extinction in a matter of minutes.

One of the larger fragments of the asteroid struck the moon, causing it to shift its orbit. That created drastic tidal shifts on the planet, which led to tsunamis. The damaging floods drowned the coastal cities. Meanwhile, smaller fragments of the asteroid continued to rain down upon the planet crushing anything they fell on beneath the massive weight of each piece.

There were fires raging that would continue to burn, until they eventually burned themselves out. By then, entire regions were destroyed and hundreds more were dead.

Somehow, through some miracle, there were survivors. Brendon and Jakayla opened their eyes and listened. It was quiet outside, aside from a ringing car alarm. The vibrations had ceased.

"I think it's over," Brendon whispered. He pushed open the closet door and peeked out. It seemed safe, but darker than it should be. He got to his feet, and then held out his hand to help his wife up. She took his hand and stood. They exited the closet together.

Both looked to the bedroom window. The glass had completely shattered. Brendon stepped to the window to look outside. The sky was blackened with dark smoke, which blocked out the sunlight. It looked like there had been a really bad fire and the smoke was still thick in the air. The air quality wasn't very good, so he covered his mouth and nose with his t-shirt. Down on the street, he saw a crashed vehicle out front. It had knocked over a utility pole, which was now blocking the main entrance of the building. He couldn't tell if there was anyone in the driver's seat. The smoke in the air was too thick like a toxic fog, so visibility was poor. It looked like the doors of the car were closed. He peered up and down the street and saw that every window had shattered on the entire block. The building structures seemed to be intact from what he could tell. The car alarm was coming from the next block.

He wondered where all the people who were screaming earlier had gone. He figured they probably went to seek shelter from the quake and the smoke. Finally, he saw a figure walking along the sidewalk through the smoke. His instinct told him to keep out of sight, so he backed away from the window.

"What's wrong?" His wife asked. "Why is it so dark and smoky out there?"

He whispered, "Fires. I think. It's too quiet out there. I expected to see people helping each other, but the streets are mostly empty." He moved away from the window and faced his wife.

"Mostly?"

"Shh," he shushed her. "There was a guy, or something. I think he was carrying a weapon. I don't know. It's really hard to see anything. I don't think he saw me."

She became worried. "Are you sure?"

"Yeah," he lied. "Besides the front door is blocked. No one is coming inside that way."

"Our windows are wide open and we're next to the fire escape," she reminded him. There was panic in her eyes, as she whispered the words.

"I'll board it up with something, but later, after he's long gone. I don't want him to hear or see me doing it." He rubbed his hand over his head in frustration ruffling his short curly brown hair.

She stepped closer to him. "I'm scared, Brendon. What are we going to do?"

"We'll just wait, until someone comes to rescue us. First responders are going to be pretty busy for a while, but they'll get to us. In the meantime, we should be okay in here. Come on." He grabbed her hand. "Let's go to the living room." He wanted to assess the damage from the quake.

When they stepped into their living room, it was a mess. Instinctively, Jakayla began picking things up from the floor. Many items were broken. Brendon checked the barricade at the door. It was still firmly in place. He added another piece of furniture to be sure.

The couple spent the next hour cleaning up their apartment as best they could. They saw that the power had gone out, but that was to be expected. They hoped it would be restored eventually. Sadly, that would not be the case.

Later that day, Brendon removed the shelves from the wall and used them to board up both front windows. First, he made sure there was no one outside by watching the street for nearly an hour. It was still too smoky and dark to see anything clearly. The air was getting hard to breathe. He hoped it would clear up by tomorrow. He hammered the shelves into place, while Jakayla found new places for the items that had been displayed on them.

During that night, they refrained from using candles. They didn't want anyone to know they were there. Instead, they sat quietly in the dark and waited for daylight. Little did they know there would be no daylight for at least another two decades. In the meantime, they were hopeful.

They hardly slept that night out of fear and panic. Jakayla was too scared to sleep, while Brendon was too worried someone might climb up the fire escape and force their way into one of the windows. The next day was no different. Outside was completely silent. The car alarm had stopped sometime during the night, after the battery died. The eerie silence seemed a bit more calming. It also made it easier to hear what was going on outside.

Jakayla did the best she could to make them dinner without being able to cook. There was food from the refrigerator that had to be eaten soon, otherwise it would spoil. At the same time, Brendon reminded her that they needed to try and save food because there was no way to get more. Not for a while, at least. The food they had needed to last them, until help came.

Over the next few days, they rationed their food. However, they had other problems to worry about. The air quality was getting worse. The smoke had found its way into the apartment. They still had running water, but it was brown. Outside was no longer as quiet as the first couple of days. The silence had been replaced by the occasional scream or gunshot. It was disturbing. They had no idea what was going on out there with the windows boarded up. In a way, they really didn't want to know.

On the fourth day, there was a fairly noticeable aftershock from the quake. Fortunately, it only lasted a few seconds. Nothing was damaged in the apartment, but it was enough to shake them up. They spent the rest of the day huddled in each other's arms.

A week had passed since the asteroid struck. Another aftershock occurred that morning, which only shook the building slightly. There had been a few aftershocks by this time. Most of them weren't too bad. There was still no sign of emergency workers in the area. It seemed more and more evident they would never arrive. The screams and gunshots outside had become less frequent. The couple had mostly tried their best to ignore them. The smoky fog was still blocking out the daylight and making the air increasingly toxic and difficult to breathe.

More importantly, their food supplies were running out. They tried to stretch what little they had left over for as long as possible, but by the next week, they were down to mere scraps. Plus, the water had stopped running. The pipes were bone dry.

Jakayla felt frustrated and overwhelmed, as she asked, "When are they going to come for us? It's been like two weeks already. We're almost out of food." She was becoming desperate. They both were, at this point.

"I know, baby," Brendon replied. He tried to reassure her. "We need to be strong. I think we're on our own."

"For how long, though?"

He looked at her and didn't reply. He didn't know what to tell her. It made him sick to think about it, but he had a sinking feeling they were going to die in that apartment. He pulled her into his arms and caressed her. He desperately wanted to make her feel safe, but he wasn't sure he could do that anymore. *He* didn't feel safe. They were starving and filthy. It was unhealthy to breathe the air. There was no way they'd be able to survive another week without food or water, but they did have poison.

"There is one thing we could do," he suggested, almost inaudibly. He was actually thinking out loud.

She turned to face him and stared naively at him. He kissed her gently on her forehead and almost didn't want to tell her. Maybe he could just do it when she was asleep. No, he could never betray her trust. Something this significant had to be a mutual decision. He needed to give her the choice he was barely ready to make himself.

He told her about his idea, "The longer we stay here like this, the more we're going to suffer. If the air quality doesn't finish us off, starvation will. Both are dreadful ways to die, but there is something we can do to make it easier on us." She waited for him to finish. "We have poison. It'll be faster."

She swallowed nervously. Somehow, it didn't sound like it would be painless.

After some debating, they agreed to take another night to think it over.

The next day, they put on their wedding clothes. He still looked handsome in his tailored dark suit, although a bit leaner than before.

Less muscular. She was still beautiful in her white lacy gown. At least, he thought so. She had never looked more beautiful to him. He lifted her veil and kissed her lips tenderly.

"I love you, my beautiful Jakayla," he said softly. "Thank you so much for making me the happiest man in the world, these past few years. My life would've been so empty without you, but instead you made me feel rich. You gave my life meaning. I'm so very grateful for you." He touched her cheek with his trembling hand.

She hugged him hard and declared, "Oh, Brendon! I love you more than life itself. You've always been so good to me. Thank you. Thank you. Thank you. If we can't live the lives we want to live, then I will gladly go into eternity with you, as long as we're still together."

"We'll always be together," he responded, while holding her tightly. "Forever."

They cried.

Finally, when they were ready, they swallowed the poison. They laid together on their bed and held hands. It would only take a few moments before it took effect. In the meantime, they stared up at the white ceiling and reminisced about their first date. It was a beautiful summer day spent at a carnival near the beach. The rides were fun, but not as much as their first kiss on the boardwalk, while gazing at the sunset. That was pure bliss. He even won her a few prizes that day, which she still cherished. They imagined the whole thing on the ceiling, as if it were a screen showing them a movie.

Jakayla closed her eyes and smiled.

"Focus on that wonderful memory," he told her. "It was one of the best days of my life. I knew from that first moment we kissed that I would love you forever." He waited for her to respond, but she said nothing. The room was silent. He couldn't even hear her breathing anymore. Tears formed in his eyes making his vision blurry, so he closed them. "I'm so sorry." The words barely slipped from his mouth. He fought back the tears. He took a deep breath and said, "Rest in peace, baby." He squeezed her hand tight and took another drawn out breath.

In that instant, he was gone, too. There was no pain. Only sleep and eternal peace.

TOMORROW NEVER KNOWS

Twenty years ago, the world nearly came to an end when an asteroid struck. The disasters that followed decimated most of the landscape, leaving every city in ruins. Billions of people were killed, and the entire world was left under a smoky cloud of darkness that only recently subsided giving way to nearly forgotten blue skies, once more.

In the years following what became widely known as the *Big Apocalyptic Event*, small pockets of survivors were forced to seek shelter in underground bunkers, where they would remain for generations. When the food stores ran out during that first year, they had to send groups of explorers out into the dark decaying world to search for food and supplies. At the same time, they learned to reacquaint themselves with how the world had become... a harsh wasteland.

For those first few years, the toxic air quality did more harm than anything else, making it unsafe to be outside for too long. Several months ago, after the air cleared, there were still other dangers to worry about. Savage nomads roamed the lands looking to take what they needed at any cost. Wild animals also searched for food, and weren't against hunting down a human. However, the most feared threat was the alien space crafts that flew over the ruined cities at night in search of humans. They called them sky ships.

The survivors learned quickly to avoid these dangers, while going out on hunts and supply runs. They usually went out in small groups since there was safety in numbers. Some groups chose to only go out during the daylight, so they could see the dangers that were out there and either face them head on or avoid them. They agreed it was best to take chances on running into random nomads and animals, than to deal with the threat of alien sky ships.

A few other groups thought differently, opting for night missions, instead. After years of dealing with the darkness, they were used to it. They reasoned it was easier to hide in the dark from the sky ships flying overhead, while hardly having to worry about nomads, who also tended to hide at night. It was a risk they were willing to take.

This is the story of one such group of hunters, four men in particular. These brave men reside in an underground bunker with their clan, which currently has twenty-six survivors remaining. Mostly children. Their bunker is located beneath their former city, which is now a mere husk of its once former glory, littered with hundreds of abandoned buildings. It's unbelievable how drastically a city can change when it is abandoned for two decades. Being able to see it during the daytime has shed a new light on things.

In recent months, the entire city has gradually become overgrown with greenery and is beginning to resemble a garden more than a city. The plants and trees had been starving for sunlight, and now that it has returned, they are overindulging themselves and spreading like a plague across the ruins. The heavy rains that followed the return of daylight played a large role in that rapid growth spurt.

Len, Mac, Harris, and Stark made their way through the desolate junglelike cityscape in search of animals to hunt. They hoped to catch something before daybreak. Night hunts were never easy, since the animals were harder to track. However, it was far more peaceful, so the animals felt safer. All one had to do was find where they nested. Stark was pretty good at doing just that. He had a nose for these things.

"Wait." He stopped the others with his deep voice, although he tried not talking too loudly. He bent down, after smelling a familiar stench nearby. His shoulder length, shaggy, dark brown hair fell over his sleepy brown eyes when he touched the ground. He had a mustache and thick sideburns, too. He shifted his hair with his other hand and said, "Here. This is fresh." He pointed to a pile of shit. "That's deer scat." He stood up and looked around them. "It can't be far." The four men were standing in the middle of an old thoroughfare. It was fairly wide. There were small one-story buildings scattered along the left and right. Old stores and businesses mostly. Ahead, the road was long and dark, veering off to the left around a tall apartment building. "Let's keep following this trail," he suggested. "We might catch up to it."

The others agreed silently and followed him. At age twenty-nine Stark was older than his buddies, which meant he had years of experience. They trusted his instincts when it came to hunting.

As the youngest, twenty-year-old Harris trailed at the rear, watching their backs. He had shoulder length black hair and was the quietest of the group. What he lacked in experience, he made up for with his skill using a longbow. He had quick reflexes and rarely missed a shot. Len and Mac flanked Stark, keeping an eye on the buildings. They watched for nomads, just in case. On occasion, some dared to lurk around at night hoping to catch hunters and explorers off guard. These four men were far from being off guard. Each was armed with long zipguns that fired small round stone pellets. Len and Mac also carried large jagged hunting knives, while Harris kept his longbow flung over his shoulder.

Len and Mac were equals in many ways. Each was multitalented. Both men were expert fishermen and skilled hunters. Both knew how to fight well with their knives. They were best friends and were always together, so they normally trained together. Each was in his mid-twenties. In a way, it had always been a healthy competition between the two friends dating back to their childhood, which had been spent almost entirely in the bunker.

Stark was the only one of the group, who remembered how the world was before.

Len pushed his thin wireframe hand-me-down glasses up his long nose and wistfully examined the abandoned businesses along his side of the street. His long, greasy, light brown hair bordered his lean face. He saw a small museum and mused, "I wonder what kind of relics we'd find in that old place." His voice was also deep.

Mac raised an eyebrow and looked over his shoulder to what Len was talking about. He had shoulder length black hair and a full beard. When he saw the museum he responded, "I doubt we'd find anything useful. I've got a feeling it's nothing but old naked statues, dusty portraits, broken junk, and other old nonsense. Nothing we need.

That's for sure. I wouldn't worry about it." He shrugged it off with his easygoing attitude. "Let's focus on the hunt. We might actually catch something tonight."

The last two hunts by other hunting groups hadn't been very productive. These guys hoped they would have better luck. They were counting on it and their clan was counting on them.

"Right. The hunt," Len smirked. "Thanks for reminding me, Mac. I thought I was out here for a damn evening stroll. The sun returns from its hibernation and we're still messing about at night."

Mac chuckled at his friend's sarcasm.

Stark whispered back to them, "You two might want to keep it down, before your chatter scares away my deer."

Len snapped to attention, "Yes, sir, Mister Stark, sir."

Mac laughed, "Oh, it's his deer now. Excuse me."

Harris giggled, but Stark ignored their comments and continued forward. He was too focused on the hunt to goof off. That could wait, until they were back at the shelter eating venison stew.

They soon rounded the bend and came upon a dark grassy clearing near the trail, which was across from the tall building. Stark took a moment to study it wondering if the deer could be living there.

At that moment, there was a loud humming coming from the nighttime sky just over the tree line at the far end of the clearing. Stark's eyes moved upward and saw the lights. The men had been out at night enough times to know what that sound meant. No words were necessary. Instinctively, they ducked into the tall apartment building behind them and closed the door. Unfortunately, there was no way to lock it.

A dark triangular shape was suddenly hovering over the large clearing. It was about half the size of a city block. Bright lights adorned each corner of the vessel making it look like three stars descending to the ground. The ship landed, while the men peeked through the broken windows of the door. A ramp opened at the bottom of the ship and light from within the doorway pierced the darkness. Just then, two dark, muscular, bipedal figures emerged and stepped down the long ramp to the ground. The light shining down from the doorway made them into silhouettes, but from a distance they appeared humanoid.

The men watching from across the road remained silent. The last thing they wanted was to be captured by aliens. By this time, they knew seeing a sky ship usually meant you weren't going home. Not many had escaped capture. It was almost unheard of to see a sky ship actually land. It was fascinating to watch. Regardless, the men hoped these aliens weren't planning to stick around too long.

Unexpectedly, Stark sneezed. He immediately covered his mouth and nose, but still managed to make a slight noise. Mac stared at him in disbelief. Len shook his head disapprovingly, but didn't take his eyes off the aliens. He watched with dread as one of them turned toward the building where they hid.

Harris stepped away from the door and whispered, "Oh, my sweet lord. We're going to die."

Mac quickly threw his hand over Harris' mouth to shut him up, but it was too late. The dark figures were crossing the road.

Len turned to the others and issued instructions. "I got a plan, but we'll need to split up. There are two of them and they look strong. We probably won't be able to fight those blokes, but we can outsmart them. Mac. You and Harris check to see if this place has a back door. If it does, head outside and be ready. Stark, you're coming with me. We'll lead them upstairs, and then jump out of one of the second floor windows, while Mac and Harris cover our escape from outside."

Stark complained, "Are you nuts?"

"There's no time to argue," Len said. "In a second or two, they'll be coming through this door, and then all bets are off! Now, move your asses!"

Mac agreed, "Listen to what the man said." He pulled Harris by the arm and they hurried toward the rear of the lobby, where they found a back stairwell leading down to a door that led to the back of the building. Stark and Len ran up the stairs to the second floor. They pushed open an apartment door that was already ajar and hurried to the nearest window that faced the side of the building.

Len looked out of the window. The drop didn't look too bad, as long as they hung onto the ledge and dropped down. He turned to Stark and said, "You first. I got your back." He could tell Stark was about to say something, so he interrupted him. "Go! Before I leave you here to face them on your own."

Stark climbed out of the window and held onto the ledge. He let himself drop to the ground. As he got to his feet, he checked the area, but didn't see Mac or Harris. He began to panic.

Suddenly, Harris called out to him from across the street, "We're over here! Run for your life!"

Once again, Mac threw his hand over Harris' mouth. "Would you stop making so much bloody noise? Are you deliberately trying to get the two of us killed?"

Stark noticed them hiding behind a burnt car and hurried over to them. They were aiming their zip guns at the building. It turned out none of the aliens had followed them out of the rear door, which likely meant they were both heading up the stairs. Len still hadn't exited the window. They wondered what was taking him so long.

Inside the apartment, Len was aiming his zip gun at the door just as one of the aliens stepped through. He only hesitated for a second when he noticed it looked like a lizard, and then he fired his zip gun's pellet right into its face hitting it directly in the eye. It screeched and backed out of the door. It was quickly replaced by the other alien, who shot a net at Len, right before he was about to jump out of the window. The net wrapped tightly around his body and he fell to the floor, unable to move.

He shouted, "Do I look like a bloody fish to you?"

They didn't find his comment amusing, especially not the one who was still holding his eye in pain. In fact, Len didn't like the way they were staring down at him. He wondered how this hunt had gone so wrong. It was never good when the hunters become the hunted. Still, he was glad the others were able to get away. Maybe they could warn the rest of the clan. He wasn't sure what was going to happen to him, though, but he had a feeling he was going to be someone's dinner.

The other three were still waiting for him to climb out of the window. They figured maybe he was forced to hide, so they waited. They hoped he'd appear in the window, sooner or later. Either that, or he'd come swaggering out of the back door, while the aliens wasted their time climbing the six floors to the roof. It was almost funny. At least, it would be, once they saw Len exit safely. Len would've preferred that.

Instead, they saw him finally leaving the building, two minutes later, except he was being carried over the shoulder of one of the aliens. Both were walking out of the front door, which was barely visible from where they were hiding across the street. The one carrying Len took him to the sky ship, while the other one came around the corner looking for them. His yellow eyes inspected the area and focused toward the rear of the building. He waited, until he was rejoined by his companion, which didn't take long.

Mac, Harris, and Stark remained hidden behind the burnt car. They prayed the dreadful reptilian creatures would walk past the car and ignore it. Harris peeked from under the car and could see they were doing just that. For some reason, they snuck into the rear door of the building and entered.

"They went back inside," he told the others.

Stark nodded, "This is our chance to move. Come on." He didn't wait for them to respond. He stood up and ran toward the clearing. Mac and Harris hesitated, but then followed him, wondering what he was up to. They stopped when they reached the trees along the edge of the clearing.

Mac asked, "Why in the world did you choose to run closer to their sky ship, instead of further away? Are you trying to get us all captured? Between you and Howling Harris over here, it's no wonder we're still alive." He shook his head unable to believe how careless his friends were being.

Stark ignored his comment and explained, "I don't intend to leave Len in there. I feel like it's partly my fault they got him. If he went out the window first, it'd be me in there."

"Oh?" Mac was surprised. "Exactly how do you plan on rescuing him from a sky ship filled with musclebound lizard faced aliens?"

"With a little help from my friends, of course. Surely you didn't think I was planning on going in there alone. Did you? We need to do this as a team. Len never would've left us in there."

Mac felt guilty and nodded in agreement. "Yeah, you're right. We can do this. We have to… for Len. So, what's the plan?"

Stark stared back at him and frowned regretfully. "Well, I was kind of hoping *you'd* come up with a good plan. I think I'm fresh out of stupid ideas for one night."

Mac grinned and patted him on the shoulder. "I guess I can come up with something on the fly. We'd better move fast, before those two gator heads find out we're not in that building." He led the other two across the clearing toward the sky ship. They were sure to stay low to avoid being seen.

Once they reached the ramp, they hurried inside.

Stark had to practically push Harris up the ramp to keep up with Mac. Harris wasn't too keen on the idea of infiltrating an alien spaceship, even if it was to save their friend.

He asked, "What are we supposed to do if we run into one of those things?"

Mac turned back and answered in a whisper with his eyebrow raised, "We kill them."

They followed what appeared to be the main corridor toward the rear of the triangular ship. The interior of the ship was dark and humid. The walls were smooth, metallic, and moist with condensation. There was steam radiating from meter wide exhaust vents that were scattered along the outer walls every six feet. The floor was a mesh grating to help drain the water, so it could be recycled. Small red emergency runner lights lined the ceilings, making them the only light source in the winding corridor.

Mac commented, "These guys sure like it warm in here. Uh oh. Get back. I think one of them is coming." He turned back and pointed. "Quick. Let's duck into that alcove."

They did as he told them. One of the Reptillan aliens approached. It paused and flicked its tongue. Suddenly, it smelled the salty sweat of the human intruders. Its yellow eyes zeroed in on their location. Mac didn't wait for it to react. He leapt out of the shadows and jammed his long hunting knife upward into its neck. They locked eyes for an instant. The thing looked extremely angry.

"Uh oh," Mac uttered.

It reached up and grabbed him by the neck with one strong hand, lifting him several inches off the ground. Mac twisted his blade and pushed it deeper, while struggling to breathe. The creature relaxed its grip and dropped him. He backed away from it, as it fell against the wall and gradually slid to the floor.

Mac retrieved his knife and took a breath. He then beckoned for Stark to give him a hand. Together, they dragged it into the darkened alcove, hoping the body would go unnoticed. At least, until they found Len and were able to get away. The thing was clad in light body armor, making it quite heavy.

"Whew! That was a close one." Mac caught his breath, while rubbing his throat.

Stark shrugged, as he wiped his sweaty hands on his pants. "Could've been worse."

Harris complained, "We're sneaking around an alien sky ship filled with *dragon people*, looking for our friend, who they captured, *probably to eat*." He emphasized the words. "Mac almost got *strangled* by one. Who knows how many more are in here? I think this is *already* worse!"

Mac shook his head in disagreement. "My friend, this could get so much worse. Pray that we live to see another day."

"Guys, how about we just find Len and get out of here?" Stark suggested.

As if right on cue, they came across a suspicious looking door with a strange symbol on it. Mac took a chance and pushed the button to its right. The door slid sideways and opened revealing a small room with a few cages. Len was sitting inside one of them. It wasn't tall enough for him to stand.

I Stand Alone

Mac was pleased to see his best friend was still alive. "Len! Are you okay?"

"Yeah, I feel fine," he smirked. "I didn't really need any help. You know? I was just about to escape before you fellas came along, but thanks anyway. You saved me the trouble."

"Right!" Mac nodded. "Of course, you were." He laughed.

"Well, don't just stand there looking pretty. Get me out of this bloody thing."

The others searched for a key.

Len explained, "That lizard bloke hit that red switch over there on the wall to close the cage. I imagine it should open the bloody thing, too. Give it a shot."

Stark hit the switch and the cage door sprung open.

Len crawled out and got to his feet. "They took my zip gun and knife."

"Here." Harris handed him his zip gun. "I'll use the bow." He pulled it from over his shoulder to get it ready.

"Thanks, kid." Len took the weapon and checked to make sure it was loaded. Once he was satisfied, he said, "Let's get out of here, before they drag us halfway across the universe to whatever swamp pit they came from."

What they didn't know is that the other two alien hunters had returned to the sky ship, after not finding their prey. The ramp had just closed. They were preparing to depart.

The four men came face to face with the two Reptillan hunters in the corridor. There was no time to fire any of their weapons. The aliens charged at them and a fight ensued, but the close quarters made it difficult to get a shot. Harris tried to aim his arrows, but he couldn't risk hitting any of his friends.

Len broke the zip gun over the head of one Reptillan. It only pissed him off. Mac was trying to grab the other one, but the scaly skin was too slippery. It was focused on Stark, who was alternating punches at each of the two aliens.

Suddenly, they felt the ship lifting upwards. Harris lost his balance and tried grabbing onto the smooth wall with little luck. They were now in panic mode. Even if they won this fight, which was beginning to seem unlikely, the sky ship had taken off. How were they going to get off?

Harris shouted the obvious, "We gotta do something! They're taking off!"

Len shouted back, "Do we look like we're sitting on our asses having tea? How about you make yourself useful and shoot that bloody bow at these green coldblooded bastards?"

Frustrated, Harris tried to aim an arrow, again. This time, he saw a clear shot and took it. The arrow shot into one of the alien heads, right between the eyes. The thing went still and dropped to the floor. At that point, the other three were able to overpower the second one. They beat him into unconsciousness, but that wasn't good enough for Len. He grabbed Mac's knife and stabbed it several times.

The three sat on the floor huffing, as they tried to catch their breath. They each had fresh bruises on their faces.

Harris reminded them, "We don't have time to rest! We gotta get out of here!"

Len stood up with a look of determination on his face. "We need to find the pilot." The others nodded in agreement. He kept the knife, as he rushed through the corridor with his friends right behind him. He wasn't sure where he was going, but he knew it wasn't back the same way they came, so he went forward.

Soon, they passed the exit ramp. Harris looked at it and had no idea how to open it. When he turned to look, the others were gone. He had to hurry to catch up to them. They continued past the ramp, following the winding corridor, until it led them straight into the cockpit. The door was open. There were two more Reptillans sitting at the controls with their backs to them.

Stark aimed his zip gun and shot the co-pilot in the back of the head, before they were spotted. In a desperate attempt to throw them off balance, the pilot turned the sky ship drastically upward. It shot forward with a jerk. They all had to grab onto something to avoid falling. Harris went sliding back down the corridor and dropped a few arrows from his quiver.

Len was too determined to let a few fancy flying maneuvers stop him. He grabbed a nearby chair and held on tight. He had a clear view of the pilot, so he aimed and threw the knife, hitting the pilot in his shoulder. The knife went deep and was stuck in place. The pilot groaned.

The sky ship leveled out and stopped moving. The pilot desperately punched in a three digit key code on a touchpad. A small screen lit up and began flashing brightly. There was a beeping alarm echoing throughout the ship, which was annoyingly loud.

Len used the opportunity to rush toward the pilot's seat. He grabbed the knife, pulled it out of the shoulder, and slit the pilot's throat. He then pulled the body from the seat and sat down.

Mac shouted, "Quick! Try to land this thing, and shut that damn alarm off!"

"That's what I'm bloody doing, mate," Len replied. "I think." He looked over the controls and had no idea what to touch. There were so many buttons, knobs, and levers. The small eight inch rectangular screen kept flashing, which was making him nervous. It was also distracting. The alarm was growing louder and becoming deafening. The others were covering their ears. Len began pressing a bunch of buttons randomly. The sky ship made a strange mechanical noise, as the landing gear was exposed. They all froze, not knowing what made the loud noise. Len then grabbed a lever and pulled it toward him.

The sky ship suddenly dropped and went into a nose dive. All the systems seemed to shut down, except for the alarm and flashing screen. They all yelled and held on for dear life, while Len frantically tried pushing the lever back in the other direction to no avail.

Within seconds, the sky ship smashed into the ground and there was a massive explosion that flashed so brightly it's mushroom cloud could be seen from miles away. The shockwave of the crash combined with the self-destruct sequence started by the pilot spread across several city blocks and leveled the entire neighborhood, thoroughly destroying every single building in its path. The sky ship and its stowaways practically disintegrated upon impact. There was almost nothing left of them.

When the rumbling was finally over, everything fell eerily silent. There wasn't a sound in the air. All that remained of that area was a square mile of desolation and rubble with tiny bone fragments scattered throughout the debris. A large portion of the already decayed city had been completely obliterated. The rest of the night continued on as before, until the sun came up.

No one from their clan would ever know what happened to the four unlucky men. Most of the clan would eventually die out over the next few years. The remaining stragglers practically became nomads themselves, in order to survive. The last of them would eventually be killed by a lone teenage girl, who ended up in the wrong place at the wrong time.

THE HUNTING PARTY

It has been thirty years since the *Big Apocalyptic Event* shook the world and changed life for everyone. With the world in ruins, scattered groups of survivors struggle to exist. Some have remained hidden away in underground shelters, only sending out small groups to gather food and supplies.

Abram is the top hunter of his clan, as well as one of the oldest and wisest of his group. His tall muscular build also makes him the toughest. At age forty, he knew the world how it used to be, but that was a long time ago when he was only ten. Since that time, he has lived in an underground shelter for thirty years with the people, who have become his adopted family. His clan.

At least twice a month, Abram ventures out to explore the aftermath of his old world. He enjoys these little sojourns into the wild. While seeing the city ruins is depressing, it also keeps him grounded in reality. He never wants to forget what he lost. Remembering the past is his way of paying tribute to all those who died in those first years when the world was engulfed in darkness.

As the top hunter, he's taken it upon himself to train the others. It is thanks to him that many of his clan know how to hunt, fish, and fight so well. Those are his main skills and he excels at each.

His long reddish hair, full beard, fair skin, and green eyes make him look more like a Viking nomad, especially considering he even dresses like one. He prefers wearing animal skins over the typical hand-me-down clothing the other members of his clan opt to wear. He can usually be seen carrying his longbow and a big axe. Only his boots are of the old world, made from tough leather with metal buckles.

He paused from his walking to gaze up at the bright sun, basking in its gentle warmth. He still felt amazed that it had returned, after two decades of darkness. The past ten years with daylight have been so fantastic. He would never again take the sun, its light, or its warmth for granted. There was a time he thought it would never return. At least, not in his lifetime. He counted himself lucky to experience sunlight, again. Not to mention just being alive, after the devastation his world has been through.

Seth asked if he was okay, since he was taking so long just standing there. Seth was much younger and in decent shape. He had medium length, light brown, curly hair and blue eyes. He carried a long spear engraved with his personal marking, an odd S-shape that he created himself.

Beside him was his girlfriend and life partner, Abby. The two had just become life partners several weeks earlier, after falling deeply in love over a period of years. Abby had long, dark brown, wavy hair, chestnut brown eyes, and a cute nose surrounded by light freckles on her rosy cheeks. She enjoyed using a slingshot whenever they went hunting, which she kept in the back pocket of her worn faded jeans.

Abram looked at the couple and smiled. "I'm good," he answered. "Just enjoying the warm sun on this cool day is all." The temperatures had been dropping gradually over the last few weeks. Winter was coming, although they still had time to hunt and fish, before the cold became an issue of concern.

The trio continued walking along the trail through the ruined city on their way toward the water road. Each was wearing backpacks filled with rations and supplies. It was customary for anyone going out on a hunt to bring a backpack. There were plenty to choose from at the shelter. Many were left over from the original survivors who fled there, decades earlier carrying whatever belongings they could carry.

Abby asked, "What was it like when the sky was only filled with darkness?"

"It was miserable," Abram replied, as he thought back on those dreary days. "You know how we normally avoid being out here in the darkness? Well, imagine having to go out at night and dealing with the constant threat of sky ships. Not being able to see what's hiding out there in the darkest shadows." He pointed to the windows of the abandoned buildings they passed. "It was pretty scary."

Seth commented, "I have to admit, it's still a bit scary coming out here, even in the daylight. I always worry that we may run into a crazy nomad, who takes us by surprise." He eyed the darkened windows above them, and then the doorways that were dangerously closer. Instinctively, his grip tightened around his spear.

"It's okay to be scared," Abram said. "Every time we come out here, we're risking our lives. We only do it because if we don't, we'll starve. To me, that makes it worth the risk. And we all have to put in the effort, including you younger folks. There's going to come a day when Troya, Christian, Avery, and I are no longer around. You two and Evangelina are the last of our youth. You need to be capable of taking care of yourselves. That means coming out here and hunting, or fishing."

"We know," Seth agreed with a nod of his head.

Abby admitted, "Evangelina has gotten very good at hunting. I don't know if I can ever be that good." She wasn't jealous. Evangelina was like a little sister to her. She was actually proud of her skills.

So was Abram. He grinned. "Yeah, that girl is good with those knives, but don't fret. You'll find something you're good at. Just keep experimenting. You're not too bad with that slingshot."

She shrugged, "I guess, but I'm terrible with a bow."

"Hmph. Archery is not for everyone." The big man smiled.

Seth held up his spear proudly. "Which is why I use this bad boy."

Abram nodded his approval. "That's a good weapon for hunting and fishing. The only problem is once you throw it, you've got nothing. If you can't get it back, you're screwed."

"True," Seth frowned. He suddenly felt less confident about his spear.

Abram said, "This is why it's good for us to work as a team. We all have our strengths and weaknesses, but together we are stronger. Also, it doesn't hurt to carry a backup weapon."

Curious, Abby asked, "What's your weakness?"

"I can easily run out of arrows. The axe is only good at close range. If I had to fight something that was a fair distance away shooting at me, I'd be in trouble. All my muscles wouldn't save me from being shot by an arrow, or hit by a rock from a slingshot." He glanced at Seth and added, "Or from getting a spear chucked at me."

Seth nodded and felt better about his weapon.

When they reached the water road, they stopped to take in their surroundings. They each enjoyed the view of the river. However, they weren't there to fish today. They were hunting. "Real meat" needed to be on the menu, as per Troya's request. She was the clan's cook, so she was boss when it came to food. She was also the oldest of them all, which meant she had a better recollection of how the world used to be. Abram had a great deal of respect for her. She was like the clan mother.

Seth asked, "So, which way?" He looked at Abram and waited for him to answer.

Abram looked north for a long minute, and then looked south. There were smaller trails in either direction. The north led to the forest. It was a good direction for finding meat, except sometimes there were too many mongrels that way. They always traveled in packs, making them dangerous. The south was also good for hunting. They often came across deer near the southern ruins.

He looked at the ground to check for prints and saw the slightest indentation facing south. It wasn't even a full print. Considering it hadn't rained in days, the ground was dry and hard. Whatever left that partial print had to be big. That was good enough for him.

"South." He pointed.

He began walking and the others followed. As they made their way south, along the water road, they remained alert. Abram taught them not to be complacent, while hunting. There was always a chance for danger no matter where you were, whether it be the ruins or a trail passing through the woods. No place beyond the shelter was safe. It was important to remember that fact.

They walked south for several minutes, until the trail gradually veered away from the river, which meant they were getting closer to the southern ruins. After a few more minutes of walking, the trees began to part opening up to a wider trail. The ruins ahead were now visible. Abram always described the southern ruins like the broken fingers of a hand pointed upward. That's pretty much how it looked.

Abram found another partial print in the dirt. He bent down to examine it. He wasn't quite sure what he was tracking, yet, but it was big and heavy. He hoped it was some kind of cattle. It had been years since he last ate beef. Maybe even a fat pig. Pork would also be great.

The three hunters pressed on. At last, they reached the southern ruins. The trail continued into what had once been a main street long ago. Now it was mostly overgrown with weeds and grass. Even the buildings had grass growing within. Vines latched onto the walls and spread across like spider webs, only they climbed all the way up to the rooftops. Some buildings even had trees on top. It was surreal.

Abram looked at the many large entrances to the vacant buildings and all of the broken windows at the ground level. Whatever animal they were tracking could be hiding inside any one of those structures, or behind them. Some of the buildings were much taller than the ones at the ruins closer to their shelter. The southern ruins were definitely larger. That also meant there was a higher potential for danger.

The group stood silent momentarily. They listened to their surroundings for any sign of their prey, but all they heard was the sound of birds chirping from their high perches. For a moment, Abram thought about shooting one with an arrow. It would certainly be easy enough. He saw so many. However, he still had beef and pork on his mind. Birds would be good as a last resort, in case it got too late. It was still early in the afternoon, so there was time.

They cautiously moved forward along the old cracked street passing between tall empty buildings. They watched everywhere around them, while listening to every single sound. Seth and Abby both felt nervous being there, although they had been there before. There was just something about the southern ruins that made it seem like the buildings were closing in on them. Evangelina's father, Christian, always felt like that old city was uninviting and they were unwelcomed. There were so many places for someone to hide amongst the destroyed structures. It always made them feel vulnerable.

Abram led the way, as they attentively peeked into the different buildings. He held his bow and arrow ready to strike. Seth kept his spear ready to stab. Abby had her slingshot in her hand with a large stone to use as ammunition. It wasn't much, but she was good at it, as Abram said. His compliment gave her a small boost in her confidence.

She felt like the whole process of peeking into the buildings one at a time was becoming tedious. Fearing it would take too long, she took it upon herself to peek into a few as well. She stayed close to Seth. Well, a few feet apart from him. Not too far.

He saw what she was doing and began doing the same. He tried not to trail too far behind Abram, who didn't seem to notice how the distance between them all had gradually begun to grow. He was too focused on finding beef and pork. By the time he finally glanced back at the others, he didn't see Abby.

"Where's Abby?" He inquired. He relaxed his bow.

Seth turned and was about to say she's right behind him, but he saw she wasn't. Suddenly, they heard the sound of agonizing screams coming from a nearby building back where they came from. It practically sounded like she was being torn apart.

Abram hesitated, reluctant to rush into an unknown situation. He immediately assumed it might be whatever large animal they were tracking, only it was deadlier than he expected. Maybe it was a bear or a mountain lion. Seth, on the other hand, didn't think twice. He rushed straight toward the sound without thinking of his own safety. His mind was only on his girlfriend. He didn't want her to suffer a second longer than necessary.

"Abby!" He shouted, as he tore through the doorway of the building, where the sounds came from. By this time, the screaming had stopped. Abram caught up and grabbed him by the shoulder. He tried to stop him from going in too far. There was a foul stench coming from within.

"Wait! We need to be careful," Abram warned.

Seth hesitated only for a moment, but then entered. As soon as he did, he spotted her body on the floor in a pool of blood behind an overturned empty vending machine. Her arm was barely connected by its socket. Her chest had been ripped open. She looked like she was missing an ear along with part of her scalp. There was no question she was dead.

"Abby!" He hurried to her side, but then stopped in his tracks when he heard a low growl coming from deep within the shadowy recess of the lobby. It was too dark to see anything that far.

Abram heard it, too. He began pulling Seth back toward the doorway. He had to use force, since Seth was frozen in place. "Come on. It's not safe in here."

"B-but what about Abby?" He was thinking about her, but his eyes were searching the darkness for whatever growled.

"Unless you want to end up lying next to her, you need to use your brain, kid. Come back out here toward the light. Let's do this right."

Seth allowed himself to be pulled back outside. For a split second, he could've sworn he saw a tall shadowy figure moving around in the darkness. He swallowed nervously. Before he could say anything to Abram, he felt him slap his shoulder hard to get his attention. He looked over his shoulder and saw they weren't alone. He turned around and came face to face with five other humans, who were standing just outside of the building in the middle of the trail.

There were three men and two women. They weren't dressed like typical nomads. Their clothing looked civilized. Three of them were armed with bows, while another held a large metal pipe.

Abram asked feeling defensive, "Who are you people and what do you want?"

They never got a chance to answer.

Suddenly, there was a tremendous howling roar coming from within the building, followed by loud crashing noises. Seth turned back around and saw something large charging at them. Abram yanked him back so hard that he fell on his ass. Abram dragged him out of the way, just in time. Within seconds a huge sasquatch covered in long black mangy hair came bursting from the building.

Seth screamed, "Holy shit!"

The sasquatch went for the other group, who stood out in the open. It snatched up one of the unsuspecting females as if she were a ragdoll, and then tossed her across the street causing her to smash into the wall of a building. She died instantly.

Seth got to his feet and threw his spear as hard as he could. It struck the sasquatch in the upper back. It turned and snarled at him, before yanking out the spear and snapping it in two like a toothpick. It charged at the group of humans, who quickly ran around the corner of the nearest building. They found themselves in a wider area that had more obstacles, so there was room to fight and take cover. There was an old rusted metal dumpster, a tall metal lamppost wrapped in vines, a small cluster of trees, and a car with no wheels. It seemed like a good place to make a stand.

They all knew even if they spread out and ran off in different directions, some of them were going to die. At least, this way, they could work together and try fighting the monstrosity. Maybe together they'd have a chance. The thing stood just over ten feet tall, and was about three feet wide at the chest. Just one hand was the size of a dinner tray.

This was going to be a fight for their lives. Each person took up a position and those with arrows began shooting it. Abram had pulled Seth with him behind the car. He shot one arrow hitting the monster in the neck. It kicked the car with such force that both Abram and Seth were knocked over.

It pushed through the trees and reached for the other female, who was about to shoot an arrow. It grabbed her by the waist and literally tore her in half. The male holding the pipe got in close and struck it with two hard swings. Just as he went for a third, the sasquatch grabbed his arm and lifted him in the air. It took a huge bite from his face, and then swung him and tossed him like a toy. His arm came clean off.

The sasquatch shoved the car to the side with ease, just as Abram was getting back to his feet. It clawed him in the chest lifting him in the air and knocking him back to the ground. Seth tried to crawl away, but it grabbed him by the leg, held him up and took a bite out of his thigh. It then dropped him and went after one of the other males.

One guy must've felt particularly brave because he stood in the dumpster and shot two arrows at once, which merely bounced off the sasquatch's back. It turned and grabbed his bow from his hand taking a few fingers with it. It then flipped the dumpster on its side. The guy rolled out holding his hand in pain, but it wasn't over for him, yet. It grabbed him by the back of the neck and squeezed. His throat was crushed. It then slammed that body to the ground hard, before picking him up, again, and tossing him at his friend.

The sasquatch approached that guy and clawed his face to the bone, before taking a bite out of his shoulder. He had been the last of that group. All five of them were dead.

Seth was still trying desperately to crawl away, but the sasquatch stomped on his back breaking his spine. It then kicked him several feet away. It went toward him and lifted him up by the leg it had bitten. It took another bite. This time, from the calf of the same leg. Seth barely screamed. He was so weak from the pain. He soon fainted. The sasquatch lost interest in him and tossed him across the street.

Abram struggled to get back to his feet. He noticed his bow was broken, although he still had his axe. It was just him. He was the last one left. The sasquatch knew it, too. It was coming toward him. Abram stood up and brandished his axe. He let out a vicious battle cry that made the sasquatch hesitate.

For an uncomfortably long moment, the sasquatch stared into his eyes with blood dripping from its teeth. It snarled at him and made fists with its giant hands. Abram knew he was about to die.

From out of the blue, there was a loud howling roar. It came from behind him. Even the sasquatch looked surprise. Abram managed to turn and almost dropped to his knees when he saw another sasquatch. This one was covered with long shaggy brown hair.

"Oh, great," he grumbled.

As if one wasn't already bad enough, now he had another one to worry about. They were probably going to fight over his corpse to decide on who gets to eat him. He knew this was a fight he wasn't going to survive, but he planned to go out swinging. He held his axe firmly as all three stood facing each other.

The black sasquatch definitely didn't look happy when the brown one showed up. It became even more aggressive than before. It grabbed a fallen tree to use as a weapon and roared at the sky. The other one roared back and lifted the dumpster. It held it high for a second, before tossing it at the black one. The black one was too slow to move out of the way and the dumpster hit it on the leg. It was injured. The brown one hurried forward and pounced on it. At the last second, the black one swung the tree and struck it.

Abram was surprised. It was as if they had forgotten all about him. For a moment, he considered using the opportunity to flee, but then he looked at Seth's broken body and he thought about sweet Abby's corpse, which was still in the building. Then there were the other five, who were lying all around him. He hated leaving them all like that. It was against his beliefs.

He decided to try helping the brown sasquatch. He wasn't sure if any good would come from it, aside from there being one less sasquatch to focus on. He found another bow and began shooting arrows at the sasquatch. The brown one turned angrily and faced him. He hoped it didn't think he was aiming at him, too. He dropped the bow and raised his hands to show he wasn't a threat.

The black sasquatch used his uninjured leg to kick the brown one away, while it was distracted. It got to its feet and brought the tree down on the brown one. It looked like it was even a challenge for the brown one, who was slightly smaller. Probably younger, too.

Abram had to help turn the tables, so the brown one could gain the upper hand. He went behind the car and found the metal pipe. He picked it up and shouted at the black sasquatch.

"Hey! Over here! You big ugly bastard!" He regretted his actions, as soon as he did it.

The black sasquatch began lumbering toward him. Abram waited until it got close enough, and then launched his axe at its chest. It made contact and stuck. He then held up the pipe ready to fight. The black sasquatch howled and pulled the axe free, tossing it aside.

The brown sasquatch had managed to pick up one of the other fallen trees. It swung it hard at the black sasquatch knocking it in the back of the head. The force caused it to bend over. Abram swung his pipe downward hitting it on the back of the head, again. It dropped to its knees.

The brown sasquatch rushed forward and began beating it in the back with the tree. Abram retrieved his axe and felt brave enough to move closer. He swung the axe at the black sasquatch's hand, which was on the ground. He chopped off two large fingers. The sasquatch howled in pain, but then it moved unexpectedly fast. It shifted its body and swung with its other arm catching Abram in the chest with its big claws, again. Once more, he was lifted in the air and knocked back. The axe flew from his hand.

The brown sasquatch jumped on the back of the black one and bit into its neck, tearing out a huge chunk of meat. The black one twisted its body and tried to push the brown one off, but it was off balance. It fell down, as the brown one straddled it. The brown one began pounding it in the face with both hands. It pummeled its face repeatedly with punches for nearly a minute. Eventually, the brown one grew weary and had to stop to rest.

It looked down at the black one, whose face was covered in blood. It picked up the pipe and stabbed it into one of its eyes. The black sasquatch went limp.

The brown one turned and saw Abram was still lying on the ground. It walked off to one of the buildings and dropped down with its back against the wall. It was seated in a position, so it could see Abram. It took the time to rest. It watched both Abram and the black sasquatch. None of them moved.

Several minutes went by. Abram began to stir. He groaned from the pain. There was blood covering his chest. He was also bleeding from his nose from when he was thrown. It felt like he had a few broken bones, as well. It hurt too much to move. Still, he had to try. First, he spit out a tooth.

He noticed the black sasquatch appeared to be dead, considering it wasn't moving and the pipe was lodged into its eye, standing upright. Meanwhile, Abram was still struggling to stand. It wasn't easy and it hurt like hell. Instead, he managed to crawl toward the dead sasquatch and used the pipe to help himself get back to his feet. He then pulled the pipe free, so he could use it to help himself walk.

That's when he noticed the brown sasquatch was seated nearby, watching him. He stiffened, and then closed his eyes. He waited for what was surely to come next. He was about to get thrashed. He lacked the strength to keep fighting, so he was ready to give up. Hopefully, it would be a quick death.

After a few seconds, Abram opened his eyes. He was still alive. When he looked, the brown sasquatch was still sitting there. Watching him. They stared at each other for a few seconds, until Abram turned away. The fight was over. It wasn't going to kill him for whatever reason. Not yet at least.

Good. It gave him time to pay his respects to the dead. It was a struggle, but he gradually began collecting all of the dead. One by one, he painstakingly dragged their battered corpses and placed them in a neat pile near the closest building. He made sure to gather all of their body parts, as well, so each body would be complete. It was a grueling process, especially considering how much pain he felt from his injuries. He had also lost a lot of blood and hadn't bothered to tend to those wounds.

At last, he was nearly done with his self-appointed task. There was only one left. Abby.

Her mangled body was the farthest away. He had to go around the corner to retrieve her remains. The brown sasquatch stood up and followed him, wanting to keep him in sight. It watched curiously, as he dragged the girl's body from the building all the way back to the pile. He had to keep stopping to rest. It took every ounce of strength he had left to place her on top.

When he was done, his body was completely drained. He couldn't go on anymore. He dropped to his knees. He could feel his breath leaving his body. He stayed there on his knees for a long time, unable to move.

The brown sasquatch looked on with interest from nearby. It was fascinated by the strange human ritual.

In Abram's mind there was another battle being fought. He wanted to get back to his feet, find his backpack, and use his matches to burn the bodies. Burning them seemed appropriate, if he couldn't bury them. Unfortunately, his body wouldn't allow him to move anymore. It was done. Every system was slowly shutting down. His heart beat slowed to a near crawl and his vision became foggy.

He closed his eyes. Unless they were already closed. He wasn't quite sure. It was hard to tell. He felt so numb, as if all the pain had gone away. For a moment, he didn't know where he was or what he was doing. He felt lightheaded, and could feel himself slipping away. He was dying.

There was a fleeting moment of disappointment because he never got a chance to find out who the other people were. Had they been from a clan based out of the southern ruins? If so, was it a large group, or was it just them? While he really wanted to know, he realized it didn't matter anymore. Nothing mattered now.

The brown sasquatch watched him fall flat on his face. It expected him to get back up, but he didn't move. He was gone. It moved closer and stood over his body. For a while, it just watched him. It looked at the pile of human corpses with fascination, and then looked back down at Abram. Finally, it bent over and gently picked him up, cradling the body in its arms. It placed him beside Abby, and then stepped away.

After a while, it turned away and walked toward the dead black sasquatch. It bent over picked up the detached fingers. It ate each one whole. Next, it jammed its own fingers deep into each eye socket of the hairy black corpse. Once it had a good grip on the skull, it slowly dragged the body away.

It walked for a very long distance, until it was far from the ruins and deep in the woods. By this time, it was getting dark. It had dragged the body of the black sasquatch the entire way from its skull.

Finally, it released its grip on the corpse and sat down on a rock to rest.

When it was done resting, it lifted up the limp muscular black arm and began biting into it. It took bite after bite, chewing, and swallowing each portion. It took its time eating its large meal. It kept eating over the next two hours, until there was nothing left. It even dined on the bones, crunching and grinding them into powder with its powerful jaws. By the time it was done, there was no trace of the other sasquatch.

The brown sasquatch sat there and rested for another hour, in an attempt to digest some of its meal.

It was nighttime when it finally stood up, ready to move on. First, it turned up toward the stars and let out a dreadful long howl. The sound echoed throughout the woods and reached the southern ruins, but there was no one there to hear it.

THE MEEK SHALL INHERIT THE WORLD

Eons ago, during the time before humans, there was the sasquatch. When the creators from above planted the seeds of life on the planet, the sasquatch was among the earliest bipedal species. However, it became the failed experiment because it did not evolve fast enough. The sasquatch was content living a primitive lifestyle amongst the wild. And so came the birth of humanity.

The sasquatch was spared and remained as part of the wildlife that would share the world with humanity. When the humans evolved they quickly proved to be amongst the most intelligent species on the planet. Humanity eventually conquered the world, taking it little by little. They built villages, which grew into towns, and then became great cities. Governments were established and countries were formed. Humanity had become the prime species.

Meanwhile, the sasquatch had withdrawn from the rest of the world. Rather than share the world with humanity, it hid away and chose to remain invisible. Its kind lived in the wild and were careful to leave no trace of their existence. They did not build villages. Instead, most of them lived nomadic lifestyles keeping to themselves. If one died, it was eaten by the others to leave no trace behind for humans to find. They largely feared humans because humans killed everything. They ate anything. They conquered all.

A young sasquatch learned early on to avoid humanity, at all costs. Its life depended on it. There was no telling what would happen, if humans got a hold of a sasquatch, especially a youth. Perhaps, it would be placed in a zoo. There would surely be experiments performed on it. Of course, there was also the threat of death. Humans would certainly kill the sasquatch because it represented a threat to its existence and its environment. Maybe they'd even eat the sasquatch. If they liked the taste of its meat, they would hunt the sasquatch into extinction. They would likely hunt the sasquatch, even if they didn't like the taste. They would do it out of fear, or to claim trophies, such as teeth, skins, skeletons, and heads to mount onto their walls. It was the human way.

Therefore, the sasquatch would choose not to interact with humans, if possible. It would learn to stay far away from humanity. On occasion, a sasquatch might become curious and want to take a peek at the humans. Of course, doing so was extremely risky for any sasquatch, so it did not happen often. There were also times when a sasquatch was spotted by humans. In these rare instances, the sasquatch would usually run off and hide, before more humans arrived. One human was dangerous enough, but a group of humans could prove deadly. Very few sasquatches were bold enough to stand up to a human, even though they were so much smaller. It was widely known that humans tended to carry powerful weapons that could bring down even the mightiest sasquatch in an instant.

One fateful day, the creators from above became extremely angry at humanity. As a show of their great strength, they threw down enormous rocks from the sky at the human civilizations destroying most of them. As if that weren't enough, nature had also grown furious with humanity for their lack of respect. The world shook violently, volcanoes spat forth their lava, and the oceans beat down on the coastal cities drowning thousands of humans. By the end, humanity was nearly erased from the planet.

The sasquatch did not truly understand what humanity could've possibly done to anger the creators from above in such a way that they would unleash their wrath upon the world, leaving it under a shroud of darkness many years to follow.

Not long afterward, the last of humanity took to hiding in the ground like frightened rodents. The great prime species had fallen. They had been harshly punished and reduced to the same level as every other creature on the planet.

The sasquatch saw this as an opportunity for its species to emerge from their hiding places. There was no need to avoid humanity as much as before. The humans had been humbled and lost much of their strength. They had grown weak. It was time for the sasquatch to spread out and claim the land.

One such brown sasquatch inhabited the woods near the ruins of a once great human city for a long time. With the fall of humanity, it roamed around the darkness for too long, but did not like the air for it had grown foul. The brown sasquatch chose to remain hidden in the safety of its cave. It howled at the creators from above demanding they give back the sun and blue skies, but they did not listen.

The brown sasquatch and all its kind continued to howl up at the creators from above, but for so long they were ignored. That is until a miracle occurred. The creators from above finally listened to the sasquatch and took pity on its kind. They returned the warm sun and fabulous blue skies, along with the clouds and daylight. There would still be darkness, but only at night, as it should be. Even the air was better than it had been for far too long.

At long last, the brown sasquatch felt brave enough to roam the lands, once more. For a while, it was content with the tranquility of the rolling hills and lush forests. There was more than enough food to keep it fed for a lifetime.

But then it remembered, humanity was nearly extinct. There was no reason to live a limited life, as before. And so, it eventually wandered closer to the great ruined city. It became curious at the sight of the large vacant spires stabbing upward. It gradually ventured closer and ultimately into the ruins. After the fall of humanity, the city had been abandoned. In that time, it was nature who reclaimed the land. It was time for the sasquatch to take it.

For a long time, the brown sasquatch explored the city, moving about vigilantly, in case humans decided to return. Naturally, they had. It seemed there was no getting rid of them. The brown sasquatch stayed out of sight. It noticed there was a tribe of human hunters that stalked the ruins in search of food, but they only did so during the daylight. For some reason, they feared the darkness. Perhaps, they had enough of it. The brown sasquatch decided to watch the humans, rather than interact with them. This was the old way of things, so it's what seemed right.

In time, the brown sasquatch became fascinated by the small tribe of humans. In a way, they became a form of entertainment for it. Sometimes, they scavenged through the old piles of wreckage from the old city. Other times, they only sought to hunt deer and birds. They always carried around their little sticks to defend themselves.

Unfortunately, there came a time when the brown sasquatch would no longer be able to enjoy its entertainment. It seemed a larger black sasquatch had appeared in the woods from the west. At first, the brown one was willing to share its territory with this newcomer. It had been so long since it had seen another of its kind. Besides, there were plenty of deer to hunt for the both of them, even with the added competition from the humans. The woods were vast and endless.

However, the black one was greedy. It wanted the entire territory, including the ruined human city for itself. It viciously chased the brown one away. The brown one did not wish to fight another of its kind. It did not understand why they could not simply share the land. After all, it was enormous and plentiful.

When the brown sasquatch tried to return sometime later, it was attacked with boulders and was almost injured. It nearly got crushed by two large ones that had been thrown by the black sasquatch. The brown one fled and decided to stay away for its own safety. It knew the black one was much stronger.

Sadly, after a while, the brown sasquatch became lonely. It longed to see the human tribe. It had come to enjoy watching their exploits. Now, there was nothing to look upon but the same trees, water, rocks, and sky overhead, which made the brown sasquatch upset. It wasn't sure why it gave in to the black one's greed. It was unfair. It had claimed the land, first. The brown sasquatch became outraged. It decided it was time to reclaim its territory. This time, it was ready to end the life of the black one, if necessary.

The black sasquatch had made its den in an old hotel lobby within the great city's ruins. The lobby was large and deep. It was also very dark, which was exactly how the black sasquatch preferred it. For many days and nights, it stayed within its den isolated from the world.

When it smelled a group of humans nearby, it became irritated. It wanted to be left alone. Yet, there were humans outside carrying sticks, while hunting on sasquatch land. They were also making too much noise with their mouths.

The black sasquatch was smart. It used the shadows of the darkened lobby to hide itself. As soon as one of the humans got too close, the black sasquatch snatched it up and tore into its flesh. The frail human screamed, until the black sasquatch silenced it forever.

It thought that would be enough to scare the other humans away, so it could return to its peaceful slumber. Instead, more humans arrived, as usual. The black sasquatch became furious. The audacity of these humans to intrude upon its lair. The black sasquatch would teach them it was a mistake for them to ever return to the city they discarded like trash. It attacked them with such vicious ferocity that they didn't stand a chance. They tried hitting it with their sticks, but it ripped them apart. It took bites out of some and left deep claw marks in others. They tried to hide behind their hard creations. The black sasquatch tossed each aside and easily grabbed them. It slaughtered all but one.

The last one was bold. It was a strange red hairy human warrior dressed in animal skins. It seemed reasonably strong and fearless for its kind. It had used different weapons to fight. Not just sticks, but a sharp claw thing. When it realized it was the last of its kind, it dared to challenge the black sasquatch with its little claw thing.

That's when the brown sasquatch showed up. It had also chosen to return, after being chased away twice already. This time, it looked ready to fight.

The black sasquatch turned its focus on its old opponent, instead. It practically forgot about the red hairy human. The human was insignificant, compared to the reckless brown sasquatch. The black one knew it would tear it apart with ease. It grabbed a fallen tree, which it would use to beat some sense into the other one. It then roared up at the creators from above for sending the brown sasquatch back at a bad time.

The brown sasquatch roared back and picked up a large human creation and threw it at the black one. The large thing struck the black one on the leg injuring it. The brown one then took advantage and leapt onto the black one, but the black one swung the tree at the last possible second hitting the brown one.

They both fought savagely. This was going to be a fight to the death.

Unexpectedly, the red hairy human intervened by throwing his little sticks at them. It reminded the black sasquatch of its challenge. The black sasquatch would oblige, but first it used the distraction to kick the brown one away. The black one stood up and smashed the tree down on the brown one.

Again, the red hairy man issued a challenge to the black sasquatch. This time, he was hiding behind one of the large human creations and brandishing a longer stick. The black sasquatch was fed up with the red hairy human. It decided once it rendered the human useless, it would go back to beating on the brown sasquatch.

However, in a turn of events the brown sasquatch and red hairy human worked together. They both attacked the black sasquatch. First, the red hairy human threw his claw thing at the black sasquatch's chest. It howled in pain and yanked the weapon free, tossing it aside. At that point, the brown sasquatch attacked the black one from behind using another tree, while the human struck it with its stick. The black sasquatch had fallen to its knees. That's when the human retrieved the claw thing and used it to remove two fingers from the black sasquatch's hand.

Again, the black sasquatch howled in pain. It lashed out at the red hairy human with its claws and tossed the human away.

The brown sasquatch then jumped onto the back of the black sasquatch and bit into its neck, tearing out a huge chunk of flesh. The black one twisted its body around, while trying to push the brown one off, but it was off balance and fell down. The brown one quickly straddled it and began pounding its face with both hands repeatedly.

When the brown sasquatch grew tired, it stopped to rest. By this time, the black one was covered in blood. The brown one grabbed the red hairy human's stick and plunged it into the black one's eye. The black sasquatch's long life had finally come to an end.

The brown sasquatch propped itself against the wall of a building to rest. It was exhausted from fighting. While it rested, it did not take its eyes off of the black one, just in case it surprised it by coming back to continue the fight. It seemed unlikely. The brown sasquatch also watch the red hairy human, who was lying nearby. Was it also dead?

A long moment later, the red hairy human began to move. It made grunting sounds from its mouth. It was barely able to move, and appeared too badly injured to stand on its own. Rather than rest, it insisted on moving. The brown sasquatch watched with interest, as it crawled over the land on its belly toward the lifeless body of the black sasquatch. The red hairy human grabbed the stick from its eye and used it to help itself stand. It then removed the stick and used it as a third leg to walk. Humans were simply amazing with their relentless resourcefulness.

Next, the red hairy human did something odd. It began to drag its dead to one area, one at a time. It stacked them into a neat pile, making sure to include even the small pieces that were torn off by the black sasquatch. This tremendous effort drained all of the remaining energy from the red hairy human because it dropped down to its knees, where it remained for a while, before falling flat on its face.

The brown sasquatch stood up and walked over toward the dead humans. It looked down at the red hairy one. It appeared to be dead, as well. The brown sasquatch lifted up the limp body and placed it onto the pile. It seemed appropriate.

It turned away and walked over to the black sasquatch, which still appeared to be dead. It bent over and picked up the severed fingers. It began eating the pair. The bones were easily crushed by its jaws. Once each finger had been devoured, it stabbed its strong fingers into the black one's eye sockets. It grabbed a hold of its skull and began dragging it away.

The brown sasquatch grudgingly dragged the black one's bulky body through the ruined city streets, and out into the woods. It continued dragging the body over grass, dirt, and stone through the woods for over an hour. When it finally got far outside of its territory, it stopped.

By this time, it was nearly dark out. The brown sasquatch let go of the skull and breathed deeply. It felt so tired. It sniffed the air around it to make sure they were alone. There were many scents in the air, but none were human.

Once it was satisfied there was no one around, it sat down on a large rock to rest. It felt so good to sit down. Dragging the heavy corpse such a great distance took a lot of effort, not to mention it was still tired from the fight, which had been brutal.

After several minutes of resting, it grabbed the black muscular arm of the corpse, lifted it up, and bit into it, taking out a big chunk. It began to eat, piece by piece. It had been a longtime tradition for a sasquatch to eat its dead. There could be no evidence left behind of their existence, even though it really didn't matter anymore, since there were a lot less humans left. It was how things were always done. There was no other way.

The brown sasquatch was no fool. It had a feeling there might be other human tribes hiding out there somewhere waiting for their time to emerge from their hibernation. Humans were too persistent to know when their time had passed. They could also be cruel and vicious hunters, and even greedier than the black sasquatch. They would want all the land for themselves, as always. If they saw a dead sasquatch, they would think the land was available for the taking.

It was not. It belonged to the brown sasquatch. Now that the black one was out of the way, the brown one could return to its territory unchallenged. Even the humans were gone.

The brown sasquatch made sure to eat every bit of the black one's remains. No matter how long it took. It took its time chewing and swallowing each mouthful. At first, it enjoyed the hearty meal, but after eating for two hours, it was full.

When it was finally done, it sat there on the rock beneath the stars. It needed to rest for a while, so it could digest some of the food, at least. It remained there for another hour, before it was ready to move on. It would return to its territory, where it would stay. As it stood up, it still felt so full. It became angry at all humankind because it had to eat so much. It was their fault.

It glared up at the nighttime sky and unleashed a powerfully long howl, which echoed throughout the entire wooded region. The sound even reached the ruins of the great city about two miles away.

Days later, the brown sasquatch wandered through the ruins. As before, it walked cautiously, half expecting to see more humans. However, there were none. It wondered where they were hiding. Surely, there had to be more humans out there somewhere. Each day, it cautiously searched the ruins. It was always the same. There were no signs of living humans. Only the things they left behind long ago.

As the days turned to weeks, and the weeks turned to months, it eventually surmised there were no humans left. The tribe was gone and there were no others to replace them. If there were, they would have come by now. The land finally belonged solely to the brown sasquatch, as it should. It howled up at the creators from above to thank them for this triumph.

In time, it gradually began to let its guard down. It had come to enjoy roaming through the city ruins freely, for quite some time. However, the serenity would not last.

After spending hours looking for deer and finding none, it returned to the ruins. That's when it finally smelled another human. The scent seemed to linger in the air, although the human was already gone. Still, the brown sasquatch searched the area. It found no one. Only traces of a scent.

Over the next few weeks, it was the same. The brown sasquatch would smell the same human scent, but it was always too late. The human would be nowhere to be found. Who was this human and why did it keep coming back to these ruins? It did not belong here. Where did it come from? The brown sasquatch became frustrated. Was this human trying to claim the ruins for itself? That was unacceptable. The brown sasquatch would find that human and scare it away, or kill it, if necessary.

One day, after hunting in the woods for deer, it returned to the ruins to dine on the nice big buck it caught. It had taken shelter within one of the buildings because it noticed the sky had darkened. It took its time eating the deer. There was no need to rush.

Later that night, it rained heavily. It was a thunderstorm. Outside, thunder shook the ground, while flashes of lightning turned the night into day several seconds at a time. The brown sasquatch easily fell asleep to the soothing sound of the steady rainfall.

When it woke up the next morning, the rain had already stopped. It left the building and instantly noticed the familiar scent of human flesh in the air. It was that same human it kept smelling, but this time the scent was strong. The brown sasquatch searched everywhere, but could not find the human. It tossed objects aside during its search thinking maybe it was hiding beneath something.

Its persistence paid off. The smell of that human was particularly strong near one of the nearby multistory buildings. The brown sasquatch ducked, as it entered through the small opening near the ground. At last, it saw the human! It was a small one, but not a child. The small human saw it, too, and made a sound through its mouth. The brown sasquatch roared loudly to scare it away and showed its fangs to let the small human know it meant business.

They stared at one another briefly, before the small human turned to run. However, instead of leaving the structure, it went up the stairs deeper into the building. The brown sasquatch became annoyed at its defiance. It wasn't in the mood to squeeze through small spaces to get to that small human, but it might have to do so. It easily bounded up the steps after the small human and stopped at the next level, where it heard something slam shut mere seconds earlier. It sniffed the air and knew the small human was hiding behind the closed door.

Was it trying to lead the brown sasquatch into a trap?

The brown sasquatch took a chance and smashed through the door, breaking it into several pieces that went flying across the room. The small human flinched from its position near a small opening in the wall. When the brown sasquatch spotted it, they locked eyes.

Was the small human thing actually daring to issue a challenge? The sasquatch was impressed by its bravery, unless the fear it showed earlier was only a trick. This small human revealed its claws and took a battle stance. The brown sasquatch was honored to accept the challenge and snarled.

As a show of its strength, it tossed a wooden human creation across the room, before letting out another roar. It then heaved its large chest and tightened its fists, ready to fight. It studied the small human for any reactions, but that small human did not move. It valiantly stood its ground near the opening in the wall.

However, it was another trick. The small human deliberately led the brown sasquatch toward the small opening, where it stepped out of the way at the last second, and then leapt onto the brown sasquatch's back, attacking it with ferocity. The brown sasquatch fell far down with this small human riding upon its back.

That's when it stole the gift of sight using its sharp claws. The brown sasquatch realized the small human was actually a brave warrior just like the red hairy one with animal skins from the distant past. The brown sasquatch slammed hard into the ground. The fall stunned it, but that was not nearly as bad as the loss of sight. Everything went black. The darkness had returned, only worse than before.

The little human had surprisingly proven to be stronger and wiser. The brown sasquatch was left in a state of confusion and pain. How could the small human have stolen the gift of sight? It must have had great power to take away that which belonged to the sasquatch since birth. It actually had the same power as the creators from above, only more powerful. They made it dark, but the sasquatch was still able to see. This time, there was nothing but complete darkness. And sound. And smell. At least, all was not lost.

As the brown sasquatch pushed itself up, blood was dripping from its damaged eyes. It shook its head trying to recover. It got onto one knee and still felt confounded. It was also in great pain. Eventually, it was able to stand. It tried looking around, but there was nothing to see.

It began sniffing and easily picked up the small human warrior's familiar scent. They both stood facing each other, once more. Each was breathing heavily from the fall.

The small human warrior used its mouth to make noise. It said, "I'm sorry about your eyes, but you attacked me. I didn't want to fight you." The words came out softly.

The brown sasquatch did not understand its language. It wondered if the small human warrior was attempting to communicate with it. If so, what was it saying? The sound was soft and gentle, almost comforting. Not aggressive. The brown sasquatch waited for the small human warrior to attack, but it did not. Was the fight over? If so, the small human warrior was the victor.

The brown sasquatch slowly turned away. It listened for movement. There was none. It began to walk away, taking care with each blind step. It smelled the grass and trees that were nearby. It could feel the flat road underneath its bare feet and had a feeling it knew which way it was going, so it kept moving forward. Fortunately, it knew the ruins well. It walked away from the small human warrior, hoping it would not continue the assault. The brown sasquatch was already too hurt to keep fighting. It felt the moisture dripping from its eyes and knew it was leaking life blood.

It kept walking for a long time. Amazingly, it only bumped into a few things along the way. For the most part, it did rather well. The entire time it walked away, it was trying desperately to figure out how it was going to survive without sight. Would the blindness be temporary or was it permanent? It was a mystery, and surely a punishment. Was the small human warrior sent by the creators from above?

The brown sasquatch finally found a place to rest and sat down. It no longer smelled the small human warrior. It faced upwards and let out a sorrowful howl at the sky complaining to the creators from above. Why did they allow this to happen? Why was the brown sasquatch being punished? Why?

Much time had gone by, since the incident with the small human warrior. The brown sasquatch had become the blind sasquatch. It was gradually growing accustomed to survival without sight, although the complete darkness was still depressing. At least, it still had its other senses.

Somehow, each of its other senses had become more enhanced. It could now smell things from further away and easily identify any potential threats. When it really took the time to listen, it heard every little sound within a mile radius. Whenever it touched things, it could easily tell what it was feeling, even if it didn't know what the thing was called. Even its sense of taste had improved.

Still, it was not easy living without sight. The darkness was an unseen torture. It was so much worse than the years of darkness brought about when the sun was gone. The blind sasquatch longed for that simpler time. It was so much easier to deal with, than the pitch black that constantly surrounded everything these days.

The blind sasquatch continued to roam through the ruins and the surrounding woods on a daily basis. It needed to relearn its surroundings. The only way to do that was to be out there feeling it. Smelling it. Listening to it.

Almost every night it howled up at the creators from above. It begged them for its sight to return. It made all kinds of promises in return, but they always ignored the requests. The blind sasquatch knew to be able to see, once again, would be the greatest gift of all. If only that gift could be granted. Usually, after it was done howling, it would go to sleep.

Every morning it would awaken with the hope that when it opened its eyes, there would be sight, again. It never seemed to happen. Instead, the darkness was always there. Waiting. Taunting. That damn deep blackness. It kept the beautiful world hidden away.

The blind sasquatch had no specific place it called home anymore. It had no idea how to locate its cave, which was too far away. It filled much of its days by roaming the ruins. It seemed easier to get around knowing there were structures on every side. Each building had a distinctive smell, which made it possible to find shelter for the night or whenever it rained. The damp smell of mold and mildew combined with rust was a big help. The blind sasquatch did not know what these things were, but it had come to know the smells over the years. They were familiar and that was sufficient.

One evening, as the blind sasquatch was drinking water from the river, it paused. It sniffed at the air and smelled mongrels. It knew very well they probably smelled it, as well. It identified at least two running along the water. They were approaching. There was no point in trying to avoid them. Besides, they were entering sasquatch territory, which meant their lives were forfeit. It had been a long time, since the blind sasquatch had mongrel meat for dinner.

It waited eagerly to meet them head on. This would be its first fight, since being blinded by that small human warrior. That was a defeat it would certainly never forget. It still felt confident it would do well against the mongrels. They had a certain way of attacking. Mongrels always felt the need to either growl intimidatingly or immediately attack and bite down on their prey, except the blind sasquatch had no intention of becoming anyone's prey.

From out of nowhere came another familiar scent. The blind sasquatch was surprised. It was the small human warrior! The smell was unmistakable. It was coming from over the water. The blind sasquatch turned toward the river and let out a howl. It sensed the small human warrior was somehow riding the water and moving further away at a rapid pace.

Suddenly, the barking of the mongrels grew louder. As did the sound of their many paws padding along the dirt trail. The blind sasquatch prepared itself for the oncoming battle. It might get bloody, so reactions had to be speedy. It would have to listen for their every movement and their distinctive heavy breathing. It had to feel the warmth of their foul breath upon its body to know where their mouths were at all times. Its large hands needed to be ready to grab, and they were.

One mongrel began running faster, as it approached. It was on the attack, which meant it would likely leap up at the blind sasquatch. It waited, until it felt the mongrel was within grasp. It then reached out with its hands and blocked the mongrel's attack. It immediately grabbed the mongrel by its thin hind legs and slammed it against the ground several times. The mongrel whimpered weakly, but it soon stopped. The blind sasquatch knew it was dead.

It listened for the other one, but smelled it moving further away. It had run into the water. It was swimming away probably toward the small human warrior. The blind sasquatch did not follow. Normally, it avoided the water because it could not swim. Ever since it was blinded, it definitely had no desire to step into the cold wetness. It was well aware how deadly the water could be.

It stared blindly across the river trying to sniff out the small human warrior. It had already moved too far away. The blind sasquatch wondered if it would ever return. Not many things crossed the water these days. Chances are it would never come back.

The blind sasquatch knew it was for the best. Perhaps, it was a small gift from the creators from above to make amends for the loss of sight.

That night, it dined on the dead mongrel. It ate well. It thought about the other mongrel that swam away. It also did not return. If it went after the small human warrior, it was probably dead.

The blind sasquatch was alone, again. That night it howled up at the sky, this time questioning this new turn of events. Of course, the creators from above never answered. They often flew overhead at night in their great brightly lit mechanisms, but never bothered with the blind sasquatch. Not even before it was blinded.

Why waste time on the failed experiment?

In time, the blind sasquatch realized it was currently the primal hunter of the land. Master of the ruined city and its surrounding woods. There was no one left to challenge it. No species strong enough to dare. It had inherited the world.

Ironically, it could no longer look upon the many wonderful colors and enjoy the land's immense beauty. It could feel the tall trees and ground beneath its huge bare feet, but never see either. Food could be smelled and tasted, but never seen. While it could feel the warmth of the wonderful sun, it could never see the brightness of the blue daytime sky. It could howl up toward the stars, which it knew were twinkling back, but it could never see them. Not anymore.

The blind sasquatch knew this was both a reward and a punishment. At last, it understood this was the price to pay for becoming master of the land. The price was high. Just as the humans were forced to pay their price thirty years earlier.

ABOUT THE AUTHOR

Jason Medina was born and raised in the Bronx, NY. He worked as a police officer in the NYPD for 23 years at the 26 precinct in Harlem, before retiring in 2014. He first started writing stories at the age of 5. It was not until 2012 that he would write his first book. He has continued to publish new books nearly every year, since then.

While he has a love for history, his books mainly focus on horror or the paranormal, such as his locally acclaimed *"Ghosts and Legends of Yonkers"* and his *"Undead Novels"* trilogy. However, he has written a detailed three-volume set of historic books about the abandoned Kings Park Psychiatric Center on Long Island.

Jason currently resides in Yonkers, where he has lived since 2000. He is a trustee of the Yonkers Historical Society and a member of their Archive Committee. He also volunteers his time at a local historic museum and for the Yonkers Public Library.

Not only is Jason a writer of books, but he is a poet, an artist, musician, photographer, and a paranormal investigator.

He can be contacted through his email: *Ginvestigators@aol.com*.

www.JasonMedinaTribalPublications.com
www.YonkersGhostInvestigators.com